The Devil in Ermine

Isolde Martyn

For my dear Ricardian friends, Julia, Angela, Jenny and Babs, and in memory of Harold Cadell

LIST OF HISTORICAL CHARACTERS APPEARING OR MENTIONED IN THE BOOK

Henry (Harry) Stafford, Duke of Buckingham
twenty-eight years old; the last legal heir of the House of Lancaster

Catherine (Cat) Woodville, Duchess of Buckingham
Harry's wife and the mother of his two sons and two daughters; twenty-seven years old; younger sister of Queen Elizabeth Woodville

Lord Stafford (Ned)
Bess
Harry's two eldest children

Pershall
Bodyservant to Harry; bastard son of one of Harry's Staffordshire retainers

Ralph Bannaster
Servant to Harry, with a farm holding at Lacom, in Shropshire

Sir William Knyvett
One of Harry's councillors,, married to Joanna, Harry's aunt

Sir Nicholas Latimer
Harry's chamberlain

Sir Thomas Limerick
Harry's steward

Sir Richard Delabere
Harry's henchman

Dr Thomas Nandik
Cambridge scholar and necromancer

Edward IV, King of England
Yorkist king since 1461, save for a brief exile in 1470-71

Richard, Duke of Gloucester
King Edward's youngest brother and Harry's cousin; thirty-one years old

Anthony Woodville, Lord Rivers
Harry's brother-in-law; eldest brother of Queen Elizabeth Woodville; and tutor to the Prince of Wales at Ludlow

Elizabeth Woodville, Queen of England
Harry's sister-in-law; King Edward is her second husband. She has two grown-up sons by her first marriage

Edward, Prince of Wales
Son of King Edward and Elizabeth Woodville; twelve years old; and has his own household at Ludlow

Prince Richard
Youngest son of King Edward and Elizabeth Woodville; Duke of Norfolk. Nine years old and lives with his mother at Westminster

Thomas Grey, Marquis of Dorset
Sir Richard Grey
Sons of Queen Elizabeth Woodville by her first marriage

William, Lord Hastings
Lord Chamberlain and close friend of King Edward IV

Francis, Lord Lovell

Sir Richard Ratcliffe
Sir James Tyrrell
Henchmen of Richard, Duke of Gloucester

Sir William Catesby
Legal advisor and councillor to several noble lords

John, Lord Howard
Heir to the Duchy of Norfolk in the event of Prince Richard's death

Margaret (Meg) Woodville
Bastard daughter of Anthony Woodville and Gwentlian Stradling; married to Robert Poyntz

Robert Stillington, Bishop of Bath and Wells
Former Lord Chancellor; friend of George, Duke of Clarence

Anne Neville, Duchess of Gloucester
Wife to Richard, Duke of Gloucester and daughter of the late Earl of Warwick ("the Kingmaker")

Lady Margaret Beaufort, Countess of Richmond
Mother of Henry Tudor, pretender to the throne; married to Harry's uncle before her third marriage to Thomas, Lord Stanley

Thomas, Lord Stanley
Steward to King Edward IV; royal councillor; and married to Margaret Beaufort

John Morton, Bishop of Ely
Royal councillor; formerly a supporter of the House of Lancaster

George, Duke of Clarence
King Edward's younger brother; executed in the Tower of London in 1478

Cicely, Duchess of York
Harry's great aunt; mother of King Edward, George, Duke of Clarence and Richard, Duke of Gloucester

Sir Ralph Assheton
Supporter of Richard, Duke of Gloucester

Henry Tudor, Earl of Richmond
Son of Margaret Beaufort; twenty-six years old; fugitive in Brittany; has an illegitimate claim to throne but his Beaufort bloodline is banned from succession by Act of Parliament

The Vaughan Family
A rumbustious family, living at Tretower, south of Brecknock (Brecon). Wales

Elizabeth Lambard, Mistress Shore
Former mistress to King Edward; friend to Lord Hastings

Anne Neville. Dowager Duchess of Buckingham
Harry's late grandmother, who gave him in wardship to King Edward in return for the restitution of her husband's lands

Warwick the Kingmaker
father-in-law to King Edward's brothers, George and Richard; made Edward king in 1461, later switched his allegiance to the House of Lancaster. Slain at Barnet in 1471

William Herbert, Earl of Pembroke
Loyal to King Edward; slain in 1469. Harry was briefly in his household

Sir Henry Stafford
Harry's uncle, second husband of Margaret Beaufort; died in 1471

King Henry VI
Former King of England of the House of Lancaster; reigned 1422-61 and briefly in 1470-71; mentally unstable; 'died' in the Tower of London in 1471

Sir Humphrey Stafford
Nobleman loyal to Richard, Duke of Gloucester

Walter, Lord Ferrers
Yorkist nobleman with a house at Weobley, Herefordshire

PROLOGUE

I am to be charged with high treason.

They are taking me to Salisbury and King Richard will be there. The last time we met I was dressed so richly that whole families could have lived for years upon the cost of that day's clothes. Now where am I? Riding with my wrists bound to the saddle pommel, and a borrowed, shabby mantle straining across my back.

God's mercy! Has someone ridden ahead? Every village we pass through spews up its lousy inhabitants and they all ooze out to stare at me as though I am a captive monster.

Enough, I must value each hour on this road. When I see Richard, I shall have to speak skilfully, swiftly. I need to marshal my thoughts like soldiers in my defence, be clear on what has happened, make some straight skeins out of the tangle of events.

Richard will listen: the stars that presided over his birth gave him a sense of justice so profuse he cannot help but listen.

May Almighty God give me eloquence and may the King forgive me.

1

Before the strange messenger arrived, I could have been struck by a lightning bolt and made no difference to England's history. But in April 1483, the planets that favoured my birthsign moved into unparalleled amity. In one day, one hour almost, my fortune changed.

Instead of attending King Edward at Westminster Palace, I had taken leave and returned to my castle above the town of Brecknock–Aberhonddu as the local Welsh call it. I was weary of hanging about the royal heels like an idle dog. Being Duke of Buckingham and the last legal heir of the House of Lancaster might engender envy in some but they would be misguided. I hungered for the respect that comes with high office, the respect that had been accorded to my grandsire, the first duke, but Edward gave me no opportunity to prove myself. At twenty-nine years old, it was little wonder I was so discontent.

On the afternoon of the day the messenger rode into Wales, I admit to frolicking. My servants had done their best to alleviate my tedium by finding me two pert wenches in a hamlet south of the town. These twin girls were pretty as briar roses, fragrant, black-haired, blue-eyed, mischievous and, mercifully, clean. I was welcomed into their dwelling, where they blindfolded me and tormented me so exquisitely that I could not tell who nuzzled me or which one of them sat astride me first.

When I was sated, their sweet whispers and girlish laughter lapped around me–as gentle as perfumed bathwater after a day in the saddle. One of them slid from the bed to stoke the cottage fire. The other girl fetched sweetmeats and, while her sister fed me, she teased me to hardness once again. I might have stayed longer in their company but Sir William Knyvett, my uncle by marriage, rapped upon the cottage door and straightaway let himself in.

'Harry, are you going to be much longer?'

'You wish to join us?' I asked, but something in his face made me toss aside my delightful rider and reach for my shirt.

'And have your aunt strangle me with one of her garters? No, Harry, it's John Shenmore—the bailiff you sent to Abergavenny, remember. He has just has been carted in with broken ribs. He was attacked down by Tretower on his way back this morning.'

'The Vaughans?' I asked. It had to be the Vaughans, the greediest marauding whoresons this side of the Black Mountains.

'Aye, who else?'

'Excellent.' I turned and gestured for my clothes. 'We can ride down tomorrow and whack the hell out of them. It may not be as satisfying as sitting on the Royal Council, invading France or—'

'Or risking the pox,' Uncle Knyvett cut in. He moved aside to let the girl bring me my gipon and underdrawers. 'Good, were they?' His stare was appreciative

'Very good, eh, *cariad*?' I smiled down at the girl as she knelt to slide my feet into my woollen stockings. I thanked her in Welsh and carried her sister's hand to my lips. 'So, is Shenmore badly hurt?' I asked Uncle Knyvett. No doubt extra payment would ease the fellow's pain.

'He'll mend.'

'Come, then, I am done here.'

I teased the wenches by striding to the door without giving them payment. But as I grabbed the latch, I turned, laughing, and paid them double their worth, amused to see their dismayed mouths tilt into merriment again.

It was a shock to leave the warm stew of the wenches' abode. The chill wind scourged our backs. April still had the breath of winter. Last night's toss of snow garlanded the hedgerows and the road was hard with frost beneath our horses' hooves. As we neared the river, I glanced over my shoulder. The clouds above the ebbing sun had parted over the mountains in a splendour of gold and vermilion as if Christ's return was due. Was it an omen?

I gave spur to my horse and hastened across the drawbridge of my castle with new heart. The murrey sandstone walls were blushed a deeper hue beneath that glorious light and the grisailled windows of the great hall were conjured into a hundred tiny, shining mirrors. I do not exaggerate. I had never beheld such an immodest configuration of clouds and I tossed my ambler's reins to a stableboy, hurtled up the stone steps and stood gasping on the battlements. But already the beauty of that sky was fading. So soon? Did it mean nothing? Oh God, surely there had to be some worth to life instead of the constant yearning that obsessed my soul.

'Your grace?'

Pershall, my bodyservant, had come to find me. His dark blue eyes were concerned. He had reason; I do not usually behave as though stung by a gadfly.

'Observing me for signs of fever, Pershall? I came to see the sky.'

'Not like you, my lord.' Impertinent, disbelieving, he stared across the rooftops of the town to where the hills reared like an angry sea, and instantly dismissed the fading clouds. 'Were the girls not to your liking, your grace?'

'Most satisfactory, Pershall. Quite imaginative.' I guessed the blindfold had been his suggestion.

'Thank the saints for that. Well, I should stay up here a bit longer if I were you, my lord. Your youngest is bawling fit to wake the dead.'

I narrowed my eyes against the rising wind as I looked towards the great ridge of Pen-y-Fan, the inevitable horizon of Brecknock. It was dark and brooding now, its green-gold collar lost in the half-light. Maybe I believed in far too gracious a god. No gentle hand had clawed out those valleys and slapped those crags against the sky.

'Should be good fishing on Llyn Safaddan soon, my lord.'

I shrugged sourly.

'What about the Myddffai girl for you tonight? You remember, my lord, the red-haired wench with duckies to die for.'

Was that my reputation? Naught but a horny Plantagenet? Sweet Christ, any lord can have a warm-thighed woman who by night willingly creases the sheets she has so lovingly laundered by day. I would have given my soul to be useful instead of rutting in Wales.

Pershall would have earned a terse answer had not the barking of dogs and the trumpeting from the river gatehouse proclaimed the monthly arrival of the messenger from the Queen, my sister-in-law.

'Shall you go down, my lord?' Pershall looked hopeful.

'What for, Pershall? News of the latest royal runny nose can wait until suppertime. Go and make ready my bath.' I kept walking, the black dog of despair following behind my spurred heels like a shadow.

'Harry! Harry, where in Hell are you?'

Uncle Knyvett emerged from the upper floor of the nearest tower. For a man in his forties he was very fit but the stairs had made him breathless. 'Th…the messenger that has just come from Westminster, Harry, he's a strange one. I think you should go down. He's not from the Queen and he will speak only with you.' I shrugged, but Uncle Knvyett had the bit between his teeth. 'He's poorly clad and yet he rode in on one of the King's post-horses. Something's up, lad.'

'Then I'd better come.' Uncle Knyvett's common sense was always reliable, he was the most trustworthy of my retainers and I loved him dearly. If the messenger had a commission to change horses at the inns where the royal letter carriers swung from one saddle straight into another, then the fellow's news was urgent and official. God willing, one of my Woodville in-laws might actually have died.

I did not stride in by the great doors. I halted instead in the shadows of the minstrel gallery, wishing to observe this messenger before I questioned him. Catherine, my wife, had just come from her viols and hautboys in the solar and was standing on the dais with two of her women and my chamberlain, Sir Thomas Latimer.

A spindly, ill-clad fellow was on one knee before her, his head dutifully bent. The hall was unusually silent save for the spitting of the logs. Straining to catch any morsel that might break their tedious diet of Welsh happenings, my servants were working softly

Cat asked the stranger's name and he raised his head and looked at her not a little astonished. Maybe he could see she was behind Westminster in her garments. That was ever a quarrel between us. Cat spent her allowance on her musicians but was constantly complaining to her family that she lacked French silks and jewelled collars. Mind, if we had been summoned to court more often, I should have seen her adorned appropriately.

'I am called Thomas Nandik, gracious lady.' His Essex voice had an oily timbre to it.

'The Queen has not sent you before, has she?' Cat sounded coaxing. The man was clearly not a courtier, and one of her ladies tittered at his gaucheness. But when my duchess tried to question him as to affairs in London, the fellow hedged his answers in such an uneasy manner that my curiosity could bear it no longer.

'Who is this?' I demanded brusquely. My wife raised her blue glaze eyes to me at the gallery rail with a faint shrug. The messenger waited while my chamberlain introduced him, then he eagerly scrambled to his feet, stretching from a question mark into a thin slash of a man. This was no courtier nor courier for his daily bread. He wore no livery and his amber rosary and clerical robe hung limply over a frame that was almost as fleshless as a scarecrow's. But there was a brooding mischief in his face that hinted not at malevolence but rather that he carried some good news. I was intrigued; he had broken the monotony and for that deserved an audience.

'Well, man, what is your purpose here?'

'So please your grace, a letter for you and a spoken message to be delivered privily.'

I was tantalized. 'Bring him up!'

'YOUR bath's getting cold,' Pershall grumbled as I shrugged my riding jacket into his arms and went past him into my inner sanctum, where the yeomen of my bedchamber were waiting to unknot my points.

Master Nandik was shown in. He faltered, lanky and round-shouldered, betraying himself as uncomfortable as a Jew in a Christian chapel.

'Is there to be a new parliament, then?' I asked him while my people removed my gipon and hose.

'Yes, your grace.'

I scowled in disappointment at the paucity of his news and wrapped my dressing robe of yellow silk and coney fur about me. What message was so vital that it needed to be delivered alone? Besides, my bath was waiting.

I idly dipped my knuckles into the rosemary-perfumed water. 'You have leave, all of you.' I watched my people shuffle out past the stranger casting their annoyance at him in swift furtive glances. He was still hanging by the door like some ragged coat upon a nail.

'What is your calling, sirrah?' I asked him.

His gaze fell before mine. 'A poor doctor of Cambridge, your grace. That is, until a few days ago, when I was asked to become a messenger.'

'How very unusual. Is King Edward trying to save expenditure?'

'Not any more.' As he came forward, he drew a letter from beneath his mantle, his face suddenly wicked as any goblin's. 'Lord Hastings did not wish to send one of his known envoys, your grace.'

'Why not?' I demanded, annoyed to discover that it was only Hastings, the Lord Chamberlain, behind the mystery. Being high in the King's favour, he never needed help from me so it was perhaps a friendly alert that some of my manors were at risk–probably a warning of another Woodville scheme to acquire other people's property. Certainly, not the restoration of the Bohun lands that King Edward had always withheld from me. Or the chance to govern Wales. That privilege had gone to a Woodville, the Queen's eldest brother.

'Another fund-raising expedition into France?' I muttered. I had been left out of the last one.

He dropped to one knee and proffered the letter. 'My lord, if it pleases you.'

I dabbed my hand dry on a napkin, and took the missive from him. It was warm and sweaty from its nest of clothing. Hastings's seal was genuine. I scowled and broke it.

'*Trusty and well-beloved, I greet you well etc ... .*

Give credence to what the bringer of this letter shall relate and collect as many men as you may in all haste.' The half-smile on Nandik's lips was that of a jouster before he delivers the bloody coup de grâce.

'The King is dead, my lord.'

In shock I dropped the letter in the plaguey bathwater. The ink had run by the time I retrieved it but the date was still legible–written at West-minster three days before on the Feast of St Guthlac.

'How?' I whispered. Forty was a fair age for a battle-scarred prince, but England without old Ned was almost inconceivable. 'Was it canker of the belly? He was complaining of his digestion when I was last at court.'

'I am told he went fishing for perch and took a cold.'

'God save his immortal soul,' I murmured, drawing reverent fingers across my hypocritical heart. Sweet Christ! The best tidings I had ever heard. Edward of York's great hulk coffined at last! May all Thames perch be canon-ized!

I could imagine the scene around the royal deathbed: Edward's queen, Elizabeth Woodville, and his life-long friend, Hastings, each desperate to hold onto high fortune, staring at each other across the coverlet, both think-ing about the twelve-year-old heir to the throne far off in Ludlow. Their eyes must have met in mutual enmity; the Queen's shadow, steeple-like upon the

6

wall, threatened by the solid shape of the King's friend. Was their hatred already streaking out across the kingdom like black lightning splitting the realm?

I am getting away from reality. It must have been more mundane than that: air heavy with incense, the chaplain's whispered prayers as he gave Edward the last rites, the perfect tears on Elizabeth's perfect cheeks and Hastings supervising bowls of steaming water to ease the kingly breath.

And earlier this week, we had not sensed a plaguey thing in Brecknock. No comets. No prophecies from some old slattern. One would think that a king's death ... .

'Your grace?'

My thoughts were so full, I had forgotten Nandik. Now I waited, tense as a virgin bride, for Hastings' message.

'My lord bid me speak plainly. The Queen's grace is sending several thousand retainers to bring his highness the Prince of Wales from Ludlow to be crowned straightway. Lord Hastings bids me tell you it was King Edward's will that my lord of Gloucester should become the Lord Protector, but that the Queen is determined he shall not. She desires to become Regent and rule the realm. It is Lord Hasting's wish and his humble suggestion that you, my lord, and his grace of Gloucester should intercept the Prince and escort him to London. My lord has written to my lord of Gloucester in like vein.'

Hastings had his wits about him, by Jesu. Ha, despite the prostrating grief he must feel for his dearest friend's demise, he was damned well out to save his own skin and hang on to his rung of power.

So it was a matter of choosing between the Queen and Gloucester.

I smiled but, by Heaven, I could have whooped so loud they would have heard me in Hereford. After all these years of impotence, I was invited to play the powerbroker.

'Get off your knees, Master Scholar. You shall be well rewarded.' I gestured him to leave but he grabbed my damp fingers to his lips.

'The holy saints preserve your grace.'

'Aye, if they've a mind to.' I retrieved my hand, my mind aflame with possibilities: if Richard of Gloucester, King Edward's brother, did not reach the south in time to intercept the Prince then I might manage it for him, but I needed to be swift and silver-tongued. Whoever held the new king would win this game. And, oh God, how I hated the Queen.

Isolde Martyn

I dispatched Pershall to find Cat and I summoned my most trustworthy household knights, Knyvett, Latimer, Limerick and Delabere. When I told them the tidings, they could see the chance of fat rewards from Gloucester. Cat would be a different matter. She would not like me opposing her sister so I purposed to tell her very little of my intentions.

I wrote a swift message to Richard of Gloucester in my own hand suggesting that I could meet him on the road, somewhere we could greet the Prince together and then proceed with the boy to London. Lest the words could convict me of treason (if this horseshoe of luck swivelled upside down), I ordered the knight, who was spurred up to carry my missive, to privily assure Gloucester of my loyalty and to tell him I was acting on Hastings' advice.

I also sent a messenger to Cat's brother, Anthony Woodville, Lord Rivers, who was the Prince's tutor and in charge of his household at Ludlow, to kiss hands and assure him I should like to join their retinue on way to London. Could he advise me of their plans?

I have to say I loved Lord Rivers as much as I enjoyed a slap in the face. Posturing upstart! And because he was in charge at Ludlow, he virtually ruled Wales. A duty that should have rightfully fallen to me!

...collect as many men as you may in all haste.

Hell take it, I would have to dispatch urgent commissions of array and send out messengers at daybreak. I needed the numbers quickly.

'Fetch me every man who can write a fair hand and bring more candles!' I ordered my pages, and soon my outer chamber was like a rookery.

With writing boards slung about their necks, my erstwhile scribes perched on chests, stools and bedsteps or propped themselves against the walls. The air smelled of ink and the scratching of their quills was like the labour of busy insects. As each man finished a letter, I sank my seal ring into the soft orange wax.

My advantage was that Ludlow lay in the Welsh Marches, whereas poor old Richard of Gloucester had many more miles to cover. Even if he came posthaste down from Yorkshire, there was a good chance the Prince's escort could evade him.

It would demand cunning. I would need to keep my cards close to my chest. Given a choice, I saw myself in Gloucester's camp. My grandmother and his mother were sisters so he was my second cousin. But, more to the point, I knew, like me, he thought that the Woodvilles were jackdaws masquerading as peacocks and that they needed plucking.

8

'My lord?'

Knee deep in secretaries, I swiftly halted in mid-sentence and smiled at my wife. Cat is twenty-six years old. She is not as beautiful as the other Woodville siblings, but passing fair. Like her royal sister, she has gilt hair, eyes the hue of aquamarines and a dimpled chin. She is taller than Elizabeth, so she does not need to wear the wire-and-gauze edifices that the Queen favours.

Cat—Catherine Woodville—was yoked to me when she was eight and I was but ten. Her family, the progeny of a foreigner and a steward, is the mill-stone about her neck as far as I am concerned. She brought me nothing. No dowry even. And every time I look upon her, I am reminded of her sister, the Queen, whom I loathe. Unreasonable, I agree. Had she and I liked each other, we might have shared the shaft of marriage like two carthorses in step. Yet she has borne me children and, thanks to the diligent snuffing of candles in our bedchamber and silent fantasies in our minds, we now have four healthy infants. However, our verbal intercourse, performed in the light of day or under reasonable illumination, is unquestionably dull and lacking in passion.

'Well, Cat?' She was standing beneath the lintel of my inner chamber, still as a saint in a niche, watching me with the air of a Patient Griselda. A stance she has sculpted to perfection.

'Sir Nicholas has just informed me the entire household is to go into mourning but then he rushed off without telling me more and Pershall said it was better I should ask you directly. Whose funeral is it?'

I did not answer her straightway but led her into the privacy of my inner chamber.

'It could be Elizabeth's.' I crossed myself mockingly and then leaned against the end of the bed, folding my arms.

She closed the outer door and stood with her back against it. 'Indeed?' she challenged dryly. 'The messenger told me she was in good health when he left Westminster.'

'Certainly he spoke the truth, she being departed from the cares of this world, the pomp and … .'

'Just the truth!' she cut in. 'Who is dead?'

'King Edward, dearest.'

'Sweet Mother of God! Harry! That is horrific news. Oh, my poor sister!'

Poor! Elizabeth was the greediest bitch in England.

My wife sank onto the nearest settle, her fingers to her lips, her mind already whirring, Woodville-like, with a thousand consequences.

'You do not need to worry about what you shall wear, Cat. I should imagine the obsequies at Windsor are over by now.' Edward had spent a lot of money on St George's Chapel as his shrine for posterity.

'Well, I shall still come with you to Westminster. Elizabeth will need—'

'Elizabeth will have the rest of your kinsmen for support.' I cut in, and strode across to stand in front of her, unable to resist drawing her to her feet and framing the fine bones of her face within my fingers. 'Much as we treasure each other's company, light of my bedchamber, I wish you to remain here and have masses said for the King's grace. I intend to join Prince Edward's retinue before he reaches London and I shall have to ride hard.' It was tempting to tell her I was throwing my cap into the ring with Gloucester. I should have liked to see her Woodville lips go slack in shock and imagine they were Elizabeth's. 'Now if you will forgive me, dearest...' I swept her towards the door. 'I have a multitude of preparations to make.'

'Damn you, Harry Stafford!' she cursed beneath her breath as I urged her through.

With so many crowding the antechamber, she could not very well argue further but she took hold of one of their writing boards, perused it, and, frowning, stared about her. 'Why are you sending for so many men?'

I wrapped a husbandly arm around her shoulders and moved her out into the passageway.

'I cannot very well arrive like a pauper, *and*—whether your family cares to remember it or not, my sweet duchess—I *am* the second duke of the realm and a Plantagenet.'

'Are you? Why I had quite forgotten.' Then her fingers tightened around the golden cross upon her bosom. 'I need to write to the Queen and... and Anthony. You will be seeing him as well.'

Yes, I hoped to see Rivers—preferably wearing a noose! His neck, not mine.

'Of course, you must send your sympathies to them.'

I swung round and beckoned one of the secretaries. 'Attend her grace.'

'You will need mourning tabards for everyone, my lord, and...' She paused, realising the enormity of what must be done to array my entourage.

'Yes, plenty to do and I should appreciate your...' I forgot what I was saying as our eldest son, five years old and spoiled, hurtled in.

'I want to come with you, sir!'

Bess, his young broomstick of a nursemaid was at his heels, twisting her hands in her waistcloth, her face apologetic.

'Ned!' Cat's arm whipped out and she held the child to her skirts, although he deserved chastisement. Aware that everyone was listening, she decided to use this to her advantage. 'Let us accompany you, my lord, or perhaps we could take the road to Oxford and meet you at Westminster? Ned has seen so little of the world.' She ruffled our son's hair and the boy looked at me with her eyes.

'No! Especially since he lacks the manners of a duke's son.'

'You never take me,' he howled petulantly. 'You never take us anywhere. I'm sick of living in Wales. Why can I not go to Westminster and be a page like you were?'

'I have said no!' And let the Woodvilles destroy my son as they had tried to destroy me?

Jesu! I had been nine years old when I had blurted out that marrying a Woodville was beneath me, and they had never forgiven that. Whether it was being made to look a fool when I served in the Queen's household as a page or denying me an heiress for my bride, they had made me pay for my childish insult a thousandfold. Cat was given to me with no lands, no titles and no dowry. I, a duke with the blood of kings in my veins.

'My lord,' she began again. Perhaps something had shown in my face. 'Truly, I long to see my family again and they will think little of me for staying back here at such a time.'

'Out of the question, my dear. Your women will slow our company.' And Cat's loyalty to Elizabeth was as predictable as the sunrise. I did not need a female Judas at my elbow. 'Let us discuss this no further! To bed with you, Ned!'

If a man is not seen as ruling his wife and children, how may he rule a dukedom? I was angry with her for letting our son question my authority. Even when I went to say goodnight to my children after all the letters had been sealed, Ned was not there. I was tempted to march straight to my wife's demesne and quarrel further, but the nursery was a warm haven. The wetnurse was singing softly as she fed my baby son and my little daughters were kneeling in their night kirtles before the fire, waiting to be put to bed.

This was my precious time each day. Tonight I would tell them about a little dragon who lived on Pen-y-Fan. I loved having their soft arms around my neck as they cuddled into me before the hearth.

But the story was soon over. 'I have work to do, Princess,' I told Bess, my eldest poppet.

'I'm not a real princess, Papa,' she told me solemnly. 'But I should like to be one when I am grown.'

'So you shall,' I agreed. My thoughts, too. If a steward's daughter could marry a king, surely my daughter could wed a prince? 'God willing, my darling.' I carried her small hand to my lips. I should make sure she would have a husband who would love her. 'Now even pretend princesses must go to bed.'

I wondered then if I should ever see my beloved little maidens again after I left Brecknock. The enterprise I was resolved upon would be seen by my enemy, the Queen, as treason. Gloucester and I could have our heads chopped off if we acted against her and failed.

Ned still did not come to bed. Sure enough, I found him in Cat's bedchamber, twanging the strings of a lute. Sufficient to grate my nerves. I try to be a father to him but, God knows, I am not sure how, for I had no fathering. By the time I was Ned's age, my grandsires had been slain in the wars between Lancaster and York and my father had died of the plague.

'Be quiet!' I admonished my son and turned to my wife. 'Did you have to make that bother in front of my secretaries, madame? It is bad enough that our son is running amok without you trying to undermine my authority too.'

'Our son spoke the truth,' Cat muttered, setting down her wine cup. 'I have a right as your duchess to attend the coronation. Why are you being so difficult?'

'Well, Cat,' I murmured picking up the crystal bottle of Hungary water that stood beside the ewer on her wash table. 'Maybe it is because you are a Woodville, think like a Woodville and use the same cloying scent your sister uses, so you even smell like a Woodville.' I tossed the phial at her. 'As for you, my tiny rebel.' I caught my son by the waist. 'Bedtime and a story.'

'Truly, my lord father?' His little face was alight with pleasure.

'On my honour.' I lifted him into my arms. 'Rascal.'

'The story about how you slew the white boar.'

'No, not that one,' I said wearily. 'We'll save that one for another day.'

2

Tinker, tailor, peacemaker, kingmaker?

Collared swans and flaming cartwheels, stitched in metal thread, glinted on the sarsynett pennons above my retinue as we left Brecknock. The three hundred Welshmen, who were jingling in harness behind me, were all wearing Stafford knots, freshly embroidered, on their scarlet and black tunics, thanks to Cat and her women doing their duty.

Lord Rivers had suggested that Gloucester and I might meet the Prince at Northampton since it was on their route from Ludlow and then we could all travel to London together. So be it! I would throw my support behind Gloucester as Lord Protector but if matters went awry, I might end up on the scaffold instead of a cushioned bench at Westminster.

'I could wish a thousand men at our backs,' muttered Uncle Knyvett. 'What if Gloucester doesn't trust you?'

It was certainly a possibility. Gloucester had sent me back a polite, curt message: *no army*! He was bringing no more than three hundred retainers. He suggested I do the same.

In his shoes, I would have arrived at Northampton with half of Yorkshire to protect me. For all he knew, I could have been secretly in league with the Woodvilles to trap him. It would have been easy. With my three hundred added to the retinues marching from London and Ludlow, we could have had him bound, gagged and on his way to the Tower of London in no time.

'All I know, uncle,' I replied, 'is that it will require some deft footwork on my part.'

'Gloucester has always kept his nose out of trouble, Harry. Happen he'll just go along with the Queen's plans.'

'Not if I can help it. And the trick will be not to arrive before Gloucester, or his fur will be on end with suspicion. God willing, I'll have a chance to talk with him before the Woodvilles descend on us.'

I had already sent one of my henchmen to reserve lodging in the town but now, as we neared Northampton, I dispatched outriders ahead to sniff out the situation. If Richard had already arrived and there had been trouble between him and the Woodvilles, I might be riding in for his funeral and would need to hide my disappointment.

As we reached the crossroads with the Great North Road outside Daventry, we found a weary knight with Gloucester's boar bristling upon his surcote sitting upon a milestone awaiting us. The young man's Yorkshire dialect was thick and hard to follow after the lilt of Brecknock. He gave us to understand that his master was close to arriving at Northampton. The good feeling returned: Gloucester trusted me.

'How many men are in his Grace's retinue?' I asked his messenger.

The fellow looked down the column behind me before he offered an unintelligible answer.

'I *think* he said it was about the same as ours,' Latimer interpreted.

'What about the Prince's retinue, sirrah?'

A shake of head. So the Prince had not yet arrived.

'Return to his Grace and tell him…' I drummed the words slowly out. 'Tell-him-I-greet-him-and-we-shall-make-haste. Understand?'

Something must have sunk into his northern pate. The idiot saluted and gave spur.

So where were the sodding Woodvilles, behind us or already down the road to London? If the Ludlow retinue had already met up with the army of retainers that the Queen was sending from London to safeguard her son, Gloucester and I might be done for already.

It was beginning to rain, our pennons were starting to droop and I have to be honest and admit my stomach was churning with such unease that I had to go and relieve myself behind a hedge before I ordered my retinue forwards.

'Well, your grace, you can always order a pair of boots in Northampton, if nothing else,' chirped Pershall, ready with a flask of water. 'Either that or a roast beef repast. Ah, listen, it sounds as though one of the lads is back. Shall I brush the blackthorn blossom from your grace or is your grace happy to look like a May Day damsel?'

I swore at him good humouredly and clambered back onto the road, brushing my shoulders. Ralph Bannaster awaited me, spattered and scarlet, his horse all lathered.

'My lord, the Prince and Lord Rivers have already passed through Northampton!'

'Christ Almighty!' I exclaimed, swiftly setting foot in my horse's stirrup. My angry fingers jerked on the bridle and my poor stallion protested. Maybe this chess game of power was already lost. I could imagine my head on the block. Yes, and the Queen and Rivers would be selling Cat to a new husband, faster than it takes to spit.

'It isn't Doomsday yet,' my steward, Sir Thomas Limerick, pointed out. 'We can still keep our noses out of this.'

True, I thought, but sometimes you have to grasp Fortune with your fist and squeeze the juice out of her. Aloud, I said, 'What, Tom, go all the way back to lousy Brecknock with our tails curled around our arses?' I kneed my horse round to face the road ahead. 'No, lads, let's meet with Gloucester as promised.'

Once we reached the great street from the west, it was clear that a mighty retinue was ahead of us. The way was much troughed and that slowed us mightily.

Some half-dozen of Gloucester's knights met us a mile outside the town. Sir Richard Ratcliffe of Derwentwater was their leader, bidden to show me to my inn. I was soon to learn that he was Gloucester's intermediary. Wherever there was trouble affecting his master, dour Ratcliffe was there to fix it. For sure, he had come to inspect me, not only my demeanour but to see if my following exceeded the specified number and whether my men were fully armoured. The grey eyes on either side the hawk nose missed nothing. Unlike his companions, he was hard to charm but at least he was able to tell me that the Prince and my brother-in-law Rivers were putting up for the night at Stony Stratford, a town which lay fourteen miles beyond us on the road to London. What in Hell did that mean? Why had they not waited for us?

Ratcliffe's companion knights and esquires were full of cheer and banter but by the time we sighted Northampton's walls, I realised they had completely surrounded me, isolating me from my affinity. Ratcliffe himself was riding knee to knee beside me, within a hand's grasp of my horse's reins and a blade distance from my throat. Uncle Knyvett made an attempt to force his horse up beside me before we reached the town gate but the Yorkists subtly kneed their amblers to block him. I glanced round at him and shook my head imperceptibly.

Clearly, my cousin Gloucester was as edgy as a boar who hears the snarl of hunting dogs. The guards holding the gate wore the White Boar badge and everywhere along the street, his men-at-arms stood outside the inns and hostelries. I was unnerved and angered by my cousin's suspicion; this place was where my mighty grandfather had been slain fighting for the House of Lancaster. Maybe I would not leave here either.

'You can tell that tanning is the local livelihood,' observed young Strangways, one of the White Boar esquires, wrinkling his nose.

Yes, Northampton did smell and the cobbles, dappled with horse turds from the Prince's retinue, added to the stink. The townsfolk, still shovelling the dung into hand barrows and wooden pails, had to be shooed out of our path despite the trumpets.

'Ah but I hear they breed good oxen in these parts,' I remarked, determined to appear at ease. 'I daresay we can expect beef for dinner, Ratcliffe, unless your lord has any other plans for me this evening.' I met his stare evenly. He smiled.

'You'll be wanting to change into clean apparel when you reach the inn, my lord. I'll inform his Grace that you shall be joining him as soon as you are refreshed.' It was a command not a statement.

'I suppose he is putting up at the castle?'

'No, my lord, it lacks comfort. He prefers *The Bear*. My lord of Warwick always stayed there.' And Richard, as page and then esquire to Warwick the Kingmaker, would have known it well.

The inn awaiting me was clean and the servants efficient. The town knew its duty to travellers. However, by the time I had dealt with bowing and grovelling from the mayor and aldermen who had turned up in their official chains and houpelandes to honour me, it was almost past the supper hour.

'Pray ask my lord of Gloucester to start supper without me,' I ordered Ratcliffe, who had remained like an unwanted shadow, and I hastened up the stairs and strode along the gallery above the courtyard, unbuttoning my riding doublet as I went. A hungry man kept waiting for his food is more easily annoyed, and I needed Gloucester open to persuasion. For an instant I thought Ratcliffe had ignored my order but then he nodded in his rather sour way, doffed his cap and loped back to his master.

Pitchers of hot water and fresh towels were waiting in my chamber, thank Heaven; it would be hard to negotiate my future smelling of sweat and horseflesh. Pershall had already lain out fresh apparel for me and seen that my coffers had been brought up. I flung out my arms to my servants to disrobe me and then I dismissed them except for Pershall. As he went to work lathering my stubble, I told him to cease his chatter. I needed time to gather my thoughts. Tonight I had to make sure that Gloucester would trust me and convince him how badly he needed my support.

I could not use wine to soften my cousin's wits. He was known to be a man of great sobriety so I would have to rope him in with the right arguments—no easy matter when the execution of his brother George, Duke of Clarence's still lay between us like a swollen river. That was the only office King Edward ever gave me, and a filthy, defiling one it was too, compelling me to head the jury of peers that sentenced the Duke to death for treason. Gloucester had rarely come to court after that. He had made no secret that he blamed the Queen for poisoning King Edward's mind and had openly said that one day he would avenge his brother's death. Maybe that was the other reason why the Woodvilles were hurrying the boy to London. They sensed revenge was in the wind. Well, as long Gloucester did not rattle his hackles in my direction.

'Your grace!' Bannaster's voice came from outside the door, interrupting my thoughts. Pershall let him in. I twisted round to curse the pair of them but then I saw who was with them. Francis, Lord Lovell, another loyal friend of Gloucester's. I knew him already. He was about the same age as I and, like the dog on his badge, a tail-wagging, amiable man.

We shared a common grievance. Neither us had been happy with the wives forced upon us. I remember one night in London when he had come down from the north in Warwick's entourage. We happily coincided at a tavern in Thames Street and drank ourselves under the board in mutual commiseration.

'Lovell!' Thrusting aside the hot towel, I rose to shake his hand warmly. '*Viscount* Lovell now, I hear. Congratulations! Come to hurry me up, have you? Is the duke growing hungry and too polite to begin without me?'

'You are looking well, your grace, albeit half-shaved.' His voice still had the burr of Oxfordshire despite his upbringing in Yorkshire.

I grinned and submitted once more to Pershall's razor.

'How is the Lady Catherine?' he asked.

'How is Lady Nan?' I countered.

He smiled wryly, his glance taking in the sparse furnishings and white-washed walls around us. 'This is bearable. Any bed lice?'

'I gather they've moved on to Stony Stratford,' muttered Pershall beneath his breath.

Lovell laughed and then his attention returned to me. 'I am sent to warn your grace that the Duke has an unexpected guest for supper.' I raised an enquiring eyebrow, unprepared for what came next. 'No less than your fine brother-in-law, Lord Rivers. He rode in about the same time as you did, so my lord of Gloucester apologises that he did not come out to meet you.'

'God's Truth, what is going on?' I grabbed the towel and began hurriedly dabbing away the soap. Pershall quickly filled a bowl with the hot water set ready for me and Lovell frowned as he watched me frantically sluicing my neck and armpits.

'We wondered that too, your grace.' He was eyeing me now as though I might be harbouring secrets. 'Imagine, Lord Rivers has ridden back all the way from Stony Stratford this afternoon to pay his respects to the Lord Protector.' The title had not been used in England for a long time. But that thought was pushed aside. It was what Gloucester might be thinking about me that had me concerned. Was he suspecting that Rivers and I had planned some kind of ambush?

'How is Lord Rivers then? Full of wit? As friendly as a starving whore?' Was I trying too hard? Tumbling over my shoe beaks trying to sound innocent?

Lovell did not answer. The turret of the nearby Grey Friars was ringing out the hour.

'I think you had better summon your tiring men, your grace. Supper grows cold.'

My servants rushed back in and swarmed about me to tie my points, loop the knopfs of my doublet and urge my boots to slide on. Arms folded, Lovell waited, lolled against the side of casement. It did not escape me that he kept glancing sideways to the courtyard below. What was he expecting? Rivers to arrive with a spare dagger in case I had forgotten mine?

'Is the Pope coming as well?' I jested, checking my dress in a silver hand mirror.

'If he does, he'll have to sleep in a stable.' Some of Lovell's friendliness was seeping back.

'Do him good then,' I chuckled. Grabbing my hat, I made for the door, with Lovell following.

'My lord!' One of my bodyservants held my dagger scabbard across his palms. This might be my Last Supper if aught went wrong but I needed to convince Gloucester I was trustworthy.

'Go to supper!' I ordered them, ignoring the fool.

'But you *will* need this, my lord! ' Pershall, smiling, tossed my mantle to me.

Knyvett and my household knights fell in behind us. I was still straightening my hat brim as we reached Richard's inn. Lovell abandoned us at the door to the fulsome welcome of the landlord while he went to announce my arrival to his master. To my astonishment, Gloucester came in person to greet me, pulling aside the gaudy arras of the passage to the private dining chamber and stepping down with arms held out.

'Cousin of Buckingham, a thousand welcomes.'

Hell, he looked the worst I have ever seen him. He had been grieving, of course, and he was not a man who looked well in black; more a rust, moss and amber fellow. Instead of embracing him, I plucked off my hat and dropped to one knee, thankful the flagstones were clean. My henchmen did the same.

'My Lord Protector,' I murmured reverently, touching my lips to his ring.

'I thank you, Harry.' His voice was soft, moved with gratitude. He gripped my hand, drawing me to my feet. Then he stepped forward to greet Uncle Knyvett, Latimer and Delabere, and asked one of his pages to lead them out to join his household knights. Returning to me, he flung an arm about my shoulders. 'Come, cousin! You must be famished, and the beef is tender...' he glanced round to make sure mine host had been hustled out of earshot and added, 'for Northampton.'

'I thought to find you in poor spirits, your grace,' I said, and saw his long chestnut lashes flicker down defensively.

'I have done my mourning, cousin, and now must do my duty.'

I endeavoured not to freeze at as a voice behind me said, 'Which you will do *magnificently* as usual, Dickon.'

Sweet Mother of God! Rivers!

'Well, now here's a surprise,' I boomed. 'I thought you ahead of us on the road.'

Cat's big brother left the brass rings of the dividing curtain rattling as he emerged out of the inner chamber like a peacock butterfly from its chrysalis. The ash blonde hair and the expensive silver embroidery panels on his doublet made him look like a Burgundian courtier rather than a man in grief. His hanging sleeve rustled as he held out a hand to me. A plethora of gems, including a lodesterre as large as a sword pommel glittered on the long, thin fingers that reached out to clasp mine. Imagine a torch held in your face! That is what I felt as his aquamarine eyes studied me with a penetrating brilliance that reminded me sharply of the Queen.

Mind, I saw now that there were plentiful silver threads in his hair and the flesh above his feline eyes was looser. He still had an athlete's body and could best my inches. Damn him! It irritated me that I could still feel vulnerable. Just standing before him was like having his fingernails claw my scars.

Not visible scars, though. He was too clever for that. It was he who had made my journey to manhood a torment, encouraging his younger brothers and the Grey boys, the Queen's sons by her earlier marriage, to discomfort me in front of the court. The sudden elbow knock that would make me stumble, or an ankle hooked about my foot so that I tipped a ewer of hot lavender water into the lap of King Louis XI's envoy. These may sound like pinpricks but a regime of maliciousness and loathing corrodes the soul. There were so many Woodvilles and there was only one of me.

I was not alone in feeling soft and fragile within my shell. I sensed discomfort ripple through Gloucester as he stood beside me, and so I turned my face reassuringly. My cousin's skin glimmered moon-white beneath his mourning brim as he glanced from Rivers' countenance to mine.

'Is the Prince here as well?' I asked, glancing towards the arras.

'No,' Rivers replied, sounding surprised by my question. 'His highness is lodging in Stony Stratford. Did no one tell you?' Belittling me, making me feel like an outsider, had always been his game.

Gloucester took breath to correct him but Rivers breezed on: 'Yes, Harry, I know we had promised to meet with you here but any fool could see that Northampton was not going to be able accommodate everyone. I decided it was better for us all to be comfortable.'

You silver-tongued liar! I silently screamed at him. *You must have planned this the moment you heard that we were coming to meet you.*

'That was thoughtful,' I replied.

'Shall we dine?' Gloucester said curtly and left us to follow him along the passage while Lovell and Ratcliffe closed in behind myself and Rivers, ready to catch any snatch of words which might pass between us.

The trouble is when you expect slurs and sneers, you read them everywhere. Rivers gestured for me to precede him but even his acknowledgment that I had that right was like an insult.

'How is our Catherine?' he asked.

'In good health and our latest babe is thriving,' I replied, over my shoulder. Both of his wives had been infertile but he did have a lovechild by some slut of a noblewoman south of Bristol. 'Cat would have liked to come with me.' Yes, it was petty of me to remind him I had power over 'Our Catherine' but to resist that temptation would have been like holding back the tide.

'How miserable of you not to bring her, Harry. The Queen would have been overjoyed to see her again. You must promise us you will let her come to London in sufficient time to have a new gown made for the coronation.' That was a return jab, a reminder of my wife's lament that I kept her in rags; a reminder, too, of the intent to crown the prince as soon as possible so as to dispense with Gloucester's protectorship.

I smiled and took my seat at the board. It was set for just the three of us. Hunger was making me irritable but my capacity to put up with Rivers increased at the appearance of a platter of perch swimming in hot spiced sauce. My winecup with filled with an excellent claret–hard to come by since we had lost hold of Bordeaux.

My cousin was watching my face as I tried it. He knew I had a more sensitive taste for wine than most Englishmen. Along with hawks and hounds, wine had always been a safe choice of talk between us.

'It has travelled passing well, would you not say?' he asked and this gave Rivers a chance to sound forth on wines he remembered from his pilgrimage to Compostela. The man shoved his knowledge down other men's throats like a scullion stuffing a capon's arse. I had heard it all before from him but it helped loosen Gloucester's reserve. By the time the local roast beef coffyred in pastry with a glaze of egg and saffron arrived, the conversation was flowing like the River Honddu after a summer thunderstorm.

My cousin let us have our heads, making little comment on our opinions. He skilfully kept the conversation light; perhaps he wanted to forget his fears for a little space, to pretend that his brother Edward still lusted in London and that we three noblemen were met together like chance travellers. *Three unwise men seeking a king?*

The servants removed the dishes from the board and the cloth, sullied with gravy, was whipped away exposing the naked oak shining like a Carthaginian's well-oiled skin in the firelight. Lovell returned, sent for his lute and curled himself in the window seat, and as we began to give our attention to his music, Ratcliffe prowled in and sat down beside him.

Was Lovell's song a warning? I do not think so. Judging by his expression as he sang and his nimble fingers on the strings, it was one he knew well.

> *There is none so wise a man*
> *But he may wisdom know;*
> *And there is none so strong a man*
> *But he finds equal foe;*
> *Nor there is none so false a man*
> *But some man will him heed;*
> *And there is none so weak a man*
> *But some man shall him grieve.*

Rivers lolled in his chair as he listened, stretching out his long legs, but Gloucester sat tight-lipped and concise in his mourning clothes, staring into his winecup like a man who bore the sorrows of all Christendom upon his shoulders. He sat so still, as if a heart no longer beat beneath his sable mantle; his face as pale as the pearls upon the brooch on his hat. I looked away, knowing he mourned where I did not, that he had travelled far longer than I to this time and this place.

'Pox take it, Lovell, that's far too sad,' exclaimed Rivers, his voice fisting into our reverie. 'Play something to liven us up! Ned would not want us to be in the dumps and I swear he would say as much, were he to be looking at us now.'

Rivers was probably right. 'Ned' would have slapped his puny brother around the shoulders and clashed his wine goblet into ours, but I saw

Gloucester flinch—the telltale twitch of muscle beneath his left eye—as though on Rivers' lips, the shaping of his beloved brother's familiar name was a blasphemy.

'Your grace?' Lovell leaned forward.

Gloucester stirred. 'I daresay Lord Rivers is right.' Only the corners of his mouth lifted. 'After all, you shared more leisure time with him than I did, my lord.' And I swear Rivers did not note the ambiguity, for his Woodville sense of self was higher than any spire.

'Know *The Cricket and the Grasshopper*, Lovell? Play that.' Rivers straightened and raised his cup. 'To Ned! May God take him to his bosom.' The Devil morelike, I thought, but I touched my goblet rim to theirs.

'Now this is supposed to be a true story', began my brother in law, 'save it was told to me by an Irishman. There was an English bagpiper went over to Ireland with the army of Richard of Bordeaux and one day he decided to slip off on his own for a bit and travel about the country. Anyway, off he went with his pipes slung on his shoulder and just as he was sitting down to have his dinner in a wood, three wolves began to accost him. He threw some meat to one and some cheese to another, hoping they would go away but still they slunk nearer and nearer. He was so afraid that he grabbed his bagpipes and began to play to give himself courage. The moment they heard the noise, the wolves ran away. "A pox on you!" he shouted after them. "If I had known you loved music so well, you should have had it before dinner."'

'Hmm,' I applauded dryly. 'An' if I had been one of the wolves I should have made off too for I cannot abide such pig squeal either.'

'No, you never did have much feel for music, did you,' Rivers observed. I hoped he was not going to dredge out the story of how he and his brothers had slipped a mouse in the lute that my mother had sent me, when I had been summoned to play before the Queen and her ladies. Elizabeth and Cat had been in the jest as well.

'I did not think they ever had wolves in Ireland,' said Gloucester with an innocence unlikely to offend. He could do that skilfully and before Rivers had time to argue or even weigh up whether it was a slur, my cousin turned to me. 'I am surprised at you saying that about the pipes, Harry. I am sure it is because you cannot have heard them played really well. Holy Paul, a good piper can almost draw the soul out of your body.'

'You'll not convince me,' I insisted. 'I have not your ear for music.'

25

'Harry would not know the difference between a thrush and a crow,' muttered Rivers silkily but Gloucester ignored the interruption.

'Lord Howard poached a wondrous piper off Lady Margaret Beaufort. I'll have a word with him when we reach London and see if he can arrange some entertainment for us.'

Well that *would* be something to look forward to. I changed the subject. 'Well now,' I asked with innocuous cheerfulness. 'What are the arrangements for tomorrow?'

'We talked about it before you arrived,' replied Cat's brother. 'We can all leave together tomorrow morning. There'll be no need for an early start. His highness was not feeling well and I should like him to sleep in. One of his teeth is nagging him and, of course, this has all been a huge blow to him.' He crossed himself. 'As to us all.'

My heart to testicles and shoulder-to-shoulder gesture was perfunctory. 'And tomorrow he will be surrounded by uncles he hardly knows,' I murmured.

'Hardly that, Harry. I have told him all about you.' It was a pinprick deftly given. 'Would you be offended if I leave you now, dear brothers?' Without our agreement, he pushed his chair back and towered over us. 'I am–if you will pardon the crassness–as sore-thighed as one of the Bishop of Winchester's pretty geese after a busy night.' Gloucester's lips tightened disapprovingly but Rivers did not appear to notice. 'May you sleep well, Dickon.' *Dickon*! Even I had never spoken to my cousin so familiarly.

Gloucester escorted Rivers to the door where, the one so tall, the other so slight, they said good night with a shake of hands.

'Goodnight, Harry,' my brother-in-law called out to me. Not bothering to rise, I raised my winecup to him in valediction. *To your damnation, Rivers!*

'What o'clock is it?' asked Gloucester, stretching and wearily drawing his fingers down his cheeks to his chin.

'Nine has not yet struck,' replied Ratcliffe. He picked up the wine jug, offering to refill our cups. My cousin shook his head.

'I should let you find your bed.' I scraped my chair back, ready to rise.

'No, no,' answered Gloucester, gesturing me to remain. 'Cast your eye over this.' He stooped and fetched out a wooden box from beneath the table. I guessed what it contained and sure enough, he lifted out a book swathed in soft cloth. As soon as he unwrapped it, I could see instantly that it was one of Caxton's, for I recognised his device with its lozenge borders exquisitely tooled upon the cover. Gloucester set it before me and I unfastened the gilt clasp with reverence and turned to the first page. It was Rivers' translation of *The Dictes and Sayings of Philosophers*, printed at Westminster twelve years ago. It was impossible to get such a book now; no one parted with them. I fingered it in awe.

'A priceless gift.'

'He brought it with him,' sighed my cousin, with the tone of a man who had just accepted a bribe against his conscience. 'I already have a copy. Would you like it, Harry?' Indeed, I would, but such generosity made me hesitate. 'No, truly, take it,' he said, waving aside my thanks.

I turned over the first leaf that boasted more lozenged artistry, and read Caxton's introduction.

'See, even William Caxton does not know what to make of Rivers,' I snorted and looked up to see if Gloucester agreed. 'He is a very learned fellow and yet...' I let the silence speak before I added, 'There was little sign of the hair shirt tonight.'

My cousin grinned. 'Not on the outside, but if Purgatory is waiting for him then his underclothes should manage to strike a few years off the punishment.'

'Like a night of adultery and a good flail in the morning?' I suggested.

'Some people do both at once,' cut in Ratcliffe, and we all laughed.

'My masters, it is getting late,' yawned Lovell, leaning his fair head against the neck of the lute. I swaddled the book and pensively slid it back into its case. What was truly going on in Gloucester's mind? Did he suspect Rivers and I were in league, ready to crush him like a flea, between our thumbnails? Had he believed that supper had been but a mummers' entertainment and reality would be a cold breakfast of daggers?

I had had enough of side-stepping.

'Before you retire, Richard, I should like to talk with you about tomorrow.'

The hammer had struck the anvil. It sparked a sharp look from him.

'Yes, I suppose you would.' He touched Lovell's shoulder. 'Thank you for the music, Francis. Get you to bed.' Then he raised a questioning eyebrow at Ratcliffe.

'I'll be within call,' growled his human hound and, with a curt inclination of his head to each of us, Ratcliffe followed Lovell out. At last there was just Gloucester, standing before the hearth, and myself at the table.

I stayed seated. My cousin was the runt of the Yorkist brothers. I was a nearly a head taller than him and I wanted him to feel comfortable and superior as he listened to me. I scrubbed my finger across the moist circle left by my cup upon the wood, wondering where to begin.

'So, tomorrow?' Gloucester sighed and once more put his hands in the small of his back and stretched. Since puberty, his spine has become curved and I know it pains him greatly at times.

'I am not sure what is going on in this place,' I declared honestly. 'I do not know what you believe of me either, Richard.' I had not called him that since boyhood, but I was the second duke in England after him and I needed him to remember and respect that.

He looked round at me, his thoughts a locked door. 'What would you like me to believe?'

I took a deep breath. How do you convince a man you had no hand in his brother's execution when it was your mouth that sentenced him to death?

'I should like you to know that although I sat as steward at George's trial—the only office I was ever given, I might add—I did not support the death sentence. Unfortunately, we were given no choice. The King and Queen wanted him dead.' Edward and Elizabeth had made that clear.

Gloucester's mouth was a tight line. He came back to the table and poured us both another drink. It was some moments before he spoke.

'He was a risk to the succession, Harry. If Edward had died earlier, George would have tried to take the crown.'

His opinion surprised me. Not just his stern conclusion but his calm in discussing it. At the time of his brother's imprisonment, he had been vehement in George's defence even though the man had been a ranting drunkard.

'Your brother was his own worst enemy.' I leaned my head upon my hand remembering the bitterness that had raged. Condemning a fellow duke to death had made me feel vulnerable. I felt vulnerable now.

'Yes,' said Richard of Gloucester. 'A taste of blood is dangerous. Once there is a failure to respect the value of human life...' He drew a downward spiral in the air.

'Especially a duke's,' I added. 'We are supposed to be inviolate. I think we should close ranks.'

'Do you indeed? And you think me at risk, I presume?'

'I know I am,' I replied gloomily, dropping my gaze. 'I have had a bellyful of the Queen and her kin and they know it. I have been kept standing in the corner of the schoolroom for far too long, cousin.'

He smiled. 'St Paul has the truth of it: *"When I was a child, I spake as a child, I understood as a child, I thought as a child: but when I became a man, I put away childish things."* I do not think Edward treated you decently either, Harry.'

Oh, he was kind, so kind that I wondered if he was going to be able to sidestep the grave the Queen was digging for him in London.

I cleared my throat. 'To speak plainly, I was wondering if you would consider betrothing your son to my little Bess.' Looking up to see his reaction, I found nothing in his face to reassure me.

'Ah, so it seems I have to purchase your loyalty, after all.'

Damnation on my frank words! I should not have rushed the matter.

'No,' I said irritably, showing him that he had bruised my honour. 'It is just something I have been thinking of for a long time. I want the best for her.' This was not going the way I wanted. The catlike way he was watching me, I felt I was already arraigned for treason. 'Clearly, you believe I am in league with the Woodvilles and this is a trap,' I muttered unhappily.

Then to my astonishment, he laughed. 'Get off your high horse, man. No, I can guess why *you* are here although I have not completely fathomed Rivers.'

'I should think—'

'No, not yet,' he hushed me. 'We are talking about you, Harry. Why *are* you here? Revenge?'

I stared evenly back at him. 'Partly.'

'No, do better than that. Revenge is not enough. I want other reasons.'

'Very well, then.' I stood up, warming to my purpose. 'It is time the old nobility reasserted itself. There are others like me with ancient titles yet we have been denied our rightful place at the royal council table by the Queen's creatures. I want my rights, cousin. I have waited long enough.' I paced to the shuttered casement and back. 'Besides, you need me tomorrow.'

'Do I?'

'If you imagine Rivers came back to—'

'Kiss my hand? You are doing a tailored job as well, I might say.' He was leaning against the table watching me. The candles lit his face from below. Cynicism had its tendrils into him like lichen on granite.

'So, Harry? The Prince's company could have reached St Alban's by now thinking me lullabied into sleep by Rivers and your worthy self.' Well, he would have been a fool not to suspect me. 'For all I know,' he continued, 'the Queen may have offered you Wales and the chancellorship of England.'

'Yes, she could have, Richard, but she didn't. God's truth, cousin, do you want my loyalty or not?' The room was silent save for my fractured breath. 'Hastings asked me to support you and here I am!'

He came across to the table and ran a hand across the case that held River's book, his expression pained.

'Forgive me for saying this, Harry, and do not take offence, but you've never fought in a battle, have you?'

'No, cousin, I have not. Do you doubt my combat skills?'

'Not at all. That's not what I'm trying to say.' I watched his fingers slide wearily across his cheek bones before he spoke again. 'Battles are a savage waste and I never want to fight another one.'

Was he suddenly lily-livered?

'Look,' I said, 'if the Prince should reach London ahead of us and be crowned before you are sworn in as Lord Protector, Elizabeth will become Regent. Once that happens, she will find some way of arraigning us for treason. You and I shall be hauled to the Tower to have our heads chopped off and she will make sure our sons shall be kept as powerless as I was.'

'You forget the Royal Council, Harry.'

'The Royal Council is already stacked, cousin. You know that Hastings is having a hard time of it. I tell you they will make Elizabeth Regent. And if you think England will be better for it....' I shrugged, fuming.

He sucked in his cheeks. 'You think I could make a better task of ruling England?'

'By Heaven, yes!' *With me to help you.* 'You could arrest Rivers tonight to be sure.' There, it was spoken at last.

He made no answer. The room was growing cold. I crouched to poke the dying embers and set two small logs across them but maybe I had left it too late.

'There has to be evidence.' The words came from behind my shoulder. 'If one acts without evidence, it is tyranny. I need the Royal Council's approval not their disgust.'

'I can see that.' I straightened, brushing my hands, certain now that he and I would be arrested tomorrow like a pair of hapless poachers. I had thought him a strong man but I was wrong. His inopportune sense of justice was making a eunuch of him.

He crossed to the casement and glanced out behind the oiled cloth that hid the street.

I was angry. Was there any use in arguing further? Looking at him now with shadows of weariness cradling his eyes and his lank hair, dull as tarnished copper, I glimpsed how the Londoners would see him after the glorious, towering Edward, and my soul began to ache. I had thought that my change of fortune lay with Gloucester, but God had been mocking me.

I drew breath to take my leave when there was a loud rattle of an outside latch, the growl of voices and the clank of armour in the passageway.

'What the—' My stomach panicked. Was it Rivers' men come for us? But Gloucester was watching me, his gaze narrow.

Christ's mercy! So he had suspected me to throw in my lot with Rivers. I was to be arrested.

Jesu! I had not even a dagger to defend myself. I eyed the poker but Gloucester stood once more before the hearth. There was nothing I could seize to hold my enemies at bay except the book box.

Ratcliffe burst into the room. Two armed men in white boar surcotes were behind him, escorting a fellow in a servant's tabard. It was stitched with the Woodville magpie device.

Gloucester seemed hardly surprised. Was the man being brought in to make false witness against me? I hugged the box against my breast and tried to stay calm.

'Your grace.' The fellow tumbled to his knees, clearly exhausted. Had he tried to outrun Gloucester's dogs? Would he grovel for mercy? No, something else was going on here.

Gloucester was smiling. 'Be seated, drink first and then speak freely. This gentleman with the bookbox is his grace of Buckingham.'

Feeling stupid, I put the damned thing down and waited, albeit still tense as a loaded crossbow.

The man drank almost to the dregs and knuckled his lips. 'It is like this, your grace. The Prince's retinue have orders to leave early tomorrow morning without you, and Lord Rivers is here to delay you. It is certain they intend to crown the Prince the moment they reach London and prevent you becoming Lord Protector.'

'How many of them are there? Have the Queen's men from London arrived yet?'

'Aye, they came in this evening under Sir Richard Grey's command.'

My cousin's eyebrows had risen. 'Grey, eh.'

'An' I can't swear to numbers, my lord, but it looked like close to a thousand, and every jack of 'em decently armed. I'd estimate they have over two thousand altogether. It will be nigh impossible to reach the Prince.'

My breathing had returned to normal. So I was not a suspect but an ally still.

I cleared my throat. 'And we have only six hundred between us, cousin.'

My tone told him that we were already dead men. Rivers probably had a force waiting to ambush us before we reached Stony Stratford. My only consolation was that it was Sir Richard Grey in charge. I had been expecting Dorset, the Queen's oldest son, to head the escort.

Gloucester made no answer and the messenger took a last swig.

'How can you be so certain of their intention, sirrah?' I demanded. 'Are you privy to their council?'

The fellow glanced to my cousin for permission before he spoke. 'Because, my lord, I have been a bodyservant in the Prince's household this last year.'

Gloucester's cheeks were twin concaves and there was a sheepish glint to his eyes as he watched me.

'Have you agents in my household, too, my lord of Gloucester?' I asked rather huffily.

'I do not think so,' he laughed, and clapped a hand on his spy's shoulders. 'My thanks, loyal friend. To bed with you and sleep well.'

'So!' He clasped his hands gleefully and turned to Ratcliffe. 'Dick, set your men stealthily about Lord Rivers' inn. We mustn't panic him. The moment there is any stirring, wake me, whatever the hour. Tell Huddleston and Scope to post guards on all the town gates and posterns. None of Rivers' men must have a chance to warn Grey.'

I stared at my cousin, feeling as though my sails had gone slack.

'To bed, Harry,' he exclaimed, grasping me by the forearms. 'I suspect we shall have to rise early, very early.' I gazed at him in delight. I was no longer in Brecknock but at the throat of history.

'You played me like a fish, you whoreson,' I said affectionately.

His hazel eyes gleamed. 'I remembered there was another Duke of Gloucester, Humphrey, Hal of Agincourt's brother, and he was Lord Protector—'

'—and his nephew's queen had him poisoned,' I finished.

'It is not going to happen to me, cousin, be sure of that.' For an instant, I saw the glitter of tears about his eyes but it could have been my imagination.

3

'Your grace! Wake up!' Bannaster was shaking me. It was still dark, Hell take it!

'My lord, his grace of Gloucester's man is below.' That was Pershall. The wet cloth he scoured across my stubble was unnecessary; danger can wake a man as fast as smoke in the nostrils. A piss and a mouth of ale later, I stumbled down the outer stairs. Knyvett and Limerick were already rousing up our retainers. I bade a dozen to accompany me and the rest to make ready to depart.

I met with my cousin outside in the courtyard in the drizzling gloom of pre-dawn. His broad collar was up like a dragon's ruff around his neck and he looked even more haggard than he had last night. Dwarfing him was a plump citizen, fidgety as a hen about to lay and looking exceedingly uncomfortable in the torchlight. I recognised Master Lynde.

'Why is the mayor here?' I whispered, plucking my cousin's sleeve, as I followed him out beneath the lane archway into the street.

'To bear witness that justice is being meted out. Rivers tried to leave. I have no qualms now in arresting him.'

My heart leapt. 'Where is he now?'

'Confined to his inn. Come, there's little time.'

He walked fast. I kept up with him, determined that the world would see I was in this with him. Lynde and a score of his armed men fell in behind us. Our footsteps echoed ominously in the silent street. I had never felt so alive in my life.

ARMS folded in a sulk, Rivers was leaning against a trestle in the candle-light of the inn's main chamber, where the air hung heavy with last night's ale. Although a night's growth silvered his chin, he still looked very much the courtier and his emerald dressing robe, which swirled with embroideries of golden pilgrim shells, looked to be of heavy Syrian silk. Of course, his hair was suitably unkempt as if he had been awakened by our knocking and no doubt his travelling clothes had been swiftly tidied away as proof of his innocence.

'Dickon,' he exclaimed, letting irritation and puzzlement swathe his features. 'What is going on?' Then he recognised the mayor and I swear the blood ebbed from his face even though he continued with an air of nonchalance. 'Is there some felon gone to ground? My servants tell me you have the inn surrounded.'

'Yes.' There was an unpleasant silence

The Queen's brother gasped like a landed fish. 'Why, I went out myself to see what was going on and two men in your livery thrust me back with pikes.'

'In your dressing gown or was it your riding gear?' I asked. At that, he looked from my cousin's face to mine and discovering how much I hated him, turned back to my cousin's brooding countenance. There was no more 'Dickon' in his address.

'What is amiss here, Gloucester? I cannot be under suspicion. I came back all the way from Stony Stratford especially to sup with you.' He swung round angrily on me and anger was unusual for Rivers. 'Is this your interference, Buckingham? What poison have you been putting about?'

I moved so that the trestle was between us and leaned across at him.

'You were fully clad earlier, my lord, and we know you gave orders to your men last night that you would be leaving Northampton before we were astir.'

'No, that's a lie. I swear to you I have only this instant been awakened.' He threw that at Gloucester and swung round to face Lynde. 'Master Mayor, as the Lord God is my witness, these are false accusations.'

But the Mayor of Northampton stood silent. At a nod from his master, Ratcliffe stepped forward with two soldiers at his elbows

'Raise your arms, my lord!'

Rivers stood seething as they searched him for weapons.

'Enough!' Thrusting aside his robe, he unfastened his beltpurse and plucked out a folded square of parchment with dags of sealing wax clinging to it. 'This is a letter that King Edward, your brother, signed on his deathbed giving me full powers to escort Prince Edward to London with as many men as I choose. Master Mayor, witness that I have done naught but my duty.' Ratcliffe handed it across to Richard, who carried it to the candle.

'I have no quarrel with this, Lord Rivers.' He passed the parchment to the mayor. 'However, as uncles of the blood royal, his grace of Buckingham and I see it as our duty to escort our nephew to London, yet you sought to prevent us.' He took the letter back from Lynde and whisked it into the candle flame.

'Christ Almighty, Gloucester! The King loved us both. You cannot do this.'

But Rivers, who had beguiled many princes of the world with his verses, his jousting and his handsome looks, had overplayed his hand.

'You will remain here under arrest, my lord, until this matter is fully investigated. Master Lynde, I pray you command my men as your own in this matter.'

Gloucester nodded to the mayor and strode sternly out through the line of soldiers. Lynde bustled after him as though the instructions had not been enough.

I lingered at the door and turned.

Cat's brother was standing dazed among the ugly scrubbed trestles like a battered tree after a tempest. He had underestimated Richard and he had underestimated me.

'Adieu, Rivers, I'll carry your love to Elizabeth.'

He made no reply to me, no pithy answer worthy of the philosopher or pilgrim, but just stared expressionless at me. It would be the first time I could leave his company not feeling like a fool.

'Harry.'

I turned.

And then he spat.

MY cousin was already mounted, his mouth a grim line of impatience. On horseback, with his collared mantle lending him more substance and the long crocodilus of our retinues tailing out behind him, he looked what I hoped he was, a man about to take possession of a kingdom.

'Is aught wrong, my lord of Buckingham?' he asked. The torches must have lit the raw wound of emotion in my face as I slid into the saddle and took my horse's reins.

'No,' I answered hoarsely, unclenching my jaw. 'Let us be quit of here.'

He twisted round and gave the order to move off. As swiftly as any army might, we rode down Watling Street.

Darkness and drizzle are poor companions and we made little speed until the dawn. It was about half-past the hour of eight when Richard waved a halt and signalled to one of his captains. The man instantly rode back along the column.

Uncle Knyvett urged his horse up alongside mine. 'How is this going to be played out, Harry? We are nearly at the causeway to Stony Stratford.' He was jumpy and with good reason. I was wondering the same myself. It was a few years since I had passed through the town but I remembered the causeway being narrow, a good place for an ambush.

Richard heard us and turned in his saddle. 'If they are expecting Lord Rivers at any instant, they'll have lookouts. We do not want to disappoint them, do we?' One of his knights claimed his attention and he turned away with a tight smile.

'Clear as Yorkshire mud,' muttered Uncle Knyvett. 'Am I missing someth—'

I laughed. 'Look!'

A horseman bearing River's scallop shell banner galloped up from behind us and foot soldiers, wearing the stolen liveries of his company, swarmed past us to halt panting, ahead of our horses. They regrouped themselves tightly behind the banner, glancing back over their shoulders. It was fair-haired Lovell that they were waiting for. Garbed in Rivers' hat and riding cloak, he spurred past us to head the procession.

'Well, it might work,' muttered Uncle Knyvett grudgingly. 'Morelike, the Woodvilles have the child halfway to London by now.'

'And leave Lord Rivers to our loving kindness? No, I do not think so.'

'Mother of God, Harry, the Queen's grace has sent over a thousand men to safeguard her fledgling. Are you sure my lord of Gloucester knows what he's up against?'

'I trust his judgment, uncle.' Then I added an honest addendum. 'God's truth, but sometimes it is hard to tell betwixt what is thought out and what is improvised.'

Uncle Knyvett's answer was an exasperated sigh as he checked that his sword could slide freely. Then he took off his cloak so if need be he might wind it round his left forearm as a buckler. I felt like doing the same but with

Richard a few paces away and the rest of our retinue needing confidence, I resisted the temptation.

We gave Lovell about a hundred paces start and the ruse worked, for we heard a horn sound ahead of us. Nevertheless, my mouth was dry as I sighted the causeway chapel and the first inn of the town. My spurs almost tangled with Richard's as we led the way across the narrow causeway.

Well, no one attacked us but any fool could realise Stony Stratford was a confounded death trap. All I could see, once we passed the Eleanor Cross, was the narrow, unbroken strip of taverns and merchants' houses, with Lovell's men heading towards a huge plug of people, stoppering any escape.

Sweet Christ! I had not seen as many people since the Queen's coronation when I was scarce out of infant skirts. I swallowed, my hand longing to clamp round my sword handle. Would I die this morning as I had feared in my dreams last night? Had it been like this for my grandsire at St Albans, forced up against somebody's front door or cornered in a yard, hacked to death between a rainwater barrel and a housewife's washing?

'Christ ha' mercy!' I must have said it aloud for Richard turned his face to me. The whoreson did not have a twitch of fear in his entire body.

'Time to send our heralds, I believe.' He lifted his arm and immediately the captain behind us set a horn to his lips. Our trumpeters blared and Lovell's men split rank, fluidly swerving aside to let our heralds through. We followed.

I could see now that scores of townsfolk stood at the edge of a huge pack of liveried retainers and in their midst, beneath the drooping pennons and damp banners, were a thicket of horsemen, who were reining round to face us in some concern as they saw our banners. Our heralds rode straight in, looking to neither right nor left and hubbub ensued as the townsfolk gave way, tearing like a threadbare cloth before their horses.

My stallion threw up his head. He must have felt my fear running down the taut rein. Sweet Jesu, I had never been so afraid in my life. Either side my stirrups, the Woodville men-at-arms stared, their mouths roundels of confusion beneath their brimmed sallets, but a yell, that's all it would take, and they could drive their baselards into our horses' breasts and drag us down. I was praying hard. The stretching crowd seemed endless. To my right a great ganglion of retainers was bulging out into a marketplace. Beyond that was the river. Nowhere to run.

We drew close enough to see that our young quarry was astride his horse. Judging by their gestures, several nobles about the Prince were in fierce argument and a young man with long blond hair was staring at us in consternation—Sir Richard Grey, Cat's nephew, the Queen's son from an earlier marriage.

Richard dismounted and I did so, too. The way before us was insufficient to walk abreast and I followed him dry-mouthed, feeling like Moses walking the bed of the Red Sea while God held back its might. But not for an instant did my cousin hesitate. He might be a runt in stature but he was cursed tall in courage.

'God save your grace' whispered like a litany as we passed, and word that Gloucester was come hissed out through the crowd like wind through reeds. The townsfolk began huzzahing.

The twelve year old Prince was staring at us and then he recognised his uncle and inclined his head. A pretty young stripling he was, too, with the leggy look of a young colt. The cap and mantle of the mourning blue, reserved for kings, favoured his complexion and the Woodville ash-blond hair. As Richard reached his stirrup, the boy, with genuine pleasure, extended his hand for his uncle to kiss.

Then it was my turn.

'God bless your highness.' Since he did not dismount, I did not kneel.

Golden lashes twitched above eyes that were a chillier blue than his father's. There was no cheer for me, only puzzlement. I had not seen him since his little brother's wedding to the Mowbray heiress five years ago, just before George's trial. He must have been only seven years old; now he was almost thirteen.

'My lord,' he said politely, but with little warmth in his greeting. Such a Woodville already! I discreetly lowered my stare to his little cross of pearls and rubies. By Heaven, he clearly had no notion of who I was or if he did, it was a studied insult. I was not at all pleased.

'This is his grace the Duke of Buckingham, your highness,' intervened a man wearing a the broad-brimmed hat of a churchman. I lifted my head and received a placatory smile. It was Alcock, Bishop of Worcester, President of the Council of the Welsh Marches, wondering which side of his bread to butter.

40

'Yes, another uncle, your highness.' I nodded, with my teeth showing. 'It has been a long while since we met.'

'You are welcome, Uncle Buckingham,' Prince Edward said, a spark of memory flaring. But he was frowning beyond me at the noblemen from his entourage who were rapidly dismounting to greet his Uncle Gloucester. 'I though we were leaving now,' he said loudly. The irritation edging the choir-boy voice seemed to be directed at his half-brother, Grey.

Richard heard the complaint and swung round to face him. 'Have you been waiting long, your highness?' he asked cheerfully.

'An hour at least. Where is my Uncle Rivers? You said he was here, brother.' Another verbal cannonball hurled at Grey, whose mouth was still catching flies. Rivers' banner had disappeared but Grey was staring north-wards across the crowd in utter puzzlement. His pallor matched his name.

'Dear me,' said Richard smoothly. 'I thought it was my lord of Buck-ingham and I who had delayed you, your highness.'

'No, Uncle Gloucester. It is my Uncle Rivers. He should be here by now. You must have seen him on the road. Did he not sup with you last evening?'

My cousin glanced northwards without concern. 'He is delayed, I fear. Shall we go to your inn and take refreshment?'

'But we have to leave now, Uncle Gloucester.' There was a stamp of foot in his tone.

'Do we, your highness?'

'Why, yes, madame my mother expects us in London. I am to be crowned.'

'And has your highness had breakfast?' Richard asked and glanced round in friendly fashion at the royal followers.

'No, uncle.'

'Then let us have breakfast,' I interrupted, making it a song for three voices.

What could our little uncrowned colt reply? Would his stepbrother, Grey, or his hoary treasurer, Vaughan, assert we must hurry? Not Grey, who had many a time smuggled spiders into my winecup when I lived at West-minster. He suddenly discovered his bootcaps of immense interest as I stared along the unhappy cluster of officers from Ludlow who had usurped my rightful dominance in Wales. 'Sir Richard Vaughan,' I exclaimed, singling out the man who had been given my duties in Western Wales. 'Maybe you think otherwise?'

Pale as a newly hewn tombstone, he looked round at me, and saw Richard studying him, too.

'No, not at all, your gra…, your graces.'

Those around him shuffled and murmured. Not one of them was prepared to stick his neck out. Had Rivers been in command there, history could have been written differently and I might already have an obituary.

Ah, it was a sweet hour. I was hard put not to grin with satisfaction as I watched the Queen's knights stiffly consign their horses' bridles to their servants and follow us. The crowd parted, cooing. An uncle at each elbow, the future King Edward V walked between us back in the gentle drizzle to *The Rose and Crown*. Most appropriate. A blushing rose; you could see where the white paint was fading and the old Lancastrian red was showing through.

At first, I thought Richard was handling the business like a master, steering everyone into privacy away from a public quarrel. Without even a bloody nose, he had outfaced and outmanoeuvred the entire Woodville retinue. It was checkmate with a soaring, illuminated capital 'C'. There was no question now that I should throw in my lot with his.

I could not resist hurling a discreet smirk in Uncle Knyvett's direction, but seeing Grey being prodded along behind us, I have to admit that he was not a worthy Goliath to our David. Elizabeth's mistake. She should have sent the Archbishop of York, a prince of the Church, not her commoner son. You do not fight eagles with a jackdaw.

ONCE inside the inn, Richard abruptly held out his arms to his nephew. Time for an embrace and thump of each other's shoulders in mutual grief.

'I cannot tell you how sorry I am about your father, lad.' I could hear the Yorkshire dialect in my cousin's voice as he let genuine emotion overcome him. Droplets glistened on his lashes, and, for his part, the Prince could be heard gulping back his tears. 'I loved him so much, Ned. England has lost a great king.' Uncle Gloucester drew back, swallowing. 'But look at you.' He buffeted the boy's chest. 'Almost a man.'

They were both sniffling and the grief was epidemic. Someone behind me blew his nose loudly and there was a little patter of applause. All eyewipingly moving unless you had no future except four walls and a pail to piss in and Grey looked as though he needed a pail.

My belly was rumbling but Richard decided some sort of formal speech was due. I would have been happy with a five minute eulogy on the late king, and, besides, Stony Stratford's *Rose and Crown* was hardly the hall of Parliament, but my cousin's endorsement of our common grief rapidly turned into a sermon.

Heaven help us! It was as if his control, dammed up while he thought himself in peril, suddenly broke. All his resentment at bearing the weight of administration in the north and campaigning against the Scots, while down in the south his brother tweaked Mistress Shore's duckies and grew fat with indulgence, spewed out.

I am paraphrasing somewhat. Richard's phrases were somewhat dryer, but the meaning was the same—the exclamation of the Labouring Brother against the Prodigal Son. Bitter as gall! And he openly blamed the Queen's kinsmen, especially Rivers and the Grey boys for encouraging King Edward in orgies of lewd carnality and wine bibbling.

God's truth, I thought, here's a different side to my cousin's coin. Just last night I had called him a 'whoreson' in play. I knew better from now on. I must cut my cloth to suit the times.

Richard had reached his peroration.

'Arrest them!' he commanded, pointing at Grey, Vaughan and Haute in turn.

'Ned!' shrieked Grey, flinging himself on his knees before his half-brother. 'Forbid it! You are the King!' He clutched the Prince's hose so tight that it was a wonder the boy's points did not snap.

'Uncle Gloucester,' intervened the boy, confused and frightened by Grey's vehemence. 'I do not understand.'

'You are the King, not him!' Grey repeated, shaking the royal legs. 'In God's Name, save us!'

The boy drew himself together. His voice wobbled but he managed to argue.

'Your pardon, Uncle Gloucester, but if the king my father appointed these lords to administer my household and the Welsh Marches, I do not see why anyone should doubt his judgment, for they have committed no offence against me. And they were certainly not in London giving my father any evil counsel but with me at Ludlow. If my Uncle Rivers were here, he would tell you so.' What a clever lad. Heaven help us if he was crowned too soon. The selfish note in his voice irked me, too. He sounded more put out by the threat to his household arrangements, than concerned for Grey.

I stepped forward clearing my throat. 'Your highness and your grace, will you hear me, please?' I asked, bowing deeply, and most of those present thought I was going to speak on Grey's behalf.

The Prince nodded, looking relived at my intervention.

'Do stand up, nephew,' I said to Grey, drawing him to his feet and wrapping my arm about him. 'Wait over here, if you please.' I left him beside Ratcliffe and turned to face the boy. 'Your highness, I wish to say two things. Firstly, that your household officers at Ludlow were people appointed as teachers to educate you; they were not appointed to counsel you as king.' I waited for Bishop Alcock to twitch or interrupt but his mouth was clamped shut. A pity!

'Indeed,' I continued, 'I believe no one in this place would doubt that it should be the greatest and wisest lords of this realm who should attend your royal person and sit on the Royal Council.' I ignored Vaughan's furious countenance. After all, once being treasurer to Dead Ned did not mean he had a right to be so again.

'The other matter is this. Your father, God rest his soul, appointed his grace of Gloucester as Lord Protector but there has been a conspiracy to thwart your father's wishes and these gentlemen here are at the heart of it. So, I regret to say, is your Uncle Rivers.' That drew a protest from Grey. I turned. 'Until these matters are investigated, sirs, I ask you to give yourselves into custody. If you are innocent, you have nothing to fear.' I swung back to the Prince. 'They need to answer questions, your highness. It is a formality, nothing sinister.'

'My loyalty is to my brother the King,' exclaimed Grey, but he was not coming up with any arguments to defend himself. If he had had his wits about him, he and the boy should have been ten miles along the road by now.

Now perhaps we could get on with breakfast.

'But I am still confused!' muttered Prince Edward. 'What conspiracy?'

Your turn, I indicated to Richard.

The tempest that had rocked him was gone and he was calm as any earnest magistrate.

'We have evidence that these knights and Lord Rivers planned to arrest your Uncle Buckingham and myself on the way to London in order to prevent me becoming Lord Protector.' His tone grew stentorian again. 'I did not come with an army but Rivers did. So did Grey here. Do you *need* two thousand men against my three hundred? What other possible motive could they have had?'

'To honour me, perhaps, Uncle Gloucester,' the boy replied and swallowed, but he had been well-schooled in speech-making. Encouraged by Grey's desperate look, he flexed his wings again. 'My lords and gentlemen, let us all journey to London together and you may air this matter before my lady mother and the royal coun—'

Over my dead body!

'Your pardon, your highness,' I interrupted. 'It is not the business of women but of men to rule this kingdom. Your father left no such authority to your mother.'

'Edward,' said Richard gently, wrapping his arm about the boy's shoulders. 'I never failed to obey your father's wishes and out of the great love I have for him, I would not fail him now. Shall you be content with your father's wishes or not?'

The Prince looked wretchedly towards his half-brother and then back to his Uncle Richard and again to the watching faces, then his shoulders sank. Ha!

'I am content with the government my father wanted.' His expression begrudged his words but it was enough. The air seemed to rush back into the chamber as though we had all been holding our breath in unison.

'His grace of Buckingham and I shall breakfast with his highness upstairs,' my cousin declared and with that he swept the tearful boy to his chamber, while I made sure the rest of the Prince's officers were herded together in the taproom with our soldiers on all the entrances. I gave orders to feed all of them. Men are more open to change on a full stomach.

Alcock was the only bishop among them, or so I thought until I recognised the small man beside him. Ah, yes, Robert Stillington, Bishop of Bath and Wells. I remembered Stillington from the time of George's trial. Dead Ned had booted him off to the Tower for 'utterances'—though our jury never heard what they were. Why he was lurking in this company of Woodville supporters was a puzzlement that I would leave to another time.

Upstairs, it was clear that the new King of England had indulged in a good blub, for the boy's nose and ears were red, and Richard, sitting next to him on a settle, had damp blotches on his mantle.

'It looks like it is clearing up be a fine afternoon,' I observed, falling back on our English habit of commenting on the weather when there is nothing else to say. I leaned out over the sunny sill of the jutting gable, rejoicing that I was not bleeding across a doorstep. Down below the townsfolk were still loitering, waiting for another glimpse of the Prince. A young woman blew me a kiss and I smiled back, and then I drew a tight breath.

Across the street a monkey tail of cheerful Woodville retainers was stretching down the street and one of Richard's bannerets was riding up and down directing more to join it. Curious, I leaned out further and saw that it led to the back of a cart flanked by pikemen in my cousin's murrey and blue. A chest was open in the back and some sort of largesse was being handed out. Devil take it! The whoresons were being paid off! Some were disappearing into *The Cock* and *The Crossed Keys* or eyeing up the cluster of young townswomen, who should have known better. Others were saying farewells, preparing to leave. Sweet Mother of God, my cousin had the cunning of Ulysses.

Oh, I had a lot to learn, I could see that. I closed the window, feeling as useless as teats on a ram, and turned. Somehow I would have to find a way to tip the balance of our alliance so he owed me a thing or two.

My cousin raised a complacent eyebrow at me but I shook my head and took off my hat and mantle, and then I unbuckled my purse.

'Did I hear something about your highness having a nagging tooth?' I asked kindly, going down on my haunches before the Prince.

'I'm not a three year old, Uncle Buckingham.'

'No, of course not.' But I was justly reprimanded. It was not my little lad Ned I was dealing with. 'This,' I said, holding a shiny bezoar stone cabuchoned in my fingers, 'came from the belly of a creature that has a neck like a spire and lives beyond the boundaries of Christendom. It was given to me by Lord Hastings when I was your age. I assure you it works. You sleep with it under your pillow.'

It was clear he did not want a gift from me but he muttered his thanks and kept it.

'You might enjoy a rest later, Edward,' murmured Uncle Gloucester. 'What time did they make you rise?'

'Six. I was waiting saddled up outside for hours.'

'So much for sleeping in,' I remarked. 'Ah, here at last is breakfast. I am starving.'

A procession of servants carried in pottage, newly baked bread and local cheeses.

'I'm not hungry,' our new sovereign said sullenly. My cousin pulled a face at me behind the boy's head and I shrugged.

'What do you intend to do now, make for London?' I asked as he washed his hands thoroughly in the ewer.

'No, not until I have word from Lord Hastings that it is safe. I am not going to walk into a charge of treason.'

'*Lord Hastings*, uncle?' The royal pitcher had ears. We had found the magic word to open his mind.

'Yes, Edward, it was Lord Hastings who warned your Uncle Buckingham and myself that your kinsmen would try to prevent me becoming Lord Protector.'

'I do not understand any of this.' Well, Edward, welcome to Westminster, where we smile like the crocodilus and never say what we really think.

When our sulky fledgling fled to the privy, Richard shook his fingers as though burned and grinned at me.

It was a poxy breakfast. The pottage was oversalted, the heart of the bread was undercooked and the cheeses lacked flavour.

Afterwards, Richard sent for a writing board and began busily scratching out a letter in his own hand to let Hastings know what had happened. Meanwhile I fidgeted, unwilling to stay cooped up with a petulant Plantagenet. Then Inspiration pinched me.

'I suggest we ride back to Northampton.'

Prince Edward looked up from his book and rolled his eyes as though I were a lunatic. But journeying back at a leisurely pace would give everyone something to occupy us and *The Bear's* food was better. 'I expect the people will go a-maying tomorrow. You could join them, your highness.'

'I cannot contain myself, uncle,' he retorted arrogantly. 'I am supposed to be riding to London to be crowned not watching some foolish apprentice in a wig with apples up his doublet.' *Brat!* He aped his Uncle Rivers' mannerisms.

'My apologies,' I retorted dryly, receiving an encouraging nod from Richard. 'But if it is Maid Marion in Northampton or a foul dinner here. I know which I would choose.'

'NORTHAMPTON, *full of love, beneath the girdle but not above.*'

Back along the road we went but the rain had gone and April was fleeing with the frisk of a lamb's tail. I remember the fleecy clouds like bulging pillows and the air's gentle warm embrace like a lover's arms.

The evening proved mellower than the morning and in the warm parlour where we had feasted the uncle we now honoured the nephew. I fetched out a fine pair of gloves that my little Bess had spent a week embroidering with white roses and tiny sunnes-in-splendour. Richard had a painstakingly-written letter of sympathy from his ten year old son, and the Prince received both graciously.

To humour him, Richard ordered food from our table to be sent across to Rivers. That pleased our colt and he grew more trusting as the wine brought a flush to his cheeks. We obviously could not be that cruel to think so considerately about our prisoner. But Rivers haughtily rejected the supper, suggesting it might be sent to Grey instead. The latter lacked the full Woodville sulkiness; the platter was returned clean.

'I must write to the Royal Council as well and explain matters,' declared Richard, as our trenchers were removed. 'It might be wise if you wrote to them too, Edward, to reassure them that we shall be in London as soon as possible.' He sent a page out once more for writing materials. 'Being king, you will discover, is not all crown-wearings and royal progresses but signing orders and dispatches and keeping yourself informed as to what is happening in every corner of your kingdom. Can you read swiftly?'

I could see he had missed his calling as a schoolmaster.

'Of course.' The Prince looked insulted. 'I can read Latin, French and Greek and Uncle Rivers taught me some Spanish as well.'

His uncle ignored the boasting. 'You might also like to consider whether there is anyone at Ludlow you wish to reward for their service to you. No haste. Think it over for a few days. Ah, here comes the parchment, let us *both* write to the Royal Council.'

Oh, it was so homely. The pair of them sat together at the board, like a pair of scriveners, noisy as mice with their quills, while Lovell and I played chess.

'I have finished, uncle.'

Richard scanned the boy's letter. 'Excellent! Your first dispatch as king. Show me your signature. No, not on the letter.' He pushed a virgin parchment in front of him.

Tongue pressed between his teeth, our new king wrote, *'Edwardus'*.

'Finish it,' coaxed Richard. The boy glanced at him, then nodded and added *'Quintus'*.

'Let me see,' I remarked, strolling over to join in leaving Lovell to decide whether to take my bishop. I glanced over Prince Edward's head at the large, spindly letters. Before long, his signature would take up half the paper. 'There's uncertainty there but a growing sense of worth. You can judge a great deal from a person's script, their emotions as they write and so forth.'

'Can you so?' The lad shrugged. 'Go on, Uncle Gloucester.' He dipped the quill into the inkwell and handed it across. My cousin smiled, thought for a moment, and then in Italianate hand, wrote: *Loyaulté me lie*.

'French,' crowed the boy. '"Loyalty binds me."'

'And much more, Edward.' He wet the shaft again and wrote *R. Gloucestre* underneath and bracketed the lines together. 'My pledge to your father renewed in your service.'

So endearing. I bit my tongue to stop myself uttering, 'Ahhhhh.'

'My turn,' I declared, holding out my hand for the quill. I glimpsed the Woodville glint in the boy's eye as he handed it to me. It reminded me of Cat's expression when I asked for one of her women to mend a tear in my hose.

It was easy to follow my cousin's example. I wrote my device: *Souvente me souvene* and beneath it, *Harre Bokingham*. My script cantered flamboyantly in comparison to Richard's dainty trot.

'"Often remember me",' translated the Prince. 'That's an odd one to have, Uncle Buckingham.'

'It certainly is. I inherited it along with a Welsh castle and cobwebs.'

'Your move, my lord,' Lovell called out.

He had left his king vulnerable. 'Checkmate,' I said, moving my bishop down its oblique road. I buffeted his defeated lordship and turned to the royal letter writers. 'Will your royal highness grant me leave to go to bed?' I bowed with a flourish and looked beyond him to the potential ruler of England.

'Goodnight, Harry.' Richard's expression thanked me for my support that day. Mind, we were not through the perilous mire yet. We still had the Queen and London ahead of us.

THE walk back to my inn washed sleep from my mind. My henchmen were laughing at some jest but I was replaying the morning's triumph over and over and my Plantagenet blood was fizzing with the firecracker we had loosed among the Woodvilles.

Revenge, such a sweet word! News of this day would reach Elizabeth and she would rage in her chambers, screaming with fury. The cold wind from Northampton would ripple up her fur and she would know her summer was over.

I needed a woman that night, a long-legged, local wench. The trouble was if word reached my righteous cousin across the way, it would lower his opinion of me and I could not afford the risk. Not yet. In London it would be different. Our gables would not be grinning at one another across the gutters, and Pershall would be able to find me a girl without the whole world knowing. Still the itch was there; even Cat would have been worth nuzzling.

'My lord duke, good evening to you.' The Cambridge scholar, Nandik, was waiting for me at the foot of the stairs. A human cat ready to rub against my bootcuffs. He had already bought himself a better doublet and new boots and his dark hair was several inches shorter.

'My lord, I write a fair hand. Do you need letters prepared or is there some other way I may serve you?' Poor wretch, I had forgotten I had asked him to wait up for me. I nodded to him to follow us up to my bedchamber.

As we drank on, he proved quite a wit, pumping out scurrilous tales of pompous Cambridge deans.

'Do you know it's the Devil's Eve?' he asked as the Grey Friars' bell struck midnight. We all crossed ourselves.

'Ah well, I am sure all the Northampton housewives will be flying on their broomsticks to the nearest common,' I quipped. The thought of the tapster wench at *The Bear* naked astride a broomstick was definitely appealing. Imagination would have to be my solace when I climbed into bed.

'Have any of you ever met a witch, a true witch?' asked Limerick.

'I met the Queen's mother,' I chuckled. 'Oh come, do you not remember the old besom was investigated for wi…' I hiccoughed, 'witchcraft back in '69, but, beshrew me, I have had it to here with Woodvilles for today.' I sliced a wobbly finger across my throat. 'To Fortune, the comely wench!' We soon emptied the jug.

I turned my inebriated attention to Nandik. 'Did you study ast…ast—'

'Astrology, my lord? Aye, it was part of my studies.'

'Then c-can you…? No, no, uncle, let me finish! Can…can you cast a horoscope for me, Nan…Nan-dik?'

'Given the correct information, your grace.'

'Wh-wh-en we reach London, cast mine for me, Nan-hic-dik, good man. He's a good man, isn't he, eh?'

'Without accurate co-ordinates, my lord, it may mean nothing but, pray you, see this.' The fellow took a folded paper from his bosom. My horoscope?

'Christ forbid!' snarled Uncle Knyvett, but I snatched it before he could.

'What does it s-say?' I asked, blinking at the hurly-burly of spheres and Latin. 'I think I need spectacles.'

'At twenty-nine, my lord?' That was Delabere chiming in. 'You're in your cups.'

'Am I? No wonder I c-cannot read the poxy thing. Interpret, if you please, M-Master Scholar. You have terrible handwriting.'

'Fame shall exceed your wealth. '

'Pah! F-Fame! Half of England has…has never heard of me.'

'What about the other half?' quipped Latimer.

I laughed. 'Well, they haven't either. You're a p-poxy flatterer, Nandik.'

'No, your grace, it is true. You will go down in the chronicles.' Then he mumbled something about being careful of Rivers, and that therein lay my fate. Well, I'd already dealt with that danger.

To be honest, I am not certain that was the entire gist of our conversation, for in the morning I had a sore head and a poor memory. Nor did I resurrect the matter with Nandik that day but secretly I resolved to give him the correct hour of my birth and let him draw the chart anew when we reached London.

Any man could have made the same prediction as Nandik. However, that night in Northampton was Satan's Eve. I wonder now if the Devil did crawl out of Hell to listen to our idle words.

4

Our new monarch endured the penance of watching Northampton's May Day celebrations. Together with Mayor Lynde, it was my chore to attend Prince Edward, who proved quite amenable until afterwards when I laughingly refused his request to see our Woodville hostages. He threw a tantrum and retired to his room to sulk so I took myself off on a local pilgrimage. First to my grandsire's grave in the Church of the Grey Friars, and then to the guildhall where Lynde dredged up two elderly aldermen, who had witnessed the battle of 1460 and agreed to show me the actual place where my grandfather was slain. To be honest, I am not sure that they even knew but they pointed out some laneway flagstones where I could say a prayer and leave my flowers of remembrance. Still high on yesterday's bloodless victory, I was no longer as mindful as I should have been of Grandfather Buckingham's bloody end—how Fate can strike the seemingly inviolate. My lesson from his demise? Choose the most likely victor!

As the sombre afternoon dimmed, Richard, with the typical Plantagenet impatience that all of us possess, tired of dictating letters to the individual members of the Royal Council assuring them of his honesty. He called his officers and mine together and we began feverishly to plan our action if London chose to support the Woodvilles.

Our main strength was that we held the boy. However, with only a few hundred men between us, and both of us far from our eyries and unable to drum up more soldiers in the blink of an eye, we were still very vulnerable. Richard had already dished out all the coin he had brought with him to pay off the Queen's men and I was reserving mine for London.

Hasting's sweaty messenger arrived just after nightfall.

Although hardly recognizable beneath an outer covering of dust, this ambitious grub was known to me. Sir William Catesby of Northamptonshire was one of the new generation of gentry who had taken the law as a career and were making it slightly more respectable. He had inched his way onto many a noble's estate council, including mine (maybe he thought I had potential) but he was Hastings' protégé. Now, despite the hard riding, his slate eyes were alert as those of a shrinekeeper glimpsing a pair of wealthy pilgrims.

'My lord of Buckingham.'

'Catesby, it's good to see you again,' I exclaimed, offering my hand. His smile was even more toothy for Richard, as he dropped to one knee before him.

'Your graces, Lord Hastings thought it best to send someone well known to you, so that you shall know I speak the truth.' I thought a lawyer only spoke what his fee dictated but I was not going to argue that one.

'You must be exhausted, man,' said Gloucester, gesturing him to rise. If he was panting to hear the news, he hid it well.

'Your graces, we advise...' he began. 'Your pardon, I mean Lord Hastings advises that London is now safe for you to enter. The good news is that the Queen's grace and the Marquis of Dorset have been trying to rally support from all the lords and prelates in the city for the coronation, and the bad—'

'That is good news?' I interrupted.

'Indeed, yes, my lord of Buckingham, for not one of the noble lords wanted to have any truck with her.'

'Numbers are not everything, Catesby,' answered Richard. In view of his cunning and timing yesterday, I had to agree. 'Tell us the bad news!'

'The Queen has sent half the treasury to sea with her brother, Sir Edward Woodville.' Richard swore, but he let Catesby continue. 'That is why she could not hire an army or bribe anyone and, of course, two thousand of her most reliable supporters are already here with you, your graces.'

'*Were*,' I corrected, but my thoughts flickering with dismay.

'What about the other half of the treasury?' exclaimed my cousin, out-racing me to the next question.

Catesby's Adam's apple shifted nervously. 'I regret to say my lord of Dorset and the Bishop of Salisbury's men carted it to Westminster Sanctuary.' The whoresons!

'Hell take it, that's not possible, Catesby,' I protested, imagining how many chests of gold plate and coin were involved. 'You can hardly get a bench through the door let alone a great coffer. It would take them days.' The sanctuary was little better than an old keep, a couple of upper storeys, that was all. I had winkled Cat out of there to consummate our marriage.

54

'No, I swear it's true, your grace. The Queen demanded a wall be hewn down so they could stow it as swiftly as possible. She has claimed sanctuary and the Marquis of Dorset, my lord bishop and other friends are there as well.'

'Very cosy. They must be wading thigh high in goblets,' I snorted.

We had been outwitted. No government could rule without money.

Richard looked fit to strangle someone. 'What about the royal children?' he asked.

'She has Prince Richard and all your royal nieces with her. I am informed the little maidens were none too pleased. Princess Elizabeth was heard to argue when the Queen was saying how much she feared you.'

My cousin's face softened for an instant but then he lifted his head again, his voice like a dagger sheathed in pretty velvet. 'And where, pray, were Lord Hastings and yourself while Dorset was looting England's treasury?'

Catesby's face reddened beneath the dust. 'They outwitted us, your grace. You must understand that Lord Hastings has been utterly distraught over the death of your royal brother. What happened was the Queen bade my lord come to her at the palace and declared that he should serve Prince Edward best by serving her, and while my lord was distracted by her arguments, Dorset was meddling at the Tower.'

'And where were you, sirrah?' I asked.

'I was disputing with Archbishop Rotherham, your grace.'

'About what, Catesby?' cut in Richard. 'The price of wafers?'

'About the Great Seal, your graces. I should explain that Archbishop Rotherham had given the Great Seal to the Queen and Lord Hastings ordered me to find the Archbishop and persuade him to fetch it back from her.'

So not only would Richard as Lord Protector lack funds to rule the country but the seal of authority to do so. It was a mess.

My cousin turned his back on us. 'You have leave, Catesby!' he said in a choked voice.

'Your grace,' Catesby protested, almost grovelling. 'Lord Hastings acted against my advice and you must understand—'

'Oh, we do understand,' I answered for both of us.

'No, I must explain, my lord of Buckingham. The Bishop of Salisbury came to see Lord Hastings early yesterday asking him to negotiate a peace between the Queen and his grace of Gloucester.' He glanced respectfully at my cousin. 'He kept Lord Hastings talking for over an hour before the Queen sent for him and by then Dorset had organised the carts and had his men positioned. We had no cause to distrust them at that point, you see.'

We saw alright. Dorset had the brains his brother Grey lacked, and the Queen's sweet-talking brother, Bishop Lionel, possessed as much cunning as the serpent in the Garden of Eden. Lord Hastings should have been on his guard.

'Very well, Catesby.' I saw him to the door. 'Thank you for your loyalty. You shall be well recompensed when we reach London.' He bowed low over my hand and had barely closed the door behind him when my cousin whirled round.

'Holy Paul!' His fists struck his sides. 'Hastings is plaguey well in charge of the Mint. He should never have let them within spitting distance of the Tower.' He paced the floor, fidgeting angrily with his rings. 'The fool! He should have foreseen that Rotherham would give the Great Seal to Elizabeth. The old wretch is a Woodville creature, always has been.'

'Calm yourself, cousin,' I soothed. 'I am sure Lord Hastings will have sorted everything out by the time we enter London. A pity he fell for the ruse, though.'

Yes, we both owed Hastings a debt for alerting us to the Queen's animosity but one has to be practical. 'Maybe he's getting too long in the tooth,' I added, stirring the pot further. 'All sentiment aside, Richard, that's something you should bear in mind when we reach London. We cannot afford such errors.'

Richard stopped his pacing. 'Well, we should be in London within two days and God willing, things can't get worse. I'll write to the Archbishop of Canterbury tonight requesting him to get the Great Seal off Rotherham, and he can organise the Royal Council to take care of any remaining valuables my sister-in-law couldn't squeeze in.'

You're an optimist, I thought, but I held my tongue.

'What are you going to do with our prisoners, cousin?'

'Keep them hostage out of Elizabeth's reach. She'll lose a brother and a son if she wreaks any more mischief. Rivers can go to Sheriff Hutton, Grey to Middleham and Vaughan to Pontefract.' All his northern strongholds, and since the Woodvilles' supporters were mainly southerners, it seemed a sensible solution. 'Do not look so disappointed, Harry. I'll keep them salted for the winter.'

I smiled. 'Crated was what I had in mind.'

I BADE Northampton farewell next morning right cheerfully beneath a sky as blue as the Our Lady's robe and we rode off at an ambling pace with the Prince in our midst like a young queen bee carried to begin a new hive. When we arrived at St Albans, the townsfolk were waiting beneath the clock tower with an address of loyalty which much pleased young Edward. After the dinner generously provided by the Abbot of St Albans, Richard took the boy on a ride around the town for a lesson in military strategy.

St Albans had seen two battles fought between York and Lancaster and I needed no reminding that my grandsire Somerset had been wounded at the first and then slain at the second. In fact, this royal progress was becoming a pilgrimage of my family's defeats.

Our future king silkily raised the matter after supper had been cleared.

'Yes, it is true both my grandfathers fought for Lancaster,' I admitted. 'We all pray that under your wise and just rule, England will never again suffer such civil strife.'

'But Henry VI was a lunatic, my lord of Buckingham. Why did your family stay loyal to him when he did not know his left hand from his right?' A good question. The obnoxious brat.

'Many reasons, I suppose, sire. He was anointed king and son to the illustrious Hal of Agincourt, and I believe my grandsire was quite fond of him.' *Did Uncle Richard tell you that your father had him murdered?* I longed to add.

'Did you murder him, Uncle Gloucester?'

Richard choked on his wine. 'No, I did not. Why would you think that?' he spluttered, when he could speak again.

'I cannot remember where I heard that,' murmured the Prince with studied candour. 'But Uncle Rivers told me that sometimes kings say things, you know, like King Henry II wishing aloud that Thomas Becket was dead, and then his knights murdered the archbishop in order to please him.'

'I hope you are not going to wish us to murder anyone on your behalf, your highness,' I said dryly.

'No, of course not, but I wondered if my father wished King Henry of Lancaster dead and—' He looked at his uncle.

'No,' protested Richard, crossing himself. 'Much as I loved your father and honoured him as king, there is a moral limit to loyalty.'

The boy nodded and turned to me. 'So there are limits to an oath of fealty.'

It was a foul way of trying to win an argument.

'There are limits to the day too and it is high time your highness turned in for the night,' I told him and Richard looked relieved. It was tempting to put my foot on the royal backside as the child rose from the board.

'Holy Paul, Harry,' my cousin said softly, as the latch fell, 'who has taught him so?'

'Someone who wanted to blacken your good name, Richard.'

He paced, twisting the ring on his little finger. 'I was at the Tower of London the night that the old king died. I cannot deny it.'

'Cousin, forget the matter. A few dogs bark but does the moon care?'

'The House of York has blood on its hands, I know that.'

'The House of Lancaster does too. Forget what the boy said. It is the future that matters.'

'I should like to see King Henry's body reburied as befits a king.'

'Then make it a resolution, Richard. Tomorrow you will be Lord Protector.' I opened my hands as though our world sat within my palms.

'Aye, and with no money to rule and a royal council wondering the truth of what happened at Stony Stratford.'

'Indeed, it will not be easy but we have come this far with God's blessing.' Jesu! I was beginning to sound like the Pope! I patted his shoulder reassuringly

He placed his hand over mine. 'Thank you, Harry. Without you—'

'You would have done the same.'

NEXT day we rode past the common at Barnet where Richard, King Edward and Hastings had defeated the mighty Warwick. My cousin had led the vanguard of the army at eighteen years old so he was well able to reconstruct the battle for his fascinated nephew. We heard all about the struggle through the bog and how King Edward's sunne-in-splendour was confused with the Earl of Oxford's star. Richard even took us to the very place where the mighty Kingmaker and his brother had been slain.

I could add nothing. I had been about sixteen and safe in Brecknock– probably tupping Cat–while eighteen year old Richard stumbled up the foggy rise in his heavy armour.

The Prince listened attentively, occasionally including me with an arched look that reminded me more and more of his accursed mother. It was clear that Rivers had daubed plenty of muck on my honour at Ludlow and I was not able to compensate for imprisoning his Woodville relations by being a great soldier like my cousin.

'My Uncle Rivers told me that you are good at the dance, Uncle Buckingham,' the boy said slyly. 'You shall have to show us when we reach London.'

'That was when I was your age,' I countered waspishly. 'I shall have more important things to do than caper with the ladies.' Or so I hoped.

'He told me you once spilled potage into the lap of King Louis's ambassador.'

'Aye, and I made myself scarce for the next hour.' What use denial or telling him it was Dorset's foot hooked about my ankle that sent me flying.

'Did my mother have you whipped for it?"

'Whip a duke, your highness?' I replied with disdain, disliking him more and more.

It seemed that all that lay between me and a return to rot uselessly in Brecknock was Richard surviving as Lord Protector. Of course, if my cousin won over the boy completely, he would not need me. I had better ensure he would.

**

AS we reached the rise south of Barnet, excitement surged up my spine. Ahead lay the selfish city of London. From the filthy laneways of Southwark to the marshy fields of Millbank, I knew it well. Indeed, I could have named each turret and spire that lay between the Tower of London in the east and the royal Palace and Minster in the west.

Richard reined in. 'There lies your great city, Ned,' he said with pride. 'I do not love it like your father did but I pray Heaven you will deal with its citizens as well as he did.'

'A shade less amorously perhaps,' I murmured.

The corner of my cousin's mouth lifted in a tight grin. The Prince made no comment. After being immured with tutors at Ludlow for months on end, he was both awed and excited by the prospect.

'Come on!' I exclaimed, aching to be within those stinking walls. I spurred my ambler down the hill and the boy's steed followed. I should not have been upset if he had toppled off and broken his Woodville neck, save that the blame would have been all mine. I slackened pace and, when he joined me, we slowed to a more decorous progress. As we reached the flat I began wondering whether my ears were deceiving me: I could hear shawms and tabors.

'It seems as though we are about to be welcomed by someone.' I turned and gestured for the message to be relayed back down the retinue to Richard, who had dropped back to speak with Lovell. I waved up Ralph Bannaster. 'Ride on ahead. See who comes!'

The boy was looking anxious.

'What's the matter, sire?' I asked.

'If it is my Lady Mother come to welcome me, she'll be angry with me because of my Uncle Rivers and my brother Grey.'

'With you? I do not think so.' If Elizabeth was around the next bend, I would eat my hat including the ruby brooch and liripipe.

'At twelve you hardly have to worry about a woman's opinions, sire,' I told him confidently. 'Whether she be a queen or a tapster wench, her task is to give comfort to her menfolk and not concern herself with making decisions.'

'If that is so, Uncle Buckingham, why do men call the women who give them comfort their "mistresses". Uncle Rivers said I should probably have one when I am fourteen. '

'We must talk about this again,' I lied, as my men came back smiling. 'Look, here comes the Mayor.'

The Lord Mayor of London and aldermen were in sight all tricked out in their scarlet gowns and black hats. Behind them, to the beat of drums and drone of shawms, came the venerable greybeards of the city, two by two on foot in mourning robes of violet broadcloth with sprigs of rosemary pinned on their breasts and staffs in their hands.

A thousand blessing on the city fathers! Their coming condoned our arrest of the Woodvilles. As the procession reached us, all the burgesses snatched off their caps and shouted, 'God save the King!' and Richard and I dismounted and escorted the lad to greet his kneeling citizens. Then we invited the Mayor and alderman to join us at the head of our company.

Within half a mile of the gates, we found some of Hastings' men waiting for us with four covered wagonloads of pikes and weaponry they alleged had been gathered from secret caches around the city—carts so overloaded they looked like monstrous shirted hedgehogs.

Hastings' captain drew my cousin and I aside. 'My lord has ordered us to proclaim to the people that these have been taken from the Queen's kinsmen and that they were to have been used against you, your graces. So, where would you like them to go in the procession, my lord of Gloucester? At the front or in the vanguard?'

'At the back, thank you.' He looked like he would have an apoplexy. 'Wait, surely these are nothing more than the arms stores my brother was preparing to use against the Scots.'

'Certes, your grace,' answered Hastings' man, 'but I assure your grace that the Queen had every intention of using them against you.'

'But even *I* who live in Yorkshire know of these stores, sirrah. Do you imagine the Londoners—?'

'My lord cousin,' I cut in hastily, 'the good citizens have been waiting for hours. Let us not delay them further. Let the carts follow and there be an end to it.' Hastings, I thought, you have just made another error of judgment, thank the Lord.

'Very well,' agreed Richard grudgingly. 'I only hope Lord Hastings can provide us with better evidence than this if the people demand it.'

'Of course,' purred the officer and jingled off to manoeuvre the carts back into a laneway so we might proceed. I held my glove to my lips to stanch my laughter as a polaxe fell off and had to be poked back in. Hastings' fellows had even daubed the Woodville device on the canvas of the wagons. Any fool could smell the fresh paint.

'So subtle!' sneered Richard. 'Holy Paul! I do not want to antagonise Hastings but I'll not have our entry into London marred by these infernal proclamations.' He swung round to his herald. 'Send some of the drummers to the back and tell them to play loudly! Thank God you don't come up with such foolery, Harry.'

I smiled but was still crossing my fingers that Hastings truly had London by the throat and this was not some damnable trap about to spring. What if he had made a last instant alliance with the Queen?

My belly was still tight as we passed beneath the portcullis at Aldersgate, but then the bells of St Martin Le Grand and all the little churches close by began to peal and within minutes every belfry in London rang out its welcome. The very air thrummed with music and the ground shook with the hooves of our horses like some monstrous drum. My heart thumped furiously at the glorious tumult.

As I waved and smiled among the cascading petals, there were few shouts for Stafford, just one or two who remembered my grandsire and sensed the old times were come again. In our sombre black, we two uncles were but a dark wall behind the Woodville princeling's blue and gold splendour. The Londoners were falling in love with him. A wonder that they did not collect the holy dung when the Prince's horse lifted its tail.

Souvente me souvene!

Ha, I vowed, I was going to carve my name on the trunk of England and shake the tree with all my strength.

The first garland startled me as it fell about my neck and then there were scores. The women, ah, the women, like window boxes of posies, clustered in the casements, leaning their bosoms out of the jutting windows above the bright falls of cloth. They blew me kisses and hurled their flowers. But one in particular, I glimpsed, as she stretched forth from below the gable—a beautiful young woman with auburn hair plaited about her head like a crown and a mouth made for kisses. There was astonishment in her face and I swear an alchemy passed between us as we stared at one another. I doffed my hat exuberantly but she did not smile. She looked shocked as though she felt the jolt of attraction like a thunderbolt. Ah, she was so exquisite.

'*Harry!*' Richard's gloved hand grabbed my arm, hauling me out of collision with an alehouse pole. Prince Edward looked round and giggled.

I tried to remember the house, the street, but my mind was whirling. I should think no more upon women, I told myself. They are no more for men than meat and drink. The precipice of power was dangerous; it was there I must concentrate all thought. And yet I longed for a woman's soft whisper against my hair and her arms about my breast, and it was not of willing strumpets that I thought but of the auburn-haired gentlewoman.

'Better than I hoped!' My cousin's excited voice broke through my reverie. 'They are behind us, Harry!' I must have looked around, for he added with affection. 'Dolt. Not that "behind us". I mean the Londoners! This is almost as good as when Ned and I rode in after our victory at Tewkesbury.' Of course, blood-stained heroes with royal captives hauled in their wake.

It was not just the commons who came in their masses to huzzah. All the noble lords, in London for the coronation, were come from their great houses near the river, and sat on horseback along Cheapside, their heads meek and uncovered. They greeted their unanointed king and swung their horses in behind us, one by one, until almost every peer rode in our company. Their titles read like a roll of the shires of England. Gloucester's sister and her husband, the Duke and Duchess of Suffolk and their son, the Earl of Lincoln, the earls of Northumberland, Arundel, Surrey, Kent, Huntingdon and Nottingham. Even, Clarence's son, little Warwick with his moon face and doltish mutterings, rode his pony with us.

The crowds were thickest around St Paul's Churchyard. In the full warmth of the afternoon, the stink of the people was almost nauseating. A triumphal progress is a wonderful experience but a surfeit of unwashed bodies was not to my carefully protected taste. However, it was a penance I did not mind and I fervently prayed to the Almighty that there would be more days like that and greater.

What's more I thanked Him that I had not sat on my hands in Brecknock. If Cat and my Welsh farmers could have seen me!

Yet, it was a relief to approach the Bishop of London's house where Prince Edward was to lodge. I was hungry and had it not been for the tumult, my hungry rumblings would have been heard down in Thames Street. But then we were waylaid by St George and eight virgins eager to read poems of welcome. No, I'll revise that. There were seven virgins, because the third from the left looked lewdly about her. The second was pretty with fair hair to her knees and a mouth like a rosebud. The rest were broomsticks or dumplings. Ah, I forgot St George. In faith his costume must have been made for an earlier occasion or else a smaller hero. I swear he would have burst his points if he had blustered for much longer for he would have weighed heavier than a dragon in any balance.

Prince Edward replied to the virgins with dignity. Rivers had tutored him well: Cat's brother deserved that much commendation. It was the kingling's umpteenth speech that day and all of us had smiled like bridegrooms until our faces ached. Knyvett handed the boy coin (supplied by me) to scatter to the poor and another cluster of beggars emerged like maggots from a hidden corpse. The boy's lips curled slightly at the sight and he quickly threw the largesse amongst them, dismounted and hastened towards the bishop's door.

The cloying virgins had all been cleared away and in their place, miraculously manifested, stood old Bishop Thomas Kempe. Tufts of white hair were escaping from beneath his mitre. He was like a large ancient pussycat, blinking newly-woken from a sunny sill. And at last, appearing in the great doorway of the bishop's house, came that grinning prince of players, Lord William Hastings. Nimbly, he came down the steps to the courtyard, swept off his hat to his friend's son and knelt humbly on the mucky, uncomfortable cobbles. I had not realised he had gone so bald.

Hastings the great lover, the Pandarus of Westminster, Master of Strumpets and Revels! Bejewelled, befurred, bereaved, bestowing and between. Yes! Between the Prince and Richard, between Richard and I.

As I have said, three is an uncomfortable number.

Rarely so dully clad, Hastings was not flattered by his mourning garments. The lines from edge of mouth to nostril were deep drawn in the glare of day, and shadows cradled his eyes. He lacked Rivers' resilience against the corrosion of age, but for an old man of over fifty, he still had a face that was pleasant to look upon, and that, despite the dissipated love-nights at Westminster and the continual search for concubines, was remarkable. In fact, when he put his hat back on his shining pate and smiled, he would have passed for a man ten years younger.

I had a qualified respect for Hastings. He had leapt upon the Yorkist carque long before it had set sail for rebellion and clung on despite storms that washed others away. His luck had arrived when Edward of York had found in him a soul mate. Although there was eleven years' difference in their ages, they had explored bosoms together but not each other's. In the sunlight of King Edward's favour, Hastings had built an army of retainers.

64

Some he employed for wages, other wealthier friends he bound by favours. In return for his patronage in matters of litigation and influence with the King, he could summon them to arms. With equal competence, he could conjure up a full week's entertainment for a foreign dignitary, and his record for love-making was said to be seven times in one night. Lucky old whoreson, he had married one of Warwick the Kingmaker's sisters, too, and even if he had neglected her, he had begotten a family that he greatly loved.

I had been envious of him when I had been the Queen's ward at Westminster. The old goat had always seemed so blithe, so plaguey cheerful, whereas I as a page had loathed everything—my situation, my life, myself. What's more, I hated the compassion I read in his eyes whenever Dorset and Grey made trouble for me; and I hated his friendship with the King that made him invincible to the Woodvilles' machinations whereas I was so vulnerable, so friendless. He could have stood up for me to the Queen and her kinsmen; instead he gave me his pity.

Certainly, after days of Richard's calm company, Hastings' presence now was like a thunderstorm. It was my turn for a flood of exuberance, albeit tempered by the initial formality due to my rank.

'Welcome, my lord of Buckingham!'

'I am grateful that you wrote to me, my lord,' I replied sincerely, grasping the proffered hand.

'How could I not, your grace? You are the highest nobleman in the realm saving the royal family. It is I who must thank you for trusting my advice.' He buffeted my chest. 'You are looking so well, Harry. It's too long since you were at Westminster.'

'I am here now to make amends.'

He understood the significance and laughed. 'By Our Lady, and so you shall!' He flung his left arm about me and we joined those around the Prince. 'Now, your royal grace,' he boomed, happily breezing back into his duties as royal chamberlain, 'the good bishop has had your rooms made ready. Are you hungry or shall you like to rest first?'

'We should like to dine now, if you please, my lord.' *We*? Oh very regal. The London's huzzahs had made the colt's head swell already. 'My lord Hastings,' he piped, flexing the Plantagenet muscles further. 'We had hoped that my Lady Mother and my brother and sisters would come to greet me. Why are they not here?'

Hastings caught Richard's warning glance behind the Prince's head but before he could answer, I interrupted:

'Yes, God's Truth, here is thoughtless rudeness to his grace's tender years. Surely out of motherly love the Queen…' I gestured as though words could not describe her unkindness.

'Unfortunately, my liege,' Hastings began, choosing his words with care, 'the Queen's grace has gone into Westminster Sanctuary and taken Prince Richard, Princess Elizabeth and your other sisters with her. Your Uncle Lionel and the Marquis of Dorset are there as well.'

We had not shared that news earlier so our vaunting twelve-year-old was thrown off guard and not yet man enough to hide his disappointment.

'But why, what has she to fear from me, from any of us?'

'Well spoken, your royal grace,' agreed Richard, raising his voice. 'There is no reason for the Queen to deny her presence to her son and king. Perhaps we should not ask *of whom* but *why* she is afraid?'

No one answered, Hastings shrugged and old Bishop Kempe tactfully intervened.

'Let us partake of dinner. I am sure that a growing lad like your royal grace is hungry.'

As we all swarmed into the great hall like horse flies following a foal, the Prince repeated his questions to Hastings.

'To be honest, sire,' I heard him reply, 'the Queen did not take the news of my lord of Gloucester escorting you to London in good heart.' No, I'd wager she let some ripe Northamptonshire oaths rend the air—a few veils ripped and shoes thrown perhaps.

Fortunately, Hastings was not going to deal in trifles; his integrity was at stake.

'To be truthful, your highness, she is afraid because she tried to raise an army against your Uncle Gloucester and snatched away most of your father's treasury.' *Snatched?* Huzzah, Hastings!

'I do not understand,' protested the boy, his eyes beseeching the Lord Chamberlain to tell him better news. Here, he seemed convinced, was one lord who had no hand in the arrest of his Uncle Rivers and Richard Grey.

'I am sorry, your highness,' declared Hastings sadly, ushering him to the table and seating him at the board, 'but you would not want me to lie to you and there is much you need to know and understand. To put it plainly, your mother seeks to rule the realm on your behalf contrary to your father's will. It is wrong of her and now that she has failed in her desire, she is afraid of my Lord Protector.'

Wearing an insouciant expression, although smug might be a better word, the Lord Protector made himself comfortable next to his nephew.

'I mean her no harm,' he said candidly, summoning a page to bring a basin so the Prince might cleanse his fingers.

'Of course not,' agreed Hastings, laying a reassuring hand on the boy's forearm, before he took his place on the bench. 'You should be aware also, sire, that your uncle, Edward Woodville, has seized much of the wealth your father left and has taken the fleet to sea. Surely that is proof of a conspiracy?'

'The Devil he has!' I exclaimed, pretending to look in consternation at my cousin. He still had to take Hastings to task on his lack of vigilance. He eyed the basin and sent me an expression that told me he would love to hurl it with its rosewater contents at his cheerful lordship. For now he took a deep breath and said softly:

'Do you not see, Ned, that people are no longer as straightforward as once they seemed? When there is power at stake, men change. You are no longer a schoolboy but master of thousands of people and much wealth. I fear you must learn many hard truths from now on.'

Out of sight, Prince Edward's fingers were crushing the tablecloth. 'Uncle, I should like to speak with my mother.'

'Summon her, sire. You are the King,' he answered grimly, his mouth curled stubbornly down.

Time for me to join the measure.

'Yes, command her to attend you, highness, and let us see if her love for your royal grace is greater than her fear of my Lord Protector.'

The lower royal lip pouted: 'It is plain you have no love for her, Uncle Buckingham.'

Well, why not proclaim it to the world?

'You mistake me, your highness! I mislike anyone who seeks power for its own sake and not for the good of the realm,' I announced, and busied myself with eating in the silence which followed.

Richard cut across the tension. 'We must convene the Royal Council at once, my lords. This land must still be governed despite family squabbles. What *is* the precise location of the Great Seal, Lord Hastings?'

The Lord Chamberlain finally had the grace to look apologetic.

'We have it back now, my lord. Chancellor Rotherham did cause us some difficulty by delivering it to the Queen when he heard of Lord Rivers' arrest, but my lord of Canterbury has it safe now and Rotherham is no longer chancellor. The Royal Council agreed on that.'

Whoops! Solved but not forgotten.

I enjoyed the dinner after that. When we eventually reached the cherries and wafers course, my cousin excused himself to Prince Edward.

'Sire, there is much to do. If you will grant me leave, I shall go to Crosby Place and with your royal consent summon all the lords spiritual and temporal to meet tomorrow. Then I shall publicly take an oath of loyalty to you and pay you homage as king.' He had raised his voice so all could hear him. 'It is for the Royal Council to decide whether to appoint me Lord Protector as your father's will decreed. I shall abide by their decision, whatever it is. Therefore, I beg you all, let no man address me as Lord Protector until I am acknowledged as such by England's peers.' There was cheering as he bent over Prince Edward's hand.

'I thank you, my lord of Gloucester,' replied young Edward solemnly when all the cheers and table slaps had ceased. 'I see now that your advice is both fair and wise.'

Ah, so touching. Richard's eyes were moist.

'God save your royal grace.' His voice was husky with emotion. 'The times are hard and we must do our best.'

I WAS glad to take my ease that night at my London house, the Manor of the Red Rose in Suffolk Lane. I had a thousand things to think about: firstly, speaking to the Lombard bankers about raising a loan, and then all the bread-and-butter matters. Tasks like having my barge refurbished, summoning a host of tailors, purchasing better horses and taking on extra cooks and servants for the banquets I intended to hold if my luck held.

The laughter of my carousing henchmen reached me from the house as I walked alone in the garden. They thought Dame Fortune my godmother. I knew otherwise; the Queen was like a wraith on the edge of my vision. Once her son was crowned, she would have my head.

My only protection against her would be to use my cousin as a shield and meantime build up an army of retainers, but that would require a vast amount of money. I could count on Gloucester rewarding me for my support for he was known to repay good service generously, but how long would that take? With the treasury echoing, he would need to confiscate lands and offices from the Woodvilles, and would the Royal Council agree to that? Besides, the inheritance that Dead Ned had always withheld from me could not be passed to me by a lord protector. The Bohun lands could only be handed over by a king. A *grateful* king.

I should have to think on that further. Meantime, the Royal Council was going to be a cursed nuisance, not to mention Richard's plaguey regard for legality as well! If, as it seemed, he was only prepared to work within the framework of the council, then he was going to have no more power than a cripple with his wrists lopped off.

The third weight that was dragging on my liberated wheel of Fortune was Hastings, who was out to prove himself indispensable to his new masters. With his huge net of retainers, his popularity with the Londoners, and his grasp of the daily bread of kingship, he would be far more useful to Richard than I.

And then I stood beneath my rose arch with a foolish grin on my face. Between Hastings' life-hardened plates of self-assurance I knew a chink where a rondel might find a tender and deadly opening.

5

Cheapside is the beating heart of London and as we doglegged through to Bishopsgate next morning, I was hoping to sight the proud maiden with the auburn hair. Ha! Did King Solomon feel so perplexed trying to find his favourite concubine among his hundreds?

No one in London keeps to their path. Meandering slopsellers, lurking harlots, choosy housewives and maidservants burdened with buckets from the conduit. I searched their faces. With my banners known now, curtseys and smiles came my way but no haughty green eyes were raised to mine.

'Seems as though you've won hearts already, Harry,' Uncle Knyvett chuckled. 'See, we'll be having St Anthony's pigs bowing soon. Here comes one now.'

'Where's your respect?' I countered laughing, drawing rein to avoid the scavenging beast. Even blowing the horns, it would take us an age to get through. 'Devil take it, let us go the longer way past London Stone.' I had plenty of time before the Royal Council session.

'Please you, your grace, I cannot thank you enough.' Doctor Nandik urged his nag forward to my stirrup as we turned into St Swithin's Lane. He had earned himself a place in my retinue this morning only because my sozzled chaplain had fallen down the stairs last night.

'Think nothing of it, master scholar,' I said indifferently, in no mood for hand licking but he kept riding at my heel, looking about proudly, the cheeky beggar. 'Can you feel the vibration in the air, my lord?'

'Vibration?' A less hungry man would have seen my scowl but there was no stopping Nandik.

'An uncanny energy. They say it happens with a new reign, the sense of renewal, a young king. Do you not sense it, your grace?'

By Sweet Jesu, he was right. That morning there was a difference, a change about the city, some unnatural force like the unleashing of energy I had felt that day when he had brought news of the King's death. But this was considerably more powerful.

'Does it not demand blood?' I asked him. 'Do not men say that King William Rufus, the Conqueror's son, was slain in the New Forest as part of a ritual sacrifice to ensure the land's fertility?'

'Aye, my lord, and there are still some Earth-goddess worshippers among the people who may believe so, but did not the Lord Christ have to die before the seeds of Christianity could germinate?'

'Hmm, maybe it is just that the ambitious scramble around frantically at the start of a new reign,' I replied waspishly. Nandik was just such a presumptuous cur.

'Yes, my lord,' he muttered.

'Or it could be that Lent is over and we are all full of good red meat again and energy for our labours?' suggested Uncle Knyvett.

But I did feel the power in the air! If a man had the will and the ability, he could achieve anything; outwit two thousand men!

We passed Oxford Place. It was looking rundown; a reminder of failure. The earl who had owned it had not supported Dead Ned and was now a prisoner in one of our fortresses outside Calais. Before that he had been snuffling round France and Brittany for charity. I was never going to end up grovelling before foreigners, I resolved.

CROSBY Place, where the Royal Council was gathered to meet that morning, did not belong to Richard. A wool merchant, the late Sir John Crosby, had built it over twenty years ago and the present owner was content to rent it to Richard whenever he came to London. My cousin preferred to put up there rather than at his mother's at Baynard's Castle, a damp old palace down by the river. I now understood why. The house stood near to one of the city's northern gates so he did not have to traverse London with his packhorses. But, more importantly, it was a beauteous stone and timber dwelling with comfort instead of defence as its first thought. Behind the gabled street front, there was a series of galleried courtyards. Certainly sufficient lodging to house my cousin's retinue.

Sir James Tyrrell, one of my cousin's officers and brother-in-law to Uncle Knyvett's eldest son, saluted me in the stableyard. He did not escort me to the great hall. Instead we passed through a second courtyard, beneath a small archway and into a garden that was overlooked by a lodging wing on one side and a mighty wall on the other.

I halted, taking in the serenity of this little paradise. Scents of bruised lavender and freshly scythed grass eddied in the air. A miniature meadow drew my gaze. It was starred like a firmament with tiny flowers and at its heart stood an arbour of lathed trellis thick with twining rose. The wall on the north side sheltered fruit trees: quince, apple and pear, thick with blossoms. Borage, heartsease, woodruff and comfrey flowered modestly along the path. Within the flowerbeds rose spires of purple foxglove and unawakened buds of golden St John's Wort. I breathed in the beauty and promised to lavish more love on my gardens at Brecknock and Thornbury, my manor near Bristol.

'Your grace,' Tyrrell prompted. So, I was not supposed to linger.

Why is it that people are always surprised when I demonstrate an interest in plants? Some men collect tapestries, others paintings or silverwork. Is a love of natural beauty unmanly or alien to a thirst for temporal power? The times when I escaped the poisonous air of the Woodvilles, the gardens of Westminster revived me. This one was perfect.

Tyrrell turned to the right and we entered a whitewashed passageway that flanked the great chamber and ended at a small oaken staircase. He led me up to a spacious room overlooking the garden. Its mullioned windows on the south side had been thrown open to gather in the sunshine.

Some half-dozen of the duke's henchmen were sitting about a table, untidy with breakfast platters. They all rose, bowed to me and withdrew, except for Lovell and a man who was busy at the furthermost window, his back turned. He was feeding crumbs to a crowd of birdfolk. They jostled each other on the sill, quite unafraid of the duke's favourite hound, who was salivating for a share. Seeing me, the dog sauntered across to smell my boots, and wagged his tail.

Lovell leaned across and shook me by the hand.

'I can see we've sat at breakfast far too long, Dickon,' he called out. 'My lord of Buckingham is here.'

'Good morning, Harry.' It was Richard who stood at the open window. He looked round and here was the greatest marvel of any wonders I had seen that morning. Gone was the miserable black cloth, and in its place my cousin was clad in an open cote of dusky red brocade stitched with golden leaves and berries. Across his tilted shoulders lay the Yorkist collar of sunnes with the pendant silver boar glinting brightly, as though, like its master, it had slept well.

73

Richard's face above the high shirt collar was youthful again and the haggard expression he had worn like a favourite garment over the last week had been discarded. It was reassuring–if he had been sounding out support on the Royal Council, he had found no large rocks so far to shipwreck his intentions.

'Harry,' he exclaimed cheerfully, shaking me by the hand. 'Holy Paul! I see I had better finish my breakfast. Time must be getting on. Though don't imagine I have been idle this morning.' I now knew him better than to think that. 'Sit down. Would you like to try some of our cheese from Middleham? My wife had it sent down as a surprise.' I cast a suspicious eye at the whitish crumble but I tried some out of politeness, making myself comfortable on the cushioned bench. Richard leaned back using the table like a misericord and finished his white bread. Part of the crust went to the dog drooling at his feet. I looked round. Lovell had gone and we were alone.

'I'm glad you arrived in good time this morning, Harry. It occurred to me last night that I've given you scant thanks for all your help this last week.'

'A pox on that,' I protested. 'The success was all your doing.'

'*Our* doing,' he insisted, 'and I thank you heartily. You shall not go unrewarded, believe me.'

'Cousin, I have had sufficient payment in seeing the demons who tormented my childhood brought low.'

'And yet you seem in poor spirits.' Yes, my chin was on my clasped fingers and I was staring somewhat morosely beyond a Venetian glass bowl of pickled French walnuts. 'Have some.' He prodded the glass towards me.

I sighed and selected one. 'I feel like a child. My Saint's Day is over and the gifts are all opened.'

'I'll keep one for you,' he promised with a grin. He poured me out some methyglyn, which I detest, and pushed the pewter mug into my hands. 'You've no reason to be in the dumps, Harry.'

My long fingers imprisoned the cold contours of the tankard. Richard's dog sat down by my chair and thumped his tail hopefully. Both the hound and his master waited.

'How can I explain?' I murmured softly and let the silence grow before I sighed. 'There are already a plaguey score of wretches outside my house wanting to know if I'll speak to you or the King on their behalf. All my life no man has ever been kind to me unless he wanted something. God's Truth, Richard.' I swallowed. 'What I mean is…these last few days I—' Here, I broke off again. 'All I know is that it has made up for a hell of...' I could say no more and shielded my face with the heels of my palms. The dog uttered a whine of sympathy, rested his head on my knee, exercising his eyebrows in concern.

I am not sure if Richard was embarrassed by my outburst. Most men disdain any show of weakness as womanly but you have to show your belly to the leader of the pack to make him feel safe. I heard him slide off the table and walk to the window. His hound left me.

'You think me your friend, do you, Harry? Yet I fall into the company you've just condemned. I *needed* your support at Northampton and Stony Stratford.'

'No, you did not!' I burst out miserably. 'You had the balls to brazen it out. Anyway, you do not need me now. Devil take it, what can *I* offer you that you do not have already here in London?'

He was leaning back against the casement, watching me with concern.

'Oh God, Richard, I know I'm sounding like a cursed milksop.' I paused, amazed at my own outburst. I had not planned to say that. 'Look, by noon today you'll be confirmed as Lord Protector and your nephew will be crowned in a couple of weeks and all I'll have to look forward to is back to dreary Wales.' *And the black dog of despair!* I paced to the window and turned. 'You know, I actually revelled in what happened at Stony Stratford, not merely seeing Rivers and Grey get what was coming to them but in using my dull mind for once, acting with you, pitting our wits against the Wood-villes, but now there will be wiser men than I to help you make decisions, men like Hastings.'

It was then he answered me with words that made my heart leap in gratitude:

'Hastings is not of the blood royal.'

I bit my lip to stomach my emotion. 'Oh, cousin, for that I thank you!'

He came back to the board. 'You are a muttonhead, Harry. You grow too introspective and look for offence where none is offered. Do you imagine I shall shoo you into a corner like Loyaulté here and—*Oh Holy Paul!*' I followed his startled gaze to the hourglass. He snatched up his hat, pointed the dog to its cushion and made for the door. I almost collided with him as he turned suddenly. 'You know what happens this morning is vital? I'm not Lord

Protector yet and if we lose control of the council we're both likely to end up in the Tower under a Woodville axe.'

We! The most beauteous word in the world! 'Yes, Lord damn it! You know you have my support.'

His smile was silky. 'There, you see, I need you. Haven't you forgotten something?'

I rushed back to grab my hat and gloves and mustered a smile as he waited for me.

'That's better,' he said kindly. 'Now, come on, cousin, let us be proud of our Plantagenet blood.'

I told myself that I had acted better than any player, that no one could have eavesdropped and faulted my sincerity. I was no better than Richard's dog, loving him out of necessity and yet—And yet something buried in my conscience told me the words this morning had struck true, that deep within my soul I wanted my cousin's friendship more than the entire world.

But I set those troubling thoughts aside as I followed him down to the great hall of Crosby Place. To hell with sentiment! I had to concentrate now on retaining my position as his principal supporter, and since time and distance are enemies to friendship, he was going to have to keep me by his side. I would stir up sufficient turbulence to make sure he had no choice.

MY entrance into the gathering of royal councillors in the Lord Protector's company was just as I had schemed, but its triumphant manner was his making. We came in together through the side door onto the dais as two cousins, two dukes, two smiling equals!

The hall instantly hushed and the assembled royal councillors turned to us and bowed. No one was seated at the long trestle table yet. Our tardiness had given them time for gossip and speculative discourse.

I let my cousin go ahead of me to the centre of the dais otherwise I should have dwarfed him. Besides, I owed him that acknowledgment and to have stepped forward with him would have been an unpardonable ascension in the eyes of my peers, a body not known for their swift acceptance of matters new and persons untried.

'My lords and gentlemen, welcome to you all,' declared my beaming cousin, stepping down.

A wave of good mornings lapped us. Hastings, whose presence was always obvious from his height and noisy laughter, detached himself from the company of Lord Stanley and large old Morton, Bishop of Ely, and came forward to clasp my cousin by the hand. He saw him made comfortable in the chair of estate at the head of the table and then turned to me.

'My lord of Buckingham.' He gestured me to be seated at the top of the bench on Gloucester's left hand, opposite my great uncle, Archbishop Bourchier. I could have embraced Hastings for his forethought.

'Content, Harry?' my cousin teased quietly, but before I could reply, John, Lord Howard appeared at his elbow and they instantly had their heads together talking about the missing fleet.

I had intended to watch the councillors taking their places, who sat with whom, but I should have been philistine to ignore the beauty of the hall. Because it was so recently built, there was light a-plenty. Remembering how gloomy all my halls were, I looked up with envy at the huge glass windows with their elegant five-leafed tracery. They let the sunlight surge in to play upon the black and white tiles and turn the motes of dust, stirred by our every movement, to flecks of gold. With all the light came warmth and so there was no need for the great fireplace behind us to be lit this morning, whereas in Brecknock there would have been few times when a fire did not burn in my hearth.

Without question, though, it was the wondrous oriel window with its extravagant use of glass that made me slack-jawed. If ever I could afford it, I resolved I should find a mason to install one at Thornbury, maybe a double one. This creation was magnificent, almost too bright to look at. The stonework above the window was exquisite, if a trifle exuberant. Plumes of ribbed stone soared to meet a complex star with a coat of arms, probably Crosby's, on the central boss. As for the rest of the hall…

'Is that not a glorious ceiling?' I exclaimed, as my great uncle of Canterbury seated himself opposite me.

He twitched a bushy eyebrow upwards. 'Impressive, excessive and wasteful! Crosby could have built a cathedral for the cost of this monstrosity.'

'It is beautiful.'

'Beauty is for God.'

I doubted he skimped on luxury. 'I suppose your palaces don't hold a candle to this then?'

He uttered a snort and muttered something about rising damp at Lambeth.

Perhaps his rebuke was good for it thrust me back to my purpose, to take measure of this gathering, to know my colleagues better than themselves, to render them predictable. But I was not the only one who did so. Ratcliffe, my cousin's loyal retainer, was up in the minstrels' gallery watching us all like a hawk on his daytime perch. I do not know if he had been sent up there for that very purpose but his master, noting my gaze, sent him a glance that bade the man come and be seated.

Looking down the table, the Royal Council were predictably drawn from the three major divisions of our hierarchy. Noblemen made up the largest group. We had a card hand of bishops, mostly caesarean clergy more interested in high office than high mass. Finally, in the minority, there were the commoners at the end of the table. This was the most vulnerable group because they owed their positions to favour and needed to continually prove themselves invaluable.

The hall hushed as Richard turned to face us, tossing his hanging sleeves behind him. Two secretaries drew up stools at oblique angles from his chair and everyone became attentive. Once Ratcliffe swiftly took his place with an apology, the doors adjoining the hall were closed and I heard the clink of steel as Richard's guards positioned themselves outside.

While my uncle of Canterbury delivered a prayer followed by an unnecessary homily, I reshuffled the councillors into their affinities. Among the lords, apart from myself, Richard could probably rely on his brother-in-law, John, Duke of Suffolk, and Suffolk's son, the Earl of Lincoln; Francis, Viscount Lovell, of course; and Lord Howard and his son, Thomas. And Hastings?

Lord Hastings was sitting with the men he had been speaking with earlier, both officers of the late king's household; his former brother-in-law, Lord Thomas Stanley, now married to Lady Margaret Beaufort, my erstwhile aunt, and opposite the pair of them was the podgy bulk of Morton, Bishop of Ely. Sir William Catesby, less dusty than I had seen him last, was further down the table.

The latter caught my glance and nodded a greeting. How devoted was he? What would make him heave Hastings off his back?

The scions of the Woodville party were noticeably absent. With two of her kinsmen in sanctuary, three in prison and one at sea, Elizabeth had left herself no glib defender. Old Rotherham, Archbishop of York, was in no position to command a hearing after his foolishness over the Great Seal and he looked like a child about to wet himself, expecting a rebuke at any moment. The other obvious Woodville supporter had to be Master Oliver King, the Prince's tutor from Ludlow, who had been sensibly reticent about his loyalties since Stony Stratford. Being a mere schoolmaster, his views were not likely to be taken seriously anyway.

Richard moved the meeting along firmly. Dead Ned's will was accepted and not one voice protested against my cousin becoming Lord Protector. There was little redistribution of offices: the post of Lord Chancellor was bestowed upon Russell, Bishop of Lincoln, an ecclesiastic with a sharp legal mind, who was guaranteed not to do anything exciting. The Privy Seal went to Gunthorpe, the learned Dean of Wells, and John Wode, the Speaker of the Commons, one of Richard's supporters, became Lord Treasurer. Lord Hastings was to continue as Lord Chamberlain, and Lord Stanley as High Steward, both posts that brought them into close contact with the new little king.

The appointments marked a smooth beginning to the protectorate but there was as yet nothing for me. I shared disappointment with the plump, dewlapped face belonging to Bishop Morton.

I could admit to some respect for him. The wily old fellow's past was a see-saw. He had supported the House of Lancaster until Dead Ned annihilated them and then, because he was too long in the tooth to keep snuffling round foreign courts like a beggar, he grovelled to Edward and hopped onto the Royal Council. Definitely not a man of the cloth. I doubt he could tell you what the inside of his cathedral looked like even if you slammed him naked against a wall and threatened a flogging.

Well, even if Morton might have preferred Elizabeth as regent instead of Richard, he certainly could not have faulted our new Lord Protector on his efficiency. My cousin had brought himself up to date with every dispatch and tidied the agendum into a reverse order of urgency. God's Truth, he handled the Royal Council like a cunning wife, deferring to them the decisions on lesser matters. It had me wondering if he had played me the same way at Northampton. Any rate, the charm and gloves, of course, were to soften these worthies for the more controversial issues still on the table–the date of the coronation and the fate of Rivers, Grey and Vaughan.

With all the invitations to be sent out, the ceremonial clothing to be made, and the fuss and megrims that go with peacetime coronations, he announced that it seemed sensible to delay the crowning until Tuesday 24th June, almost two months hence. Most of the council mercifully voted for what seemed such a wise recommendation. I was able to uncross my fingers. It would have been folly to crown a Woodville king with the fleet missing and that hornet Elizabeth refusing to accept the impotent role of queen-dowager. Having a postponement extended the opportunity to seize back the former and settle the latter.

It was only when Hastings raised the subject of the boy's lodging that at last I found a voice.

'Since his mother has looted Westminster, let his highness go and live at the Tower. Is it not customary for a king to stay there anyway before being crowned? And the city will be delighted. Besides, he'll enjoy looking at the shipping and the lions.'

I hoped they would maul him.

Across from me, my great uncle stirred. 'But surely if our little king moves into Westminster, the Queen might be induced to leave the sanctuary.' No, not Westminster! His mother would be smuggling messages across the yard to turn the boy against us.

'You are an optimist, uncle. It would be like asking the Pope to move to London.'

'Practicalities, archbishop,' Hastings exclaimed, waving what looked to be a list. 'My lord of Buckingham is perfectly correct. I have gone through the palace inventory and I can assure you what is left is not fit for a king to sit on let alone eat off. It is a wonder she did not take the throne.'

Someone muttered something about close stools and there was a rumble of laughter further down.

'Then that is settled,' said Richard swiftly and moved on to the final matter which he had saved until last hoping that dinnertime hunger would keep the discussion short. 'I think you all realise now that there was an attempt by the Queen's kin to take the government of the realm completely into their own hands. The seizure of the fleet, the rifling of the treasury and their seeking refuge in sanctuary are, I think, sufficient proof. Given that evidence, I feel that the events which took place during his highness's journey to London are no longer subject to misconception. My lord of Buckingham and myself were outnumbered but fortunately not outwitted. We ordered the arrest of Rivers, Grey and Vaughan without your permission, my lords, but as God is my witness, the times demanded swift action. I now submit that action to your approval. Is it your wish that these lords be set at liberty?'

'God forbid!' exclaimed Hastings. 'Keep them where you can watch them.'

'Some might say they should be tried for treason,' I pointed out. That went down like a carque with a gash in its side.

'Arraign 'em for conspiracy!' Hastings again, trying to tilt the balance.

Howard and several of the earls nodded but old Archbishop Rotherham with his chancellorship gone had nothing to lose by disagreeing.

'My lords Gloucester and Buckingham, there is no proof that Rivers and Grey intended to take you prisoner. It is highly appropriate that the Prince should have brought a large retinue from Ludlow and flattering to his royal person that Grey should ride to meet him with a large number of followers.'

'For Heaven's sake, Rotherham!' snapped Hastings, slapping the table. 'We argued all this out before Grey left London. He did not need to take so many.'

'Let me finish if you please, Lord Hastings.' Feathers ruffled, the archbishop jutted his shoulders like a nesting hen resettling. 'What I am saying is that you cannot try someone for a crime that has not been committed. You cannot hang a man for wanting to murder, only for the deed itself.'

'Isn't that what treason is?' I asked dryly. 'Wishing you had one king instead of another.'

'It was not a proven act,' persisted Rotherham. 'Did they raise one sword against you, my Lord of Gloucester? Did they?'

'I cannot say that they did, Rotherham, but they would have done if we had not forestalled them. I'd stake my duchy on it.'

'And I mine!' I exclaimed.

The new Chancellor, Bishop Russell, cleared his throat. 'May I ask what charge you wish to bring against them, your graces?'

'Treason,' I insisted. 'Treason against the Lord Protector!'

'Without wishing to take sides, my lords, I feel I must point out that such a charge would not stand up in court.' Russell gestured apologetically. 'Your grace is only confirmed as Lord Protector from today.'

Oaths exploded from Hastings and myself, but our freshly-minted chancellor raised his hand for silence. 'His grace of Gloucester assures us that he intends to rule with the assent and advice of the Royal Council.' My cousin inclined his head solemnly. 'Therefore, *ipso facto*,' Russell pressed, 'there could be no treason against the Lord Protector until an hour ago.'

'What would you have us do then, chancellor?' I asked smoothly. 'Release Rivers and Grey so they can raise an army to "rescue" the Prince from us? Why in Hell are the Queen, Dorset and the Bishop Salisbury skulking in sanctuary if they are innocent? My lords, let us be sensible about this. There was a conspiracy. The Queen tried to become regent and failed. It is obvious Rivers and Grey were behind her.'

Rotherham sucked in his cheeks and shuffled the papers in front of him with lowered gaze.

'Aye, let's not talk so soft—' The Duke of Suffolk who had been busy cleaning the nails of his left hand with the forefinger of his right, ceased his preoccupation, shifted his large bulk and leaned forward. 'If there is still a danger, let Rivers and the others remain in custody for the time being. Blust me, a few weeks won't hurt 'em. You'll see, they'll have had enough of it by the coronation and they'll be quite glad to stop jannicking around and accept my Lord Protector is going to govern this realm.' He grinned at Richard and added, 'With the advice and consent of this council, of course.' His great hand slammed down on the table, 'An' now if you don't mind, I'm for my dinner!'

I caught my cousin's side glance and responded with an almost invisible shrug, and he followed my gaze down to where the Warden of the Cinque Ports had already nodded off. It was long past noon, a lot of rumbling had been coming from the part of the table where most of the bishops were sitting.

Letting out a deep breath, our new Lord Protector smiled at Suffolk. 'As you say, my lord, there is no need for haste in this matter. And as for dinner, well, I thank you all for your attendance and good counsel and wish you a hearty appetite!' He scraped back his chair, and we all rose and bowed towards him. The meeting was over.

I took my time leaving the board. I wanted to watch the handshakes and polite exchanges. Richard, I observed, departed with Howard, and Morton and Rotherham hastened out together. No one else was in a hurry especially as the doors were opened to let in servants bearing flagons and wafers.

Lord Stanley came to pay me his respects. He was a silent doleful type but one that bore watching because he was always safely washed ashore whatever the political tide. Here he was, Steward of the Royal Household once again.

He asked after Cat and the children.

'And how is Aunt Margaret?' I enquired solicitously. 'Are her wrists still bad?' I hoped so. Margaret Beaufort, mother of the fugitive Henry Tudor, was like the worst sort of mother superior (and I don't mean the ones that ride to hounds and wear silk chemises beneath their habits).

'Doesn't complain,' Stanley said nasally. He gave one of his habitual pauses then added, 'Damp weather hasn't helped.'

'Has she tried a copper amulet? We have an old woman at Brecknock who suffered terribly until one of the bards told her to wear copper, so her son had one fashioned for her and she says the pain almost completely went. She could hardly move her fingers but now she can sew again.' A miserable old hag, she is, too.

'I'll tell Margaret, thank you.' Another tedious pause. 'She's down for t' coronation. You are welcome to come by.'

'Thank you.' I had rather gouge my eye out with an iron brand.

I dislike it when I hear the sound of someone's phlegm being dragged up their throat. He looked to spit it up onto the great hall tiles and then thought better and tugged a cloth from his sleeve.

'I'll have an amulet made,' I offered. 'I'll be curious to see if it works for her as well.'

'A kind thought, lad. Here's Hastings.' He departed holding the joint of his finger against his left nostril trying to snort away the blockage in his right. I turned with relief to Hastings' suaver attentions. Catesby was beside him, anxious to bow over my hand. He greeted me and discreetly withdrew.

'Bright fellow, that one,' muttered Hastings. His attention veered as he admired a passing serving wench. 'Always useful to have a few tame lawyers about the place. If it hadn't been for Catesby, I'd be a far poorer man, I can tell you. Land tenure can tie you up in the courts until the Second Coming.'

He reached out and tweaked the returning girl's bottom and received a purr of a look over her shoulder. 'Anything I can do for you while you are in London, Harry?' It was clear what he meant.

'Are you encouraging infidelity, my lord?' I replied, wondering if he knew where the demoiselle with auburn hair dwelled.

'In a dutiful Christian like you, Harry? Perish the thought.' He lowered his voice confidentially, 'You did a nice piece of work this morning, if I may say so.'

It was kind of him but then compliments are free.

'I am learning, my lord.' Oh yes, I am learning.

I WAS not sure whether to hie it back to my house for dinner. Maybe Richard would expect me to join him so I took myself back to the little garden and sat down on the stone seat. The euphoria of power was still in my breathing, the black dog of despair was chained back at Brecknock and I was able to open my senses and let the beauty of the world fill my heart.

A male dove with puffed-out snowy breast and spread of tail feathers disappeared up the path in pursuit of his haughty she-dove. I smiled, thinking of my own quest for the green-eyed girl. Master Dove's conquest would be a fleeting pleasure, over in an instant. If I ever found her, mine might be also, for love had ever eluded me.

The sweet voices of the black nuns of St Helen's in their chapel beyond the wall of Crosby Place rose in an anthem, gently rousing me from my reverie. A bumble bee overladen with tiny buckets of pollen flew clumsily past me humming a descant and a ladybird in scarlet and black Stafford colours landed on the pleats of my green doublet and trundled cheerfully over the velvet furrows until I found a better place for it to foray. I sat there watching its progress in utter contentment until Tyrrell's arrival sent the doves panicking up from beyond the hedge in a rasp of wings.

OUR new Lord Protector was pacing the upper chamber, his thin lips tight with displeasure. 'Dorset has fled the sanctuary!' he exclaimed on seeing me.

'Has he indeed?' No wonder that Lovell and Ratcliffe were looking whipped. 'When did this happen?'

84

Lovell snorted. 'Last night. Damn whoreson has to be in the city still. An apprentice recognised him down near Aldersgate and raised the hue and cry but he got away.'

A map of London lay pinioned by candlesticks upon the board. I wandered over to peer at it. Loyauté pattered after me, nudging my hand for attention.

'Ah, talking of whores,' I murmured, 'doesn't Dorset's new lover, Mistress Shore, live around there?'

Witty Elizabeth Shore had been Ned's mistress. The third panel of a lascivious triptych.

'We've had her house under watch,' Ratcliffe answered. 'In my opinion, he's hiding out in the fields. If I were in his shoes, I should head down the river. He'll be looking for a ship to join Edward Woodville at sea.'

How far could Richard be pushed? I looked up from fondling Loyauté's scruff. 'I say loose the dogs on him while he's still in the open!'

'But...but he's a nobleman,' protested Lovell.

I felt no compassion. If Hastings had been Dead Ned's whoremaster, Dorset had been the King's devil, tempting him to excess. I met my moral cousin's stare.

'*Do it!*' he told Ratcliffe.

Huzzah for Richard! I could have hurled my hat in the air like some sweaty apprentice.

Another Woodville almost in the pot!

6

The dogs never sniffed out Dorset although the packs ran hither and thither from Clerks' Well across to Shoreditch every day for a week. Somewhere along the warrens that flanked the Thames, the Woodville rat had found a rope betwixt quay and ship. Nevertheless we sent agents down to Devon to keep watch on his wife lest he send to her for money. No doubt he would skulk in France or Brittany until our new king came of age and then he would come back to scavenge.

London was too busy feasting to care a jot. Prince Edward's household was set up in the royal apartments at the Tower and the royal councillors divided their time between there and Crosby Place like cheerful bigamists.

'Have a care, Harry, or you'll be getting a belly on you.' Uncle Knyvett jabbed a finger into my waist as the tailors measured me for my coronation clothes. He was right: life had been a whirligig of banquets, all part of the game to discover whether my 'good lordship' would prove more useful than Hastings'. Whoever had the ear of the Lord Protector needed to be fed and watered. A good job Richard had two!

The grovels were never blatant, merely causal references between the loach in green sauce and the suckling pig with hot codlings, or a meaningful look above the raised cup. Knights, merchants, the desperate and the despicable, they hopped about my Lord Protector's friends like hungry fleas.

Out of my alliance with my cousin was growing something greater than respect. I feared it might be the altruistic friendship that forgives shortcomings and I found it disturbing. Why? Well, isn't friendship a form of slavery, a shackle of sentiment that clouds reason and dulls ambition?

As if to counteract these spasms of purity, I burned the candles to their stubs as I caressed the pretty flesh that slid between my bedsheets, imagining each wench to be my elusive green-eyed sylph. And then one morning I was getting into my barge on the watersteps of Baynards Castle after a honeycakes and kiss-your-hand-audience with Proud Cis, Richard's mother, the Duchess of York, when I saw *her*.

Her. Mid-river, rowed by a water boatman. The girl who had been haunting my dreams. She was sitting stately as any princess with some plumpish, heavily-veiled woman beside her.

I hauled my dawdling Uncle Knyvett onto the barge, grabbed my helmsman by the arm and pointed. 'Matthew, follow that boat!'

YOU would not think we could lose her but we did. The little craft swiftly wove in among the merchant barques off Queenhythe, whereas my oarsmen battled to keep our lumbering barge clear of the mooring ropes and the swarm of small wherries bearing folk to the city. By the time we reached the landing steps, she and her companion had disappeared.

'You can't go chasing after virgins, Harry,' muttered Uncle Knyvett, as we resumed our journey back to Dowgate. 'Didn't you listen to your cousin's lecture in Stony Stratford? It's all wedding rings and fidelity from now on.'

'Would you like a swim among the turds?' I countered sweetly. '*He's* not married to Cat Woodville.'

But Uncle Knyvett was right. I had more important matters on my agendum.

'What was the harvest from the taverns last night?' I asked Pershall as he dressed me for dinner at Goldsmiths' Hall.

'Interesting, your grace. The lads all went out stealthylike, without the livery, as you requested.'

'And the gossip?'

'Gossip is "Uncle Dick from up north" would like to make himself king. Aye, and they're giving a new thirly-whirly to the old scandal about her ladyship of York.'

'The Flemish archer?' I smiled dismissively. I was more intent on wondering what I could do to ensure that Richard fulfilled the alehouse prophecy.

'No, my lord, just you wait on… While you were seeing her grace this morning, I chewed some cud with one of her grooms, an ancient what used to go on campaign with the old duke. Seems to me his lordship was away slaughterin' the Frogs or some other poxy whoresons when King Ned was conceived.'

'Godssakes, Pershall, you never asked him direct?'

'No, of course not. Circumloc… well, whatever, is one of my many talents.'

'Hmm, but if—'

'Aye, *if,*' he cut in. 'It would mean that them little princes have no royal blood, your grace, and your cousin of Gloucester is the rightful heir. But the funny thing is the rumours aren't coming from the Lord Protector's affinity, not with him being her son and so forth. No, indeed, my lord, there was a fine brawl at the *Swan* with some of his grace's White Boar fellows defending my lady's good name. No, my money's on someone else trying to stir up mischief. It wouldn't be Lord Hastings neither. His men are all puffed up like courtin' pigeons about serving the new king.'

'Hmm.' I blew out my cheeks pensively. 'Ask Sir Nicholas to give our lads some more ale money for tonight and tell them to fan the flames–the talk about Proud Cis and the archer–hot as they can.' I wanted people speculating that if Dead Ned had no true Yorkist blood, then the Prince had none either.

Pershall bowed. 'It shall be done. An' I should hire a food taster if I was you, your grace, and afore you say it, I'm not putting my hand up for the extra wages.'

'*Pershall?*'

He grinned at my perplexed face. 'Word is the Queen would like to poison you and your cousin Northern Dick.'

And who was spreading that one?

PERHAPS Richard did have a food taster or maybe the Queen lacked imagination. I survived supper at Crosby Place next evening and returned to find a huffy Pershall roosting on the stairs to my bedchamber.

'You might have told me you had made an arrangement, your grace,' he muttered, springing to his feet. 'An' what with Lord Hastings havin' sent you a pretty harlot for supper tied up with a ribbon.'

'An arrangement? What arrangement?'

'Well, you tell me, my lord. But all I know is there's two of 'em up there. I know you like a threesome o'times, my lord, but I don't think those two are like to get along. Morelike scratch each other's eyes out. I've put 'em in separate rooms so you can have one at a time if you'd rather. Do you want to bang on the floor when you've finished?'

I stared at him in amazement and then with a deep breath, thrust my hat and cloak at him and headed softly up the stairs. I went furtively to the nearest door and glanced in. A young woman was lolling against my pillows, grooming her nails. It was the serving wench that Hastings had goosed that first morning at Crosby Place (and probably had a leg over since). I did not want his leftovers.

'My cousin will have a visitation from God if he hears of this,' I muttered. *'Pay her off!'*

'I daresay it will be noisy removing her.'

'*I* shall be noisy if you do not. You and Bannaster shift her hence or you can both look for another master.'

'But she's a beauty,' whispered Pershall to torment me.

'So is the Queen.' I turned to him again. 'You say there are two? Where in Sweet Christ's name is the other one?'

Smirking, he pointed to one of the guest chambers and then, with a grin, strode across and opened the door.

'My lady, his grace of Buckingham.'

I could have kicked the grinning sot from here to Greenwich. He had left me with no choice but to go in.

Sometimes Fortune smashes her fist into us as though we are butter. That's how I felt. Before me stood the young woman with the auburn hair and green eyes.

She curtsied formally, her gaze modestly on my toecaps and then she lifted her lashes and looked in my face with eyes like sanded emeralds. I had the impression of fragility but her healthy, honey skin denied that. Nor, I hazarded, was she untouched, for there was no rigidity in her bearing but a gracious confidence. I had been wrong in thinking her scarce out of childhood. I was wrong in every way save that she was very beautiful.

'My lady,' I began, for unquestionably my visitor was no ploughman's get and the flattery would do no harm. 'I pray you be seated. Shall you take some refreshment?'

She shook her head. 'Thank you.' Her voice was as I had imagined, soft and rich yet with a recognizable burr of the west that was quite delightful. 'Your man has looked after me very well, my lord. I did not think to wait so long.' Her lips tightened and for an instant she betrayed some uncertainty.

'It is almost curfew, my lady.'

'Unfortunately, yes, my lord.'

I swallowed. I was growing hard just drinking in her beauty. In my imagination I was already stripping away the triangle of green silk covering her breasts, sliding my hand beneath her generous collar.

'I do not seek to delay you, my lord. I...I am here to give you a petition.' That shot my gaze up from where her necklace of coral and crystal lay above her delicious cleavage.

'A petition?' The flare of disappointment in my eyes must have been high as St Paul's spire save that she was too busy drawing out a sealed parchment from beneath her belt to notice.

'I apologise that I deluded your attendants, my lord, but the matter is vital.'

'I see.' I reached the window and opened the lower lights. How absurd that anything but self interest could have drawn her here. I took a deep breath of the chill air, thankful my shaft was subsiding to flaccidity.

'Your grace, *please?*' Passion and despair fought in her voice.

'I do not usually consider petitions at this time of night, demoiselle,' I answered over my shoulder. 'Do your parents know you are here?'

'I doubt it since you have imprisoned my father.'

I turned abruptly. 'I have not imprisoned anyone.' Except a Welsh whoreson, who had been cutting the leather straps of our horses' harnesses in the fall, and was still locked up in Brecknock keep.

'Then one of us is a liar, my lord of Buckingham, for my father is Anthony, Lord Rivers.'

'*What?* Rivers does not have a daughter.'

'Yes, he does.' Defiance blazed in her voice as though her entire life had been a battle for respect. 'Acknowledged before witnesses. I'm his bastard.'

The bastard from Bristol way. I could only stare at her, cursing Heaven for a very bad jest. Oh Jesu, *a very bad jest.* Tainted blood. My wife's niece. Another damned Woodville.

'My name is Margaret.' I felt the scarring in her, heard the pain of childhood. Some compassion must have flowed out of me for her head jerked upright as though I had openly voiced a slur upon her virtue. So she did not want my pity. I could understand that.

Rivers' daughter. Did she love her father whom she must have hardly ever seen? Did he love her? No matter, I would no more set him free than I would bare my throat to a bloody-fanged wolf. Just my cursed luck, why did she have to be a Woodville?

She had set the petition on the small table and stood watching me with her hands clasped between her breasts. In the silence between us, the sudden unpleasant thumps of wall and stifled curses beyond the door echoed louder than cannon fire.

'Is that the cat being put out for the night?' Margaret Woodville asked dryly. She meant to rile, a corner of her mouth twitched almost imperceptibly.

'Something like that,' I managed to answer, wishing I might cross to the aumery and pour myself a throat-searing mouthful.

The haphazard knocks and grunts receded down the stairs. My visitor's mouth finally serifed into a faint smile. Oh, Devil's arse! She had seen the other wench.

'I should have thought a man like you would have better taste.' Then she instantly looked ashamed and murmured an apology. But it had been like having my cheek scratched by a diamond ring. Give her due, the wench had courage but if she wanted mercy for the paradox she called her father, she was dancing with the devil.

'I do have taste, mistress. It is mirrored in my eyes at this very moment.' She did not like that but before she could insult me further, I added swiftly, 'But, of course, you are here to discuss some means of twisting the screws on me.'

'Is there any, my lord?' A coin of hope flung in a saint's spring. Did she not know the saints do not listen? *I might*, however. Playing games with her could be amusing.

'There is always hope but I cannot help you, mistress. You would be better speaking to the Lord Protector since it was on his orders that your father was arrested. I am sure if you throw yourself on your knees and wash his shoe beaks with your tears...'

She flicked a disdainful glance at my clean ones and picked up her unopened letter. 'I beg your pardon then for disturbing you, your grace.' Too proud to bargain.

'Believe me, I am sorry I cannot assist you.'

Resentment chilled those green eyes. *Cannot or will not?*

I took hold the door handle and nearly collided with Pershall. The whoreson had been eavesdropping.

'Ah, there you are,' I said with sweetness, observing the parallel scratches down the left side of his neck. 'Seek out Bannaster and ask him to give this young woman an escort to...?' I looked round at Mistress Woodville with a querying eyebrow.

She hesitated, but the thought of making her way back alone across the city dismayed her more. 'St Martin Le Grand, your grace,' she admitted. Presumably the Queen drew the line at accommodating bastards in Westminster Sanctuary.

'Ah, near Aldersgate?' I returned towards her.

'Yes, my lord.'

'Seen hide or hair of your cousin my lord of Dorset then, mistress?'

Her cheeks sunk into concaves. 'No, my lord.'

I do not think it was my sudden proximity that made her eyelids shield her eyes like pretty visors.

'But there was a great to do, Mistress Woodville. A hue and cry within and without the gate, all over the ward you are dwelling. Surely you must have heard that?'

'I heard the baying of dogs, my lord, out in the fields.' Her chin rose and those green eyes were staring up into mine without blinking.

I drew a deep breath. Another world, another name, I would have kissed her.

There were voices at the foot of the stairs.

'It sounds as though your escort awaits you. Join the petitioners at Crosby Place, mistress. Who knows, his grace may be moved by your arguments–if you have any.'

'Or the King might,' she countered bravely. 'He is my cousin as well.'

A tight smile from me. 'A little cousin still, but I am sure he will listen.' I gestured that she proceed to the door and stood there with my hand upon the latch but half out on the landing, she turned.

'Please.' Just the touch of her hand on my wrist was like a summer fire on dry kindling. 'I truly beg your pardon for my rudeness. Please may we speak again?'

Could Samson resist Delilah, her breath sweet, her eyes moist? A Delilah Woodville? No, he could not.

'I am sure our paths will cross again, demoiselle.'

ATTENDING the morning court of an uncrowned twelve year old in his apartments at the Tower of London was like watching a score of grown birds feeding a cuckoo chick. As soon as I could leave without giving offence, I made my excuses and withdrew with my retainers.

Uncle Knyvett gave me the wink that he wanted a word so I gestured our entourage to go towards the water gate where my barge was waiting, and let him pluck me by the elbow. He drew me aside beneath the cherry trees of the inner bailey.

'A waste of a good morning,' I commented, staring up the walls of the Wakefield Tower where Henry VI had been murdered.

'You can say that again. By the saints, Harry. This whole business is woolly. Do you know what I mean? If you have a strong man as king, well, he's the King and what he commands, everyone does. But with a boy, particularly this one.' He pulled a face. 'I reckon we are looking at a future Saul not a Solomon, and it doesn't bode well for you, my lad.' I nodded and let him have his head. 'What's more, if the old tale of Proud Cis and the Flemish soldier of Rouen is true, then that pimply boy preening himself back there has no more royal blood than I do. So, what I am thinking, Harry, is that Richard of Gloucester would make an exceptional king.'

'That's treason, Uncle Will,' I scolded.

'And what else occurred to me, Harry,' continued Uncle Knyvett, as though he had just discovered that milk comes from cows, 'and I'm sure to you too, was that if the plague were to carry off Gloucester next August, then you'd be the next man for the throne.'

'Christ, uncle, does the sun go round the earth?' Me, King of England? Of course, as the last heir of Lancaster, I had dreamed of that. But there was still Richard's legitimate nine year old lad, although he was reputed to be delicate, unlikely to make old bones—unhealthy issue from two people closely related.

'Let us come at this from another direction then. What do you reckon would prevent Gloucester becoming king, Harry?'

'Apart from his grace's conscience which is as big as Canterbury Cathedral?'

He grinned. 'Aye, apart from that little hiccough?'

'Hmm, let me see, if England was governed from York, he would not have a problem, but this is London and the people here don't know enough of him to trust him. I'd say that if the Queen and Hastings decided to give each other the kiss of peace, they could whistle up the whole of southern England and the midlands against us. Gloucester doesn't see it. He thinks everyone except the Woodvilles loves him because he's been a good boy up north.'

Uncle Knyvett rubbed a hand across his chin. 'Then you just have to make sure Hastings and her ladyship do not become friends.'

'Or...' My mind was whirling. What coincidence of planets would make Richard take the throne? 'Heigh-ho, that might be the answer, uncle!' I exclaimed, shaking his hanging sleeves. 'We have to make sure they *do* become friends again.'

He pulled away. 'No, come on, that's like asking a man to believe in fairies, Harry. The woman wants his head. She'll bide her time until the boy's of age and then the moment Hastings sets a foot wrong, she'll have the kites pecking his lordship's handsome eyes out on London Bridge.'

'Ah, but they do not have to be really friends,' I said softly. 'Gloucester just has to believe they are.'

He snorted. 'Well, I haven't a poxy clue what you are raving about. I just know that my head would feel safer on my shoulders if Gloucester were really in charge.'

THE unkind hint that Uncle Dick was reaching for his nephew's crown became as common as dog dung and the citizens buzzed in like flies to investigate the stink. You could sense it riding through East Cheap to Crosby Place. The people whispered at the street corners, three here, four there, glancing suspiciously at strangers, noting the badges of the men-at-arms outside the cookshops and brothels. Hastings would have smelled it by now and I would also make sure the miasma crept under Westminster Sanctuary's door.

It was worth the trouble. A day or so later, Elizabeth, bored by the company of her children, proved herself easy bread to the mould of fear. She did just what I hoped: she decided that a reconciled local enemy might be better than a multitude of absent friends. A pretty, perfumed messenger–Mistress Shore–was summoned to the sanctuary and given a letter of loving friendship for Lord Hastings.

95

How did I know that? Well, although Richard had placed a cordon of men-at-arms around the sanctuary, he wasn't going to deny his little nieces the joy of clean sheets, and laundresses do like to chatter. So when Ratcliffe informed us that our horny Lord Chamberlain was now playing the goat with Mistress Shore every evening, I rubbed my hands with delight. It as was as good as hanging himself with one of her garters. By night she made love to the old wretch and then each morning she visited the sanctuary with sweets for the royal children and a progress report for Elizabeth. I would have wagered my dukedom that Dorset had hidden at her house as well before he sprinted out across the fields.

DANGER should make a wise man careful, but when I glimpsed Mistress Woodville in line with other petitioners at Crosby Place next morning in the drizzle, I could not resist desiring her favour. Very stoic she looked, holding up a square of cered leather above her head. Soon her arms would tire, and the rain would bedraggle her starched veil.

'Nick, there is a young woman halfway down the line in a gooseturd green gown with a long mustard cloak. Pluck her out and bring her to the other door to the Great Chamber.'

RICHARD was not pleased that I had rearranged his queue; probably due to his damnable sense of justice and the consequences of being forced to tidy his bed as a page.

'You are not going to tell me any more about this woman, are you?' he muttered, grumpy but curious.

'I hardly know anything about her either, cousin, but it's fair that you see her.' The word 'fair' hooked him. He sent Tyrrell to bring Margaret Woodville in.

'Mistress Poyntz, your graces.'

I thought Tyrrell must have found the wrong woman and my jaw slackened to see it was indeed Margaret Woodville. The little witch had never told me she was married. The loosened hair of the previous evening had been a way to gull my servants, not to mention their master.

She curtsied to us both, self-conscious like any woman of her sodden hem and dripping headdress.

'Present your petition to his grace, madame,' I instructed her. 'Then you may stand by the fire and warm yourself.'

Frowning, my cousin observed her over steepled fingers and his pile of papers. His secretaries at either end of the board inspected her with discreet admiration. Her firm breasts and graceful neck and shoulders would have turned most men's heads.

She darted me a swift look of gratitude before she loosened the ties of her cloak and fumbled nervously with the drawstring leather bag hanging from her girdle. After setting her petition before Richard, she retired meekly to stand before the hearth. Loyaulté catching the dripping edge of her cloak woke and shifted away with a look of displeasure that matched his master's.

'You are Lord Rivers' bastard daughter?' asked my cousin.

'Yes, your grace.'

'Well, I honour you for your loyalty to your father, Mistress Poyntz, but it is up to the Royal Council, not I, to grant your father his freedom.'

She came forward once more, glancing at me again before meeting the Lord Protector's scrutiny. Some pigs might fly but this white boar had his cloven hooves firmly planted.

'If your graces would speak to the Royal Council on his behalf.' Her beseeching face looked to us in turn. I kept my expression objective; Richard's was weary.

'Are you requesting me to condone treason, madame?' He leaned forward again. 'Your father's governance of the Prince of Wales must have deluded him into believing that he should govern England as well.'

'My lord, I am sure he did not mean to—' She fell to her knees. 'Please give him another chance. Let him go on pilgrimage to Jerusalem.' A reminder of the hairshirt and saints badges on her father's cap.

I think Richard winced inwardly like I did. Pilgrimages were the way Rivers made the rest of us feel wanting.

'No, madame,' my cousin replied firmly. 'He shall remain a hostage until all the monies that have been thieved by your other kinsmen are returned. If you wish to help him, I suggest you go and visit your aunt in Westminster Sanctuary and tell her that your father's wellbeing depends on her change of heart towards me, his grace of Buckingham and the Royal Council. You have leave, madame.'

What choice did she have but to hide her disappointment and rise with dignity?

'One moment, though!' He forced her to stop and turn back to us. 'What is your husband's name again?'

Another obeisance. 'Robert Poyntz of Iron Acton, my lord.'

'And why is your husband not here to support you in your petition?'

For an instant her expression might have resembled a fly's just before it hits the sticky web. 'Because he is Constable of Carisbrooke Castle on the Isle of Wight, my lord.'

'Hmm, isn't that a post that your father once held?' His knowledge startled her. 'Is your husband there now?'

'I…I am not certain, your grace. He has a good man as his deputy. I know that.'

The Lord Protector glanced heavenwards. 'Numbskulls,' he muttered, beneath his breath, and swung round on his senior secretary. 'Kendall, see Mistress Poyntz out and record where she is presently residing. When you next see your husband, madame, pray ask him to attend me.'

'I thank your grace.' A briefer curtsey.

She left unsated, and I could not go after her as I desired, for my cousin exploded immediately in a right pother.

'A pox on that damnable family! Fetch Lord Howard in, one of you! Edward Woodville is swanning up and down the Channel with half my brother's wealth and who are manning our fortresses? His bastard niece's husband for one.'

I said nothing, merely leaned back against the window with my arms folded and waited for our estimable admiral to arrive from one of the chambers off the gallery and sweeten the Lord Protector's humour.

'There's still no news, I'm afraid,' Howard announced. He breezed in, waving empty ink-stained fingers. I liked him. He was one of the wheels on which the cart of England ran. In his sixties, with a score of military campaigns behind him, he exuded dependability.

Richard came straight to the point. 'Jock, did you know Rivers' son by marriage is Constable of Carisbrooke?' Howard curled his lip and shook his hoary head. 'Holy Paul!' fumed my cousin. 'Do either of you know who's Constable of Portchester, then?'

I met Howard's glance and shrugged. All I knew was that Portchester was the sentinel castle east of Portsmouth.

The Admiral of England swished his mouth sideways, looking sheepish. 'Ahh.'

'*Ahh?*' prompted Richard, his smile an illusion.

'Sir Edward Woodville, I believe. Your pardon, Dickon, I should have found out—'

'No, *I* should have thought of it,' fumed my cousin. 'See!' he exclaimed, turning to me. 'The entire south is riddled with the Woodville pestilence. Get an order out, Jock. I want every one of the constables along the south coast replaced with people we can trust. The cinque ports, Southampton, Poole, Plym—'

'The Royal Council…' Howard began.

My cousin's fingers rose in a 'V'.

'Just a moment.' I intervened, hiding my amusement. 'Have you considered the consequences, Richard?'

'Harry, it will take very little for me to ride back home and rebuild Hadrian's Wall across Yorkshire. I am sated to here.' He sliced a hand across his throat. 'Everywhere I look, there's some Woodville toad. Didn't my brother have any sense? Good English noblemen have been starved of office for years because of one family's greed. Go, Jock, what are you waiting for! I want Edward Woodville and his ship. By Heaven, I'll have his head!'

The door closed behind Howard, but Richard still looked as though wanted to hurl the wine jug through the window. Even Loyaulté got out of the way of his pacing master.

'Isn't your wife arriving this afternoon?' I asked sweetly. My cousin just needed to get his leg over and take some pleasure.

'Humpf.'

'In God's Name, cousin, cut yourself some slack. You're not a slave on a treadmill.'

'Harry, I cannot run this blessed kingdom if I don't know what's been going on. I need to talk to King Louis's embassy and—'

'King Louis's embassy can go scratch himself. Make ready for Lady Anne. She'll be expecting a husband not a workhorse. What say I hear the petitions for the rest of the day?'

'Harry—' He was like a songbird with the cage door open, hesitant to leave. It wasn't because he didn't adore his wife but I guessed the letters and dispatches were a bulwark against the truth—that he was a prisoner now, unable to return to his beloved north.

'No one manages anything better than you, Richard, but even the Almighty took a day to rest and tomorrow is Sunday.'

He ran a hand around his chin.

'Go!' I ordered laughing.

PETITIONS are tedious but it was time I grabbed the pick and shovel for some real work. I wanted the Londoners and the royal council to see me as a man of integrity, not a wine bibbler like Dorset or a one-day-a-week philosopher like Rivers.

And speaking of Rivers—I sent for Delabere to sniff around the clericals at St Martin's before supper time and find out more about pretty Margaret. Wouldn't it sting Rivers if I played the wasp to his daughter's honeypot? No, that sounds cruel. My antennae had sensed a hunger in her just as great as mine. Had not Aristotle said that 'Love is composed of a single soul inhabiting two bodies'?

When I arrived back at the Manor of the Red Rose and found Mistress Poyntz back on my hall doorstep like a boot scraper—no, a spitting cat might be more accurate—it seemed like destiny.

Encouraging this friendship was reckless, but I reckoned that even if we did not become soul mates, she owed me at least a pennyworth of thanks.

I had her taken up—discreetly, mind—to my chambers and I ordered a private supper.

What she did before anything else was slap my face.

'NOW, just an instant,' I growled, as she struggled to free her wrist from my grasp. 'What was that for?'

'For having my husband dismissed from his post.'

'You have a poor sense of logic, mistress. I helped you see his grace of Gloucester, did I not?'

'Oh yes, my lord, you gave compassion with one hand and thieved it back with the other. Let-me-go!'

'Not unless you agree to break bread with me. Or perhaps you would like to lose Iron—' She kicked me. 'Acton.'

It was time to silence any potential scream so I kissed her. Her hand pushed against my chest but then she sighed beneath my lips and let me taste her. Her breath was sweet and I deepened my embrace. I knew how to tell a woman what I wanted from her. It worked. Rivers' daughter kissed me back, stealing her fingers round the nape of my neck and letting me draw her closer. It was some time before I raised my head at my servants' knocking.

Pershall and Bannaster were in with their platters for the side board before I had even loosed her. She sprang away from me in shame and turned her back, straightening her cap and probably trying to convince herself that she had not enjoyed the moment.

'The lady will share supper.' My tone brooked no rebellion.

Pershall winked and as the door closed behind him, my lady Poyntz whirled round on me like a windstorm, hands fisted.

'I am leaving, my lord. I have my children to—'

'Lying ladybird,' I clucked, enjoying the shame staining her cheeks. 'Your children are safe with their nursemaid in Gloucestershire. Did you imagine I should not become curious? You came to London to witness your father's triumph and then you received a letter from him begging you to intercede for him. I have to say he must be desperate if he's down to relying on you, my sweet. I told you to weep.'

'Jesu, you are a hard man.' Many a true word….? Yes, she was right.

Would she spread her wings and depart in a fury? No, the aroma of the supper viands had reached her. I caught her rueful glance at the enamelled domes on the side board.

'And you are either stupid or very brave, Mistress Poyntz,' I told her, unlocking a cupboard and taking down my richest mazers. 'I am the most powerful duke in the kingdom after the Lord Protector and you have just assaulted me.'

'Are you trying to impress me, my lord?' She flicked a scornful glance at the jewels twinkling on the mazer lids and then stared down at the dirty mark across my left shin. 'Did I draw blood?'

I looked down at my new scarlet hose and then sharply at her. Oh, yes, my vanity was bruised.

Isolde Martyn

She guessed her danger, for her beautiful eyes held a mixture of fear and exultation as she watched me from across the room. Was I the lion to be tamed by her whip and dance of feet?

'Perhaps the apt words to describe you are "impertinent and imprudent", madame.' I removed the lids from the mazers and filled them generously with an expensive claret. I was being magnanimous in allowing the wench leash, almost as much as Cat, but any hunter knows that a cunning prey makes the taking sweeter.

She accepted the wine from me, her breath levelling, and I touched my cup to hers, my expression challenge for challenge. I could see now the rubbed edge of her satin collar and the wear on her sleeve as she drank but the costly chased metal beneath her fingertips seemed to mean nothing. It was me she was examining over its edge and that pleased me.

'Why are you here other than to abuse me, Mistress Poyntz?'

'Because...because it is better than doing nothing.' The first touch of wine had moistened her lips. 'And maybe you will change your mind.'

I swirled mine before I drank. 'I'm married to a Woodville, remember. I do have some understanding of the clever cogs and greedy wheels within your family. Everything is calculated to a nicety, like now.' I looked across the rim, daring her to deny it. 'It's in the blood never to act on impulse.'

No lashes fanned down to veil her purpose. 'My mother did,' she replied pointedly, trying to convince me she was only a half-measure. 'I have been paying for it ever since.'

'Ah! So, kicking me was an impulse?'

'Oh no, that wasn't.' A dimpled smile lit her face. 'But I would not have kicked you if you'd been grey and hoary. I'd have shown some—'

'Respect?'

She nodded.

'But that is what this is all about.'

I wanted respect for my birthright. Respect and revenge, so when Pershall handed me a hand mirror, I could look myself in the face.

Her eyes were sad and I saw she knew how that felt. 'Yes,' she said softly, and lifted a hand to my cheek. 'But it comes from within, I think.'

Well, that was a matter of opinion. I drew away and poured myself more wine. 'Pray be seated if you are staying, my lady. If not, for the love of Heaven, plague me no longer and go now.' Before I behaved dishonourably.

102

I sat down by the small table knowing she would not stay. Her perfume would linger but she would be gone, the flash of auburn hair like a squirrel's flight, seen, forgotten, but instead I heard the rustle of her gown and felt the movement of cloth as she set a plate before me.

'May I serve you, my lord?'

Oh, there is a God. I lifted my head and watched her with hunger and an aching heart as she lifted the covers of our repast. Her fingers, neither so long nor unpleasantly elfin as her sire's, worked in wifely fashion. Soon my plate was arranged delightfully and then she served herself. It was astonishing to me that I could not remember Cat ever doing that; it was beneath her. Always the cutler or a servant served us.

'This is a feast,' Rivers' daughter murmured, drawing up a cross-legged chair and seating herself opposite me at the small table.

'I pawned Brecknock castle to pay for it.' I did not tell her I was already in debt to half of London. Trading on hope. 'Good appetite, my lady!'

She ate daintily, licking the excess from her lips. The western sun lit her tawny, crumpled cap and played upon the fine cheekbones; Rivers had given her good scaffolding. But while I was thinking it wondrous how she had piled her tresses into so small a space, she was thinking about her husband's anger.

'Is there aught you can do about Carisbrooke, your grace?' she asked, setting down a cleaned chicken leg.

'Fearful of being blamed?' I prodded a bowl of lavender fragrant water towards her.

'Yes, my lord.'

'Then be comforted. Your husband is not being singled out. There is to be a general change of sentries along the coast.' One nepotism replaced by another, probably with knights speaking the Yorkshire dialect.

Another silence followed but a gentle, companionable one; we might have been a modest merchant and his wife. Would life have been different if I had wed a frisky noblewoman like this instead of boring Cat with her plague of harps and hurdygurdies?

'So how long have you been married, Meg?'

Her shoulders stiffened at the sudden familiarity but she did not rebuke me.

'Five years, my lord,' she said briskly. 'We have a son and a daughter. Anthony is three and Anne was born last year. She's named for my grand-mother. And you, my lord? Have you children?'

'I have four. The youngest is still in swaddling. My oldest boy is a young rascal but I love him dearly and I miss my Bess.' Something in my voice spurred pain into her face.

Was she missing her children? No, there was more. Some hurt there to be pricked further.

'Sweet Meg, is that what Poyntz calls you?' I set my winecup down and watched her green eyes cloud like a stirred pool.

'Surely it is none of your business what he calls me, my lord.'

'Does he tell you that you are the loveliest woman in England and your eyes are the green of emeralds? No? Oh, that is truly sad. What did he receive for marrying you? The castle on the Isle of Wight?' She was looking down at the cloth. 'Or perhaps it was your father who said you were the prettiest child in England as you sat astride his leg and played at galloping. No? Then, Meg, life has given you the short straw.'

'That is not true.'

'Daughter to the Queen's brother! Why, you should become one of the princesses' ladies.'

'I am well cared for, I thank you. I do not need to beg.'

'Today you did and the time may come when you may again. England is facing civil strife because of your father's foolishness at Northampton. Your family is on the nose, Meg.'

'You are married to my aunt, my lord,' she countered. 'Doesn't that give you some obligation?'

'Unfortunately, Cat prefers shawms to my presence. We blow the can-dle out when we couple. Is that how it is for you, Meg? Come, eat some more.'

'I have had plenty, thank you. I should go home now.' Was I treading on the rotting stairs of a marriage? I tried another step.

'You should.' I agreed. 'I don't suppose your father or your husband would want you to eat in my company.' And then memory struck me. 'Jesu, I think I recall your husband now. He was sticking like a burr to my lord of Dorset's mantle last time I saw him.'

'That might be so.'

'So would he be in my lord marquis' company at the moment, do you suppose?'

The telltale tightening of her lips betrayed her.

'The Isle of Wight,' I murmured, sitting back. It was a guess.

'No.' The protest in an instant, too prompt to leave doubt.

'I think you need someone to protect your interests, Meg, and keep your manor house safe from act of attainder.'

She swallowed. 'Just what is your meaning, my lord?'

'Clear as day, I should have thought. To be frank, since your husband is conspiring with the Marquis of Dorset, are you going to compete for Lord Hastings' bed or will mine suffice?'

'Is that a true offer?' she scoffed.

'Cross my heart. Think about it, Meg, and run home now to your lonely mattress.'

Her hackles were still up but she did have manners as she took her leave. 'Thank you for supper.'

'My pleasure.' I kissed her hand like an adoring gallant. But next time...

HOW do you make an uncle king in place of the nephew when the uncle is too busy signing despatches and all you have against the brat are rumours about his grandmamma?

The morning after Meg had supped with me (don't mistake that I longed to lie with her but I had to be wiser than Hastings and tread carefully), I finally stumbled over the key to the future. The occasion? Mass with the Prince, my cousin and his lady at St Paul's, followed by a banquet at Westminster Hall. Swarms of important folk crawled out from under their stones to dine in the royal presence including Bishops Alcock and Stillington, still glued to one another's company.

I caught Uncle Knyvett's eye where he sat on a lower table and excused myself from the high table to go to the garderobe. He met me in the passageway.

'Uncle,' I whispered. 'I need a discreet inquiry on the Bishop of Bath and Wells.'

'Hoo, I can tell you about Stillington, Harry. Remember I was one of Duke George's affinity.'

'Ah, I had forgotten that! We'll talk further. Wait up for me.'

I returned to the feast. The boy king was merry and Richard's Anne was laughing. It must have seemed perfect to the commoners stuffing their noses into the doorway to gawp and salivate. It was never so perfect again. A bush of wondrous flowers while in amongst our roots the insects gnawed–the Woodville grubs turned out of their holes by the Lord Protector's spade, the Lancastrian worms who hated the Yorkists, and above it all on the leaves I sat like an insatiable young caterpillar ready to nip off the young shoots.

When I returned to my house, Nandik begged an audience with me. He had been showing a popinjay hunger since we had arrived in London, and that eve he was flaunting a blue fustian jacket and matching stomacher beneath his dark mantle. He was shaving more regularly now but with his crow black hair and swagger, and despite his learning, he still looked a desperate knave.

'Your grace, at Northampton, you showed some interest in astrology. With your grace's consent, if I had the exact date and time of his grace of Gloucester's birth, I could—'

'That is very generous of you, Nandik, but I should point out that you could have your balls cut off and stuffed down your throat for such a deed, and I truly have no wish to see your left shoulder in York and your right leg in Southampton, nor distribute your ashes after the bonfire. Have I made myself clear?'

'Perfectly, your grace.' He bowed and backed towards the door. 'I just wanted to let your grace know, however, that the current position of the planets is in the Lord Protector's favour.'

Oh, Nandik was so hungry for a sinecure.

'Thank you.' I could have consulted a bawd from a Southwark alleyway and heard the same. To content him, I drew out a rose noble from my purse. 'Here, buy yourself some boots to go with your new clothes. On your way out, tell Pershall that I am ready to disrobe, and ask my uncle to attend me.'

'Is that *all*, my lord?' He seemed astonished that I had not asked him about my own future. I did not need to. I had it already planned.

'WHY this sudden curiosity about Bishop Stillington, Harry? Thinking of becoming Archbishop of Canterbury and need a recommendation?' Uncle

Knyvett sat down on the bed while Limerick lifted off my collar of sunnes and roses and Pershall removed my shoes.

'It's those lizard eyes.' I slid my rings off into a coffer while my points were unfastened.

'Savin' your pardons, my lords,' butted in Pershall. 'Wasn't he that bishop what got tossed into the Tower when George of Clarence was shoved in a barrel?'

'The duke did not get shoved in a barrel, Pershall. He was privately executed and you are talking about one of my cousins so show some respect.'

'Yes, my lord. Sorry, my lord.'

'Oh, go and charm your way beneath a cookmaid's skirts, Pershall. Out! I'll manage now, Nick, sleep well!'

I checked the door after they had gone to make sure none of the servants might hear our conversation. Limerick had taken on new men to cope with all the extra feasting and there was a fair chance some of them had been bribed to spy on me.

'So what's gnawing at you, Harry?' asked Uncle Knyvett, yawning.

'I've been thinking about George's death all day. Is it possible that he discovered indisputable proof that Dead Ned was an archer's by-blow?'

'Well, you heard all the evidence in the treason trial, my lad.' Uncle Knyvett's sour expression told me he did not want to dredge up the sludge, but my mind was buzzing.

'But I didn't hear everything. That is just the point.' I paced, tapping my fist against my palm. 'All along, it was the King who made the accusations. I was just a cipher. Truly, it was...it was as if there was some hidden grievance between them that was never aired.'

'There was a sackful of plaguey differences between 'em. The duke drank too much to keep his jealous thoughts to himself. Can't we stow this until morning?' He slid off the bed.

'But did you not think it curious that his execution was done privily, not on a scaffold before a crowd of his peers? Since I sat in judgment on him, I surely should have witnessed his death.'

'Aye, so you should have, but I reckon King Edward was ashamed of killing his own brother.'

I quickened to my argument. 'Or maybe he wanted to make sure George made no final speech.'

'They usually order the drummers to drown 'em out, but you could be right. Do we still need to chew the cud on this one, Harry? I am heading for bed. All I can tell you is that I was not in George's confidence, thank God, else I'd be under a slab by now.'

I could understand his reluctance but I could not let go the matter. 'Wait, please think back, it is important. Who did George trust the most?'

He shrugged. 'Tom Burdett, of course. Poor devil, hanged, drawn and quartered.'

'So *he* cannot blab. Anyone else? Bishop Stillington, for instance?'
'Possibly.'
'As Pershall said, the King did shove him in the Tower for a while.'
'True.' He digested that and then said, 'So what's to be done?'
'Well, I am resolved to meet with him. And since he knows you, be a good fellow and arrange it.'

'Hang about, that might not be so easy. He is boarding at that fat slug Alcock's house. In fact, I've never seen the pair of 'em apart.'

'And Alcock is the Queen's man to his backbone. You know what, uncle,' I purred, 'I feel like some serious religious discourse after all this carousing. I believe I shall invite Bishop Alcock, Bishop Kempe and Chancellor Russell to supper.'

'Ha! Not Stillington?'

Of course not, *I* shall be seeing *him* while the other three are here. But, dear me, who is to entertain the bishops while I am indisposed?' I offered my best smile.

'No, Harry,' he groaned, raising his palms to ward me off.

'But there are just two weeks to the coronation, two weeks to play at kingmaking.'

'Play! That's an ill word for it.' He swallowed and ran a finger beneath his collar. 'Blessed Christ! I shouldn't be encouraging you. They've still got some barrels at the Tower, Harry.'

'It will not be the Tower, I swear to you.'

AT four o'clock next day, the three bishops arrived to sup with me but by the time dear old Knyvett explained that I was in bed with stomach cramps, the cooking smells from the kitchens had them salivating, and they willingly stayed to enjoy the feast without me.

At Clerk's Well, the bells of the tower of St John's were competing with the neighbouring priory to ring out five o'clock as I arrived for my assignation with Stillington. With Bannaster, Pershall and Nandik following somewhere behind me, I felt utterly at ease and rather relived to be free of my full entourage.

The footpaths across the fields at Clerk's Well were full of people. It was a fine summer evening and there was plenty happening: guildsmen rehearsing interludes, young men practising their wrestling for the August bouts at Smithfield and maidens kicking up their heels to timbrels. It is a district wholesome to the nose and more accessible than Southwark.

Stillington was already waiting beside the stone curb that ran squarely round the famous well. He was clearly used to dukes misbehaving. If he was surprised to see his grace of Buckingham in a chaplain's second best habit, then he gave no sign of it, but fell in beside me. No one took notice of a pair of drab clerics as we strode in the direction of Skinners Well. Judging by his sour expression, winkling information out of this wary churchman might prove as hard as getting a mother superior to roll in the hay.

'You had no trouble slipping the leash, my lord bishop?'

He scowled. 'I have a friend I visit at the priory. Will this take long?'

'As long as we like. After all, there is no need for Alcock to restrict you any more since the Woodvilles have lost their cudgels. I daresay you are feeling more secure about your future now.'

'My future is in God's hands.' Oh no, not piety as a buckler!

'Then you have changed your stripes, bishop,' I clucked. 'I thought your major sin was speaking out. Since when have you become so meek?'

He folded his lips tightly. Well, it was a daft question so I offered to buy him a beef pie.

'No, I do not want a beef pie,' he said tersely. We walked in silence until he finally said, 'Perhaps you would like to come to the point.' Ah, that was a show of interest at last.

Because I was missing supper and my belly was gurgling, I rebelliously stopped a pretty pie peddler. The bishop averted his eyes from the wholesome charms above the tray.

'Here.' I thrust a pie into his hands. 'Let us just say my guilty conscience is prompting me to look after you and at last I have the opportunity to do so.'

Stillington glared at the pastry crust and then at me.

'You must understand that I was *ordered* to proclaim a death sentence upon your friend the duke,' I explained to him. 'A verdict I bitterly regret. But for his sake, I should honestly like to make amends.' A lie, I am afraid, but I hoped it might thaw this stubborn cleric.

'Aye, by the Blessed Virgin, it should not have come to that,' he muttered, his eyes fixed sorrowfully upon the path and he bit into the pastry.

'But now we have a change of government, my dear bishop. Our Woodville bitch is muzzled but, of course, there is not the slightest doubt that if she regains her authority she will have you murdered.'

He choked. His eyes watered and his thin lips were flaked with crumbs by the time I had thumped him back to normal breath. Still distressed, he wiped a hand across his mouth and cast the remainder of the pastry to a stray dog. I unstoppered the leather flask from my belt and passed it over to him.

'King Edward shielded you, is that not so, bishop? He did not trust you enough to give you high office again, but he wouldn't stoop to your murder. I hope you say a daily prayer for him.'

'I pray for all of them.' He handed back my bottle and we walked on. His head was bowed, his clasped hands, like Pontius Pilate's, writhing in the generosity of his sleeves.

Time for pressing my seal on this softening wax.

'The dead are dead, Stillington. It is the living that need you. Pray for Richard of Gloucester. And if you want to save your own skin, by Heaven, you had better make sure Gloucester stays in power, and there is only one way to be sure for all time.' I took a deep breath and a guess. 'Give him the proof he needs, Stillington. The apple from the Tree of Knowledge. God's mercy, you helped him when he was courting Lady Anne. Why won't you help him now? He needs to know for his safety. For his son's safety. He's not a jealous drunkard like his brother was, but honourable and just. Things need not go wrong this time.'

Stillington did not answer.

'For the love of Christ!' I almost shouted, clapping my fists to my temples. 'You did not hesitate to give the apple to George, pips and all, though the damned fool did not deserve it. God's truth, bishop, why do you wait now, when the occasions is so ripe?'

He continued walking, his eyes on the path before him, and the stray dog danced backwards in front of us, slobbering for further dainties. I began to think that any secrets were an illusion on my part and that I had been punching into thin air.

'My lord.'

At last! I glanced down at the old man, my fingers crossed. He was running his tongue over his thin lips like a reptile. But when he spoke, it was not the assurance I sought.

'Am I to pray for you as well, my lord duke?'

'Certainly, if you can spare any.' I answered with brittleness and not a little astonishment. 'What is the matter? Do you not trust me? Heaven preserve me, do you think this is a snare set by Bishop Cock-and-Balls?'

He swallowed, clearly discomforted. 'You are married to the Queen's sister and... and you are the heir to the House of Lancaster.'

'Yes, and I have been behind Gloucester like a loyal shadow ever since King Edward died. If you doubt me, ask him. In any case, I do not want your secrets, Stillington, take them direct to him. I'm not a messenger boy.'

'No, but you want the Bohun inheritance and only a king can give it to you.'

For an instant, I was struck to stone like Lot's wife and then realising we were standing on the path like quarrelsome lovers, I shook myself back to civility and turned on my heel.

THE three bishops were still consuming some of my best Rhenish and malmsey when I slunk through the postern gate as stealthily as any cut-throat. My head was still reeling. I was confused, afraid and exposed, as though Stillington had peeled back the skin of my face to show the ugly mess beneath. I walked into my bedchamber, my palms to my eyes. The urge to scream and kick shook me.

'Your grace? Harry?' A pair of slender arms encircled my waist and a woman's cheek nestled against my back.

'Meg?' I whispered, turning, my heart lifting like a lark. 'Meg! Oh, my darling, you should not be here.' My fingers touched her soft hair where it blessed her cheekbones and I feasted on her loveliness like a weary pilgrim come at last to kneel and wonder.

'I was careful, my lord. No one saw me. I hid when your servants came back to turn back the bed covers.'

'Oh beautiful, beautiful Meg.' I kissed her then, savouring each caress of her lips on mine, and it was some time before either of us spoke again.

'Your grace.' She surfaced from our depth of ocean first.

'Harry to you,' I whispered, drowning in the green deep of her gaze.

'Harry.' She tugged at my sleeve. 'Look.' A strange mournful sound broke through the enchantment.

'Meg?'

'No, that was not I. Look!' She turned me and I cursed.

The skinny dog had followed me home. It had nosed open the un-latched door and stood halfway in, head and tail downcast. Only its eyes were raised in hope. I stared back and the beast's tail gave a faint, questioning wag.

Meg put a knuckle to her lips, reeled away and collapsed laughing on the chest at the end of my bed. The dog regarded her with reproach and fixed its baleful look once more on me and I began to laugh, too, and suddenly the world seemed good and wholesome again.

'Lord's sake, a morsel of pie and it has followed me all the way from Clerk's Well.'

'Clerk's Well.' That made her laugh more. 'What in Heaven's Name were you doing in Clerk's Well, my lord,' and then she bit her lip. 'Forgive me.''

Stillington's lie was adaptable. 'I have a friend at St John's Priory.'

Her eyes sparkled. 'Would you take me there?'

'He smells and they do not like women visitors,' I teased.

'No, to the meadows, I mean. Here, boy,' she snapped her fingers coax-ingly at our forgotten visitor and it came forward cagily, with an eye on me. It knew on which side the bread was buttery.

'Hmm, I might.' Our gazes danced together. I could hardly breathe, jealous that she was caressing the dog when I still had to beg for her favours. 'Are you staying the night?' It was too direct perhaps but she glanced up at me through her coppery lashes.

'Would you like me to?'

'If Poyntz isn't likely to run me through with his sword.'

'If my aunt your duchess will not slay me with her bodkin.'

'Oh it would not be a bodkin. She would probably knock you over the head with a hurdy-gurdy if she cared, but she doesn't, Meg, not a whit.' I opened my arms and she was in them within an instant.

'I should hate you,' she whispered lovingly, winding her fingers through the hair at my nape. 'Oh God, make me hate you.'

'Your father is a knave and your uncles are vipers but I want to buy you the moon and stars.' For those words, she kissed me and smiled. Excellent! I gently loosed her arms from my neck and strode to the door and slid the bar across.

Meg was feeding the dog when I turned. She held some out to me as well.

'You, madame, are a liability,' I muttered, slapping a wedge of cheese onto a hunk of bread. 'I have a trio of venerable bishops in my hall, a virtuous cousin in Crosby Place who believes in marital fidelity, I am supposed to be sick with stomach cramps and there is this dog not to mention that I am about to make love to my brother-in-law's daughter.'

'Are you?' That soft warm laugh that came from her heart.

'Divinely, exquisitely, unless you like it rough and passionate. The dog can lick your soles while I....'

'I think I would prefer "exquisitely", Harry.'

'With candles?' I asked hopefully.

'As many as you like.' She came across and undid the laces of my shirt. 'Do you take a vow of poverty on Mondays?'

'Oh this,' I shrugged, realizing I was still clad in a simple dark gown. 'I was not meeting a woman.'

'I suppose I should not ask.'

'No.' Her fingers were loosening the laces that held my hose to my gipon and then she slid her hand down my codpiece and I groaned in utter ecstasy and then I was pushing her collar down her shoulders and pulling away the flimsy covering between her breasts as I had longed to do the moment I had first seen her. My hands slid inside her bodice. Delicious pointed breasts quivered against my palm and the sweet nipples tightened as I rubbed my thumbs across them and kissed her with all the passion of my dark soul. Her fingers continued to play upon my prick, stroking and freeing me. I undid her belt, my breath quickening. I wanted her more than any other woman in my entire life. I wanted to bury myself in her, hold her, possess her and ride to the stars.

I am not sure how we reached the bed but I remember lifting her up onto it and pushing up her gown and petticoats. Tiny curls of flame hid the sweet adit between her thighs. I drew my fingers away creamy with her longing.

'Oh, Meg.' She was watching me, her eyes wide, as if I had cast some spell upon her. 'Are you sure?' I asked.

'Love me, Harry. All of me. Harry.'

I kicked the muddle of gipon and hose away and tugged my shirt over my head. She was leaning on her elbows gazing at my body.

'Man enough for you, my lady?'

'Oh yes, yes, my lord.'

I made love to her with her hair around us like a fire. I stripped her naked and caressed her, until she was pleading with me and I was at such a pitch that the world receded, and as she shattered, I released, with a loud gasp of exquisite pleasure.

We were adulterers, sinners, and Hell was waiting to welcome us in with torches lit, but entering her had been like entering Paradise.

I lay back sated, and she fell asleep with her face against my breast and her hair tickling my throat, and I was like a man blessed by God.

I WAS in a deep sleep when Pershall shook me. I awoke to straightened bed-clothes and a happy, smelly dog alongside my shins. Meg was gone.

'I thought you did not like black dogs, my lord. Isn't this—'

'Yes, it is, Pershall. All the way from blessed Skinners Well. Did you not notice the damned animal following me?'

'No, can't say I did, my lord. You see, Nandik and I were busy discussing free will an' such like.'

'Free will?' I said dangerously.

'It might scrub up into quite a handsome creature.'

'Then go and scrub it.'

'Me, my lord, I don't do dogs.'

'You do now. It goes with the position, Pershall. How about you and he enjoy yourself in the stables!'

114

Where had Meg gone, my pretty bastard? Back to being a respectable matron, the Queen's niece? Every inch of my body remembered, ached, for her. Overnight, I had become enthralled but it was not a healthy condition when I needed my wits sharp as pikes. I was still feeling off balance when Uncle Knyvett came to join me for breakfast. He would have got more conversation out of the abbot of a silent order. But then I recalled that he had done me a huge favour.

'How was supper then?' I asked, when the servants had withdrawn.

'You owe me, lad.' He placed a cherry stone upon a spoon and catapulted it at me. 'How did you fare?'

'I am not sure if our friend Stillington knows anything to make a difference.'

'Never mind, worth a try. By the way, I did not know your fellow Pershall owned a dog.'

7

I managed a few minutes alone with Richard before the Royal Council meeting and slid in an apology.

'Been behaving like a rowdy student,' I confessed. 'Stuffing myself to perdition all over the place while you've been straining your eyes over dispatches.'

He only laughed. He was so irritatingly reasonable. 'Nonsense, I've found it invaluable to have someone reliable and responsible meeting everyone on an informal level. You've done fine work, Harry, saved me a lot of time for what really matters. I can't do both and I much prefer my side of the bargain.'

It was pointless arguing with him and if he preferred to see me with a halo round my head instead of half-moons under my eyes, that was his folly.

He caught me off guard again later. It was during the meeting—a humdrum bread-and-ale session to argue out details about Parliament and the Convocation. London in June was going to be so crammed with notables that all the castles and cathedrals of the kingdom would be quite deserted and if the Frogs launched a massive assault they would easily conquer us.

Everyone droned on and on. I stopped paying attention.

'Cousin! I repeat, *Is that agreeable to you?*' The Lord Protector's stern tone cut through my musing. The councillors were all staring up the table at me with great amusement.

'Your pardon, my lord, what was that you said?'

Richard shifted irritably. There was a flicker of something I could not fathom in his eyes. 'Do we have to go through it all again, Buckingham? I have a meeting with his highness at the Tower in half an hour.'

'Your pardon, my lord, I admit that my thoughts were elsewhere.'

The Duke of Suffolk gave a great belch of laughter. 'Buckingham, we've just assented to you becoming the Chief Justiciar of Wales and you weren't even listening, you daft happ'th!' He rose and reached out across the table to shake my hand. I was dazed and could only stare speechlessly at Richard, who was laughing with the rest. My thanks were stammered and breathless.

Wales was mine! Lonely, perverse, damnable Wales, mine at last! My trusting cousin had given me the means to establish a vast net of retainers just as Hastings had achieved in the Midlands. Henceforth I could summon up an army of Welshmen and array troops from Shropshire down to Somerset, and since all castles, garrisons, appointments and incomes in Wales now fell within my jurisdiction, I should easily be able to pay my soldiers and maintain a proper ducal retinue without falling into further debt. My eyes were moist as I clasped his hand and accepted the document confirming my appointment.

'This should have happened a long time ago,' Richard said for all to hear.

Hastings' congratulations to me were noticeably tepid, so in retaliation I loudly invited Catesby, his devoted retainer, to dine on the pretext that I needed the fellow's opinion on a manorial dispute. Hastings watched us depart, with narrowing eyes.

***

NEXT day the fire really started. Bishop Stillington visited the Lord Protector and the effect was little short of a miracle. I did not hear of it until I was leaving the royal lodging at the Tower and Hastings, booted and spurred, almost collided with me in the stables. I gave him good-day and would have passed him but he thrust up a hand against my shoulder and slammed me against the nearest wall.

'Get out of here!' he roared at the grooms, and shoved his riding crop tight across my gullet. 'What in Hell is going on, Buckingham?' he snarled.

'I do not know what you mean,' I gasped in all sincerity. He was almost choking me. Yes, I could have defended myself but I didn't want to make matters worse. Getting a spray of his saliva and a close view of his sweating pores was distasteful enough.

'For Christ's Sake, boy, you poxy well know all right. *He* refused to see me. *Me*! Not even Ned ever did that to me, so what stinking, arselicker has been pouring filth about me into his ears?'

'You have picked the wrong arselicker, Hastings. *I* have no time to listen to hearsay.'

He glared, a tiny muscle twitching angrily in his cheek, but then someone else gave a loud cough and he eased his force on my throat.

Bishop Morton and Lord Stanley were standing, slack-jawed, at the rear stalls. They must have ridden in with Hastings.

'Are you not making rather a fool of yourself, my lord?' I chided softly, jerking my head towards the others. 'Unless there *is* something or someone you don't want the Lord Protector to hear about?'

'You poxy coxcomb!' he sneered loudly, grabbing the neck of my mantle. 'When I think of the many times I stood by you as a child.' *Liar!* 'I know my household is riddled with your friggin' informers.'

'You planted Nandik in mine,' I countered smoothly.

'Nandik!' he scoffed. 'That trumped-up scarecrow. Better get rid of him before the pair of you are hauled before the courts for witchcraft and treason. Ha, played at horoscopes already, have you, lad? What do you hope to learn? That *you*'ll one day be king? Nandik will say anything you pay him to.'

'Lord Hastings,' I replied coldly with all the hauteur I could muster, 'you overstep your rank. Perhaps adultery with Mistress Shore is addling your wits.'

I think he would have driven his fist into my belly but before I could hurl the old goat off me, the Lieutenant of the Tower came running in

'*My lords!*'

With an oath that would have made a virgin faint, Hastings flung me away from him and hurtled out, leaving me to ease my collar back into its original position. I brushed aside the Lieutenant's concern and sent him after Hastings.

'Sweet Mother of God! What caused *that?*' I exclaimed, turning to Morton and Stanley, who must have heard every word.

Stanley shrugged and came forward. 'Old Dick wouldn't see any of us. Seems like he's in a real puther, been running round like a dog with its balls lopped off ever since...'

'Since what?'

'Really, my son,' Morton beamed at me. 'I *am* surprised you don't know. Bath and Wells squeezed in an audience with our august Protector early this morning. One presumes it was to deliver some tidbit that he's been saving ever since Malmsey George's demise. A lovely aroma of intrigue, hmm?'

An aroma that made me ravenous.

'Where is my cousin now?'

Morton bestowed the responsibility of answering onto Stanley with a broad smile.

'Gone home to "mother".' It was not respectful but what else could you expect of a Stanley?

RICHARD was in swordplay in the courtyard, when I arrived at Crosby Place. He had forgone dinner at Baynards and seemed to be slashing at Huddleston, his duchess' brother-in-law, in the hopes of spending some of the pent-up misery that was so obvious in his face.

He was scarlet with exertion as he joined us later in the great chamber for the meeting of our inner council and he did not bother to change his apparel. His collar was loosely tied at the neck and he had merely pulled on a sleeveless satin jacket over his sweaty shirt. A far cry from his normal fastidious self.

I raised questioning eyebrows at him as he came in but he ignored me. It was a bread and butter meeting but he sped us through faster than a whore on a busy night, and then curtly announced he wanted to see me alone and disappeared into his inner sanctum slamming the door.

"I think I am about to be beaten for getting the wrong answers in my hornbook,' I muttered, pretending to be as perplexed as the rest.

'Brawling before school, I heard,' corrected Lovell with a light smile that barely masked his anxiety. 'I hear you and Lord Hastings had words this morning.'

'Search me why.' I answered. 'Is that what has angered him?' I nodded towards the closed door.

Lovell shook his head, perplexed. Howard gathered up his papers and hugged them to his chest. 'If it's aught else, do us a favour, Harry, and find out. We need to know.'

They were upset, his good men and true. Until now, we had all been heading towards the coronation upon the same barge, golden tassels, purple canopy, the lot, all happily waving but now the future seemed as hazardous as shooting London Bridge.

MY cousin, the queen bee, had discarded his jacket, and was sitting at his table of papers, with one hand supporting his temple. The chamber was hotter than a brothel and it was a wonder he could concentrate on anything. Across the table, his chief secretary, John Kendall, was struggling to consult one of the Patent Rolls. It was flowing off his lap onto the floor and an undersecretary was on his knees rolling it back up. Loyaulté was in the corner on his sack looking disgruntled, and snapping at a blue fly.

I had to wait while the three finished their business before my presence was coldly acknowledged by my cousin. Kendall deposited his burden into his assistant's arms, wiped his hands on his flanks and offered me his vacated stool. I declined to be seated.

'Open the window before you go, John,' Richard muttered, pulling savagely at the lower lacing of his shirt. He flung himself back in his chair and put his feet up on the table. While the room emptied out of the servants' door, he watched me sternly, carefully choosing his words.

'Two grown men squabbling like jealous children,' he sneered.

'Hastings attacked me for no good reason,' I replied.

'Holy-friggin-Paul! I have enough to contend with without the twin pillars of my protectorate having dogfights in public. Do not let it happen again!' He swung his feet down and took a warrant from the nearest pile but I refused to be dismissed like an erring schoolboy.

'Hastings is as guilty as Lucifer, Richard, and you know it. He is openly jealous of my influence with you, he's ingratiating himself with the Prince and he's kissing hands with the Queen again.'

He did not look up. 'I do not want to discuss it further, cousin, you can see I'm busy.'

I slammed my hand down upon the table making the inkpots shudder.

'For Lord's Sake, Richard! We are discussing the security of the realm. You know as well as I do that Mistress Shore is a messenger between Hastings and Elizabeth. She pleasures him by night and then minces down to the sanctuary by day to dandle your nephew and nieces while she gives Elizabeth a full report on last night's pillow talk.'

He swore at me but I persisted.

'He has been listening to rumours that say you are bloody enough to seize your nephew's crown. The city's edgy with it. You only have to stick your nose out of doors to smell the uncertainty. There is an anti-pope in your protectorate, Richard, with a shadow conclave ready to move in on us at any moment.'

'Oh, Christ bless us,' he said nastily, 'is this some peculiar ability learned in Wales, some fey instinct for nosing trouble or—'

'God's Truth!' I roared at him. 'Listen to me! You may be bent on self-destruction but I'm not. I know how the Woodvilles do things and right now they're gradually moving in on you like a pack of bloody wolves. The city's crawling with them. I've seen faces from the old days in the streets. They're bringing in supporters from Kent and Surrey, not to mention the new recruits who fear losing their offices to your northerners.' He opened his mouth but I did not give him a chance. 'Oh yes, I know how they do things,' I muttered. 'They tried to turn me into one of them, remember. It's Stony Stratford all over again and we need a show of strength. You must send for more soldiers from Yorkshire, men you can trust.'

'Don't talk like a fool! I can't do that,' he replied savagely. 'That would only confirm the rumours. I'll end up with more fucking enemies than I have already.'

'Then you have no alternative but to arrest Hastings.'

He clapped his hands to his ears. 'No! Arrest our greatest ally? I'll not hear of it! Christ, that would start a fire! On what proof? Just because he lies with a foolish strumpet and spends time with the Prince. He's the boy's friggin' chamberlain, for Christ's sake. You call that treason?'

'Then test him out,' I retorted, calming down. 'Make it known that you are sending for extra soldiers. If he is guilty, he will move quickly.'

He sniffed loudly and stared at the writing in front of him.

'Christ love us!' I muttered. 'We're vulnerable. Hastings' men could have surrounded the inner council an hour since and we'd have been penned like silly sheep–hauled off to the Tower with barely a blade drawn. We have to protect ourselves.'

I tugged a blank sheet of parchment from the pile and seated myself on Kendall's stool.

'To whom shall I address it? The Mayor and Aldermen of York?' Richard did not answer. He had hidden his face in his hands and there was no movement behind his ringed fingers, so I started without his consent:

Right trusty and well beloved, we greet you well, and as you love the weal and surety of your own selves, we heartily pray you to come unto us to London in all the diligence you can possible after the sight hereof, with as many as you can defensibly arrayed, there to aid and assist us against the Queen, her blood adherents, and affinity, which hath intended and doth daily intend, to murder and utterly destroy us. I paused, changed the punctuation and added: *our cousin the duke of Buckingham and the old royal blood of this realm.'*

'How about sending Ratcliffe with it?' I suggested, and finished the letter off: *as our trusty servant, this bearer, shall more at large show you, to whom we pray you give credence, and as ever we may do for you in this time coming fail not, but haste you to us hither.'*

I pushed it over to him and he slowly unpeeled his fingers from his face, read it, and then tossed it away from him. 'I see. You don't like my writing,' I jested, grabbing it up. Inside, I was angry. Why would he not confide in me? I had been behind him at Stony Stratford, for God's sake! And then I heard a muffled sob. Tears were running down my cousin's cheeks. Loyaulté trotted over and snuffled his knee, gazing up at him with a pitying whine.

For an instant, I was at a loss. Was this my cousin who had always seemed so resolute, a man of steel nerves and common sense? I must have stared at him slack-jawed. He just sat there, mechanically fondling the hound's head, staring into nothingness while tear after tear welled out silently.

Maybe Stillington had told him he was a bastard as well. Well, it was not so impossible. Proud Cis might have had another hiccough of infidelity.

'Richard!' I went round the table and crouched down beside him, unclenched his other hand from the curl of the chair arm and held it in my own. 'This is not like you. What is it, my friend?'

He swallowed, barely able to speak, and turned his face to me heavy with sorrow.

'What have I done, Harry? Am I so great a sinner? I never once failed Ned, not once, and now God—' His lips quivered but the words disobeyed him. I eased up to my feet, laid my arm about his shoulders and I held him to me until the shaking ceased, then he pulled back from me, knuckling away the moisture on his cheeks.

He needed time to recover so I went to the door and called for his page to bring us some strong drink, and while I waited by the closed door, I said to him gently, 'If you need my help, then I am here. What has changed since yesterday when we made merry?'

'Only the whole damn world!' The slender fingers clenched into fists over his heart. 'There was a time when a man might...' His hands uncurled and fell despairingly to his sides as he took a deep breath and strived to bring himself under control again.

The page scratched at the door and I swiftly took the flagon and dismissed him. I poured out some fortified wine and wrapped my cousin's fingers around the cup. He swallowed slowly and gradually grabbed back the reins of his emotions. I waited and at last the revelation came:

'Harry, remember in Northampton we spoke about my brother George and why you were instructed to find him guilty, because...because if he outlived Ned, he would try to seize the crown?'

'Are you going to tell me that tale about your mother and the Fleming is true and that Dead—' I caught my error in time. 'That dear old Edward had no right to the crown?'

'Oh that's true alright.' He laughed bitterly, filling his cup again. 'My mother was so infatuated, she could not help herself.'

So the speculation was true. I could have whooped.

Careless Aunt Cis. No sponges in vinegar. What a shame.

I tapped my fingertips together consideringly. 'Then Edward had no right to the throne but George did and so do you.'

Ha! I was tempted to ask him if he had ever reserved a barrel of malmsey at the Tower with his name on it but that would have been too cruel. Instead, I said: 'No wonder the poor wretch pickled himself. This means, of course, that you are the rightful king.'

He ignored that. 'That is not the worst, Harry.'

'God forbid! If you are not the Duke of York's son, keep it to yourself.'

But the revelation was coming now. My prayer this morning to the Saint of Lost Causes had not been in vain.

'Harry, the Bishop of Bath and Wells came to see me today. He swore to me on the Holy Gospels that he performed a trothplight between Ned and the Earl of Shrewsbury's daughter, and that when Ned married Elizabeth secretly in '64, Eleanor was still alive.'

It was so simple but it took my breath away. A trothplight was as good as marriage if made before a priest.

'No wonder the Queen wanted George silenced. It is a wonder Stillington survives.' I strode to the window, hugging my shoulders. Now there were two reasons to make my cousin king. 'Have you only the old man's word for it, though?' I asked over my shoulder. 'Eleanor's not doing embroidery hidden away in a nunnery somewhere?' Richard pulled a face. 'Ah, no Lady Eleanor,' I murmured, and came back to sit down on Kendall's stool, hard put not to laugh.

What a mess! Better than I had hoped. Dead Ned had managed to destroy his own dynasty before he had even sired an heir. To marry in secret and twice!

'Eleanor was four or five years older than Ned and a widow, just like Elizabeth. Foolish, eh?' Richard wryly shook his head, his humour raw and painful.

Foolish? I could not think of one Plantagenet king who had managed to master an intelligent woman—Eleanor of Aquitaine, Isabella the fair, Margaret of Anjou, Elizabeth Woodville, and now, rising from her grave, Eleanor Butler.

'What happened to her eventually?'

'She took holy orders, and she died four years after Ned married Elizabeth. You see, it makes my nephews bastards.'

How could it?

'Whoa, surely Ned and Elizabeth took their marriage vows again once Eleanor was dead?'

'No, that's the cursed crux of it. I do not think so. You know how slack-willed Ned could be at times.'

'Yes, but Elizabeth never leaves a blasted stone unturned.'

'That's the irony, Harry. I do not think she knows. Ned never blessed well told her. You see what this means.'

'Indeed I do!' I replied, springing to my feet and sweeping him an obsequious bow. 'King Richard III, by the grace of God.'

'No!' he snapped, recoiling violently.

Hmm, how could I persuade him? I needed a touch of Satan's methods, but the kingdom of England was already on the table.

'Forgive me, Richard, but your dilemma as I see it is purely an emotional one. The kingdom has never prospered under child kings. If you take the crown now, it will prevent civil war later when the Queen gets her tentacles back into the boy.'

He ran a finger along the edge of his table. 'I could shut Stillington away somewhere and pretend I never gave him audience this morning.'

'You could.'

I let a silence fall between us and strode across to the window. Down in the garden the duchess and her bastard sister, Lady Huddleston, were laughing as they picked flowers. With broad-brimmed straw hats to keep the sun off their faces, they looked like moving flowers themselves from where I stood. My duchess would have been with them if she had not been so dyed a Woodville, and then I thought of Meg and my heart ached that I must persuade her to return home. I was running a huge risk in seeing her.

Behind me, Richard fisted the table, so angry still. I did not want to leave him alone and I wondered about sending a page to fetch in the duchess. He had not confided in her yet but the Kingmaker's daughter might like the idea of wearing a crown—it had always been her father's dream.

'Listen, whatever you decide, Richard, I shall back you to the hilt.' I said, tracing my hand slowly along the stone transom.

'I know, Harry.'

He thrust back his chair and strode across to brace his hands against the chimney mantle. There he glared down at the bronze summer screen that hid the hearth, and toed it angrily.

'I tell you after today Hell will hold no surprises for me. There's a knotted cord about my temples and God's tightening it, second by second. You know what I want to do? I want to go home to Middleham.'

Of course he did, and second best had been going to his mother. I wonder what *she* had counselled or admitted. Mine would not even have listened; she would have swung the conversation round to buying new bed hangings.

In a while he turned to face me. 'Harry, I know you and Ned did not see eye to eye but...' That made me wince; if there were such beings as guardian angels, Dead Ned's and mine faced each other with flaming swords. I guessed what was coming. 'I loved my brother,' he was saying as though I was some magistrate that need to be convinced. 'How can I do this to his sons? Even if I disinherit them, they will always be a rallying point for any opposition. They will have to be kept under surveillance for the rest of their lives, for the rest of my life, and my son's after me. If I permit either of them to marry, then their children will be a threat to my son's children.'

Mine, too, I thought. He forgets I am in line to the throne as well.

126

'Well, then,' I muttered, 'let them inherit, but I predict they will be a constant threat to us. Wasn't that the issue at Stony Stratford?'

'But Ned's boys.' He looked so conscience stricken that I felt shamed by the blackness of my thoughts. Was the will of God an argument worth airing? Stillington being sent by the Almighty? Maybe not. Hmm, I should have asked Pershall and Nandik what they had decided about free will.

I half-sat on his table and waited.

'What's in the name of bastard anyway?' He was asking softly. 'Edward is still my brother's son.'

'But, without a scrap of Plantagenet blood in his veins. My dear Richard, bastards do not inherit. It is against the law, so is bigamy.' Ah, I thought at last. The Law! Here is the touchstone.

'I thought you of all people upheld the laws of England.' I chided. 'But let's ignore them, shall we? Why not let any jack out there can claim the throne? Heaven help us, next instant, we shall have Henry Tudor putting up his hand.' I held no mercy in my face. 'Would you not like to do things your way for a change? Implement all those ideas you have been brewing up over the years? Didn't you tell me we need a law to prevent juries being bribed and coerced, and what about your suggestion to publish the laws in English instead of Latin so that any man with schooling might understand them.'

He gazed at me in agony. 'Yes, of course I cursed well would. I have a shopping list as long as your arm. But what will history say of me if I snatch the crown from my nephews? There's plenty out there have already marked me for a villain.'

I shrugged. 'Make sure the chroniclers tell it your way. Do you think anyone now cares overmuch that Henry Bolingbroke deposed Richard II? Reign long and well and no one will give a turd.' Before I could gather breath again, he said, 'Leave it, Harry.'

I folded my arms with an appropriate sigh.

'I need more time,' he muttered, cradling his shoulders and stretching his neck back. 'Holy Paul, I can't even think straight any more.' He collapsed in his chair.

Poor wretched Richard of Gloucester! I remembered the times I had wanted to crawl into some dark place, no matter how mean, and wish the earth would heave me off its back.

Outside the heavy door to the antechamber I could hear the voices of his friends; inside his fingers tapping against the vellum were the only sound as though he was adding up each side of the ledger. I respected him that day for his integrity. I even envied him for the agony the decision gave him. But I had not underestimated him; inside his Libran shell, the man of action was struggling to be heard.

'Very well, Harry,' he said at last, his fist clenched.

'You are going to do it?' I demanded, suppressing a whoop that would have been heard as far as Smithfield. And it had been me he had confided in before the rest!

He rang the little handbell for a page and commanded that Stillington be summoned in. I had not realised the bishop was still on the premises.

'You want me to hear his testimony?' I asked, confused.

'No, I want the council to hear him.'

'*The Royal Council?* Is that not—'

'God, no, I mean our council here and if it be their advice, only then shall I shall lay Stillington's evidence before the full Royal Council when the time is right. Make no mistake, I shall not take the crown without the consent of Parliament.'

'Very well.' I should have expected this, but he was right, it had to be done properly.

'Give me a few minutes to compose myself, would you?'

I hesitated as I reached the door. 'Have you decided what you are going to do about Hastings?'

The pain in his face that he should betray his brother's sons whereas his brother's friend would uphold them unto death was plain.

'Let us wait and see, Harry. I hope with all my heart that you are wrong.'

MOST of his inner council were still in the grand chamber when I emerged. Lovell was leaning against the transom of the window, arms folded. The rest were still at the board.

'Well, what's the pother about?' asked Suffolk. He unfolded his hands from across his belly and sat forwards.

'He's on his way to tell you.'

'Thank God for that!' muttered Howard. 'Now we can swat whatever gadfly is biting him. You've done a good job, Buckingham.' Well, he thought so, but Ratcliffe was staring at me as though I was the damned gadfly and Lovell's expression had an envious tinge.

Richard came in with his usual purposeful manner but any fool could see his face was damp from a sluicing and that the skin around his eyes was red.

'It is fortunate most of you are still here, good friends. I have just summoned the Bishop of Bath and Wells. He has some information that presents us with a crisis, a grave crisis. And I ask you to carefully evaluate his testimony before you give me your advice.'

'Perhaps you could explain the situation while we are waiting, Dickon,' suggested Lovell quietly.

Richard nodded and sat down wearily at the head of the table. I slid into my place opposite Suffolk. I read amazement on their faces in all its forms as he sorrowfully explained about Dead Ned's conjugal duplicity.

Howard exchanged glances with his son, Thomas, and was the first to reply.

'Tom and I have to declare our interest. If little Prince Richard is no longer to be Duke of Norfolk, the duchy falls to me by right of inheritance. But that would be the least of my reasons for advising you to go ahead, Dickon. I know you would serve England well.'

Ah, very diplomatic.

Suffolk rubbed his chin pensively along his clasped fingers. 'Supposin' the crown does go to you and your heirs, Richard. Not wishing your son ill, but you've only got the one. God forbid anything should happen to him, of course, but you understand what I mean.'

'Not at all, that's a valid question, Will.' He considered for a moment. 'Then the crown would go to your son here. He's my eldest legitimate nephew.'

Young Lincoln turned bright scarlet. 'Me, your grace?' He looked to his father for concurrence. I had forgotten Lincoln and there was I thinking that I would be next in line.

Well at least that brought the Duke of Suffolk and his affinity on side.

'Oh, plainly this is in all our interests.' Lovell's cynical tone could have cut ice. 'I should like to be Lord Chamberlain, Tyrrell would like to be

Master of Horse. Why are we even bothering to discuss it? Half of London has already laid wagers that the boy will never be crowned.'

Richard winced.

'Could Stillington be lying, your grace?' Ratcliffe asked. 'We all know you are open-handed to those who serve you well. Happen he is hoping for Canterbury or a cardinal's hat?'

The arrival of a page to say the bishop was waiting outside halted further dispute, but before he could be summoned in, I set my hand on my cousin's sleeve.

'One matter further,' I exclaimed, waving the page to disappear again. 'The letter to York.'

Richard scowled, sucking in his cheeks. 'Harry has advised me to send for more men.'

'Devil take it, my lord!' Ratcliffe rounded on me. 'It will look as though his grace mistrusts the south.'

'If he doesn't, he should,' I retorted. 'The southern shires are all held by the Queen's friends and we have only a few hundred reliable soldiers.' There were mutters of agreement and I pursued my argument. 'It is just a safeguard, gentlemen, while we present the legal evidence to Parliament.' I swivelled to face Ratcliffe. 'And I think you would be the perfect representative to convince the good aldermen of York.'

The man's cold grey eyes examined me. Jesu! Here was a northerner who bitterly resented my influence on his master. Before he could argue, I added, 'The sooner you return with soldiers we can trust, the better.' Then I turned once more to my cousin. 'May I suggest that you keep the lid on this pot until then.'

Howard nodded agreement. 'This will take some careful strategy, my lords. You will need to get little Prince Richard out of sanctuary and into your hands before you declare both boys bastards.' He was right. And he was being damnably self-seeking, too. If Prince Richard was deprived of all his titles, Howard, as the next heir, would become Duke of Norfolk.

'And do we delay the coronation?' he was asking.

'The embroiderers' guild will be sticking pins in wax images if we do,' I retorted dryly.

Richard grabbed the reins of the meeting once more. 'All in good time, Jock. I pray you all listen to the bishop's evidence first. For my part, I cannot sit through this again.' He stood up and we all rose to our feet. 'Dick, come with me now and I shall sign the letter,' and with Ratcliffe reluctantly whistled to heel, he left us.

'I wonder how long this will take,' muttered Howard. 'Is it true, I wonder?'

I pulled a wry face as I rose to let Stillington in. 'My lords, to put it in a nutshell, what matters is not whether the bishop's tale be true or false but what we make of it.'

***

I HAD invited guests for dinner next day, but Pershall drew me aside before I entered the great hall to greet them.

'Your strumpet's back, your grace.'

I smiled through clenched teeth. 'Call her a strumpet, dear Pershall, and I'll whistle in every stinking dog in London for you to lather.'

'Very well, the *virtuous* lady that slept in your bed all night.'

'Hmm, I hope no one saw her come in.'

'No, my lord. I put it about that she was *my* doxy like you requested. In fact they believe that she granted me favours on your bed.'

'I'll strangle you later,' I murmured sweetly, cursing that instead of making love, I must welcome Mayor Shaa Alderman Billesdon, Master John Russhe and several other merchants–all worth cultivating.

Poor Meg! There would be no way I could excuse myself from the table for several hours.

OF COURSE, she was irritable at waiting so long. She thrust her chin high at me the moment I entered my bedchamber.

'I'll not play the whore to you again,' she hissed, her veil bobbing with anger upon its precarious wires. 'How dare you send me this!' and she flung at me the necklet that Bannaster had delivered to her lodgings on my orders. 'What was I supposed to do with it? Wear it when my husband comes home? Pawn it like a whore? Do you think I have no honour?'

I laughed at her fierceness and dropped the offending trinket into the purse on my belt.

Such irony. I might have thought myself a kingmaker but here was fiery Meg, waiting to carpet me like a disgruntled wife.

She stood glaring at me with knuckles on her hips and tendrils of hair escaping from her satin cap. 'Did you think I lay with you only to coax you into freeing my father?' There was no 'my lord' or 'your grace' in her conversation.

'Did you?' I teased tritely, although I dreaded her answer.

'Ha!' she scoffed. 'You took advantage of my distress and I'm to be paid off. Go and find a queue of virgins to deflower. I hope the pox gets you and the moths eat your ermine and if you don't stop blocking my way, I shall resort to what my mother taught me.'

No woman had ever made me laugh so much. I reeled back against the door.

'You are wonderful,' I exclaimed. 'Worth at least a golden necklace.' I was ready for her fist as it shot out from her side and caught her hand. 'There is something I have to say to you,' I whispered, drawing her with me towards the cushioned window recess, 'and I want you to calm yourself and listen.' Something in the seriousness of my expression exacted her grudging obedience. I tugged her onto my lap.

'I will be honest with you,' I stroked a finger over her wrist and up the silk of her inner sleeve. 'I find you delightful company but you are someone else's wife and I am a man of state, a busy man, so busy that lust, like food and drink, is hastily dealt with.'

'Ha! Either I am obtuse or you are verbose, my lord.' She struggled to stand up but I held her tight.

'No, sit still and listen. Love, sweet Meg, demands courtesy and gentleness. Love demands time. The contemplation of the beloved…' I turned her face to me, 'to the exclusion of all else and I do not have that time. In other words, I am resolved to send you home to your children, ladybird.'

'You are not my keeper.' Her lips crushed into a pout. "Sides, I am not a bad mother, if that is your game to make me feel so. My babes are well cared for by their nurse and my mother, too. And you forget why I came here.' She grabbed my chin. 'I am intent on staying so long as you keep my father a prisoner, else my mother will not forgive me.'

'He is not my prisoner, Meg, and your mother puts too much faith in you. Loathe as I am to lose you, you-must-return-home.'

'Say you so.' The she gave me an arched look, and clasped her hands to my cheeks. 'Are you afraid of Gloucester finding out?'

'I am a grown man, sweetheart.'

And then the minx began her own games, diving her hand between her skirt and my short cote, feeling for my cock, which began to crow and rise upon his perch. She twisted round and undid the flaps of my codpiece to seek him out.

I groaned with pleasure as I felt her hand ease his comb back and forth.

'I have a meeting with the Hanse merchants at suppertime,' I gasped.

'How unfortunate,' she whispered. 'Then I cannot let you forth in such an unresolved state.' I was so hard I could have hung my hat upon my member.

'Meg,' I groaned as she scrambled away from me, but she was only gathering up her skirts to mount me. She pushed me back into the cushions of the daybed and rode me so deliciously that I could only think of her darling cunney encompassing me and when at last I poured my seed into her, it was like heaven on earth.

She disappeared behind the garderobe corner to cleanse herself and came and mopped me too so there was no spoiling of my hose. 'There,' she murmured retying my flap and tugging down my doublet. 'Go to your meeting.'

'You are a little witch,' I complained, sitting up, feeling around for my hat.

'If that is so, you, my lord, are my broomstick.' She found my hat for me. 'Can you sup here tomorrow?' Her pretty green eyes both beseeched and promised.

'I am not sure.' I resisted looking at her further and ran my fingers along my hat brim. 'The Gloucesters and I are invited to Lambeth Palace. This is what I mean, Meg. This is my work.' I stood up and she nestled against me, wrapping her arms about my neck and teasing her fingers through my hair .

'Then I shall steal in here before curfew.'

I could not forbid her though I knew I should. 'Do so, but be very careful, sweetheart,' I whispered, undoing the garland of her arms.

RETURNING next evening, I let my attendants disrobe me before Pershall brought Meg in. I opened my arms to her, lifted her veil and kissed her thoroughly.

'My beautiful love.' I unclasped her belt and freed her of her gown. We scarcely made it to the bed. Afterwards when I was spent, we lay together between the sheets. For a while, I cradled her head against my shoulder in a husbandly fashion and then she wriggled up and leaned herself upon her elbow, twirling a lock of my hair between her fingers.

'Ha–rry, I...I have been to see my aunt.'

That sluiced the lethargy from lovemaking clean from my mind. She meant Elizabeth. Jesu! Now she would be on Captain Nesfield's list. The instant Ratcliffe returned from York there would be questions.

'Did you give your name to the guards?'

'Not my real name, no. Why do you ask?'

'No matter.' I raised myself on an elbow, too, to read her face the better. 'So tell me, was there room to sit down among the coffers? You know she's gotten half of Westminster Palace stuffed in with her?'

'She looked well enough. Pale, of course, from too little sun, and thicker in the hips from want of exercise.'

'Well, that's no one's fault but hers. What did she have to say?'

'That Gloucester is a greedy dog and covets the crown, and that you love no one but yourself and hang like a dag upon his arse.'

'Very loquacious of her. And you believe that?' I ran my hand down the lovely slope of her back and thigh. 'As you see, my walls are mirrored with looking glasses.'

Her cheeks dimpled with laughter, as she glanced at the scarlet tester above us and the tapestry of Lancelot and Guinivere on the wall.

I smiled. 'Lady, I need no mirror but your eyes.' I kissed her with finesse for some time and then I asked, 'Was Mistress Shore there at the sanctuary?'

Nothing showed in Meg's face but beneath my fingertips her body tensed.

'Mistress Shore is a free spirit, Harry. I know naught of her comings and goings.'

'Yes, she flits all over the place. A regular butterfly. I hear she has moved in to comfort Lord Hastings.'

'I know—'

'Naught,' I finished for her. 'Never mind, Meg, I'll not question you further.'

'*Is* the Duke of Gloucester hungry for the crown?'

'I know—'

'Naught. I suppose I should not ask.'

'No, you should not,' I said sternly. 'This bed is free of faction and I'll not have it defiled with foolish gossip.'

'You are calling the Queen of England a gossip?'

'Why not? If I am "vain", she can be a gossip! But Westminster Sanctuary is hardly Cheapside. She must feast hungrily on any scraps that visitors feed her. I hope you did not tell her about us.' She gravely shook her head, thank Heaven. 'Do you carry messages for her?'

There was no subterfuge in her face. 'Oh, I do a few errands. I took her in some Paris thread.'

'So you have been there before?'

'Yes, of course.' She stroked a finger down my chest. 'Harry, why would she call you "vain"?'

I rolled on to my back. 'Oh, because there is not a scrap of liking between us. I was made her ward for a while.'

'But did you not have family of your own?' I did not answer. She shook me. 'Har—ry, I am interested.'

'My Grandam Buckingham sold my brother and I as wards to King Edward in order to get her lands back after Grandfather Buckingham's attainder.' My lips must have tightened.

She sensed the hurt stoppered up in my breast. 'It might be cleansing to tell me more.'

I stared up at the brocade canopy and remembered being led up to the scarlet and gold canopy in the Painted Chamber at Westminster Palace and the two huge glittering figures awaiting me. The terror and the humiliation. Imagine this giant of a man turning you upside down for sport in front of a creature who seemed all jewels and soaring headdress, except for her eyes; I remember those eyes, eyes like a goshawk's.

'My younger brother and I were in my Lady of Exeter's household to begin with, but she was having an *affaire de coeur* and the King gave me as a ward to the Queen.' I gave a deep sigh. 'Let's leave my past alone, Meg.'

Stirring those embers gave off noxious vapours, vapours that made my belly panic as though I was a little page at Westminster again. I had done everything wrong. I fell asleep at Elizabeth's coronation, complained about having to marry her sister, and after that her claws were out.

Then there was the mortification of my wedding when I was eleven years old. The Woodvilles had mocked me before they put me naked in the marriage bed to touch legs with eight year old Cat. Truly, I have more scars on my soul than beggars have scabs.

'My memories are not good,' I lied. 'Let us stow the matter, Meg, please. Your father and your cousins, the Greys, were never kind to me.'

She snuggled into me. 'What happened to your brother?'

'Died before manhood. I do have some half-brothers and sisters but I hardly know them. My mother fell in love with an esquire called Richard Darrell, quite below her, so they were never were invited to court and I hardly saw them.'

'My poor Harry, you must have been very lonely, but you had Gloucester as a friend.'

'No, actually I hardly knew him until a few weeks ago. He was in Warwick's household up in Yorkshire. That's where I should have been, instead of fetching your aunt's gloves or cleaning dung off her shoes. But whenever Gloucester and I coincided at Westminster, he was always very amiable to me. We used to talk about things like boys do, horses or hawking.'

Now my pretty questioner leaned on her elbow as though she might discern more secrets from my expression. 'My aunt the Queen never liked him either, did she?'

'Your aunt was jealous of the King's great love for him.' Yes, Dead Ned had shooed the Woodville jackals away from his little brother but he let them maul me.

'So you spent your entire time at the court after that?'

'Yes, save for a brief while as esquire in my lord of Pembroke's household at Raglan. I was very happy there and his lady and daughters were gracious and kind. Lady Margaret Beaufort's son, Tudor, who is now an exile in Brittany, was an esquire there as well. She visited him once or twice.' Hardly at all, but more than my mother ever did. 'She was married to my uncle in those days.'

'Hmm.' Meg stroked her finger through the hairs on my chest. "So why could your uncle not have been your guardian?'

'Don't you understand how it works? I was worth too much as a ward. Now are you done raking through my past? Remind me to recommend you to the Lord Lieutenant of the Tower as an interrogator.'

'Thank you, I shall look forward to his offer. So you remained with my lord of Pembroke until you took over your own household?'

I shook my head. 'Warwick put pay to that. When he rebelled against King Edward, his men slew my lord of Pembroke and I was back in your aunt's household again.' I found her hand and carried it to my lips. 'I cry you mercy. Can we be done with this?'

'Not yet. Don't you see it helps me understand you better?'

'Don't probe too deep, my dear,' I warned her, kissing her shoulder. 'You may find I am just a rainbow bubble of vanity. A pin's prick and pfft!'

'I don't believe that for an instant, Harry Stafford, and do not try and distract me either.'

I groaned and flopped back heavily against the pillows.

'Ha–rry.'

'What you have to remember, Meg, is that your aunt and your father did not treat me with kindness.' Never in a million million years, would I have imagined myself lying naked with Rivers' daughter, telling her such a thing. 'At Westminster it was French nods and calumny, never honest trust. They taught me to love beautiful things but not how to love.'

'Are you saying that you have never fallen in love, my lord.'

'Yes, of course, I have. There was a milkmaid at Raglan. Ouch!'

'My father knew how to love.'

Ha! Rivers was one person who did understand vanity.

'Father would have married my mother had he been free.' I did not correct her; all married men say that.

'And is your mother married to another?'

'Indeed not, there has only been my father and she is still deeply in love with him. It is for her sake just as much as mine that I want him pardoned.'

I did not want to ride down that bridlepath again. 'I daresay your mother's parents were none too pleased.'

'Oh no, Harry, they supported her decision. After all, being the lover of the Queen of England's brother is better than being the wife of a nobody.'

'I suppose so.' I wondered if her husband Poyntz would agree with that remark.

She leaned over and kissed me. 'Do you trust me?'

'Yes,' I lied, running a finger along her lower lip. Much as she delighted me, I would not tell her anything that could be useful to her aunt.

'Do you think you could love me like my father loves my mother?'

'I think I might manage that.' The only way to deal with a woman when she is delving too deep is to kiss her. They cannot kiss and talk at the same time.

8

The Royal Council met in Westminster Palace at ten next morning. My cousin and I were hoping to gain their permission to fetch Prince Richard from Westminster Sanctuary. It was crucial that we had possession of both the princes before I made my arguments to Parliament that Gloucester should by right be king. What point in deposing the older prince, if the Queen still held the younger?

It proved to be the stormiest session of the Royal Council that I had ever attended. On the surface of it, nothing could have been more reasonable than my cousin's suggestion that Prince Richard should attend his brother's coronation. No one argued with that but we spent an infernal time debating the question of extricating the boy from sanctuary against his mother's wishes. Richard was determined to send Chancellor Russell to negotiate with Elizabeth, however, he made it quite clear that if that failed, force might be the only way.

At that suggestion, all the bishops puffed up their feathers at the idea of sacrilege, and the old story about St Peter manifesting in person to consecrate the abbey was dredged up. It is incredible that the imagination of some drunken fisherman out on the dusky marshes hundreds of years ago should affect the decisions of grown men in this day, but there it was. It annoyed me so mightily that I made the first of many speeches that were to direct events within the realm. What loosened my tongue was Russell blethering about Elizabeth's fears as a mother.

'Womanish fear!' I exclaimed loudly. 'Don't you mean womanish perversity, chancellor?' I stared down the board at where he sat with the other bishops. 'I dare swear by my very soul, my lords, that she does not need to *fear* anything, either for her sons or herself. There is no man here who wants to got to war against women.' I smiled and added smoothly, 'Would to God some of her kinsmen were women, and then we should have some peace.

'However, what does concern me,' I continued after their chuckles had died down, 'is that if Russell's golden eloquence fails to convince her, she may well try to smuggle the child out of the kingdom, and what fools we shall all look then if she succeeds. The little prince will be at the mercy of the King of France or any foreign prince who desires to see our country riven by civil strife once more. I say we should get the child out by any means rather than have him slip through our fingers.'

Russell cleared his throat. 'Even assuming you may be right in the long term, my lord of Buckingham, nothing will make me change my mind about breaking into the sanctuary.'

'And do you suppose that *I*, Lord Chancellor, would dare what no one else has dared? I have no argument against the rights of sanctuary but I've never heard of children needing sanctuary. Has this little boy committed any crime? No, of course not. By the law of this realm, he has neither claimed sanctuary nor has it been granted to him and I think if the child was asked to make the decision he would tell you that he would rather not be cooped up in there with no room to play.' I warmed to the crux of my argument. 'So, my lords, if Prince Richard has not asked for sanctuary, it is not breaking the law to remove him.' I subsided feeling rather red-faced but saw to my amazement that they agreed with me. Even Hastings did not argue and that made me mighty curious.

Russell actually smiled. 'I congratulate on your arguments, my lord. Put in those terms, I see no difficulty, but let us try my way first.'

WOMEN are so unpredictable. The Queen agreed to Russell's proposal but begged that her son might stay with her a few days longer because she was nursing him through a bad cold. Russell was so relieved that he accepted the compromise gratefully, not suspecting as I did that Elizabeth might be planning to move against Richard in the next day or so. I knew full well the only thing she ever nursed in her entire life were grievances.

Russell came to tell us the good news while we were dining with Prince Edward at Aunt Cis's board. The Prince was pleased and while he was safely distracted showing his grandmother the tricks of the monkey his Uncle Richard had given him, my cousin the future king drew me aside. We agreed then that we should double the guard around Westminster Sanctuary and widen the net we had set to snare Mistress Shore.

Sweet Mistress Shore! Our men had been waiting to intercept her since the day Hastings had quarrelled with me. But either he was being cautious about who shared his bed or she had been indisposed with her monthly course. But at the end of the week, at last our patience was rewarded. On Thursday just before curfew at nine o'clock Richard's men followed Shore's pretty butt to Beaumont Inn, Hastings' London house, and kept watch until my men took over from them just before daybreak.

It would not be easy to arrest so famous a woman for treason. Not without a hubbub. That meant we had to plan our interception carefully. Her practice had been to go by boat from Beaumont Inn, where Hastings lodged, to Westminster Palace steps and then up to the sanctuary. Usually a couple of Hastings' servants preceded her to the quay to whistle up a wherry. Hastings never gave her the use of his barge; that would have been too public.

That day there was the usual early morning business at the house, servants going about their chores but something more—a rustle, if you like—in the house's undergrowth. When Hastings' retainers reached the river, my officer and his men arrested them. *Arrested?* To be honest, it was more like a few well-directed blows on their heads, then my fellows stripped them of their surcotes and put them on. The lovely Shore did not suspect anything as she left Beaumont Inn,. No doubt she was hazily languid with the night's ardour and it was not until the boat was in mid-stream and heading downstream towards the Tower that she realised. Apparently, the moist cherry lips opened and her bosom rose as she took breath for a scream but my officer clamped his palm against her mouth and his companion held a dagger to her ribs. Her hands jerked up to hurl the basket of sweetmeats she was carrying into the Thames but her aim was miserable and they fell about the bottom of the boat. My captain retrieved every sticky one of them, thank God, and kept them in his lap. It was gusty out there on the water so he made no attempt to search the basket there and then.

I was waiting at the Watergate of the Tower. Mistress Shore glowered at me with a mixture of hatred and fear as my men hauled her up the steps. I was sure she was as guilty as Hell.

'Today is Friday the thirteenth,' I told her as we threw a cloak over her head.

***

A QUARTER of an hour later I made haste up the lane, past the Wakefield Tower and across the grass to the White Tower, brushing the sugar from my finery. It was beginning to rain, as I remember.

I had not been idle. There was no time to question Mistress Shore but I dissected each of the sweetmeats. Then I left her gagged and shackled in a room above the Watergate. My men were sworn to deny access to even the Lieutenant of the Tower. All we needed was to keep news of her arrest from seeping across to the upper floor of the White Tower, where the joint meeting between the councils of the Lord Protector and the Prince had already begun.

The cobbles were slippery in the drizzle and I was breathless as I arrived at the foot of the outside wooden stairs to the keep. I paused as if to catch my breath, taking off my gloves. It was the pre-arranged signal to Tom Howard, who was in charge of Richard's escort that morning. He was with two of Richard's northern captains, Pilkington and Harrington and some dozen White Boar men outside the royal lodging. They were laughing and talking as if nothing was untoward, but he was watching for my signal and came across instantly.

'Good morrow to you, my lord.' His voice carried cheerfully. I nodded at the question in his eyes.

'It is a very good morning.' Then I said softly, 'I want you and your men up outside the Council Chamber in a few moments. No fuss and no noise, you understand?'

Tom was no fool; he wanted to inherit a dukedom. 'Leave it to me, my lord.'

Meanwhile I hurried ahead up the narrow twisting stairs as fast as I could. The meeting was already in session. The guards would have let me through instantly but I gestured to them that I wished to recover my breath. I was listening. Hastings was there. I could hear him telling the others some tale of how he had met an old acquaintance by chance on the Tower's wharf, and that the last time they had met he had found himself in some sort of danger.

I thrust the halberds aside and burst in. Hats and mitres swung round on me with an array of amazement and disapproval.

'My lord of Buckingham!' exclaimed Richard, like a schoolmaster, interrupted by the arrival of a late miscreant pupil. 'Whatever is the matter?' I could see concern in his eyes, concern that a rising had broken out, that we were already outnumbered.

'Gloucester, I must speak with you!' My voice was passionate.

He turned courteously to the long table of faces. 'Excuse me for a few moments.'

Outside the chamber, he almost had a fit at the array of soldiers clogging the stairs and crowding into the antechamber. He glanced at Tom Howard and then at me.

'What in God's Name—'

'We have the evidence we need. *Read this!*' I said, pulling the small drawstring bag from my doublet. Spread wide, it revealed the tiny scrap of vellum surrounded by the broken honeyplum. Richard took the tiny ball wonderingly, opened it out and scanned it twice, dismay growing in his eyes. It was a promise in Hastings' hand. A promise of reassurance to Elizabeth. 'We arrested the harlot Shore this morning,' I told him. 'She was taking that message to the sanctuary.'

Richard's gaze was hard now. Immediately, he swung about to one of his secretaries who was in attendance in the antechamber. 'Ask Sir William Catesby to come out here.'

Catesby came through the doorway, took one look at Richard's stern visage and the armed men beyond, and swallowed hard.

'I want a second opinion,' snapped my cousin brusquely. 'Is that Hastings' handwriting?'

Catesby's fingers shook as he examined the tiny scrap of vellum. He nodded nervously but we needed to creak the words out of him.

'I should say so, yes.'

'But could you swear it?' demanded the Lord Protector. Catesby's Judas eyes met my cousin's hawklike scrutiny.

'Yes.'

'So be it,' replied my cousin, biting his lip. There was no time for reconsidering. In a low voice, he gave Tom curt instructions, then he and I returned to the meeting. Catesby hung back, preferring to wait outside.

We took our places with obvious heaviness of spirit. Hastings watched me with dislike and I could not resist licking my sticky fingers, but he seemed unaware of the cannon shot about to explode around him. Richard looked ill as he faced them, as grey as he must have looked when the news of King Edward's death had come to him at Middleham.

'There is a plot to destroy myself, my cousin of Buckingham, and those amongst you whose friendship I hold most dear.' His gaze swept sorrowfully over them but his eyes probed for signs of guilt. Bishop Morton raised a surprised eyebrow, Archbishop Rotherham shifted uneasily and sweat dribbled down the forehead of Lord Stanley even though that it was a cool, damp morning. At the end of the table Doctor Oliver King, the Prince's tutor, peered at us above his spectacles and swallowed hard.

'Who are they then?' prompted Hastings. He always hated silences. 'Let them be justly punished.'

Richard looked at him in sorrow. 'The Queen, her son Dorset, her brother the Bishop of Salisbury, my brother's harlot, Shore, *and others*.' Hastings dropped his gaze to the table. 'They have tried to paralyse the proper form of government in this land and they have sought to countermand my brother's will. You, Morton, Stanley, Rotherham and Doctor King are bloody traitors.'

Morton had spine. Indignation quivered in every fold of his jowls but Stanley could not help looking to Hastings.

'What have I done to injure any of you?' shouted Richard. 'Hastings!' The cry was wrenched from him. 'You were my friend. How have I offended you?' He flung the message scrap before him.

Hastings' eyes never left my cousin's face as his fingers blindly found the leather scrap. As he lowered his head to read it, his eyes flew wide in horror.

Outrage and anguish laced my cousin's voice. 'Hastings, Hastings, how could you side with that witch Elizabeth and that strumpet Shore against me?'

'No, no!' exclaimed Hastings, shaking his head vehemently as he recoiled from Richard's fury. 'I am no traitor!' But under cover of the board, we did not know he had drawn a dagger. 'If there be a traitor here, it's *you!*' He lunged at Gloucester.

'Treason!' I roared.

Lord Howard leapt up to grab Hastings' mantle. Tom's men burst in, swords drawn and there was a fine old scuffle because we had not made it earlier clear to them who they were to arrest, and everyone was yelling, with myself bawling orders at Tom, trying to make myself heard above the din.

Hastings drove the rondel upwards but Richard managed to swerve and grab his forearm, forcing the blade away, though it took all his strength and being shorter, he was at an awkward angle. I was too far away to help. It was only when Lord Howard managed to get his arm round Hastings' throat that Richard was able to force the dagger from his grasp. The guards seized Hastings, pinioning his arms behind his back.

My cousin righted his chair and collapsed in it, gasping. 'Take him away!' he commanded huskily, pointing at Hastings.. 'I never want to see his face again.'

'You heard!' I ordered.

'You!' Hastings' venom fell on me. 'You fucking spawn of Satan, this is all your doing.' I gave a nod to the soldiers and they dragged him out towards the stairs.

My cousin's shoulders sagged. It was over. His brother's friend had betrayed him. His anger was spent.

'And what of these, your grace?' asked Pilkington, prodding Morton none too gently to his feet. Stanley had been grabbed from beneath the table and looked quite foolish, his hat over one eye and his cheek bleeding. Rotherham's face was furious. Either arm held, Oliver King politely requested that one of the soldiers find his spectacles. Morton was humming, as if he did not care a jot. A pity Dead Ned had never set the precedent for lopping bishops.

From his chair, Richard studied his prisoners like a weary god on Judgment Day and then he straightened his head, turned his face to me and said with a cold loftiness. 'Cousin, will you see that these traitors are taken away and closely kept?'

'With pleasure,' I smirked, overseeing the hustling out. 'I'll have the Lieutenant of the Tower find you the best quarters, gentlemen.' I gave Master King a slap on his thin back that sent him staggering. We still could hear the curses coming from Hastings further down the stairwell. It would have been a dog's job getting him down and right hazardous. The stairs twisted like a rope and he was not a small man.

I came back brushing my hands. Richard had subsided onto the carved chair and had buried his face wretchedly in his shaking hands. Lovell's hand was on his shoulder, and Howard was declaring what everybody needed was strong liquor. I grinned and hurried downstairs after the clanking guards. I caught up with Hastings' escort in the guardroom on the ground floor where they were waiting for the Lieutenant of the Tower to allocate a cell.

'Find a priest to shrive 'em and fetch the executioner!' I barked.

Hastings flung continual obscenities at me while Stanley shook and wet himself. The priest arrived in a hurry.

'Get this traitor outside,' I growled. 'He can say his confession in the rain. It won't make any difference, will it?' The priest gave me a furious glare and followed the struggling Lord Chamberlain.

I turned my attention to Stanley. My fingers grabbed the opening of his cote and jerked his large bulk towards me. 'You fool!' I sneered. 'Shall you be next?'

He spluttered and writhed within my grasp, begging for his life.

'Your life!' I flung him away from me into his escort's clutch with an oath. 'Well, you shall have it. I shall intercede with the Lord Protector on your behalf. Loose him.' They dropped him and he sagged between the soldiers. 'You are lucky that you never came so close to Gloucester, Stanley. He finds it easier to forgive his enemies than his friends.' I jerked my head meaningfully towards the door they had dragged Hastings through. 'See that Lord Stanley is more comfortably housed than the others,' I ordered. Stanley beseeched God to shower blessings on my head.

I pulled my mantle about me and stepped outside.

Across the cobbled yard on a strip of grass, Hastings was kneeling before the priest, his face sour with something that was not repentance and he scowled at me as the chaplain murmured absolution.

'Finished? Good. There should be a block of wood over there that will do us nicely.' I pointed towards a pile of building materials. Two of the men-at-arms ran across. They attempted to carry a wooden block but, finding it beyond them, one of them began to kick it with his foot. The headsman came hurrying out with a huge axe in his hand.

'Make haste!' I bawled at him. It had to be done quickly before Richard had second thoughts. Ratcliffe, the only man likely to have had the presence of mind to stop me, was on his way to York. Grand Aunt Cis would have wished me to advise my cousin to hold Hastings for trial but that was not what I wanted.

146

The anger in Hastings suddenly subsided. This was the end for him and reality had at last driven the sharp knowledge home like a blow in the belly. With dignity he knelt down once more on the muddy grass and two of the soldiers dragged the block into position. It was scoured and criss-crossed like a cook's chopping board.

'Have you a last wish, traitor?' I asked.

He did not turn his head, his eyes were taking in the unfeeling clouds and the summer leaves on the cherry trees close by.

'Yes, I have,' he said softly, his blue eyes growing watery. 'Ned promised me that I might be buried at his feet. I was ever at his side in life and I would be loyal to him in death.' Tears ran down his cheeks or was it merely the rain?

'I shall tell his grace,' I promised.

'And one thing more, Buckingham. I curse you.'

'At least you no more pity me. Are you done now?'

'Yes. *Yes*! In God's Name, strike hard!'

LONDON did not give Richard any time for inner flagellation. The news ran fast as a summer grassfire. The Lord Mayor came galloping into the Tower, white-faced, expecting the worst and my cousin gave him audience among the debris of the meeting chamber.

It took me a while to compose myself before I could face my cousin, for although the soldiers had swiftly bundled Hastings' headless body into canvas and slung it into a cart, the ruddy puddles had churned my belly and I could not leave the garderobe in the royal lodging for a while .

As I returned to the keep, I met Howard halfway down the White Tower's spiral staircase. Unfortunately the torches of the stairwell lit my face.

'Not like dancing at Westminster, is it, lad?' Was that sympathy or an insult?

I swallowed. 'I never realised there would be so much—'

'Blood?' He finished for me. 'Never been on a battlefield, have you?' One sideways shove to where the step petered to nothing and he could have sent me tumbling down to my death. Instead, he retreated to the small recess above to let me pass.

'Harry.' The soldier's edge to his voice had softened. I looked back down on him. 'You'll not be the only one with a conscience tonight. Do not blab to Dickon that you know, but he has just sent off Assheton with an order to Ratcliffe for the execution of Rivers, Grey and Vaughan. To punish Elizabeth, I imagine.'

I clambered on up like a blind man.

I had been readying myself to endure Richard's self-recrimination and to carry the full blame for Hastings' death, prepared to quote precedents to justify myself, to point out that like Henry II before him, my cousin had made a statement that was easy to take literally. Instead, I passed the soldiers and entered the chamber in shock. My cousin was as guilty as I was.

Christ forgive! How would I explain any of this to Meg? There was still time to send a counter order to save her father. But looking at Richard's face in the antechamber, I already had my answer.

He looked haggard enough to convince a dozen lord mayors that there had been an attempt on his life, but he was fully in control.

'Draft a proclamation,' he was saying to Kendall. 'Set down that there has been a conspiracy, an attempt on my life by the Queen's supporters, and that the Lord Chamberlain...' He looked hard at me, 'is dead. There is to be no need for any panic. Everyone should go about their business as normal. Say that Hastings and the Queen plotted to overthrow the Royal Council, mention that Hastings was an evil councillor to my brother, that last night he lay with Shore, one of the conspirators, et cetera.'

It sounded like a fabrication although it was the truth, and his secretary's expression told him so. 'Do what you can with it, John. Ask Lord Howard's advice if you need help. I wish Ratcliffe were here,' he said, blaming me further.

'Howard has gone. What are you going to do about Shore?' I asked as Kendall bustled away to get an army of scriveners busy so that the whole city might hear the official news within the hour.

Richard looked at me sourly. 'She's still here? Oh, I care not, send her to Ludgate gaol. Let her do penance as a whore.'

'In a shift with a candle! That should draw the crowds.' That provoked a sullen lift of eyebrow. 'If you will be advised by me, Richard, I suggest you send Morton away from the south as you have done with Rivers. I have a strong keep at Brecknock.'

He shrugged haughtily. 'I'll consider it.'

Encouraged, I overstepped the line. 'We might as well flog this matter and get it over. Are you going to request Parliament to draw up an act of attainder upon Hastings?'

His face contorted like a mask of Rage.

'Holy Paul!' he roared. 'You are as greedy as the fucking Woodvilles! And which of the late Lord Chamberlain's manors does your grace have his eye on?'

'No,' I protested sincerely, backing away. 'I mean, is it not usually—'

'Must we persecute a whole family because of one man's failings? Oh, my God, it will be bad enough trying to explain to poor Aunt Kate why Hastings was executed without the proper process of the law! Oh, this was done ill, very ill.'

I could not answer him. His mercy in this instance shamed me but I was not going to buckle beneath his insults. If I stared back with arrogance, it was at his provocation. I had removed Hastings from his path, taken the ugly decision from him.

'I am sorry,' he muttered, storming away with an angry toss of his hands as though everything had slid out of control. When he turned round again, he was himself again, with a soldier's backbone. 'I am going to Westminster to see the Chancellor and make sure there are no misunderstandings. In view of this crisis, I am going to suggest the Royal Council send out writs postponing the coronation.'

I was not at all pleased. 'That is madness if you want to keep the guilds on side.'

'I did not say there would be no coronation, Harry, just a matter of *whose*. We need a few days for things to calm down. You can clear up things here. Tell Kendall to send out a summons to all the royal councillors for a meeting here tomorrow morning and you had better have your evidence of the conspiracy ready.' I nodded obediently like one of his men-at-arms. Ha, should I have saluted?

There was, of course, little real conspiracy. He did crush it in the egg.

'What about Stanley? Shall I arrange for his trial for high treason?' That brought him to an abrupt halt in the doorway. He turned, his expression sarcastic.

'Another beheading? I thought, Harry, that you had promised to ask me to be merciful.'

I raised my head up defiantly. 'Who told you that?'

'Catesby was on his way down just as Stanley was grovelling to you.' His eyes challenged me to deny it. Catesby, it seemed, was springing phoenix-like from Hastings' embers, anxious to be indispensable to my Lord Protector.

I slung my cloak over my arm. 'Well, I have changed my mind. Stanley's a plaguey time-server. He never got off his arse to draw his sword for your brother and he won't for you either.'

'Two things, cousin,' lectured Richard, his hand poised on the door ring. 'One, the Stanleys can bring several thousand against me in the field, and two, the realm is sufficiently purged, and if it is still sick then it is not worth the bloody fucking remedy. Good day to you.' With a curt inclination of his head, he left me. The soldiers followed him and I was left alone.

I walked into the empty council chamber, and stood staring at the long candlesticks lying like fallen saplings across the overturned benches, and the ink puddles on the table, still dripping onto the floor. Hastings' hat was lying under the table. I did not touch it. I wondered if his spiteful ghost was already watching me.

Over by a window where a scrivener had sat, I found a sheet of paper that had not been trampled, and retrieved a quill from the fallen pot. I set them on the part of the table that had not been sullied, righted the bench alongside and lit a candle from one of the torches in the antechamber. Outside the rain beat upon the windows and cleansed the yard. Inside there was no sound but the scratching of my quill.

Forcing myself to do the task was healing. I was concentrating so hard that I did not hear anyone come in.

'Lord Howard said I should find you here.' Uncle Knyvett quietly sat down beside me with his back to the table. 'You do have secretaries, you know.' He watched me wave the letter to dry the ink, fold it and drip sealing wax upon the overlap. 'I heard what happened. Do you want to tell me about it?'

'No,' I answered. 'I have just written to Hastings' steward offering all the Lord Chamberlain's men-at-arms service in my household. I want it to go to Thames Street straightaway.'

'Of course,' he said gravely, and thrust it into the breast of his jacket. 'I'll dispatch several men instantly to spread the word. Were you hurt in any way?' I shook my head. 'Everyone was in a real pother at the house, I might

150

tell you, and your little wench came running in distraught. Thought you were dead at first. She's waiting there now.'

I put a hand to my forehead and smoothed back my damp hair.

'I do not know what to do next,' I whispered. 'I feel utterly spent, as though some brawny fishwife has wrung me out like a dishcloth.'

Uncle Knyvett put his arm about me. 'Go out for a gallop beyond the city walls.'

I blinked around me at the chaos. 'But Gloucester left me in charge.'

He urged me to my feet. 'You just tell me what must be done here, Harry, and I'll see the Lieutenant and sort things out.'

I rode back through Billingsgate and Candlewick with a score of men at arms at my back and it seemed to me the streets were deserted, and those few citizens that were about shrank back and touched their foreheads in fearful respect.

I DID not see Meg that day, thank Heaven. Pershall, on his own authority, had escorted her back to her lodgings and pretending to be a jealous lover, paid a local horse boy to bring him word if she left or entertained any visitors. His tidings that she had been lodging at Mistress Shore's house had me furious.

'Do you need spectacles, man, or would a new brain be better?' I snarled at Bannaster, who had always seen her home before. He stood before me, staring at the knots in the floorboards, his mouth puckered like a child's. Stout hearted, he could not add up a ledger but he could crack heads together like walnuts.

'She allus said goodbye to me at Paul's Yard so I never saw her dwelling. How wuz I to know it were important, my lord. You never worried abaht it with your other whores.'

I told him to piss off and then relented and gave him extra ale money. Even then he refused to let Pershall usher him out.

'My lord, you know your manor of Yalding be up for a new steward?'

'It is not a good moment to mention it, Bannaster. Today has been... somewhat fraught. Could you just go and get drunk instead?' But he stood there stoutly, cap in hand.

'It's like this, my lord, the wife's of a mind to leave the farm at Wem and move to Kent.'

I took a deep breath. 'Too late, I fear, Bannaster, the new man's already appointed. You can go and work for him if that's your fancy.'

He curled his lower lip. 'Wouldn't suit, my lord. She allus wanted to be a steward's wife.'

'Next time, perhaps.' I was not sure how long my temper would hold. 'I should not want to lose you from the household, Bannaster, but now, if you do not mind...' I walked my fingers in the air and he finally understood the message.

Yalding! I denied Bannaster's wife Yalding! Oh God, if only I had known the consequences, she should have had every frigging acre of it the damned place and more besides.

All I desired at that moment was to drink myself to oblivion. What happened at the White Tower was repeating in my mind over and over and over. I barred my door and reached for the flagon and then I remembered George of Clarence and set it back down. Instead, I went to my private chapel but if I pleaded for heavenly absolution, none came.

I DID not want to return to the White Tower next day but there was no choice. I was glad I had kept a clear head the night before. My evidence was heard. But looking at the faces of my fellow royal councillors, I knew their acceptance of the triangle of treachery was based not on intelligent assessment of the facts but fear. Richard said not a word of his decision to execute Rivers. It was clear he was not going to tell me either.

The other matter that riled me as I strode down to By-Our-Lady Tower was that Catesby and Tom Howard, not to mention the Yorkshire henchmen too, were dogging Richard's heels, begging how they might serve him, right ravenous for rewards. I knew I had to be mature and accept that the strength of his government would be spread over many shoulders, but in cutting down the Hastings lion, it seemed I had unleashed the jackals.

I decided, therefore, to look in on Stanley and chew the cud awhile. From Richard's remark about him yesterday, I presumed that peace and reconciliation might already be gestating like healthy twins in my cousin's mind and within a few weeks, the old weathercock would be free again. Maybe I should mend matters with them, too?

Stanley did not have much to say for himself but Bishop Morton did.

He was guarded by thrice the number outside Stanley's quarters. Seated on a settle by the window with his slippered feet on a yellow footstool, he reminded me of an overweight dragon sitting on its tail. A small leather-bound prayer book rested on his paunch, supported by one podgy hand while the other snaked in and out of a bowl of strawberries on the small table at his elbow.

'Are you actually the real Morton or a changeling?' I mused aloud, leaning back against the doorpost, my arms folded languidly.

He smiled the sort of expression you see on the crocodili sea captains bring back in baths of water from Alexandria.

'They do not make changelings in my size,' he said ruefully. 'As you see,' he waved a hand towards the locked door, 'I am amply protected from such eventualities. Can you tell me for how long?'

'One never knows with you, bishop. Forever might be a good idea. Even if you were dead, I should put a guard around your grave and a couple of men at the far end of the churchyard in case you try to burrow your way out.'

Morton chuckled, a deep rumbling sound that made his bulk vibrate before the sound actually erupted, like the fire mountains that are said to lie off the coast of Naples. He gestured to the strawberries. 'Have one! Fresh from my garden at Ely Place.' I shook my head. The plump hand stilled above the fruit and then it chose the reddest, most perfect strawberry. 'You know,' he continued, talking with his mouth full. 'I think we underestimated you, my boy.' His use of pronouns made me curious. *We?*

I cocked my head on one side. 'Gloucester and I?'

'Fishing for compliments? No, I mean just you. I doubt our august Lord Protector could have managed on his own.' I waited for something more but another strawberry disappeared into his mouth. He extracted its leafy coronet from between his lips and rubbed it free of his fingers onto the table. 'A pity about Lord Hastings though. The dear Lord Protector will never get that blot off his hands, I'm afraid.'

Either he was ill-informed or he chose to absolve me. Very curious.

'I must be getting on," I said briskly. "I just came by to make sure you were comfortable.' I straightened up and turned to slap my hand against the door for the guard to let me out.

'Buckingham.' It was the way he said my name.

I looked round slowly with studied hauteur. The ugly whoreson was not even looking at me, but down at his book as if reading. 'There are two sayings in our Lord's Book that may be useful for you to consider, your grace: St Luke's Gospel, chapter 23, verse 42, and the second epistle of the blessed St Paul to Timothy, verse 5. Your chaplain will look them up for you if you cannot manage it.'

'Not all dukes are illiterate.' I glared at the tonsured head, angry with myself for rising to his jibe. He glanced up momentarily and beamed, his smile like Circe's.

I rode from the Tower amused at his contumacious good humour but wishing that all fat bishops who grinned like stone devils might be wiped from the face of the earth. Curiosity nags at you, doesn't it, like an ache in the guts and as my chaplain was still on his sick bed, I sent Nandik to look up the two references and translate them into English for me. I expected a 'pride goeth before a fall' homily but Nandik read out:

'"And if a man also strive for masteries, yet he is not crowned, except he strive lawfully." That's from the letter of St Paul to the blessed Timothy, your grace.'

An ecclesiastical sermon obliquely given, far more tactful than accusing me of executing Hastings unlawfully.

'And the verse from St Luke?'

'Oh, I did not have to look that one up, your grace. It is the Penitent Thief at Our Lord's Crucifixion. "And he said unto Jesus, Lord, remember me when thou comest into thy kingdom."'

Thy kingdom?

'MY LORD of Gloucester has had Mistress Shore's house nailed up and put a guard around it,' Pershall informed me when I arrived back. 'Not that I wish to worry you, your grace."

'Lord in Heaven!' Richard being high-handed again. 'Has he had any of her household arrested?' My collar felt tight. Had Meg been carrying messages, too?

'Apparently she-who-is-virtuous had the wit to remove herself, if that is what concerns you, my lord. My young informer offered her assistance and tells me she is now putting up at Blossom's Inn in St Laurence Lane.'

I let out a breath, so relieved Meg was still at liberty for both our sakes. The last thing I needed was Richard's suspicion, although after yesterday, he could hardly doubt me.

'I want you to send a purse to her and the instruction that she is to leave London.'

Although it would pain me to lose Meg, I needed to keep her safe.

'Very well, my lord. And your robes for the coronation arrived yesterday, my lord.'

'Did they indeed! Why did you not inform me straightway?'

'Because you were busy executing Lord Hastings, my lord. May I suggest you try the apparel on this morning, my lord, to make sure it is a proper fit and to give yourself some diversion from rearranging the government.' My tankard hit the door just as he closed it behind him. Then he opened it again. 'I have arranged for Mistress Poyntz to meet you at St Mary Bow at five o'clock this evening. I hope that meets with your grace's approval. May I advise you wear something inconspicuous. The priest's cassock again perhaps? Then maybe Cheapside may be spared the sight of her berating you.'

'Berating me?'

'She told me that was her intention, your grace.'

MEG was outside St Mary Bow, with a basket of Kentish cherries on her arm, feeling rather exposed, I imagine, for although she looked of testy humour, she was relieved to see me. The dusky skin around her eyes proclaimed she had slept ill.

'You still stand out in a crowd,' she complained, her eyes taking in every inch of me at the plain brown doublet and leather cap with flaps that covered my hair. I took her arm and then realised we were being watched from above. Standing on a balcony where fulsome bunches of herbs adorned the stone balustrade, was Dame Juliana Shaa, surveying the street like a Roman empress.

'Devil take it! Quick! Round the corner.'

What a damned cursed meeting place! Right next to Tamersilde, a building used by the nobility to watch processions.

Meg let me drag her round the corner. 'A rival mistress?' she jabbed. Dame Shaa could have rolled me into thin pastry.

'The Lord Mayor's wife. I tup the older ones on Tuesdays,' I growled and crossed myself with a prayer to St Jude that woman was myopic. A pox on Pershall! 'I knew this was folly,' I grumbled. 'Why don't I just stick my neck in the Cornhill pillory and let everyone in London hurl rotten turnips.'

'Hush, I am sure she did not notice you. She must be planning the decorations for St—'

'John's Eve,' I groaned. I had already had my invitation.

Meg ignored my peevishness and peered around the corner. 'Hush, she has gone in now.'

But I was not pleased. 'Is there somewhere where we can talk without getting–*uugh*!' A passing cart with its shouting occupants drowned my curse. My little shrew pointed to the door of St Mary's.

'I cannot talk to you in there.' I growled.' But she was already briskly leading the way into its gloom.

Within the chilly presence of numerous monuments to long dead haberdashers, we went through the ritual of holy water and lighting candles to Our Lady. Then Meg knelt and, putting her hands together, stared devoutly at the window above the altar and started praying. I settled beside her, seething with impatience.

'Why have you not gone home to Gloucestershire like I bade you?' I demanded when she was finally done.

'To get rid of me, I know.'

'No, curse it, for your own—'

'What is going on, Harry? What about poor Lord Hastings? God rest his soul!'

I looked swiftly about me lest any had heard her. Was she a lunatic to rant at me so?

'And I suppose Mistress Shore is murdered too?'

'Do not talk such folly!' I snapped. 'No one's been murdered!'

Her shoulders sank in relief, but as footsteps passed behind us, she crossed herself vehemently and began to finger her rosary. We both stared forward like a couple of stone mourners on a tomb.

'She will survive,' I muttered, when it was safe to speak again. 'Probably shogging the gaoler by now.'

'That is not amusing. Where is she?'

'Safe in Ludgate and do not go near her!' The swift jut of chin told me that she would disobey me. I should need to put a watch on Meg Poyntz. To shame me further, she made great play of praying for the whore.

I had closed my eyes, wondering why the Almighty had deliberately plagued my life with difficult women, when my sleeve was fiercely tugged

'And what about my father? Did you persuade the duke to let him leave England. Harry, *please*, answer me?'

I tried to meet her eyes but I could not. The stained-glass Christ I was staring up at did not look sympathetic either. 'It is not good news, Meg.'

'Oh!' She would have stormed away but I kept a tight hold on her, cursing my stupidity yet again for meeting her.

'May I assist you, my children?' An elderly priest had seen our quarrel.

I instantly buried my face in my hands and Meg put a hand on my shoulder.

'My brother is troubled, Father. He has come to pray to the Lord Our God to weaken his anger against his enemies.'

'Wrath is a deadly sin. Do you want to confess, my son?'

'Thank you, not just yet.' My voice was muffled. I did not dare look up. A dry hand descended upon my head and a benediction was uttered. The sandals shuffled away, and I was able to strip my fingers from my exasperated expression. 'This is ridiculous. Let us go back to your inn.'

'I am not at your perpetual disposal, my lord.'

'For Blessed Christ's sake, I did not mean that.'

'Hush!' she scolded piously. 'You are in His House. And in His Name, answer me, you did intercede for my father, did you not?'

'Meg!' I groaned.

'Tell me!'

'I swear to you in this holy place that I have not been privy to any decision-making.'

But she was no fool. 'Stop playing with words, Harry.'

'Very well. He is to be executed, Meg. I was too late to stop the order. Gloucester gave it without consulting me.'

She clapped a hand to her lips. 'Blessed Jesu!' I thought for a moment that she might retch but she was winding up her anger. 'I cannot believe this. You of all men had the power...' She crossed herself with duty and speed–and fled.

Isolde Martyn

I found her leaning her shoulders against the side of the church with tears pouring down her cheeks and splashing her bosom. I reached out my arms but she knocked them aside.

'Don't you dare touch me!'

'Abuse your aunt not me, woman! Your father was hostage for her good conduct. Instead she conspired."

'*Conspired?*' she hissed. 'What, to keep her children safe? Oh, I thought that you would help me. *I trusted you.*' She was close to screaming at me.

I glanced behind me. A hairy old beggar was watching us, too far away, thank God, to hear our conversation.

'Bridle your temper!' I snarled. 'Or, by Heaven, I'll have you thrown into Ludgate alongside that gossip Shore!'

She spat. 'You devil! You are...you are filth, my lord of Buckingham.' She would have run but my hand was an iron manacle about her wrist.

'If I deserve the gutter, so do you! By Heaven, you strumpet, I daresay you only lay with me to save your father.'

'That's not true.' Her sobbing stilled and she glared up at me like a little girl, resentment mingled with guilt in the shiver of her lips.

I looked down into those beauteous green eyes, awash with tears, and dreaded to find treason in her. 'Filth, am I? I thought for just one precious week of my life that there was more than self-interest in a woman's embrace, that despite my part in your father's downfall, that you liked me for myself.' I raised my hands in instinctive supplication as if a perverse god was listening. 'That some happy coincidence of the planets, some wondrous alchemy, made us more than bedfellows. Fare you well, Meg. Be advised and do your grieving in your mother's arms, not mine.'

Contrition flared in her face. 'No, you'll not shun me, Harry. I love you, you fool!'

She reached a hand to my sleeve but I left her. The beggar rattled his bowl as my shadow fell across him and I put my hand up to hide my face.

When I reached the safety of my house, I sent two reliable men to find Meg and take her to one of the properties I owned off Cheapside. For her own sake as well as mine. She was becoming too great a risk.

9

On the following Monday, the day Prince Richard was promised to leave Westminster Sanctuary, we drove the full weight of the Royal Council against Elizabeth. The entire council met at the White Tower and then we travelled together by barge to Westminster in full public view.

With a loud clanking of armour, the men-at-arms, who accompanied us, surrounded the sanctuary and lined the route the Prince would take to Westminster Palace. Lord Howard and my great-uncle of Canterbury led the deputation appointed to meet with Elizabeth at the abbot's house, while my cousin and I, and the rest of the councillors assembled in the Star Chamber at Westminster.

We had held some of the full council meetings here but King Edward's massive chair at the head of the board had not been occupied since his death and its emptiness still haunted my cousin. Even I felt Dead Ned's absence keenly, for the palace, unused since April, was hollow without his laughter, and miserable without his splendour.

There we waited for damn nigh two hours while Elizabeth wrangled with the abbot and the deputation. I could not sit drumming my fingers any longer so I found myself a window onto the courtyard. It was cursed hot outside. The soldiers were cooking in their steel casings, and the commoners waiting for a sight of Prince Richard were competing for the shade of the archway. At last the trumpets sounded.

Westminster Hall with its high hammer beam roof was cool and sombre; Elizabeth had stripped the expensive tapestries from the walls and Richard had not had time to see to its refurnishing. The paraphernalia of the law courts had been stowed away so the floor of the hall could be packed with our retainers.

I took my place at the dais to welcome the boy on behalf of the Royal Council and my colleagues arranged themselves like an arrow shape on either side of me. The fanfares sounded, the heavy doors were swung wide and King Edward's younger son, dapper in a mustard tunic with one leg matching and the other clad in black, stood blinking between Howard and the Archbishop, taking in the hushed hall of waiting faces. The roly-poly little knave was not at all flummoxed. In fact, he gave us a huge grin and everybody cheered. Then, hand in hand with the archbishop, he walked through the bowing ranks towards the dais. Uncle Bourchier conducted him up the stairs and I knelt on the second step down and kissed his hand and then to echoing huzzahs, I rose and kissed him on both cheeks.

Throughout my speech to the gathered lords, the child looked mighty pleased with himself and when I had done, he doffed his black cap and inclined his head graciously to the assembly. They loved him for it and there was further applause.

'What happened?' I whispered to Howard as he came alongside me with a triumphant sucked-in smirk.

'A snivelling struggle from the Queen but your great uncle's reassurances swayed her in the end. God's Rood, the performance in kissing him goodbye and telling us he had an ague and must be kept warm, and all the while the little rascal was fidgeting to get away and have a taste of freedom.'

It was time to escort him to his other uncle and with my Uncle Canterbury on one side and myself on the other, church and state guided him to where the Lord Protector stood waiting at the door to the Star Chamber, wearing that expression of foolish indulgence that some mothers have for their babies. Perhaps being his namesake, Uncle Richard had a greater kindness towards this nephew.

'Uncle Dickon!' exclaimed the princeling with delight and then he realised he had forgotten the occasion so he extended his hand regally, saying grandly: 'How does your grace?' This brought guffaws of laughter. Prince Richard looked round at everyone with bubbling satisfaction and back to his uncle, who could hardly keep his face straight as he took his hand.

'Your grace, I am in good health, and you?'

Prince Richard sniffed. 'I have had a runny nose.' Uncle Richard laughed, and flung his arm around the child's shoulders.

'Come on, Dickon,' he exclaimed cheerfully. 'Let's take you to the king's grace. Are you glad to be out of the sanctuary?'

The boy nodded vigorously. 'There was nowhere to play properly.' He looked up pleadingly. 'Uncle, would you give me a bow and arrow, please? I started lessons before...before his highness my father died and I was truly improving and...'

160

'Yes, yes, all right,' laughed my cousin, sweeping him along. 'We shall ask the Lieutenant of the Tower to have a butt set up for you and you can perhaps persuade your brother to do some practice too. He has spent too much time indoors lately and needs some exercise.'

The rest of us followed them back into Westminster Hall.

'I wish this one were king instead, even if he is keeping me from being a duke,' muttered Howard. 'There is more of his father in him.'

'Just as well he is not,' I muttered. 'Gloucester is finding it hard enough to consider deposing his brother.'

We had to remember they were bastards.

***

IF you want something made known in the swiftest time to the widest audience in London then the preacher at St Paul's Cross is your man. On Sundays, after early morning mass, crowds gather in the churchyard to hear the special sermon. There is always a famous cleric invited and often the speaker is a friar. Dominicans and Franciscans seem to attract the cleverest to their orders.

On the surface of it, my cousin was lucky that the preacher who had been engaged for Sunday 22nd June was Mayor Shaa's brother, Ralph, who had a fine reputation as an orator and was likely to draw a good crowd. Brother Shaa was amazed when we summoned him to Westminster, but as the situation was made clear to him, his eyes began to sparkle at the prospect of mitres and benefices falling from the hand of a grateful king. He spent an hour at the abbey delving through the Holy Bible for a fit text and returned jubilant and incomprehensible.

"Spuria vitulamina non dabunt radices altas nec stabile firmamentum conlocabunt.", he proclaimed, brandishing his notes. How I detest the bad breath of religious pedantry.

'I missed the meaning of that.' Richard told him bluntly.

'Your pardon, my lord. *"But the multiplied brood of the wicked shall not thrive, and bastard slips shall not take deep root, nor any fast foundation."'* We still looked at him blankly. *"'Bastard slips shall not take root".* Bastards, your graces! *The Book of Wisdom,* which follows *The Song of Solomon.'*

'Ah!' My cousin looked across at me.

'Amen," I said dryly.

'Perfect, then.' Relief shone in Richard's face as though Shaa's discovery of the verse had bestowed God's absolution. Truly, sometimes my cousin thought like a village idiot.

I HAD survived many a sermon at Paul's Yard in my youth by eyeing the London wenches. What I had also learned was that, firstly, it was wise to arrive early and, secondly, there was no use trying to charm my way up any petticoats when the girls had been listening to a two hour onslaught on sin and adultery. But the latter was far from my mind when I arrived at the cathedral that morning. Since there was no sign of the Gloucesters, I bade my retinue mingle with the gathering crowd and wholeheartedly accepted an invitation from my new friends among the city merchants to join them on their stand.

Brother Shaa had a sunny morning for his eloquence and consequently there was a large turn-out. St Paul's Yard was wearing a very different face from its weekly appearance. The stalls that usually sprawled into the very nave of the cathedral had been cleared away. In fact, the poet who called himself Piers the Plowman might have likened the scene to his fair field full of folk. Instead of the greasy-tongued touters and scabby beggars, the yard was packed with guildsmen squiring their wives and sweethearts, and clusters of apprentices. Around me, the merchants' wives with their little spire caps and fluttering veils were all in holiday humour, showing off their finery, easing their necklines lower and biting their lips to make them cherry red. But for once I was more interested in the preacher. And, Devil take it, where was Richard?

Below the pulpit, Brother Shaa waited, grinding his jaw as the hour drew close. He tarried in mounting the wooden steps, clearly still hoping that the Lord Protector would arrive. The crowd began to fidget and when his brother signalled him to begin, the wretched man hurtled through his introduction like some green esquire galloping at a quintain.

Oh, it was a botched up business. The congregation, used to chastisement for coveting each other's wives and asses, looked as obtuse as scarecrows at the mention of 'bastard slips'. As for the peroration where Shaa was supposed to point to my cousin and proclaimed that he was the very image of his father the Duke of York? Well, Richard missed the important flourish.

When he did arrive, his servants noisily cleared a way for him to a position within twelve paces from the pulpit and Shaa, seeing him at last, halted in mid-sentence and went right back to the beginning of the 'Richard is the most English of York's sons' and did the huge arm gesture bit all over again. The White Boar men around the duke cheered and so did my retainers, but most people stood with their mouths hanging open like nesting holes. I should have laughed had the matter been less sensitive.

The intelligent aldermen who understood were scowling daggers at the Lord Mayor for not letting them in on the matter earlier, and as those more canny amongst the crowd grasped Brother Shaa's meaning, an unpleasant hush fell over the great yard. The faces of the wives so charmed by Prince Edward a month earlier turned stony, while the men looked at each other with 'I told you so' expressions.

Well, thank Heaven, London wives do not have a say as to who governs England, otherwise we should be ruled by whichever underdog takes their fancy, and a change of king every Sunday.

I knew my duty. Before the crowds slunk away, I led some of my merchant associates to meet Richard, and made a deep obeisance. His cheeks were a dull red with embarrassment but he greeted everyone blithely enough. While our retainers mingled with a loud show of conviviality, he drew me aside.

'Holy Paul! What a fool I was to permit such mummery as this. I am now the laughing stock of London.'

'Not that, I assure you,' I answered cheerily. Tyrant, maybe. 'Tomorrow is the important day anyway. Just leave Parliament to me.'

That did not banish his scowl. 'I hope to Heaven you are right, Harry. By the way, Anne and I are moving over to Mother's for the week so the people will know we have her support.'

'Excellent! I applauded, patting his arm. 'Now off you go to dinner and do not worry. Leave everything t—'

'What is the matter, Harry?'

'Nothing,' I exclaimed, espying a woman who on first glance looked like Meg, and on second nothing like her. 'Leave everything to me!'

MY HEART was galloping when I took my place on the front bench in Westminster Hall next day. It was my purpose to recommend that the House of Lords that Parliament should offer the crown of England to Gloucester but some would call it treason. My intent was known and I ignored Archbishop

Rotherham's glare from the benches opposite and smiled sweetly at Bishop Alcock. Stillington was almost hidden behind the bulk of my great uncle but at least he was there and I would have no hesitation in fishing him out from that pond of mitres to give evidence.

'Blust me! You've drawn a fine crowd yonder. There are abbots come out from under their stones that I haven't seen in years.' My lord of Suffolk joined me and young Lincoln stepped over the front bench and sat down behind me. I was very glad of their company.

'Hope it goes well, Harry,' Lincoln whispered, a hand on my arm. 'You all primed up?'

'He's looking tight as a virgin's cunny,' muttered his father. 'How long do you reckon this will take?'

'I've a lot of arguments to set forward, sir.'

''Spose you have. Look, if you see old Kempe over yonder nodding off, start winding up. He's always the first to go. I remember one session when all the bishops except Lionel Woodville were snoring their blessed heads off. Well, you won't see young Lionel here today, that's for sure.' Suffolk rambled on but I could hardly pay attention.

I was cold but the sweat of my hands was ruining the ink of my notes. Would everyone be able to hear me when I spoke? Even though we were all drawn up close where the crimson woolsack sat upon the dais, the hall seemed high and vast for one man's voice to fill. Howard came to shake my hand and wish me well and so did several other Yorkist lords but the wars had thinned the ranks of noblemen. Hastings, Rivers, Dorset, of course, were missing. George's son, Warwick, had the wits of a changeling and was too young. The Lancastrian lord, the Earl of Oxford, was a prisoner in Hammes and Lord Stanley was still mewed up in the Tower. Some had deliberately stayed away, not wishing to assent to the inevitable. The inevitable. Yes, so I hoped. Richard was relying on me.

Upon the appointed hour, the mace was carried in and Chancellor Russell took his seat upon the woolsack. When he finally called me to make my address, I was so nervous that my hands were shaking. But when you believe in what you are saying, when you are prepared and have the right words, when you have the courage to look them in the eye and forget your notes, the magic begins. There was no more rustle of chasubles and soon I could hear that wonderful stillness in my listeners and knew that I had them.

God knows how long I spoke for, too long probably–Kempe did nod off–but my arguments fell on rich soil and the congratulations afterwards were heady fare for a man who had starved all his youth for a kind word. Here at last was something I could do truly well. Ah, if only Elizabeth and the rest of their kinsmen had been there to hear me. That would have shown them that the boy duke they had tried to render impotent was now a kingmaker.

Of course, I still had to address the guilds and the Commons but what was concerning me as I rode home–drained yet high–to change my attire, was that this day was St John's Eve. The streets would be full of bonfires, the Lord Mayor and his retinue would lead the procession and several thousand of the city watch would march in armour through London in a cresset-lit column carrying their weaponry. Since the watch was mainly made up of men who had seen service as soldiers, I was mighty edgy. If an armed rising was still in the offing, it would be tonight when there was no curfew and the entire city would be out carousing.

It was past nine and still twilight when I arrived at Tamersilde. I wished I might innocently enjoy the evening; instead I found myself studying the other guests, wondering if any might prove traitors. Certainly, Howard and Huddleston had made sure plenty of our men-at-arms were discreetly positioned around the building but it was useless ordering that every window within bowshot be closed or expecting that the old London archers, who would be strutting past so proudly, should leave their bows and arrows at home on wallhooks.

A goblet of wine made me feel better as I moved among the nobles and merchants but I still had a sense of danger. When Dame Juliana ushered me out to the balcony to join the Gloucesters, and I saw the bonfires being lit down the street, that sensation grew stronger.

My cousin looked utterly unperturbed. He was a figure of much splendour in a murrey doublet embroidered with tiny golden lions and roses. A reliquary hung from the collar across his chest and a brooch shaped like the special cross of St John was pinned upon his hat. He greeted me cheerfully, delighted that the Lords had agreed to him taking the crown.

We clinked goblets. 'Set for tomorrow, Harry?'

'Yes, so long as I do not lose my voice or drink too much of this.' I swirled the wine. 'You came prepared this time, I see.' Just the glint of a rondel's haft showed beneath his gold satin mantle.

'What about you?"

I lifted my hands from my belt. 'Ah, I am expendable.'

'Hardly,' said Lord Howard at my elbow. 'And God preserve your speechwriter too!'

'I have not got a speechwriter, Jock. Half a dozen lawyers, yes, and Chancellor Russell read my notes through on Sunday night.'

'Then you make a wondrous good job of it, Harry. More tomorrow, eh?' He clapped me on the back and disappeared into the throng crowding the inner room.

Anne, Richard's duchess, came out with Lady Suffolk to join us and we kept the conversation light as the crowd grew thick beneath us. Above the gables, the night sky was spangled with sparks and we could not see the stars for the golden glow of bonfires. Thames Street was ablaze with lamps above the doorways and necklaced with candelabras hung on ropes between the gables.

London was in reckless mood. The thatch might catch, skin might burn but so long as the tables buckled with firkins of ale and roast meats for passers-by, no one cared. Where we stood, the smoky air was overlain with the smell of flowers. Tamersilde's balcony and every nearby sill were garlanded. Bunches of fennel, St John's Wort, green birch and creamy lilies hung upon the balusters and adorned every front door in the street.

'I wish your father were alive to know what has come to pass, Anne,' I whispered to her as we helped ourselves to sweet pastries. 'It was always his dream to see you crowned.'

'Yes,' she said wryly, dabbing her lips with a kerchief. 'I am sorry that Mother did not come down with me but we did not know that Richard would be made king when I left Middleham.'

'Nor did any of us, Anne. Thank God, England will be secure again. Stony Stratford was a close shave, believe me, and as for last Friday the Thirteenth…'

'Yes, indeed.' She gave a little shiver. Then smiling, set her palms upon my sleeves and stretched up on the tips of her toes to sweetly kiss my cheek. 'Thank you, dear Harry, for all you have done for Dickon. Our Aunt Anne would have been so proud of you.'

Ha! Grandam Buckingham, who told me to dissemble and bide my time. Grandam who did naught to save me from the Woodvilles. Nearly twenty fucking years, it had taken me to free myself.

I straightened up, my cheeks kindling like a maiden's. 'It's not quite in the bag, my lady. There are still the guilds and the Commons.'

'Child's play for you but—Oh, our almost-king wants us back on to the balcony.' I offered her my arm but she delayed, looking down and letting her fingers pluck at the golden collar about her throat as though arranging the words before she spoke. Then she looked up at me through her fair lashes. 'What I am stumbling to say is that some men can only conquer by causing bloodshed, but yesterday you conquered the lords of England with words.'

I bit my lower lip, surprised at how delighted I was with her praise and carried her hand to my lips. 'You know what, sweet cousin? Many's the time I wished that your father had betrothed us, and given your sister to Richard.' Lord, how she blushed. 'Maybe our children shall make a match of it.'

Her blue eyes sparkled. 'I should like that, Harry.'

'Harry, are you flirting with my wife?' He took her hand and drew her forward beside him. An apprentice on stilts was waiting to give her a nosegay of white roses.

I lifted my hat to the column of old soldiers passing below. 'Of course. I shall be her highness' most outrageous flatterer.'

'And there I thought you were being sincere just now,' teased Anne.

'Of course, I was.' We exchanged glances to tease Richard. 'Nothing untoward then?' I asked him, dispensing with frivolity and sweeping a keen eye over the faces below.

Anne's eyes widened. She stared like Christ's blind beggar suddenly realizing the array of armed men that could have been harnessed against us and her fingers flew to her lips. 'Oh, Dickon,' she exclaimed, seeking her husband's arm.

'Look merry, my love, for Heaven's sake!' he growled through his smile as he acknowledged the salutes. 'The Londoners only need to smell smoke and there'll be a fire.'

She obeyed instantly and turned a cheerful face upon the merrymakers, but I could see from the tension in her shoulders that she understood the danger. That was good. Let them both realise how much they depended on their friends.

She glanced round warily before she whispered, 'How soon before the soldiers arrive from York?'

Richard met my interested stare. 'I heard word tonight that they are on their way.'

'Thank Heaven for that.' She waved to the scarlet-cloaked constables marching past but her earlier spontaneity had vanished. There were acknowledgments but no huzzahs from the ranks. 'It's not like being in the north,' she said, as though the burden of what lay ahead among strangers had at last sunk in.

'No, my love,' the future king answered grimly, 'and this is just the beginning.'

I STAYED beside the Gloucesters on the balcony as a reminder to the city that I was very much a part of England's governance. By Thursday eve, I hoped Richard would be king, suffused with gratitude, and ripe to give me my Bohun inheritance.

'You have little to say for yourself tonight, Kingmaker,' he jested, clinking goblets with me.

'I was actually thinking you need a barber.' I retaliated. 'You'll be lucky to get the crown on with that thatch. What do you say, Anne?'

'Say you so? He's worried he's going bald.'

'I am not!'

Of course three is a crowd. I wished that I had a wife—or a mistress—who would look at me so fondly. Mind, wives prattle and Anne was babbling about the move to Baynards to the mayor's dame, so I stopped listening and thought about whether I should send Meg home with an escort or risk visiting her. I was still chewing on the matter when Lady Huddleston, with a lift of eyebrow at Richard, drew Anne and the other ladies inside. It was clear something was up for Lovell skilfully herded the merchants to the other end of the balcony, leaving Howard to insert himself between Richard and I. He flung a friendly arm around each of us.

'I hate to concern you both, and there is no need for panic so let's keep a lid on the pot, eh, but there's has been a fire at the Tower of London.'

My cousin swore. 'Don't say my nephews—'

'Nay, don't wet yourselves. The Lord Lieutenant has moved them to By-Our-Lady Tower, but what happened, see, was some whoresons lit a fire as a diversion and broke into the royal lodging after the boys. One of the soldiers swears Dorset led the attack. Saw his face clear as day. Quite a skirmish.'

'And did they catch any of them?' I whispered.

'No, Harry, three killed, the rest escaped over the wall and a boat was waiting for them. Very well planned. We may have to change the garrison.'

Richard's knuckles gleamed white upon the rail. 'Have you sent out patrols along the Canterbury Road?'

'Already done, lads. The dogs are out and we are searching Southwark and Bermondsey but with the revels still going on...'

Richard nodded, chewing his lip. 'I'll go to the Tower tomorrow morning. I daresay this will happen again.'

To be sure it would. I knew I had to get my cousin crowned and anointed, and then maybe we could sail into calmer waters.

I felt my sleeve twitch. Delabere stood behind me with a small sealed letter. It was ill-timing; suspicion flared for an instant in my cousin's face.

I lifted my hands in the air. 'No daggers, Richard. I just give speeches.'

Instantly he was all contriteness. 'I am sorry, Harry.'

'Forget it, shall we? I need a good night's sleep.' I thrust my goblet into Howard's hands and went to say goodnight to our hosts. I would return to the Red Rose and change to humbler attire. With the streets full, it would be my best opportunity to visit Meg without being recognised.

But my company was attacked on the way home. One moment we were avoiding a trestle table, the next it was flung across our path and some twenty carousers thrust off their cloaks and came at us with swords. I had never had to fight for my life before, let alone with no poxy weapons but my fists and a rearing horse. As God is my witness, I fought hard but the whoresons dragged me down, and one of them rammed a fist into my belly and brought me to my knees. Lord knows whether I would have lived if Uncle Knyvett and my friends had not risked their lives. Two of my men were killed, another slashed badly below the knee, Latimer had a bloody nose and Uncle Knyvett was wounded in his right arm.

'God's Truth, it's like Brecknock after market day,' chuckled Latimer as he clambered up from the gutter, with the help of the landlord who owned the adjacent tavern, but I was not laughing.

'Did none of you catch the cut-throats?' I gasped in disbelief as Delabere hauled me to my feet. A wall of frightened London gaped around us. Maybe a reward tomorrow would loosen their tongues.

It was not until I was ripping off my ruined finery, cursing that the money I had borrowed to pay for it was wasted, that I remembered the letter.

Gloucester's arselicker

If my brother dies, so shall you!

How sweet of Elizabeth.

I SLEPT ill that night, not worrying that Elizabeth would send more assassins but angry that I was the scapegoat for Richard—it was not my signature on the warrant to execute Rivers. At least, my mirror showed me an unbruised face. Disgruntled but unbruised. I was grateful for that. Making a speech with swollen lips would not have been amusing. Or convincing!

Escorted by Lord Mayor Shaa, I entered the Guildhall that morning to the sound of the city trumpeters. His sword bearer preceded us and the mayoral retinue in their part-coloured worsted livery trooped behind us. The magnificence of the great hall and the huge number of merchants and guildsmen gathered there to hear me put me in better humour. It surely is one of the mightiest banqueting halls in Christendom, built at great expense to house the council of aldermen and the city's law courts, and a wondrous place to speak. I felt a sense of history, standing there on the dais with the sun streaming through the stained-glass coats of arms.

They needed a strong king to defend their interests and safeguard Calais, I told them, and that argument moved them most of all. I was able to leave the dais, confident that Elizabeth had few supporters left.

As I rode back to the Red Rose with my retinue, John Russhe, a merchant about the same age as me, who was fast becoming one of my inner circle, declared, 'I was going to ask you to dinner next Sunday, your grace, but you will not be available now.'

'How so?' I asked

'I gather they are booking you for the next sermon at St Paul's.'

Uncle Knyvett roared with laughter. 'You know what, Harry, I even heard one guildsman say: "That lord spoke so smoothly that he didn't even pause to spit".'

'His grace has no need to stick his nose in the air,' smirked Latimer. 'The Londoners speak so lousily themselves that they think that anyone who can string a couple of sentences together is a blessed marvel.'

'Hey now,' countered Russhe.

'Have done, you lowly commoners,' I retorted, over my shoulder as we rode down Cat Street back towards Cheapside. 'The speech only worked because I believed what I was saying. I used to spend hours as a child listening to how people used words.'

'You certainly have a skilful turn of phrase and a pleasant voice, your grace.'

'And you were pretty to look at,' teased Uncle Knyvett. He gestured to my cap with its plume of dusted gold. I grinned, glancing down at my scarlet doublet with the Stafford knots embroidered on the black satin panels.

'Rattled well, too,' added Limerick, leaning forward and shaking my collar of sunnes and roses.

'Look, if you have to listen to someone wittering on at you for two hours, it is less painful if the babbler is well dressed and pleasant to look upon.'

Uncle Knyvett chuckled. 'Do not defend yourself, Harry. You did well, right well, and I hope our future king realises how much he owes you.'

Did he? I began to wonder why I was not doing this kingmaking for myself instead of Richard, if it was this easy.

***

WESTMINSTER Hall was crammed with shire knights next morning. My kingmaking speech to the Commons setting forth Gloucester's claim is in the records. Again there was no opposition. Catesby followed the great roar of 'ayes' with the motion that a deputation from lords and commons should present a petition to Gloucester next day requesting him to become king. I was beseeched to lead it.

Chancellor Russell, who always weighed words with a miser's care, shook my hand and said I should have been a lawyer. On reflection I am not sure if that was a compliment. Others were grudging in their praise. Catesby was overheard to remark: 'Who does Buckingham think he is, the Angel Gabriel?'

The following morning was drizzly but our procession through the streets from Westminster Palace to Baynards was cheerful and loud with conversation. It would have been quicker and less smelly to have gone in barges, but public events need to be carried out with as many spectators as possible. By the time we reached Thames Street and the cook shops gave up their dead, we had a great tail of people behind us, and, despite the watchmen and men-at-arms lining the street, a riot almost broke out when we reached Aunt Cis' portcullis, and the crowd surged forward, struggling for a view. I ordered my pikemen to keep a space of about ten feet around me. I would be damned if I had to do kingmaking half-choked. Then I drew a deep breath and gave the nod to my herald. He sounded a fanfare and the parliament trumpeters replied.

My cousin did not delay this time. He came out onto the gatehouse battlements with Anne hanging on his arm and his mother and chaplain flanking them in moral domesticity. Looking up at them, I felt like the commander of a besieging army about to parley with the enemy. Of course, we had planned it like that. Richard said he wanted to enjoy the feeling of being besieged with pleas to become king and it was the obvious way to do things.

I dismounted and, snatching off my velvet cap, I swept my cousin a deep obeisance while behind me with a jingling of harness and a creak of leather, lords and commoners did the same.

Richard glanced at his wife. Gently disengaging from her, he leaned his hands upon the crenellations, a half-smile playing about his lips. There was colour in cheeks and exhilaration in the tilt of his head. Up there he looked a true Plantagenet and kingly too, as if the knowledge of our purpose had already anointed him with some mysterious, intangible charisma.

'Cousin of Buckingham, my lords and gentlemen, good morning to you all. How may I serve you?'

'Most gracious Lord Protector,' I began, 'we are here to present you with a petition from Parliament.'

Richard looked round at his family. Anne responded with a reassuring smile but Aunt Cis was sternly looking us over as if we might be about to drop horse turds on her cobbles. My cousin rested his arms along the weathered stone and stared down at me. 'Then I shall hear it right willingly,' he offered with great charm.

'Your grace—' The sudden shouting from the river was tiresome. Poor Anne gave a start of concern and Aunt Cicely disappeared to deal with the matter. I guessed its source: the citizens who had not been able to pack into the street behind us were piling into wherries to glimpse events from the river. 'Your grace,' I began again, raising my voice.

'I cannot hear you,' mouthed my cousin, cupping his ear. Then there was a scuffle in the crowd behind us and I had to wait for that hubbub to die down. It was as well that Richard had forbidden the carrying of weapons within the city or hasty tempers would have drawn blood.

'For the love of God, get back there and shut them up!' I snapped, turning on one of my captains. 'This is becoming ludicrous,' I grumbled to Speaker Gunthorpe, who was holding the petition. 'I cannot make a public presentation of the damn thing if I cannot be heard.'

'I'll see to it.' Mayor Shaa heaved himself back into the saddle and forced his horse through the cluster of dignitaries. The noise gradually dwindled to a testy mutter and he returned with a smug expression.

I took my hands off my hips and turned once more to crane my neck at my cousin. It was uncomfortable to keep looking up and I had strained my voice on the previous shout.

'We are here, your grace, to petition you to resign the post of Lord Protector.' A gasp shuddered out of the ignoramuses at the back. For an instant, Richard let outrage darken his features. Of course it was all play, but maybe it brought home to him that he was dependent on our good will for his survival.

'In what way have I offended?' he demanded in a voice that must have been heard above the battle noise on Barnet and Tewkesbury fields. His long fingers spread wide and his tone took on the just amount of indignation. 'Name my offence and I shall answer for it!'

'Oh no, your grace.' My smile was as public as I could make it. 'You have offended no man here.'

'Only the women!' called out some wag and squawked as someone clouted him hard.

'My lord, we wish you to resign your stewardship of our beloved realm so that you may instead guide us as our loving king and lord, which by your royal lineage and most worthy person you deserve to be.'

This was the tricky part. There was a hush as the crowd waited for his answer.

'You have a king already, my brother's son.' Richard flung a hand towards the turrets beyond the tenements of Billingsgate. A nice touch as the sunlight made a timely entry and lit the gems on his fingers.

'Most gracious lord, it has been proven to the satisfaction of Parliament that your noble brother King Edward IV, whom God assoil, was not lawfully wed to Dame Elizabeth Woodville and thus the issue of that union is not lawful either. Their progeny cannot inherit nor usurp the governance of this realm. There is no one, your grace, with a better right to the crown than your most noble self.'

Except me!

I bowed again, hand on heart.

Lords and commoners watched the face above them lose all trace of cheer and charm. Richard showed he was aware of his wife watching him anxiously, of his mother primly observing the people as if she was some sightless saint hewn of stone. He was staring solemnly down at us, his mind taking in each of our faces, and inwardly savouring the rising glory. We waited patiently until he at last broke the silence, his voice carrying so clearly that no man had to strain to catch the words.

'My lords, gentlemen, friends all, you offer me greater honour than any man may dream of, but I am utterly unworthy of the task so I must decline your generosity of spirit. Not only because I am conscious of my own failings but I know that if I agree, my name shall become synonymous with the term tyrant throughout all Christendom, and when all of us are cold earth and there is no one left to tell the truth, men will called me a usurper. I pray you, therefore, do not ask this of me.'

'My Lord Protector,' I replied, 'we commend you for your modesty and your sensibility but we cannot accept your refusal. It has been proved to the Royal Council's satisfaction that King Edward's sons are bastards, unable to inherit, and that your grace is the rightful heir. If you refuse our request, your grace, then you compel us to look elsewhere, and there is another willing, who dwells beyond these shores and considers he has a right.' It was right perilous mentioning Tudor but I could hardly suggest myself.

Richard went rigid. He had not been prepared for that.

Behind me, Gunthorpe gave a snort of disapproval. 'That was hardly called for, my lord of Buckingham.'

'He has no choice, Gunthorpe. Let it be seen he has no choice.'

Above us, Richard had recovered his composure and his response came loud and clear as if he wanted as many witnesses as possible to be able to testify to his words, as if he feared being in the dock on Judgment Day:

'Very well, if it is truly the desire of the Lords and Commons then I shall accept, but be certain, all of you, that you want me for your king. Be sure, for without your loyalty and your love, such kingship as I can give you rests on air.' He spread his long fingers wide in suppliance. 'I have no wish to be king.' There was a sudden jeer from the back. 'Yea, by my immortal soul,' he shouted, 'I dare swear so, for it is true whether you would have it true or not. *I repeat* I have no wish to be king but in the absence of a legal claimant with better right than I, it seems I have no choice and must obey God's Will and *yours!*'

Cheers broke out but he held up his hand for silence. 'All I ask is that you remember it was you who wanted me for your king; and I swear here before Almighty God that I shall do my best to bring justice and peace to this troubled land.'

Well, thank Heaven, that was over. I flung up my hat and caught it with a shout.

'God save King Richard!' I yelled and knelt on the muddy cobbles. Richard's friends tumbled to their knees and the courtyard rang richly with cheers, echoed by a roar of exclamation from the river and more huzzahs.

The new king reached out for his lady's hand and drew her to his side as he acknowledged the applause with the tight sad hint of a smile. I almost pitied him. It would have been much easier for me but Dead Ned's beloved brother felt every shout with anguish as well as pleasure.

As if conscious of the irony that her father had fought and died to ensure a crown for her, Lady Anne was clinging proudly to her lord and graciously enjoying the cheers. The Londoners had always loved her not just for her father Warwick's sake but because they remembered how Dead Ned had paraded her as a captive after her father's slaying.

Oh come, Aunt Cis, I chided silently. Stop standing there like a wooden chess queen! He is the only son you have left. The old besom melted at last, she kissed him on both cheeks and then with a half-curtsey carried his hand to her lips. The people clapped. Then Richard turned back to face us and held up his hand again and a hush fell.

'What do you wish me to do now, my lords and gentlemen?'

I had restored myself thankfully to my feet and now with a bow, I gestured to Gunthorpe to kneel and proffer the petition, which he did with blessed conciseness: 'We most humbly beg your grace to ride with us to Westminster where Parliament may proclaim you formally as our king.'

Richard inclined his head graciously. 'I shall be with you directly.'

His mother took control. 'My lords and gentlemen, I welcome you to my house to drink the health of the king's grace, Richard III!'

There was vociferous agreement on that and while the new king and queen went to wave to the people on the river, I led the way into Baynard's Castle.

After drinking his health, it was back through the city to shouts of 'God save the King!' The well-wishers were nearly all men, I noted. This time, it was 'King' Richard who led the way with Suffolk and myself at his stirrups. Elizabeth must have heard the noise as we arrived at Westminster Palace and I hoped someone had bothered to tell her why.

In the Great Hall, the judges and magistrates were waiting in their silks and ray robes. My cousin hesitated at the sight of the marble chair with its purple velvet cushion. I saw him swallow with emotion at the betrayal of trust he was committing so I stepped before him and gestured him to seat himself. Like the soldier he was, he took the final step, turned and sat. Applause crashed around us but I could see that for my cousin the moment was solemn, holy, and I realised he recognised, not my hand as having led him there, but the hand of God.

They were expecting a tidy little speech, merely appropriate thanks but they miscalculated. Richard, made sacred by their blessing, lectured the practitioners of the law, the self-assured judges, the clever lawyers and the burly sergeants at law on Justice. He told them it was to be the foundation stone of his reign, that men were equal were before the law, both lords and commoners alike; and that he would rule without prejudice or malice. As a gesture of his sincerity he ordered one of the sergeants to cross to the sanctuary and bring out the first of the fugitives he found there. We waited, amazed, like an audience at a mystery play wondering how this would turn out.

We heard the footsteps. All eyes swerved as the doors opened. Sir John Fogge stood on the threshold. He was a close relative of the Woodvilles and had been involved in the scandal when the Woodvilles had stripped a prosperous merchant of his possessions on a trumped-up charge. Here was testing indeed: there was no love between my cousin and Fogge.

There was fear in the twitch of the knight's left cheek as he walked in the silence up to the marble throne and saw who sat there now.

King Richard rose and offered him his hand. 'Today is the first day of my reign, Sir John, and your pardon is my first deed as king.' Fogge went down on one knee, almost dazed. 'I pardon this man as an example of the mercy and friendship I wish to prevail in this land. Let there be no more enmity among us. Sir John, you are at liberty. You may return home to Kent a Justice.' Fogge kissed his ring, stepped backwards down the dais, bowed again and marched from the hall a free man and then the hall erupted in applause.

Richard's solemnity vanished. 'Let us to mass,' he said lightly, touching my sleeve, and we filed behind him across the courtyard to where the Abbot and his monks waited bearing a golden cross and the abbey banners to lead us to *te deums* just as his brother had been led two decades before.

I hope Elizabeth was spitting.

10

By Saturday, Howard was given the strawberry coronet of Norfolk, Tom Howard became Earl of Surrey and Catesby was made Chancellor of the Exchequer, an office that could be peeled from him as swift as a scullion can disrobe an onion. My advice, I admit. A man who can change his coat and betray his master might do so again. As for me? Since we no longer had Hastings, I had the organization of the coronation dumped in my lap.

Our new king was in testy temper. Sweaty Ratcliffe and my lord of Northumberland had turned up on the doorstep with an army of Yorkshiremen, who were no longer needed, and I was blamed for it. Not only was Ratcliffe damnably sulky that he had missed all the excitement but rudely outspoken about Hastings' execution.

We rode out to Moorfields where the northerners were camped. They made a great circle around us and you could have heard their roar for King Richard back at London Bridge as he doffed his hat at them. Their affection made me envious as Satan. I had as much hope of the Welsh fêting me as fly across the Thames.

Richard was clearly purring at their devotion but inside he was seething.

'Thank the Blessed Christ, they didn't arrive last week. It would have looked as though I was seizing the crown by force.'

'It was last week you might have needed them,' I pointed out defensively.

He ignored that. 'Yes, but what-do-I-do-with-them-now, Harry? Our enemies are going to make a meal of this.'

'Simple!' Ratcliffe butted in before I could answer. 'Make them special constables for the coronation, because I tell you this, I am not friggin' well escorting them north again.'

And while Richard was going round their campfires, shaking hands, dear Ratcliffe waited until no one was within earshot and then he had another swipe at me.

'You might like this.' With a superior face, he drew a folded parchment from his doublet. It smelled of sweat and horses.

'What is it?' I asked suspiciously.

'A copy of Lord Rivers' will, your grace. Since you are married to his sister and screwing his daughter, I thought you might like to pass it on.'

By Heaven, I nearly smashed my fist into his smirking mouth. 'You have good teeth, Ratcliffe, I suppose you want to keep them.'

'You have the King's trust, my lord. I suppose you want to keep it.'

'While you were messing around in Yorkshire, sirrah, I made your master king and with not a drop of blood spent.'

'Really, my lord? I thought you personally dispatched Lord Hastings.'

I shook my head in exasperation and tried to be decent. 'I do not understand why you are trying to make an enemy of me, Ratcliffe. I thought we were all on the same side.'

'Aye, I hope so, my lord, but when I hear that you are all cosy with Rivers' bastard, it makes me wonder if the King knows of it?'

'You can wonder what you sodding well like.' I strode off to join Richard. All my life I had strived for respect for my rank and my person. I did not get it from the Woodvilles and if the northern whoresons could not treat me fairly, I should show them they were making a mighty error.

'IS HE pardoned?' Meg hurtled down the stairs into me as I entered the house, where she had been safeguarded. 'Tell me!'

I caught the shapely bundle of impetuous womanhood and turned her back towards the stairs.

'No, he's not,' I whispered. I urged her back to the upper chamber where I could speak with her in private and thrust the door closed.

'I don't understand. The usurper pardoned Fogge.'

I plucked off my gloves and tossed them onto the window seat. 'Fogge was fortunate, that's all, and never call the King a usurper.' Then I turned to face her and make matters clear. 'Your father is dead, Meg. He was executed by the Earl of Northumberland three days ago, together with your cousin Grey. I warned you they were hostages for the Elizabeth's obedience. Blame her!'

180

With her fingers clutched to her lips, she dropped onto the settle, her blue skirts settling around and tears trickling silently down her cheeks. Had I been an artist, I would have painted her in her beauty and her sorrow. Poor Meg.

I sat down beside her and made to put my arm about her, fool that I was, but she thrust me away. 'I cannot believe this, that you...' She fumbled angrily in her girdle purse for a kerchief. 'You made that foul duke king, yet my father who was a good man—'

Good! A self-centred prick. Just because he was a handsome piece of brawn on the tiltyard and could manage a rhyming couplet.

I stood up, flipped open the flagon on the table. It was a weak perry. A woman's drink.

'Sweetheart?'

'Don't you sweetheart me, you lump of excrement! Have you come to brag, Buckingham, to impress me with how clever you are? "Look, Meg, I've made a king." Well, any fool can put a paper crown on a pig.'

Excrement, was I? My laugh was patronizing. 'Oh and what did your family do for England? Procreate, that's fucking all.' I sat down beside her again but she whacked the back of her arm into my chest and wriggled away as far as she could.

'How can you be so remorseless, so despicable?'

'Ask Elizabeth and your cousin Dorset. I am actually trying to be sympathetic.'

More cascades trickled down her cheeks and splashed on to her collar. She did not—maybe could not—answer so I waited, my hands clasped between my knees, waited as she sobbed for her father, waited, longing to hold her in my arms. Slowly her breathing stilled.

'Am I still excrement?'

She nodded gravely, her little nose buried in the sodden, silk cloth.

'Use your head, my darling.' I who was supposed to be a smith of words fumbled to find the phrases and despaired. 'Oh, Meg,' I pleaded. 'It would not have made any difference. I could no more have saved your father than St Peter could have stopped the crucifixion.'

'You could have done it for me.'

'And it would have been for the wrong reasons. Loved is not purchased. It either is or it isn't.'

I was so afraid that she had used me, given me kisses and fondlings only to buy her father's freedom, that the truth was gilded lead. Desperate, I strode across and plundered the aumery, unstoppering the flask there. It was empty.

'It must have been easier, I suppose, not dying alone,' she said at last.

I thought of Hastings.

'Yes, there would have been comfort in that,' I said wearily. 'I've brought a copy of your father's will. He asked for Richard to be his executor.' That astonished her. 'To be honest, I think he had a great deal of respect for Gloucester.' She did not like that one bit and sniffed defiantly. I drew the folded papers from my belt, and laid it between us on the cushion. 'I though you should have it.'

She mopped her fingers on the sodden kerchief before she picked the papers up. 'But this is not his writing.'

'It is a copy, Meg.'

'Most of this is verses,' she exclaimed in puzzlement, looking from one sheet to the other. 'Some sort of poem.'

'Yes.' Five verses. Eight lines each. I almost knew them by heart.

It's... it's all about accepting his misfortune and...and apologising for some misdealings in property.' She read the second page again, her frown deepening. 'Bequests to the poor, something for his wife but there's no mention of Mother or I.'

'No, Meg.'

'Why did you show it me?'

'Should I have withheld it, then?'

'No, Harry,' she whispered, and more softly, sadly, 'no.'

I sighed, knowing how much she was hurting. 'Your father wanted the world to recognise him as a philosopher. Those verses are a gracious epitaph.' I watched her fingers stroke along the lines as though she might discern some intimacy beneath the ink

'But so selfish, Harry. Is this how he spent his last hours? Not thinking of us at all? My mother will be heartbroken. She ruined her honour for love of him. All her life it was nothing but him, when was he was coming to visit us, how many months and how many days until she heard his foot upon the stair, his voice in the yard? Every morning without fail, she lit a candle in the chapel and prayed for him.' She looked round at me, her eyes bitter. 'Compostela, Rome. Did he light candles for us?'

'I am sure he did,' I lied. At last she let me draw her head against my breast and I closed within my arms like a precious pearl.

WE lay together that night, our love-making a comfort and a giving. In the morning, I broke my other tidings.

'I am giving you an escort to take you home this day. Some of the King's informants know about you.'

'Home,' she echoed bleakly.

'Your children need love.' Her green eyes pleaded that she too needed love.

'I grew up without love,' I told her, 'save for my nurse who loved me dearly, and then I was taken from her and sent to the court. I know now that her mind was a nothingness but she was sweet and kind and I missed her so terribly. You must be there for your children, Meg. Teach them how to love, teach them joy in everyday things, teach them with your passion and wrap your arms about them every day.'

'Harry?' She touched gentle fingers along my wet cheekbone. I carried her fingers to my lips and then I flung aside the sheets. 'Don't go!' she pleaded. 'When shall I see you again.'

'I do not know, Meg, but I shall light a candle for you every day of the rest of my life.'

RICHARD'S coronation should have been a day of triumph for me, for I organised the most glorious ceremony that London had ever seen. All the receipts for who attended, what we wore, what we ate, the names of those who stitched our clothes or sewed our shoes are in the records of the exchequer. Maybe some day hundreds of years from now, some old chronicler may find them and see how civilized, how magnificent we were.

We practised the cushion-carrying on the Tuesday. Stanley was the worst at keeping pace, partly because he had only just come out of the Tower the night before and still had cobwebs in his brain. The ceremony of knighting the esquires took place on Wednesday morning at the Tower, followed by a banquet. In the afternoon Richard made the traditional journey through the city to Westminster Palace.

Isolde Martyn

London cleaned up its streets. Garlands of white roses were strung between the gables and looped beneath the eaves. Lavender and scarlet arras rippled beneath the wealthy men's windows and ribbons of murrey and blue bedecked doorknockers, hung in streamers and coiled in maidens' loveknots. Some commoners had hewn boughs of hawthorn and cut ropes of ivy and honeysuckle from the hedgerows to decorate their doorways. Bells, trumpets, shawms, drums, taboret pipes, hand-organs, hurdy-gurdies pealed, blared, beat, fluted and sang to the gasping air. But serrating the streets in haphazard armour were the borrowed Yorkshire soldiers, boar badges in their caps, pride in their eyes and halberds in their hands. Poor devils, they were so unwelcome; the Londoners scowled at the vowels they could not understand and debated in glances why this new king must fear for his safety.

At first sight of his Yorkshire lads, my cousin delivered me a I-told-you-so scowl from beneath his canopy but he could fault naught else. In truth, even to the fickle-minded, he certainly looked as magnificent as his brother always had. Mind, the glory was all based on loans. Just reckon what the long mantle of purple velvet furred with ermine, the doublet of white satin shot with gold, and the Spanish leather knee boots that shone like polished ebony must have cost, let alone the robes for everyone else, but I digress.

There are plenty of ways to win hearts: seven small pages, shiny-faced and so well brushed that their heads gleamed like oiled wood, marched alongside the King with such precocious dignity (the first time they had behaved well) that the crowd cooed over them like a grandmother. And Anne had some honeyed ladies in her train. Their gorgeous smiles and low-cut bodices sweetened the note of tyranny and had the men all whistling.

To be honest, I was against the new queen riding in a chariot since it meant the crowds could not see her easily. But Anne stated flatly she was not even risking an ambler so she rode in a litter. Her gown was of white damask (just like her canopy), but shot with tiny threads of gold and edged in ermine. Of course, she did not have tassels (I teased her about that later) but she did have a dainty diadem of beryl and peridot that sparkled wondrously. And there were plenty of esquires to escort her, handsome young masters in murrey doublet and hose. After her came Richard's sister, followed by all the noble ladies and maids-of-honour in blue velvet gowns purfiled with crimson satin.

184

And I? I was clad in a velvet doublet, blue and costly, embroidered with golden wheels of fortune with a diamond sewn into each blazing hub.

After the exuberant splendour of the day, the evening was as flat as a cake without yeast; Richard and Anne excused themselves early to indulge in bathwater followed by prayers and meditation in St Stephen's Chapel, while I went over the details for the crowning with Howard and my uncle of Canterbury.

At seven o'clock next morning the White Hall was jammed with haughty peers tormented by their coronets and burdensome robes as they lined up for the procession. Judging by their belly rumblings, the whoresons were hungry, too. The only creature who did not complain was Richard, who was berthed beneath a canopy of estate on his marble chair in some spiritual world of his own. Perhaps the prospect of the being ladled with holy oil concerned him. God might still hit him with a thunderbolt or the ghost of Dead Ned might materialise in the chancel and spit at him.

I had been up at dawn to help him put on the special ceremonial garments: the white shirt that was open to the waist for his anointing and over that a crimson shirt of glistening tartaryn with silver and gilt laces. His hose were sarsynett (uncomfortable, I reckon; I had opted for fine wool). It took both Howard and I to fasten the train of purple satin with its weighty lining to his doublet. Just its great hanging hood of miniver and ermine would put a strain on his shoulders. He was muscular but not a broad man.

Once he was apparelled, I spent my time playing pendulum between the Great Hall and the White Hall to make sure everyone was in the correct order, and that the regalia were being properly guarded. I can definitely say funerals are simpler, a sword, a destrier, tapers and everyone in cheap mourning hoods.

The clergy were late and the lady most aggravated by the delay was my aunt by her former marriage, Stanley's wife, Margaret Beaufort. She sent her page several times to plague me. Since she was the mother of Henry Tudor, a vagrant pretender to the crown, the wretched woman was lucky to have been invited let alone have the privilege of carrying Queen Anne's train. If Richard had not been so insistent on a show of unity, both Margaret and Stanley would have been on bread and water.

I found Margaret standing apart from the maids-of-honour with her nose in her prayerbook, fanning herself. Oh, she looked sour. I suppose she was seething that God was putting the crown on Richard's head instead of her son's. When she saw me, she tucked her book under her arm.

'Ah, at last, Buckingham!' The woman has small eyes that shaft you and a tongue like a poison dart. 'How much longer do you intend to keep us waiting here?'

'Now, now, Aunt Margaret, just a little more patience. We must not get ourselves hot and upset, must we?' She sucked in her cheeks at me–a bad habit which always makes her look like an abbess with bellyache. I noticed then her cramp-rings as she nursed her left hand against her breast, rubbing the knuckles with her right palm. Aching, I suppose.

'I have to say it, Aunt. You are looking magnificent in your scarlet.' That made heads swivel. Mouse-faced, almost forty, she blushed right enough. Lying coxcomb, was I?

'It might be better, Buckingham, if you had stools fetched for the Queen's ladies instead of dealing out fulsome compliments.'

A just rebuke. I called out an apology to the pretty creatures, clapping my hands for servants to fetch out benches.

Anne, however, was very forgiving. 'You've had enough to think about, my lord,' she exclaimed generously. 'I should have seen to my ladies' comfort earlier but everything is rather an effort.' She looked as anchored as Richard.

'*Mea culpa*,' I apologised, trying not to stare at the loose lacings of the red velvet surcote and purple kirtle across her little breasts. With her fair hair loose to her waist and a circlet of gold about her brow, she looked like a young maid from King Arthur's court. 'Hope they've warmed the oil for you, Anne.' I gave her a brotherly hug about the shoulders to annoy Margaret.

'Queen to you!' she teased back with mock indignation as I straightened the circlet skewed by my presumption. 'Yes, I shall survive.'

I went back and fussed over Margaret as I seated her. 'The old joints playing up again?' I asked cheerfully.

'Unhand me, Buckingham!' Then she added in a mutter over her shoulder, 'Both your grandfathers would turn in their graves at this day's enterprise.'

I leaned down. 'Perhaps they would, Aunt, but where were you and my uncle when I needed an education in loyalty to the House of Lancaster?'

'I hope you cursed well faint with exhaustion, boy.' I had seen gentler smiles on she-wolves.

186

'Are you all right now, Aunt Margaret?' I boomed loudly in retaliation as though she was seventy. 'Won't be much longer.' But the woman's bent fingers had snared my billowing sleeve and she whispered: 'If you had had any wit instead of a turnip for a brain, it would be you wearing the purple and maybe saintly King Harry's soul would be avenged.'

I stepped back. The twin arches of her unplucked eyebrows rose in question, but I could not answer nor would she free me. 'Cat got your tongue at last, Harry Buckingham?'

I wanted to move away but the small blue eyes had me pinioned like a butterfly stabbed upon a boy's brooch-pin.

The words came at last, spun out of bitterness. 'I did not see you waving a banner behind me, Aunt, or showing me the colour of your money.'

Her smile was warm as Circe's. 'If you do not throw in your cap in the ring, you cannot play. Enjoy walking in his shadow, child of Lancaster, before self-seekers like Catesby poison your name.'

She loosed me and I stood dazed.

'Your grace!' A small cough, and an anxious esquire piloted me off like a half-wrecked caravel to rope up at my cousin's quay. Despairing, a failed sorcerer trapped between reality and illusion, I picked up my white wand of office.

'My Lord of Buckingham, it is time.' Like a playing card in his stiff, glistening tabard, with his trumpeters at his shining heels, Blanc Sanglier stood before me, while I, like some poor fool tasting the gift of poppies, struggled to breathe and nod.

So it began like a dream, no, more splendid than any illusion: the anthems and the fanfares, the banners of Our Lady and St Peter, the great processional crosses, the ranks of mitres, the heralds and the great noblemen of the kingdom. Glad that they had taken the time to practise, the lords bearing the Sword of Mercy, the Mace, the Swords of Justice, the Sceptre, the Orb, the Sword of State, one by one began their stately march. It was Howard, the newly minted Duke of Norfolk, who bore in his hands the heavy cap of maintenance with its jewelled arches rising to a golden cross.

At last my cousin came barefooted down the steps, his pages holding the heavy purple train which it would be my task to carry. As he walked past the bowing courtiers, I forgot his height and saw only the face of a man about to become a king. He halted where I stood waiting for him and I found myself bowing as deeply as the rest.

He could barely swallow. I could see that he wanted to embrace me and yet the rich robe dragging back his uneven shoulders made it too hard.

'We did it, Harry.'

My jest tumbled out like a loving nursemaid's warning: 'Yes, now mind you do not trip.'

He waited while I acquired a comfortable grip on his train and we set off awkwardly for I was also carrying the wand. 'Not so fast, your highness. I have never done this before.'

'*Nor have I.*'

Russell and Stillington glided forwards, smelling like a couple of incense holders, to escort him to the door. After the muted light of the palace, the hot glare of the July morning after the muted light of the palace was a shock. I sensed Richard falter. Then it was my turn to be dazzled. The sun scorched me through my heavy silk robes; my hands sweated. I feared to drop his train and lose the sense of unity between us. And then my breathing eased. I set aside Margaret's shrewish rebuke. Together, my cousin and I had won a kingdom and the roar of the people was glorious. I wanted to laugh exultantly and whoop so loud that Elizabeth would hear me. *You underestimated me, you Woodville bitch. Well, World, take note! Here is Buckingham!*

The air in Westminster abbey was rich with incense and holy with plainsong. My cousin was led to pray before St Edward's shrine while Anne made her stately progress from the palace. I knelt behind Richard and then, as Anne joined him, I was startled to find Margaret Beaufort lowering herself creakily onto the cushion next to mine. She ignored me, leaned forward to make a petal shape of Anne's train and then she clasped her hands to pray. For what? Richard's death and damnation? *A turnip for a brain? Child of Lancaster? Thy kingdom?* Morton's words came to poke my brain with pitchforks as well.

I tried to pray. The words came. My mind obeyed, yet my heart felt unmoved, like the great stone beneath the coronation throne where Richard would soon be seated.

I rose mechanically. The royal couple were led to the high altar where, stripped to the waist, their bare skin was anointed with holy oil from the ampulla, the most vital and sacred part of the crowning, then they were clothed in robes of cloth of gold and seated on the thrones.

I cannot remember the sermon nor all the oaths Richard was required to swear save that they were in English so all men might know what he promised, but I remember the exquisite singing of the anthems and then the fealty.

'I, Henry Stafford, Duke of Buckingham, become your liegeman of life and limb and of earthly worship and faith and truth I shall bear unto you, for to live and die against all manner of folk so God me help.'

'Is it your wish that ye have this man for king?' asked my great uncle of Canterbury, lifting high the crown.

'Yea!' cried the abbey.

Margaret alleged later that I turned my face away when the crown was placed on Richard's head. I was not aware of doing so, only of the black dog of despair suddenly slavering to sink its fangs into my brain again as I realised that the friendship I had shared with my cousin was over.

I felt utterly desolate. However much our cameradie had been laced with high ambition, there had been something fine and good about it all: Plantagenets, cousins, dukes, court exiles with common enemies, two men thrown into alliance. Where my irreverence had taken the edge off Glouces-ter's piety, so his high purpose and trust had diluted my fear of myself. But now, he was crowned, anointed; now he held *God's* mandate to rule; now he was master and I, like the rest of his subjects, must always bow to him. Whatever he commanded, it was my duty to perform; whatever I asked of him was his privilege to bestow or withhold.

Is that friendship? No, that is a fairy tale for children! Harry Stafford was now obliged to do what King Richard ordered and in return he might hope for the gift of offices. *He might only hope.*

Sweet Christ, what was it I had dreamed of when I had left Brecknock? Revenge on Elizabeth and the desire to show the world that I was not an impoverished milksop, that I could snap a Woodville king in two and be another kingmaker? But, like every beggar, I always had the fantasy to wake up and find *myself* the king!

Was Margaret right? Had I abused my birthright, dishonoured my ancestors? Terrible thoughts possessed me. Thoughts that should have been bound with iron and buried deep. If God's Will had compelled me to push

Gloucester up the wheel of destiny, I could likewise give that wheel an extra shove and send him on a downward path once more. I, who had undermined all in setting my cousin on the throne, might now take to myself the crown, for the friendship that had redeemed me was broken now. I had lost the only hand upon my rein.

The fanfare crashed into my thoughts and I mechanically raised my coronet and lowered it again. A great shout broke and hundreds of voices chanted:

Verus rex, Rex Ricardus!
Rectus rex, Rex Ricardus!
Iustus, juridicus et legitimus rex, Rex Ricardus!
Cui omnes nos subjicio volumus.
Suaeque humillime iugum, admittere guernationis!

There! It was done. I could neither speak nor think, nor did I want to.

Anne's crowning followed and then I had to bear Richard's train as we returned to Westminster Hall. Now it was he who smiled at the crowds and I who appeared moved and introspective. The commoners surged forward as the last of the company reached the Westminster Hall and flooded in behind to gape as the ceremonial ranks broke with a unison sigh of relief. Our anointed king and queen retired to strip off the stifling gowns, the noble guests withdrew and I found myself left on the dais staring unseeing at the garlands looping the white cloths, and the great salt and platters borrowed from Crosby Place.

A friendly hand shoved a jack of ale at me. 'You look weary, Harry. Take an hour's respite.' It was decent of Lovell but I shook my head. What he mistook for integrity was my desperation to escape the Devil's whispering. 'You made a magnificent job of things,' he added. 'I think our foreign guests' jaws nearly hit the ground.'

'Ah, so that was what the noise was.'

'No, seriously, it will be hard to keep things up to your standard. As to where the money will come from...'

'That's for tomorrow, Francis. You will make a fine chamberlain. Go and see if there's aught the King needs. I'll hold the keep here.'

Nursing my ale, I sat down on the corner of a bench beside one of the marble trestles and watched the cutler arranging his knives on the nearest side-board. At the other end of the hall a sergeant-at-arms and the hall steward were trying to persuade the rabble to leave. The servants were growing angry, beseeching me to order the pikemen in and the situation was becoming ugly. I was just about to summon the guard when Howard returned.

'Not having a rest, Harry? You looked a bit strained back there in the abbey.'

'Yes, Jock, I nearly dropped the plaguey train a few times. Why did I have to carry that daft wand too? Didn't know whether I was a sorcerer or a pageboy.'

'Try carrying the crown. Almost smashed the blessed thing. You've done a grand job, Harry.' That was generous. As Earl Marshall, these ceremonies were actually his responsibility save that Richard had given the task to me. 'Yes, indeed, even old Hastings with his flair for such things couldn't have bettered you, and young Lovell just wouldn't have had the experience. Now, is there anything I can do?' Tactful of him mentioning Hastings.

'It's going very smoothly, Jock, except for them.' I jerked my chin at the growing crowd of intruders. There must have been already about two hundred of them cramming the entrance to Westminster Hall. 'Do you think some men-at-arms will do the trick or are we likely to have a riot? It will ruin it for *him* if anyone gets killed.'

The new Earl Marshall stuck out his lower lip thoughtfully then he chuckled. 'Wait on. I'll deal with 'em. I'll be back in a few minutes.'

Few minutes? Ha! The weary servants were starting to get mighty angry, beseeching me to order the pikemen in. Like the damned in hell, the crowd was writhing and pushing forward, snatching the fresh baked bread from the nearest tables. Out of patience, I summoned in the soldiers and while I was instructing them, a shout from the steward made us turn.

'Oh God in Heaven!'

Howard's great war horse was draped from mane to hoof in cloth of gold and he loomed above it, a supernatural being in gold and scarlet, like a vision from another world. Visor down, he rode his horse down the steps and straight at the intruders. Instantly, the squirming mass ceased its gyration and gasped with one voice. In ducal tones, he commanded them to leave, and rode back and forth along forcing them back. His destrier caught the jest of it, delicately planting its hooves to miss the wretches' feet by a seed's length and as the rabble frayed away so the soldiers were able to push the great doors closed at last.

I was convulsed with laughter. Howard's antics had driven away my devil too. 'There you are, Harry, we shall not have to hold our noses while we eat.'

'I'm not so sure,' I spluttered, pointing to the fresh manure splashed across the flagstones.

THE BANQUET began miraculously on time on mopped flagstones (although there could have been some lost lice and fleas hopping around the great doors). Blanc Sanglier reappeared as though magicked to supervise the fanfares, and a grinning king sat down beneath the purple canopy of estate held high by his henchmen. He was now clothed in purple as befitted his rank, brocade threaded with gold and stitched with white roses and the garter insignia. Anne had given the robe to him as a coronation gift and it almost cost the eyesight of the Tailors' Guild. Lovell and several chosen noblemen served their liege lord and lady from platters of gold. Thank heaven, I was not expected to play the page and kneel. That would have brought back ugly memories of serving Elizabeth.

Mind, being seated between my Uncle of Canterbury and my lady of Suffolk as they argued over what made the perfect latrine was not my idea of celebration. Certainly, I was as tired as an ass that had been roped to a treadmill all week but my demons would not let me be. Now that it was almost over, I felt as though the heel of God had pressed me flat. If only Meg had been waiting in my bedchamber. In her arms I might find oblivion. I longed to clasp her sweet body against mine again, bury my face in the perfume of her hair and forget the cursed world.

Applause broke around me. The King's Champion, Sir Robert Dymoke, beautiful in snow-white armour, rode up to the dais on a charger caparisoned in red and white silken harness, and rasped out his challenge to anyone who doubted Gloucester's claim.

I watched Margaret Beaufort's lips tighten. Challenge? Yes, Richard, *what are you going to do about Henry Tudor? About your nephews?* A cup was proffered to Dymoke. He took one gulp and dashed its contents on the rushes, claiming the vessel as his fee.

We sat through fire-eaters, tumblers, dancers, a play by Norfolk's troupe, songs from the royal chapel choir and last but not least a cursed bagpiper. I groaned inwardly and met my liege lord's grin. It was a relief to rise from the table and not hard to infiltrate the circle of conversation where Margaret Beaufort stood as they cleared the trestles away.

'Are you returning to Woking at the end of the week, Aunt?'

She gave me her why-should-that-matter look, but answered civilly: 'No, I shall be staying in London a little longer. Stanley, as you know, is to accompany the King on his northern progress.' Yes, I knew King Richard was not going to let Thomas Stanley out of his sight in a hurry. 'I gather you are not going a-junketing?' she added.

I spread my hands apologetically. 'I have so many responsibilities in Wales now.' Perish the thought of returning to Brecknock! It was amusing that just the mention of Wales riled her. The Tudors considered it theirs.

'What a shame,' she replied insincerely. 'Still, I suppose it would be a waste of time you going north with him. They won't be interested in you in York, will they?'

We were on the periphery of the cluster surrounding one of the Castilian diplomats and everyone was too interested in his exotic tales to listen to us.

'You are unkind, Aunt.' I whispered. 'I cannot understand why you dislike me so. I never put a frog in your bed, did I?' She shrugged. 'And here am I with a genuine admiration for you and Jasper Tudor, keeping the flame of hope flickering for Lancaster these past twelve years. It shows not only tenacity and determination but patience, a virtue which you possess in abundance, though it flowed thinly this morning.'

'You know I write to my son,' she muttered crossly. 'All the world knows it. I suppose you read every letter.'

'Only the innocuous ones you deliberately allow to fall into our hands. "Dearest Son, I wish you were here. How is the weather in Brittany?"' I watched her suck in her cheeks again. 'Tell me, Aunt, what price would you pay to have your son here? Is it worth a throne?'

'I do not understand what you mean.'

'A purely academic question which I should not like to be misconstrued.' She was not insensible of a few curious glances in our direction and forced her gaze into pleasanter creases. I lifted her hand from my arm. 'Give it some thought.'

I moved along the tables, shaking a hand here and there until I reached Uncle Knyvett and Limerick.

'The lads reported some tavern talk today that might spoil your indigestion, Harry. Do you want to hear it?'

'Certainly.' I shrugged and sat down. 'Spew it out then.'

'They are saying you have made Gloucester king so that you may later brand him usurper and tyrant and take the crown yourself. How about that one?'

'Pah, and if he is a usurper, how can I take the crown while the princes live?'

Uncle Knyvett nodded. 'Aye, Harry, but the whisper is that they will not live long. I warned you it was not kind.'

I shrugged. 'But he is king *legally*, uncle. It is Parliament who has put the boys aside.'

'All I'm saying is watch your back, lad, and you don't want to be all charm with her ladyship Beaufort, neither. What if King Richard were to start believing the gossip?'

'Yes, understood.' I patted his arm in thanks. 'She's probably behind the slander. Or else Elizabeth is still meddling.' A royal page bowed before me. 'Looks as though I am wanted.'

I went up the steps wearily to where Richard and Anne were talking with the Suffolks.

'My lord of Buckingham.' Richard raised me from my obeisance, thanking me again for all that I had done, and embraced me. 'I wanted to tell you that I have decided to make your henchman, Sir William Knyvett, Constable of Castle Rising, if you are in agreement.'

'That is very generous of you, your highness.' But why was my cousin grinning so broadly?

'We also have something for you that we are sure will please you better than any other gift.' He handed me a document, tightly rolled and wrapped by a ribbon of scarlet, its wax heavy with the imprint of the Great Seal. 'It will be official when Parliament confirms it next week.'

I unrolled the parchment and almost wept. Richard had given me the Bohun inheritance, the lands that had been withheld from me since 1471. To him it meant a loss of royal income and a show of trust; to me it was my lawful inheritance and it added some fifty manors to my possessions.

194

'And furthermore,' laughed my cousin, 'to show the world how much love and trust I have in you, you are to receive the offices of High Constable and Great Chamberlain of England.'

It took my breath away and I dropped to my knees speechless and overcome with shame. There I had been listening to Satan, and here Richard was being generous, trusting me, when I could not trust myself. I felt torn in two. No man had given me so much. No human being had ever shown so much unquestioning faith in me. God have mercy! All the deep laid plans, the childhood dreams, the stolen imaginings, the alternative within alternatives. But then...

I read no pleasure in his northern friends' faces and as I kissed Anne's cheek, I glimpsed Catesby and Ratcliffe watching me with contempt as though they found my courtesy and splendour risible. The former said something and Ratcliffe, looking straight at me, laughed. Despite the fact that I outranked them in every way, despite all I had done, they still found me something to laugh at.

Later when my expensive robes were chested and my coronet coffered, I stood alone at my bedchamber window looking across the moon-silvered rooftops. You beloved fool, Gloucester, I whispered, directing my thoughts to Westminster. You have made it too easy. You have created in me the most powerful subject that any English king has ever had.

The greater the trust, the greater the betrayal.

11

'I am making plans for the government of the south while I am away. Are you still resolved to return to Wales, Harry?'

I was standing with the King in the Great Chamber at Westminster staring uncomfortably at the image of Fidelity painted on the window jamb. He had decided to be away until October. The court would go by river to Windsor and then trundle in a royal progress up the spine of England, with some excessive crown-wearing and flourishes when they reached York. No one with any sense lingered in London in August, the month when the risk of pestilence was greatest.

'It does nothing but rain in Wales,' I answered gloomily.

'But you *are* Justiciar of Wales,' he pointed out, selecting a peach from a silver platter—there were a few valuables Elizabeth had missed.

I made a face, grinned, and helped myself to a Spanish apple. 'Yes, but you don't get these in Brecknock.'

The royal fingers aimed the peach stone at the upper window light. It missed and Loyaulté loped over hopefully. 'I shall leave Russell in charge of the Royal Council and if there is any problem, he can send for Howard. You can control the west and he the east and if the Woodvilles try anything, they should be easily crushed by the pair of you.'

I made a pile of the orange peel on the sill. 'What are you going to do about the Lords Bastard?' I meant the princes.

Richard's frown of displeasure snapped down like a visor. 'What do you mean, *do* ?' He glanced about us as though we were talking treason. On the other side of the chamber, two minstrels were playing for Queen Anne and her ladies and no one was watching us.

I spread my hands innocently. 'My liege, I am High Constable and all the prisoners in the Tower are my responsibility. What do you imagine I meant?'

'No matter. I am just racked with guilt still.' His fingers played with the ring on the little finger of his right hand, a habit that was growing. 'They are on my conscience the whole time, poor children. I can never set them free, can I?'

'No, and they are causing a lot of interest, more than the Royal Menagerie, I can tell you. If you want my advice, I should take them up to Middleham or Sheriff Hutton, wherever your northerners can keep them safe.'

He relaxed visibly. 'Much my thoughts also. I do not want to keep them caged so tightly, and up there they'd be freer. Young Ned is not speaking to me, of course. He may be difficult on the journey.'

'But there is no reason to keep him by you. Have them modestly attired and kept in one of the wagons when you leave London, ah, and I shouldn't make it known you are taking them. If Elizabeth thinks they're still secure in the Tower, she will be a while planning another rescue. Keep it a close secret, hmm?'

He nodded. 'Good advice, Harry.'

I folded my arms and leaned against the embrasure. 'I have another suggestion to make with your royal grace's permission.'

'No ceremony, cousin, speak your mind.'

'Wily old Morton is renowned for escaping. He has managed to slither out of the Tower before and I'll wager he'll try it again while you are away. Let me send him to Brecknock. The keep is strong enough and I'll watch him like a December greybeard would a May wife.'

Richard pulled a face: 'Hmm, a tad too close to some of the Tudors' Welsh cronies for my appetite. Though you are right, he'd be safer in your keeping. The University of Oxford has sent me a petition begging me to set the old snake free so Brecknock would be a good compromise. That's settled then, you take Morton and I'll take Stanley.'

'What rapture!' I put on a Cheshire dialect, mimicking Stanley's round-shouldered stoop and the King gave a right royal groan.

'You know, what that arse really wants is northern Wales,' I pointed out, 'and I'm in his way.'

'And you are going to stay in his way, Harry. The only reason I'm being lenient to the old weathervane is because his plaguey kinsmen can whistle up a fair size army. Look, how about I dangle some of Rivers' lands in front of him?' He teased Loyaulté with an oatcake. 'That might keep the growser happy.'

198

I watched the dog demolish the cake in an instant. 'Ratcliffe seems to think Lady Margaret's increased her letter writing of a sudden.'

'So I am informed. All the more reason to keep Stanley by me. There, that's all our enemies dealt with except dear Elizabeth, but she can't do anything while I've got the boys. London should be safe enough.'

'Quite so,' I took up my gloves and riding crop. 'I'll not delay you further now. With your leave, I am off to the Steelyard. I am thinking of investing in a couple of trading ventures.'

'Excellent!' He walked with me to the door. 'You shall still go and see Catesby at the Exchequer tomorrow? I want you to understand the wheels and levers. God forbid I die before my son's a grown man, but if I do, you will be Lord Protector.'

'Perish the thought,' I answered fervently, bowing over his hand.

'One thing more. Anne and I wish you to ride with us part of the way to York. Say you will.'

'I wish I could,' I protested, 'but I have so many responsibilities now that if I wore all my chains of office at once, I think the floor would give way.'

He chuckled. 'You must come. Holy Paul, with all Anne's chariots, we'll be crawling along like a row of tortoises. Join us at Oxford and ride with us to Gloucester then you can hie off to Wales.'

I carried his hand to my lips. 'Make it a command, Richard, and then I cannot refuse.'

His face saddened, 'Don't put it like that, Harry.'

***

THE King's comment about Margaret Beaufort made me wonder if I had greatly underestimated her. The rumours that I had not planted, were they all from her?

Two days later, I cornered Ratcliffe in the palace guard room. He was as helpful as a beggar with his tongue cut out but when I pulled rank as High Constable, he muttered that the bitch was as closely watched as a harem of lovely slavegirls and would my royal grace mind my own business and leave him to do his job. Closely watched, was she? It seemed that if I wanted to hold another conversation with Aunt Margaret without Ratcliffe rearing up like an adder, it had to be with Richard's full permission and before he left London.

I found him sprawled under a tree beside the combat yard watching Lovell being playfully slaughtered by Tyrrell. It was one of those sticky days that makes your hose cling and your armpits sweat, and Richard was in a sleeveless cote. He was leaning on his elbow, one hand idly caressing Loyaulté.

'Watch your left, Francis!' he shouted, suddenly sitting up and then groaned as Lovell failed to take advantage of his advice. I cleared my throat and he glanced round. The dog padded over to lick my hand.

'Harry! I thought you were inspecting the garrison at the Tower this afternoon.'

'I decided that could wait. I would appreciate a private word if your highness pleases.' I took off my hat and used it as a fan.

'Say on!' he ordered, gesturing to his attendants to fall back, but his eyes still closely followed the swordplay.

I dropped down on my haunches beside him. 'I have been thinking about your northern progress and who would be the greatest threat to you while you are gone.'

My cousin looked at me squarely. He was obviously not in the mood for such serious matters but he was too courteous a man to make light of my concern. 'The Woodvilles, of course, and a few of the southerners who were enjoying the trough too long and resent my friends taking their offices.'

'Well, that is all true but I believe that we ought to lure Henry Tudor and his uncle home. While they are still at liberty your Lancaster enemies still have a focus for rebellion but if they were out of the way, then their sympathizers would have to come to terms.'

'Do you truly imagine Tudor is a threat?' His smile chided me gently, then he sighed and returned his attention to the combatants, running a hand over his chin thoughtfully. 'I was considering reopening negotiations to ransom him from Brittany early next year.'

'That did not work when your brother tried it and it is far too costly. Give me your permission to try my persuasive powers on Lady Margaret.'

His mouth twitched with humour. 'And what riches am I supposed to unearth from my empty coffers to entice the Welsh braggart home, pray?' He groaned as Lovell missed another opportunity to break through Tyrrell's defence.

I pulled a face. 'Confirmation of the earldom of Richmond and your lovechild, Katherine in marriage.' That winded him. He lost all interest in the combat.

'Holy Paul, Harry, I'll not let my poppet—'

'Merely to bait the hook, your highness.'

He scowled, and took a draught from the goblet on the footstool at his elbow. 'Do it, but let it be one of my nieces.'

'Princess Bess?'

'No!' he snapped sharply. Bess, the eldest, was his favourite. 'No, Tudor would not believe you. Offer him young Cecily. Ah, bad luck, Francis. Well fought, James!'

Lovell staggered up to us with the sweat coursing off his scarlet face. 'I'll have to lose weight,' he lamented. 'I've not won a bout all week. Do not laugh at me, Dickon. Time you got down to some practice otherwise you'll start getting podgy like me.'

'What, our hero of Barnet and Berwick?' panted Tyrrell, scraping his shirt sleeve across his wet forehead. 'Never.' But Lovell's words had fallen on fertile ground. Richard sprang up and began to strip off his cote.

'Come on, Harry,' he exclaimed. 'If anyone needs to lose a bit of weight, it is you. Ever since we've come to London—'

'No,' I protested, appalled at the loathsome suggestion. 'It is too friggin' hot for a start and...' But Tyrrell was tugging away my doublet. Lovell pushed the practice sword into my reluctant hand. It was not manly to refuse.

I had been promising myself I would start daily lessons in sword play but I had been very slack in getting round to it. So, not at all prepared, I miserably saluted Richard before we stepped back and began to circle each other warily. Once the attendants scented what was in the wind, word spread and two earls, the Spanish ambassador and a handful of barons materialized from the buildings around the yard. Many of coronation guests had gone back to the country but there were still plenty of the northern affinity.

Richard's thin lips were parted in calculation, and I felt my throat go dry. To know I would be ignominiously defeated was unbearable. My only consolation was that his preferred weapon was the battle axe so perhaps he would not be quite so adroit with a sword. He was waiting for me to make the first thrust but seeing I would not, he launched an attack which I was able to parry successfully. Anyone who has ever fought in single combat knows that your reflexes are of the utmost importance. You have to defend, anticipate, act within the umpteenth of a second. You have to watch your opponent's eyes, his hand, his stance, in order to block the deadly blade as it mercilessly whips at you again and again and again.

I knew my cousin's responses would be faster than mine; that, being lighter, he could move more lithely. It dawned at last on my poor beleaguered brain that he was being kind to me, deliberately slowing himself down to give me more openings to thrust at him. Sweet Christ, he was doing it so I should not make a fool of myself.

His loving kindness stung me into a fury. Was I a child that I needed to be protected? I launched an attack on him that was both swift and serious. The fight was real: Richard metamorphosed into Dead Ned, Rivers, Dorset, Hastings, Ratcliffe, everyone who had underestimated Harry Stafford. A mutter rose from his war-scarred veterans and I knew I was doing well. The King of England was retreating, his blade flashing defensively. I laughed exultantly then found the tide had turned. Wave after wave of blows drove me back, pain lashed my arm and the sword whirled from my hand. My head crashed back upon the dirt and a blunt combat weapon jabbed at my breastbone. A roar went up. Behind Richard stood Catesby and Ratcliffe. smirking at my defeat.

Richard flung the sword away and grinning hauled me to my feet. I was too breathless to speak and mustered as good-tempered a face as I could. All his affinity, save good-natured Lovell, were looking with smug delight at the straw and dirt clinging to my hair and hose. Reason told me that they could not do otherwise than cheer their royal master's triumph but the serpent of jealousy writhed about my guts. Even though the royal arm was around my shoulder and Lovell was thrusting a cup of ale into my aching hand, I seethed against every one of them.

On my prie-dieu that night, I pleaded with God to dash the cup of ambition from my hands, to stop events playing so easily into my outstretched cajoling fingers but there was only silence. The Devil drove the memory of the day's shame again and again into my thoughts and I was possessed of so great a hunger for the crown, that my guardian angel could not withstand its fury. My survival through youth had been kindled by the determination to crush the Woodvilles for their mockery. Now I felt the same about Richard's henchmen.

***

Margaret Beaufort was not an easy person to find next day and when my duties permitted me some respite, I was forced to resort to asking Stanley where his wife was. I found him at his house, jabbing glumly at his dinner. Below the salt, his officers watched with interest as he invited me to join him. I sat down and agreed to a cup of wine.

'Going north soon then, my lord?'

He nodded, prodding a brace of partridges with a gingery-looking sauce congealing over them. 'You here to discuss travel arrangements? I didn't know you were Master of the Horse as well, Buckingham.' I ignored that sling-shot.

'The King desires me to have a quiet talk with Lady Margaret,' I told him.

'About what?' he asked, sorting a bone out of his mouthful with his tongue and spitting it onto the rushes. 'Am I included or is it about needlework?'

'You are not involved, put it that way. In fact, I'd stay out of it if I were you.'

He snorted morosely. 'Happen I don't have much choice.' He paused to extract another tedious bone. 'Anyroad, she's gone t' Red Pale, lad.' He raised doleful eyes to me and seeing my puzzlement, enlightened me. 'The Red Pale at Westminster, that printer fellow, Caxton.' He began once more to pick ponderously at his partridges.

'Thank you.' I picked up my hat and gloves and stood up.

'She may choose to talk about it later,' he warned me mournfully.

'That is up to her, isn't it?' I replied, wondering how in Heaven a woman of her quicksilver intelligence could bed with this exciting, cheerful lump of manhood.

'I'll know it all sooner or later.' He smiled dully. 'Waiting doesn't bother me, Buckingham.'

***

CAXTON'S fellow printer, de Worde I think his name was, ushered me into the printing house while he went to find Lady Margaret. I breathed in the smell of ink and paper. It had been years since I had come with the rest of the court to gape at the new invention Dead Ned had imported from his sister's court in Burgundy, so I watched the activity with renewed curiosity.

Several apprentices were arranging metal letters back to front in frames. Another was using a large pad to ink a completed frame that had already been set in the great press and when that was done, he and another lad turned the great screw which pressed a sheet of white paper down onto the inked surface. After the print was made, the screw was twisted up again and fresh paper was inserted and the frame containing the next folio was carried over. It was a laborious process but faster than using a whole monastery of copiers. No wonder the Lord Bastard had sneered at the book of hours I had given him. I suppose he had paid many a visit here and regarded any book that was not printed as old-fangled.

'Your grace, your presence does us great honour.' Caxton himself emerged from the stairwell. He was a gaunt fellow with the slight stoop that so often characterises the very tall. His inky fingers left a stain on my glove. 'My lady will be here in a moment. Have you had a look around yet, my lord? May I say your patronage would be an honour, and inquire if there is any learned work your grace would care to purchase or perhaps invest in? We should naturally dedicate it to you.'

'A book on gardening perhaps.' An astonished silence met my answer.

'By St Anthony!' exclaimed Margaret Beaufort, pausing on the bottom stair. 'Now I have heard everything.'

Caxton made no comment on her outburst, and promised to consider the matter if I provided the money.

'Why do *you* not write a treatise, my lord?' probed Margaret waspishly, as we left the bustle of Caxton's shop behind us. 'How to pluck a white rose at the proper season. How to pinch off the young buds.'

'You are very froward and ill-mannered for a noblewoman.'

'Ill-mannered and agog with curiosity as to why the high and mighty Henry Stafford has sought me out in a printer's shop. Is the palace on fire or is it something more important?'

'Dear Aunt,' I murmured sarcastically. We skirted two esquires playing palm ball.

'By the Sweet Virgin, must you "aunt" me with every breath? It makes me feel guilty.'

204

'Guilty?' I echoed, picking up the leather ball that had trickled to my feet. I tucked in the wisps of hair that had forced their way out and threw the ball back.

'Guilty that I never bought you a wooden horse that ran on wheels or a toy dagger to stick in your friends.'

I gave a snort of amusement. 'Heavens, my lady, when you visited us at Pembroke, your son and I were past such toys.'

That made her haughty. 'I am sorry. Life never gave me any practice at motherhood.'

We walked in silence for a few minutes. God knows what filled her mind, honest guilt probably, but I was remembering my short sojourn at Pembroke Castle as a fellow esquire of her son Tudor. Those few months in William Herbert, Earl of Pembroke's household were like Heaven after being Elizabeth's errand boy. I found the Herberts a cheerful, loving family, who treated the esquires like welcome cousins, and it opened my eyes to the greed and calumny of the Queen's household. Alas, the earl, God save his soul, was slain in the war with Warwick and I was summoned back to Westminster again.

I remembered Tudor as a quiet, intelligent boy. Not a muscular, athletic fellow nor puny either. His mother's visit for a week when he was ten meant all the world to him. I came across him sobbing into his pillow after she had gone. At least she visited him.

'Can we start again, my lady?' I sighed. 'Is it to late to become friends?'

'Who has friends?' We circumnavigated a herbal bed on separate sides.

'What was your business with Caxton?' I asked as I rejoined her and we continued on the path towards the Tyburn.

She broke off a sprig of lavender. 'I should like him to print an English translation of a French book of devotion but he says he has too much work at the moment.' Her dark skirts swished down the steps ahead of me. 'Do not be taken in by Caxton's bonhomie. He has not forgiven you for executing his patron, Lord Rivers.'

'I must apologise to him, then,' I countered witheringly. 'Gloucester and I were not considering what damage the loss of Lord Rivers might cause to England's literature when our lives were in danger at Stony Stratford. I should also point out that the Duke of Northumberland sat in judgment on Rivers, Vaughan and Grey, not I.'

'But my husband tells me you were rather anxious for the Royal Council to condemn them. But no matter, expediency dictates that one must make allowances for the action of kings. By the by, Buckingham, this pleasant little walk you insisted upon is attracting a great deal of attention. My constant shadow over there is wondering what you and I have to say to each other and I imagine he will present exciting conclusions to the King your master. Or do Sir Richard Ratcliffe and Sir William Catesby control what King Richard hears?' So she was singing that song again. No doubt she had her spies too.

'I should be very wary of Catesby if I were you, Buckingham. He has already played Judas to Lord Hastings and I'm sure he'd like to make another thirty pieces of silver.'

'Thank you for the advice.' I pulled her aside to avoid a dog turd on the path. 'Actually, the King is quite aware of what I wish to say to you. He is anxious for genuine reconciliation between the Houses of York and Lancaster. In a nutshell, your son is welcome to return to England.'

'The King', she replied, freeing her arm, 'should advise you to save your breath.' She stopped by the rail and rested her hands upon it, the lavender still clasped in her skewed fist. 'What is it you really want from me?' she asked over her shoulder.

'Trust.'

'Is that all?'

'My terms are different from Richard's,' I promised, as she started down the stairs. 'I shall stand warranty for your son's safety. It's better my way.'

'Your way?'

'You *are* planning a rising while our liege lord is in the north, aren't you?'

That brought her up short. She turned and stared at me though her features betrayed no sign I was correct. 'All those rumours,' I added. 'It had to be you.'

'I didn't start them all.'

'I started quite a few myself.'

I had her full attention at last. She ran a finger round her pointed face to ease the hard white coif. 'Why on earth should I organise a rising?'

'Because it will be the first opportunity you have ever had. Let me see, you are going to tell the Woodvilles you will support them putting their little prince back on the throne and then when the Tower is raided, pfft.'

'Pffft?'

'The boys won't be there. The Woodvilles and their supporters will say, "Alackaday, here we are with a rebellion, what do we do now?" and you say, "The princes have been murdered by a tyrant, so support my son, Tudor, instead."'

'And shall they be?'

'What?'

'Murdered?'

'No, of course not. Richard is taking them north with him. Anyway, let's continue with my hypothesis, shall we? Before poor old Richard has a chance to trundle the boys south to prove his innocence, the whole of southern England is up in arms against his alleged tyranny. So when Henry lands on the south coast, all the southern lords flock to him as though he is—forgive the heresy—the Second Coming. Meantime, you have ordered your Cheshire men south so when Richard charges back down like a wounded boar, you have him caught between two thumbs.' A boar between thumbs! I could not believe I was coming out with all that but maybe my babble had hit the nail upon the head. Margaret was staring at me as though I was a vision of Our Lady. 'Well now, is that how you imagined it, my lady?'

Her nostrils quivered as she took a deep breath. 'Listen, Buckingham, when I was first widowed—Henry's father, as you know, died when I was only thirteen—yes, I spent much of my time romancing that my baby son would one day become king and a great king too. At fourteen one's ideals are so important but as one ages those fantastic hopes strive with practicalities and eventually one compromises with life.' Her hooded eyes suddenly fixed upon my face. 'Not only is my son barred from the throne by the 1407 Act of Parliament, but he is unknown to the English people. He has no captains, no army, no ships, and you believe I would encourage him to risk his life against such overwhelming odds? Try remembering what happened to Queen Margaret d'Anjou and her son.'

Well, I could have pointed out to her that Edward Woodville was roaming the Channel with half's England's treasury available, but that was better left unsaid.

'I can see your point,' I agreed. 'But, listen, it does not have to be that way. Just send him a sweet letter saying Richard wants to be friendly. Henry shall have his earldom back and one of Edward's daughters to warm his bed.

I promise it, my lady. Does my word mean nothing to you? I am second to the King, I hold more offices than any nobleman in history and yet you still seem to see me as some little boy strutting up and down in a paper coronet.'

Her expression told me that was exactly how she had been seeing me but I sensed the wind had changed now. We moved in silence beneath the thick canopies of two venerable oaks, stepping over the roots that veined the ground. She stopped abruptly as a startled squirrel raced past us streaking for safety up the ancient trunk like a flame. I turned around. The human dog following us could not break cover to eavesdrop without being obvious. Margaret had not appeared to notice any longer. If her pebble eyes strayed over the bright summer leaves above her head, her thoughts were earthbound.

'Let me ask you this, Buckingham. If King Richard should die, what shall you do? Stand as Regent to his lad or make yourself king?'

I glanced warily behind me, took her elbow and we reclaimed the path.

'No question at all.' I answered softly. 'In those circumstances, I should claim the throne as the legitimate heir of the House of Lancaster.' I looked her straight in the face. 'Would you support me?'

She nodded. 'Yes, yes, I would, and you would safeguard Henry?'

'I should give him high office and a princess for wife.'

'All very well, my lord, but we are speaking of ifs and maybes. The reality is we have a man as king now, not a child, and if I were not the doting mother of Henry Tudor, I should say you have given England a most excellent king. Our new queen has told me of all the changes he intends and they sound fair and just. Can you do better, Buckingham? Is total lack of scruple a regal quality?'

I turned slowly, my face cold and implacable.

'Crowns are not won by caution. Neither, tell your son, are earldoms.'

12

It seems more than just a season ago I journeyed by barge to Reading and then took horse with my retinue along the road through the Chilterns. July was at her kindest; the warm air was drowsy with songs of bees and grasshoppers. About the villages, orchard trees stooped, overburdened with fruit, while the wasps feasted on the windfalls; and beyond the thickets of hawthorn and ivy, heedless of the scythes being whetted, the corn was ripening to gold and the meadows were knee-deep in buttercups. It was the time of year to tumble a willing girl in the long grass and to Hell with the consequences.

Alas, my thoughts needed to match my destination. Oxford, city of rhetoric and unruliness. I lodged my retinue at a comfortable inn on the London road and next day after much deliberation I rode in clothed in my most sober doublet. It had been tempting to wear the emerald imperial doublet with a daffodilly stomacher—clerics hate wild wood green because it is arcane and redolent of anarchy.

Hosted by Bishop Waynflete and President Mayhew at Magdalen College, my royal cousins had already spent a morning at the University Great Hall and were thoroughly soused in moral and natural philosophy when I joined them for dinner. I suggested we should go hunting in the afternoon but no, it was receptions at the other colleges, huzzahs from students with knobbed complexions and hand-kissing by shabby scholars unearthed from their library burrows. All very lofty. Mind, I have to acknowledge that my cousin is very well read and of course this monkish community adored his no-whoring-or-doing-anything-to-excess streak.

Each to his own. Lincoln, Surrey and I thieved some of the student gowns and slunk off into the city after supper. But the tavern ale did not lighten my spirits. I discovered from young Lincoln that Sasiola, the cloying ambassador from Isabella of Castile, was thick with my cousin, and there could be an alliance in the offing. Definitely time to dislodge the foreigner and request a private audience with Richard in Mayhew's parlour.

Once we had got rid of pleasantries, I came to the crux: how soon would the betrothal between his son and my daughter take place? I saw with dismay how his eyes grew troubled. Around us it was as if the books and papers fell silent in embarrassment. Even Loyaulté, belly-up at my bootcaps, sensed the sudden unpleasantness between us and removed himself to the hearth. A pox on Sasiola! I hoped his balls shrivelled!

'Circumstances have changed by a mile, Harry. I am genuinely sorry to cast cold water on your earlier proposal but you surely can understand that as our future king, the Prince of Wales, must marry a foreign princess and cement an alliance that will keep the realm secure. Besides he is only nine years old and you surely remember your own reluctance to be made handfast at so tender an age. What about Northumberland's son for your Bess and...' Cement an alliance! A murrain on that! He could take all the posts he had given me and ram them up his arse! I did not listen to the rest of his excuses. *He had promised*!

Could the fool not see that the betrothal would content my vaunting ambition? My child as queen. Had he learned nothing from Warwick the Kingmaker's rebellion? By Jesu, just some vague promise might have saved my sanity. I left the room as soon as I could.

'Hang about, Harry!' At the sound of his voice behind me, my heart lifted but he had not changed his mind. 'Anne and I are going to take the dog for an evening stroll along the millstream. Pray you, accompany us.'

I had to stow my temper.

An evening stroll? We had half the plaguey college and most of the retinue trailing behind us and it was only when we lingered afterwards on the freshly-scythed grass of the quadrangle that they drifted away and afforded us some privacy.

Richard, still sensitive to my hurt, busied himself throwing a stick for Loyaulté but Anne had been trying to fathom the reason for my rare silence.

'Are you truly sure you will not come with us to York, Harry?' she asked.

'There will be good hunting,' promised Richard, resisting the urge to wipe his sticky glove on his haunch. He made a sheepish face at me across her wired veil.

I admit I was still sulking. Pah, let him go swagger in front of his son and the northerners.

'Harry? No, listen.' He knuckled me in the chest and looked up at me as though I was a troublesome stripling. 'Do not take the quarrel between us so personally. I am a public creature now. I cannot let my selfish desire dictate policy.'

'Forget the matter,' I muttered, looking beyond him. The marriage between our children would have joined the Houses of York and Lancaster. Could he not see that?

'I need you, my friend.' Another gentle buffet. Ah, so appeasement was definitely on the agenda. He gestured to the building surrounding us. 'Look at what we can do.'

'What do you mean?' I asked, making a sullen art of being obtuse.

'Open your eyes.'

There was still some wooden scaffolding along one side of the cloister, but the waning sun had ripened the fresh wall of the Great Hall behind us to the hue of saffron and conjured the window glass to blazing buckles and jewelled pins. It lit my cousin's face as he turned to me and he seemed to burn within as if his soul was reflecting back the fire of the sunset.

'Think of all that can be done, must be done, to make England a just and fair land to dwell in. We can achieve so much, you and I. With lords like you and Jock behind me, there is no limit to the possibilities. I ask you, cousin, how do men remember King Edward the Confessor?'

I groaned inwardly; the schoolmaster was back. 'Banishing birds for disturbing his contemplations?'

'Try again.'

'The abbey at Westminster?'

'Exactly! Every night, Harry, I pray to God that men shall look back on my reign as a golden age. An age not just of good laws and justice but of beauty such as this.' Another flourish of sleeve at the architecture. 'By such as this shall men shall remember us.'

It was impossible to face down his dreams with huffs and sullens. He had clasped his queen's hand and now swung her arm playfully. 'Anne has decided to continue Elizabeth's patronage of Queen's College at Cambridge and I want to see King's Chapel finished. It shall be one of the most magnificent buildings in Christendom.'

'*Cambridge!*' I scolded, crossing myself in mock fear. 'I hope none of these doctors and demies overheard that heresy.'

Anne prodded a finger into the pleats of my doublet above my heart. 'Perhaps you should think about endowing a college, Harry.'

'A university at Brecknock,' I countered with a Welsh lilt. They could have a course on rearing godly sheep and writing poetry that was not about phalluses. Aloud I said, 'I heard that an estimate of a good reign is whether a man can leave a bag of gold hanging upon a tree for a day and a night, and return to find it untouched.'

'Or, better still, a woman can walk from Cornwall to Carlisle without fear of assault,' declared Anne.

'Indeed? Not even a tumble?' I teased her.

But Richard was too serious for my wit. 'My brother was a fool to underestimate the gold in you, Harry. He mistook you for base metal when you have such ability, such energy.'

Thank you for disclosing what Dead Ned truly thought, Richard! That's shaken my self-esteem again no end.

'Holy Paul, I thank God you had the stomach to come to me at Northampton else England shall not see what we three may yet achieve, eh Anne?'

And yet you would not unite your house with mine!

Oh Richard, Richard, Richard, what fools we were, what fools we were.

*

Boring Brecknock! Although I was now the most powerful nobleman in England, riding back into the town, I found no exuberant welcome for me such as Richard would receive from York. Naught but a formal little reception, an exchange of news; yes, some acknowledgment that I now was overlord of Wales but not a skerrick of enthusiasm, no 'Well done, my lord!'

At least Uncle Knyvett, bless him, was waiting in the bailey in front of the assembled household to offer me a mazer of wine. He had arrived direct from London ten days ahead of me.

'Did you enjoy the royal progress, your grace,' he asked in formal greeting, dapper in his London doublet of mulberry velvet.

'Yes, indeed, I met with the King and Queen at Oxford and then we ambled to Gloucester where we parted. God's truth, it was like a jolly pilgrimage after the stink and strain of London.' Apart from the hunting at Woodstock, it had been tedious. 'How was your journey?'

'Nothing remarkable, your grace.' Then he lowered his voice. 'Apart from my Lady Beaufort's retinue passing us on the road. Her ladyship was right disappointed that you were on a different road and then she insisted on having a few words with Morton. I could not very well say her nay, could I? I hope I did naught wrong in that, Harry.'

'Of course not.' I flung an arm about him and my officers fell in behind us as we walked towards the steps. 'But otherwise no trouble with our prisoner?' I glanced up at the keep wondering whether Morton was watching me through an arrow-slit. 'The worthy doctors of Oxford begged me earnestly to have a care of him.'

'No, her grace your duchess has seen him well bestowed.'

Oh, I swear she had.

Cat looked as lively as Lot's wife as I mounted the outside steps to greet her at the door of the Great Hall.

'Ah, such a pleasure to be home.'

'How many loans did that cost you?' she sneered at my scarlet cote as I strode into the solar with our little girls in my arms and Ned tugging for attention on my hanging sleeve.

'My dear, if anything gave delight to the Lombards, it was the bill for the cartload of damasks and Italian velvets that you have yet to peruse. I hope your fingers are not sticky, Ned.' Across his neat head, my wife's Woodville eyes still wished me to the Devil but the acquisitive greed in her was fully stoked.

'My lord father,' whined my son. 'Why were we not allowed to come to the coronation?'

I stooped so I was eye to eye with him. 'Ned, how could I send for you when the King's own son was absent?'

Around us, my household knights muttered approval at my reply.

Cat's expression was evil. 'Your pardon, my lord, I am confused. Whose absent son are we talking about? The usurper's brat? *Or the king's son you should have crowned?*'

13

'The only ruddy thing that has happened here since we left is a substantial increase in the numbers of fleas,' grumbled Pershall as he unpacked. Cat had deliberately let my apartments accumulate a summer of dust. One only had to stamp on the floor and a score of eager blood-suckers hopped out from the rushes. 'Do you wish me to see if I can rustle up those twins, my lord? You haven't had your leg over any wench since she-who-is-virtuous, an' I think it's puttin' you in the dumps. It ain't natural. A hearty bit of fornication—' He thrust his hips forward.

'Hold your tongue, Pershall.' But he was right to warn me.

Within a few days I was back down at the bottom of the well of misery. Soon I should be thirty years old and it felt like I had never left Brecknock. God knows, I had plenty to occupy me; dispatches from here, there and everywhere, including a letter from Richard still fussing about whether I truly understood his view that his son should marry a foreigner and hinting it might be worthwhile writing thank you *et cetera* to various worthies in Oxford. Ha, perish the thought, your highness, and there I was going to tell the deans in my own hand that their wittering made me spew. My cousin may be almost thirty-one going on a hundred but how old does he reckon me?

I was never idle. My responsibilities as Justiciar for Wales were a distraction and, of course, local matters. I had two of the Vaughans' ruffians hanged. (I'll swear they were behind the burning of my second largest barn in Newport but we could only get witnesses against them for sheep-stealing.) I also rode around my demesne with my officers to estimate the harvest and the work of my bondsmen in my absence, and I was not particularly happy with the way I found things. Thieving Welsh! Some might say I dispensed justice with a heavy hand.

I swear many of my dull-witted tenants barely knew that there had been another change of monarch let alone that I had become the most powerful man in England save for the King. All that they could mumble at me was about the hot sun scorching the grain and a murrain that was laming the cattle and giving them sores about the mouth.

Isolde Martyn

And in the evenings? Ah, the evenings. Such amiable repasts in the great hall with Catherine sitting next to me like a wooden funeral effigy! No, I lie. She wasn't inanimate. Woodville waves of scorn constantly lashed my averted profile.

'I don't care if you are now High Constable of England and can piss on Wales from a great height,' she had hissed at me as we took our places at the board on my first day at home, 'all I can see before me, my lord, is the usurper's arse-wiper.'

VISITING Morton became like a breath of Westminster. If it had not been for his presence, I might have thought the kingmaking had been just voices in my head.

The first time I went up to the keep, I found him sitting on a settle in a narrow patch of sunlight, peering over a manuscript from my personal library.

'Who authorized this?' I demanded curtly, jerking my head round to chide Bannaster.

'Lady Catherine.' Morton lowered the book. 'How pleasant of you to call, Buckingham. Enjoying Wales again, are you?' I ignored the jibe. I was inspecting the room. It had been whitewashed and there were new bedhangings. Cat's meddling again. A fire burned in the grate and the vase of meadow flowers that stood on the window embrasure looked like my daughter's gift. So hardly a prison, save for the window slit, the naked flagstones and the locked door.

'Such idleness and luxury,' observed Morton facetiously, as though he could plumb my thoughts.

I bent down to brush a streak of mud from the Spanish leather of my boot. 'Prisoners are not supposed to enjoy their captivity. Word gets out, even from Wales.'

'I think you are wise, my son, for I have a good memory for faces. It is quite possible that the flaxen-haired groom with the slashmark on his forehead who you took from Lord Hastings' household reports to Catesby still, and I am wondering if your swordmaster from Bedford is in Ratcliffe's pay, and as for her grace's hurdy-gurdy player...'

'The hurdy-gurdy player!'

216

'There was an excellent little entertainment beneath my window. The fellow has such a memorable nose. I would swear by our Holy Church that he was once in Lord Howard's employ but I doubt he serves two masters since your wife pays him so royally. No, let us forget the hurdy-gurdy player. But it would seem that our new King's friends like to keep themselves informed of each other's activities '

I smiled but I was not amused. The fat old devil was trying to tuck burrs of jealousy beneath my girths.

I strode to the arrow-slit. The poppies drooped like penitents' heads among the wilting scabious. My summer was fading too and I felt misery swirling round me like a vengeful miasma. 'Have you given thought to your future yet, Morton? You've changed your coat often enough.'

The pectoral cross, heaving on the broad, cassocked chest, rose with a sigh.

'It would be foolish to lie to you for I'm sure your grace would not believe me, but if the world had gone as I would have wished, Edward of Lancaster,' he crossed himself in memory of the dead, 'should have had the crown and not Edward of York. But only a madman would fight for the dead against the living.' He closed the book, his blue eyes distant as he nodded wistfully. 'Yet I was a loyal servant to King Edward and would have been so to his son but God's will be done. Yet as for my Lord Protector who is now king...' He broke off and looked up at me with resignation. 'I have already meddled too much in the affairs of the world and I think it is God's Will that I now meddle with beads and books and no further.'

'Bishop,' I smiled, leaning back against the wall. 'We are not overheard. Why do you think I made myself your gaoler? I am most interested in your point of view and I can assure you that no harm will come of speaking your mind to me.'

Morton folded his hands upon his paunch. 'I know full well that it is dangerous to talk about princes since innocent words can easily be misconstrued.' He lifted a finger to staunch my protest. 'Surely your grace remembers *Aesop's Fables* from your nursery days? *The Lion and the Horned Beast?*'

'What of it?'

'Remember how the lion, who was king of the wild wood, proclaimed that no beast which bore a horn upon his brow should remain in the wood on sentence of death. One creature with a weird cluster of flesh upon his forehead

217

began to run away and a fox called out after him: "Where are you going in such a pother?"

The creature made answer, "I must leave the wood. I am fleeing because of the proclamation."

"Pah, you addlepate!" exclaimed the fox. "The lion meant horned creatures. That does not include you.'

"Yes, I know this bunch of flesh is not a horn," replied the beast, "but what if the lion should decide it is a horn, where am I then?"'

'My lord bishop,' I assured him, grinning. 'I promise neither the lion *nor the boar* shall hear any of the words you speak in Brecknock.' The boar was Richard's badge.

He nodded. 'If I said what I truly thought, my innocent words would do *neither of us* much good.' Interesting.

I went to the door. 'Well, since I cannot press you...' but he had risen and moved over to the fire place, flexing his clasped fingers. His back was turned to me but still I hesitated to leave.

'Buckingham,' he said at last, 'with regard to the Lord Protector, since he is now made king, I do not purpose to dispute his title, but as for the well-being of the realm of which he has the governing and of which I am but one poor member...'

'Go on, bishop,' I said coldly. 'You are talking of the king I have made.'

'I was only going to say that although he has so many admirable qualities, it might have pleased God to have given him some of those other virtues necessary for the ruling of the realm such as Our Lord has planted in the person of *your grace* !'

He turned and his smile was broad as a cathedral door.

***

I LEFT him alone again for another few days until I could bear it no longer. From then on I began to visit him daily. Sometimes we talked about books or hunting; other times, when the conversation slewed around to something more dangerous, it was like dancing with a shadow. Morton was the master of circumlocution. Phrase built upon phrase so skilfully that it was hard to find the cornerstone of truth, let alone purpose. But each day he grew bolder. At first when he spoke of Dead Ned, it was with respect. But gradually, drawing a fine line dextrously between comment and calumny, he shook out the tales surrounding Dead Ned, George and Richard: how King Harry of Lancaster had died so conveniently of 'melancholy' in the Tower after hearing that his son had been slain by the Yorkist brothers, how Lady Oxford had found herself impoverished after his grace of Gloucester's dealings with her, and how, after George's execution, his lands had all fallen into the hands of his brother Richard. Scandals, executions and slayings—including those of my grandfathers and my Beaufort kinsmen—all mentioned with a shrug, a world-weary smile or a sudden lift of eyebrow.

Yes, I began to see more and more how the House of York had scythed the Houses of Lancaster, Beaufort and Stafford. Events that had been distant to me as a child, I could now understand as a man. Of course, Morton was trying to draw me back to my family's traditional loyalty but he constantly sang a counter tenor of rather agreeable flattery in descant to the plainsong gossip. Eventually I put an end to the game and asked him outright whether he would support me, the heir of the House of Lancaster, as claimant to the throne.

He beamed at me as though I had just been on the road to Damascus.

'My lord, I have been waiting on this day. God be praised that he has given you both courage and wisdom.' From the purse on his belt, he flourished a small sealed square of paper. 'I have had in my keeping this letter from Lady Margaret. Read it at your leisure, my son, and you shall see that since last you spoke with her, she has been praying that our Lord God might bless you with enlightenment.'

I took it without smiling and dropped it into the slit of my hanging sleeve.

'It would be a very dangerous gamble, bishop. Let us be frank here. I do not have the King's military experience if I have to meet him on the field.'

'My gracious lord, I assure you if you were to raise your banner, you would find friends aplenty. Not only has this tyrant lost the common people's trust, but he has remorselessly made enemies of those who loyally served his brother.'

But so had I. Yes, certainly, several score of Hastings' men now wore my livery, but it would take some mighty laundering to wash me white as snow again.

'Strange isn't it,' I remarked. 'I paid my cousin homage at his coronation and pledged him fealty, yet you counsel me to perjury and treason. In
your book, it looks as though an oath doesn't amount to much and I find that
a rather unsettling thought. Just suppose I risk my neck and raise a rebellion,
succeed even, how do I know that Tudor and Pembroke won't break their
oaths to me at some opportune moment.'

'Your grace, it is—'

'No, let me finish, Morton. You can play the serpent to my Adam for
all your worth, seduce me from my alliance with Richard, but the worst that
could befall you is exile or being booted back into the Tower whereas I....'

'My lord duke, if you are leading a cause that is both true and just,
God will protect you.' He grasped the velvet epaulettes on my shoulders and
peered into my face so close I could smell the perfumed comfits he liked to
suck. 'Seek out a mirror, my lord. Can you not discern how much you have
changed since King Edward's death? The realm needs your vision and guid-
ance. You are the heir of the House of Lancaster and the blood of the victor
of Agincourt flows in your veins seeking vengeance and justice.' He shook
me gently before he let go. 'I promise you Almighty God will give you the
courage, Harry.'

I stood staring down at him. There was a seriousness in his face that I
had never glimpsed before. Even compassion. He reached up and thumbed
an invisible cross upon my forehead. 'May your soul find light in the darkness
that surrounds you. Be at peace, my son.'

I swallowed and stepped back. How did he know? But before I reached
the door to flee that penetrating scrutiny, he called out to me. I turned round
with the greatest reluctance and saw his fingers were tightly clasping his cross
above his heart.

'If you decide this cup is not for you, my son, I swear by the Blessed
Christ that Lady Margaret and I will accept your decision and not a word
of our conversations here will go beyond these walls.' As I nodded gravely,
he added, 'But all I ask is that you think hard but not long, my lord. If this
enterprise is to take place, there is no time to fritter.'

I had to show that I was not lightly led. All men have their price. For
the last ten years Morton had enjoyed high office under Yorkist rule.

'I suppose a cardinal's hat would suit you, Morton?'

'Your grace, I think it would suit me very well.'

MY LUST to prove myself further warred mightily with my fear of failure and vanquished sleep. In the morning I was still hesitant in yoking myself to the Tudor arms wagon, but Morton conjured up more weaponry. This time it was missives from acquaintances across the Channel: Archbishop Angelo Cato, physician to King Louis; Adam Redesheff, a scholar at Louvain and Giovanni de Giglis in Rome, each reviling Richard as a child murderer. Pah, what of it? The foreign courts tittle-tattled like whores waiting for takers. Maybe I was a fool to listen further, but then my wily prisoner began to speak of redemption. One pebble may not bring a man to his knees but a stoning will and Morton bombarded me.

Why did I agree to play his game at last? Because the Devil inside the ermine wanted to be king; because, above all, restlessness was eating into my skin like leprosy. I no longer felt alive in Brecknock, more like some poor beaten donkey yoked in a treadmill, but every time I thought about becoming king, my imagination flared brightly and the darkness lifted.

THE HOUR after I gave my consent to captain Margaret's rebellion, Morton's prison began to resemble the Chamber of the Privy Seal. The bishop wrote letters like a man obsessed. The tip of his third finger grew swollen where he held the quill against it. The missives–shafted not only at Margaret's allies but also the men who had served Dead Ned–were cunningly worded and I suppose he had already crafted the phrases during his solitude.

I appreciated his haste. By Jesu, a woman with a babe beneath her girdle had more time than us. The rebellion had to take place before Richard returned to Westminster. Less than two months to topple a king.

He applauded the agendum I had facetiously suggested to Margaret. We would raise our banners in Prince Edward's name then give out the boys were dead. Without them, the Woodville affinity would be crazed and hot to follow us.

It was not easy doing the webspinning from Brecknock but much had already been done by Margaret. Now she wasted no time but straightaway sent her receiver, Reginald Bray, a blunt-spoken man who had worked for my uncle, to visit us at Brecknock. I told him my terms to carry to Henry Tudor.

Meantime, I dispatched Nandik with a letter to John Russhe, my merchant friend, who replied that he would sound out his wealthy acquaintances. Cat wrote to Elizabeth of my miraculous conversion to the Woodville cause, and Nick Latimer, who had ever been loyal at heart to Lancaster, visited his native Dorset and found friends there who would uphold our enterprise.

Since I held so many offices, neither the increase in couriers nor the commissions given to blacksmiths, armourers, fletchers and lorimers roused any suspicions. I sent my servants to make purchases at the horse fairs and every day I practised a full hour at single combat.

The rebellion, like a bear cub, was gradually licked into shape. Bray returned from Brittany with the news that Edward Woodville had yielded the treasury money to Henry Tudor so he now could buy mercenaries, and on 24 September I received a letter from Tudor giving me his sworn word that he would land at Poole Harbour in mid-October. I wrote back that day.

Other reassuring news trickled in: Morton's friends, the Brandons and the Cheneys agreed to fight for me and Russhe wrote that many of the London merchants considered I should make a worthy king. It only remained for Elizabeth Woodville to commit her followers. Without them we did not have the numbers.

It was because of me that Elizabeth baulked. That stubborn she-devil wanted to do her own scheming. News reached us that fifty of her friends had made a fresh attempt to rescue the boys from the Tower and Howard now had the conspirators under arrest. Of course, when we heard that, we renewed our assault on her. Tudor's youngest uncle was a monk at Westminster, so Morton wrote to him begging him to intercede with Elizabeth, and Margaret's physician, Dr Lewes, made another visit to the sanctuary. I confess by now I was growing edgy. The sand of the glass was starting to run out.

Finally Elizabeth gave an ultimatum. She requested proof of my change of heart: firstly, that I must sign a warrant for the day of the rising giving her servants safe passes in and out of the Tower. Secondly, I was required to write a letter to the Lieutenant of the Tower ordering him to release her sons. If I refused to supply either, she would take it as proof of my treachery and forbid all the Woodville loyalists in the southern shires to join us.

I knew the boys were not there so as High Constable of England I willingly signed the authority and gave the documents to Bray to deliver to Dr Lewes.

My compliance won her over. Within two weeks, families related to the Woodvilles, such as the Guildfords and the Lewkenors, not to mention Richard's forgiven sinner, Sir John Fogge, promised support. The Marquis of

Dorset was still at large and he went from friend to friend with news of the rebellion. In the west, Cat's brother, the Bishop of Salisbury, who was still being pursued by the King's officers, wrote to me that he hoped the St Legers, Courtenays and Bourchiers would join the rising. I promised him refuge at Kimbolton. Thence he fled and my cousin's soldiers never thought to look for him on my land.

Morton wrote both to the King of France (reminding him how hungry Richard had been for battle during Dead Ned's invasion of France back in '75), and to his Holiness Pope Sixtus IV, promising more contribution to the papal coffers once King Richard was deposed.

Do not think I did not have doubts. Sometimes I would dream that I was fighting Richard again in the practice yard and wake up sweating and fearful with his blade at my throat.

'Are you sure that Lady Margaret is not using you?' asked Uncle Knyvett, when I first discussed my plans with him. 'I can't see she would want you as king if there's a chance in friggin' hell she could become queen-mother.'

'She needs a captain for her army before her son lands. I'm supposed to be overcome with shame for my sins and anxious to depose the tyrant.'

'You do realise you are risking everything you've gained.'

'Well I am not, am I? If things go awry, I shall pretend I was stringing them along to lure Tudor home. But if everything shapes up, I shall be king and you can be Chamberlain of England.'

'I haven't the rank.'

'You will if I make you a baron.'

He chuckled. 'I've the greatest respect for Lady Margaret but yonder bishop...'

'He's my hostage for Margaret's compliance.'

'Aye, but in peril his cloth will save him. Nothing will save you unless you've become a closet Franciscan since I last saw you.' He plucked at my collar lacing. 'No hair shirt? I thought not.' He was right to warn me. Fire burns when you meddle with it.

'I am not a fool. I read every one of the letters that Morton sent out.'

'No code words saying: "Huzzah, we've gulled Buckingham"?'

'God's Sake, give me some slack, uncle.' The trouble was that he voiced my own fears. 'My claim to the throne is better than Tudor's. What's more

I'll marry my little Bess to Richard's boy. Hell take it, I could even put Edward V back and marry her to him. Tudor can have his earldom back and he'll be happy with that.'

'And what about Jasper Tudor, who styles himself Earl of Pembroke? What about Stanley? They will want power in Wales.'

'If I secure the crown, they can stuff Wales up their arses.'

He pulled a face.

'Not a blow was struck at Stony Stratford and yet we gained a kingdom, see,' I exclaimed in the local dialect. He did not laugh.

'But this time, Harry, Richard of Gloucester will be your enemy.'

PEPPERED with Woodvilles and buttered with Beaufort money, the date of the rebellion was fixed for 18 October and there was to be a rising on that day throughout the south. My only fear was that so great a number—and we are talking about a conspiracy stretching from Maidstone to Exeter—could keep so great a secret. My anxiety turned out to be better founded than the rebellion: before September was out, I received a letter from Richard, saying that Howard had heard all manner of wild tales and that some of them implicated me. My cousin suggested that I should meet him in the Midlands on his return from York so we could demonstrate that this talk of rebellion was idle nonsense.

I took his letter with me to the little private garden that I had made within my castle walls and set Bannaster on guard outside the gate to preserve my solitude.

I had planted the garden some years before. Like the great sightless ridge of Pen-y-Fan, it gave me solace. I sat down upon the turf seat and stared about me. It was well tended now but when I had returned in August, milkweeds had stood high between the clumps of lavender, and ivy had crawled amok among the speckled musk and orange marigolds.

I sighed and idly tugged a sowthistle out from here, a dent-de-lion from there. Out in the fields harebells and eyebrights, purple mallows and the white sprays of fool's parsley flowered at no man's bidding, while within my little kingdom the dead petals already clung to the spent daisyheads and the best was over.

Desperate, I thought of Meg. I clothed her before me in a robe of lustrous green satin and fastened about her neck a collar of jewels that matched her eyes and upon her head I set a duchess's diadem. 'Be mistress to a king,' I whispered but before I could bare her shoulders and worship her breasts with my lips, she faded. Burning against my fingers, I felt the parchment of my cousin's letter.

It was in his neat hand and I let my eye trace once more the familiar signature. It was not too late to ride to him with my list of traitors save that I knew my new allies were keeping close watch on me for signs of second thoughts. I buried my head in my hands and wished that the world would heave me off its back.

The rustle of damask disturbed me. For an instant of madness, I believed that Meg had come to me, warm and desirable. But when I raised my head from my clasped knees, it was to recognise the straight folds that fell from the girdle of my wife's gown; threads that elderberry and catkin, blackberry and medlar could bewitch into subtle colours danced before my eyes. I turned my face away to hide from her my tears.

I heard her pick up Richard's letter from where it had fallen at my feet.

'You have not answered him.'

'No, I cannot. Not yet.'

'Don't be a damnable fool! You must reply. Nothing else will content him. Say you are sick and cannot come.' She watched me haul myself to my feet. 'You must right the wrong you have done and free my nephew, the rightful king.'

Rightful king? She had forgotten that the boys' father stole the crown.

14

You think, Saints of Heaven, that I should have kept faith with my cousin Richard, but you are not sealed within my skin. The Plantagenet blood does not congeal in the sores of the dying; it is passed on with the ambition that made our first great-sire a king. That is why we rebel; Henry II and his restless prodigy, Bolingbroke, Prince Hal, Humphrey of Gloucester and Richard of York. We are all kickers against the rut. Even that pious, monkish Henry VI was as perverse as the rest. Being born a king, he did not desire to be one. As for Edward, George and Richard? Just like the rest! Contrary, wilful, we are never content with our rank at birth but need must fight with teeth and claws to swing our fortunes up a notch. And now? And now, Richard, being king, is not truly happy for he has betrayed his brother's trust and his subjects will never live up to his ideal world. And I, rich in offices and lands, must fulfil my destiny.

BY THE EVE of the day appointed for my army to march from Brecknock, I had over four hundred footsoldiers, including twenty-five Russhe had brought from London (I had expected more but others were pledged to join the Kentish rebels), fifty mounted knights and eleven arms-and-supply wagons. Several hundred archers and halberdiers were to meet us at Hereford and I could rely on a hundred more from my manors across the River Severn to come to my banner once we reached England. Together with the Woodville affinity and Tudor's mercenaries, we should be an army fit to hold off an impassioned and unprepared Richard while the Cheshire men of Margaret Beaufort and her Lancaster adherents closed in on him from the north.

I DID not like the temper of my army. The harvest had arrived late and the men had been loath to leave the binding of the sheaves to the women. Only bribes had drawn them away from the prospect of the harvest home, the corn dolls and the ale.

My other anxiety was the weather on the morrow; louring clouds bruised the sky above Pen-y-Fan. Water cascading from the mountains had swollen the bellies of the streams. Already, the roads streaking out from Brecknock were too syrupy for my peace of mind.

'What do you think, Nick?' I stared at my precious guns that had been delivered in great secrecy earlier in the week. Latimer, standing alongside me in the barn, heaved a deep sigh and pulled the canvas down to conceal them.

'I reckon they're too heavy for the road as it is, my lord, let alone if there's more rain blowing up. We can have them follow us as soon as maybe, but it will mean leaving two dozen men behind to manage them. Shall I see to it?'

I nodded. 'A cursed shame.' I could take the risk but if the carts sunk in to their axles, digging them out would be Herculean, and they were worth a fortune.

Ah, misgivings! They skittered across my mind, gnawing at my fear. Still, if aught went wrong, I should be able to talk my way out of the mess.

'What did your astrology chart foretell for October?' I asked Nandik, summoning him to my chamber that evening. He seemed surprised at my renewed interest.

'By my very soul, the death of a king, your grace.'

'All very well, Nandik,' I answered, trying not to wince at his pied hose. 'But how precise are your calculations? I am told King Louis no longer enjoys good health. The planets may be predicting a new occupant for a tomb at St Denis.'

He grinned. 'Oh no, your grace, definitely England.'

I never knew with Nandik how much was buttering and how much truth but I believed him. It is well, I reflected, as the door closed behind him. No man, not even a king, can withstand his destiny.

THE WAY seemed clear as we left Brecknock: straight east to Hereford. No piddling villagers would question the purpose of the High Constable of England. The only difficulty would be the crossing of the river Severn because the bridges were few.

My cheeks were still moist from my little daughters' kisses but I had Ned and his nursemaid with us so no one could use him as a hostage against me. My little lad was full of questions as he rode with Uncle Knyvett. God willing, I though, you will be Prince of Wales before by the Feast of All Saints in November.

But then the rain began. The Black Mountains, visored by low clouds, disappeared from sight in less than an hour and the golden leaves and vibrant coverlets of the fields shed all hue as though some apprentice launderer had boiled the vat. Our world shrank from a beauteous, broad valley to a grey passage walled by thickets spiky as the Blessed Christ's crown of thorns, and beyond that a nothingness. Many of the Welshmen grew fearful, crossing themselves and muttering to St Alud for her protection lest the Wild Hunt hurtle out of the fog.

When my horse stumbled in a rut outside of Bronllys, and the cursed rhymer in our company conjured the incident into a portent, I halted the column in the red mud. Devil take it! If I could address parliament, I could surely deal with a host of superstitious fools.

'Good Friends and Comrades-in-arms, remember the story of how William the Bastard stumbled as he landed on the beach at Pevensey. Did his cause fail? No, he became King of England. Friends, use your wits. If a man is doomed to misfortune every time his horse slips on this shit of a road then this realm will be a country of beggars.'

I looked down the column of pikes and halberds, wondering whether it would have been quicker to have hanged the rhymer on the nearest elm rather than give these louts a history lesson. Half of them were swineherds and delvers with brains as small as walnuts. Oh well.

'I promise you this,' I exclaimed. 'There are rewards to be had. Knighthoods and riches for those who march with me this day. I cannot change the weather, good friends, but I can change your fortunes.'

My captains cheered and then every man was huzzahing.

'And now,' I roared, 'for Sweet Christ's Sake, let us get out of this stinking mud and get to England as fast as we may. Forward!'

We made camp that night towards Glasbury. It was a mistake; we all rose damp and short of temper to pack up in the pouring rain. In fine weather, we should have reached Hereford in a couple of days; now we would be lucky to manage ten miles a day. Brooks that pissed little in summer were now full-bladdered. But there was other mischief afoot: saddle girths broke, tethered barrels rolled mysteriously from their canvas moorings, and a wheel came off one of the hindmost carts. Had we brought the guns, the mud would have sucked them down like a monstrous incubus.

Just past Glasbury, Limerick informed me that the wagon with the mended wheel had not caught up with us and that some of the men were missing. Well, in such conditions, I was not surprised but Morton snuffled up that little morsel.

'Desertion?' he suggested, edging his horse up beside mine. Foolish man! It was not helpful and he had those around me glancing at one another uneasily.

I was not in the best of tempers. Heavy gobs of water were splashing down my helm, spilling onto my sodden cloak, seeping down beneath my collar.

'I thought you and God were allies, Bishop Morton. Perhaps you'd have a polite word with Him about improving the weather.'

Behind the waterfall trimming his broad-brimmed hat, his expression was most discomforted. 'What I am praying for, Buckingham, is a good dinner and clean, dry sheets but I daresay that is not in the offing.'

'Why not?' I retorted with mock cheer. 'Perhaps we should halt and offer prayers, my lord.' I flung up my arm and the entire army rattled to a standstill. For once the old rascal was caught off guard. He should have thanked me for it; few men can surprise John Morton with a fresh experience.

'I hardly think the men will be in a reverent frame of mind, your grace,' he countered, and sighed in relief as we resumed the march.

My wretched soldiers, pathetic as soaked sheep in their dripping brigandines, tramped until twilight with the mud fastening round their ankles like manacles at every step. By the time we reached Hay, they were glad to disperse among the cottages for warmth. I put up at *The Three Tuns*. The landlord was so fulsome in his praise of our new king that we had to tell him that our army was for Richard's invasion of France.

It was still pelting hard next morning and we were all saddled up ready to move off when the cry of 'Messenger!' went up. I expected to behold the horseman approaching from the east but he had come from behind us, an old man who had been left behind to serve the garrison at Brecknock. I noticed with an icy feeling in my guts that he rode Cat's mare.

'God save your grace,' he gasped, dismounting and stumbled over to clutch my stirrup. Those closest saw the spreading bruise upon his forehead.

His message spewed out like vomit and I hauled him into the inn before his tidings infected every Jack in my company: tidings that Vaughan of Tretower, the fornicating bastard, was bombarding my castle with can-nonballs. What's more, the rogue had sent a company after us to pick off the stragglers. It was only when they were attacking the poor devils mending the wagon that the old messenger had managed to skirt around them and get through to warn us.

'My guns!' I exclaimed, sinking on to a settle in utter shock. 'The whoreson is using *my guns.*'

'Do you want to send back a detachment?' asked Delabere but I felt Morton's cynical gaze upon me.

'No!' I answered. Cat was capable when she roused herself. I could trust her to take care of our children, the rent rolls and all the fine possessions I had brought from London. 'No going back, we have greater matters ahead.'

'I do not like the smell of this, Harry,' whispered Uncle Knyvett, catch-ing up with me outside. 'Are you sure we should not return to Brecknock while it's still standing.'

'You think we could hot foot it there in time in this deluge?' I an-swered. 'No, I do not think so, but what you can do, uncle, is take some of our best horsemen and slit the throats of any of Vaughan's curs who are fol-lowing us and round up any stragglers. We'll wait for you at the bridge in Bredwardine.'

Uncle Knyvett is so blessedly efficient. His lads rejoined us long be-fore we crossed the Wye boasting their swords had enjoyed a brisk but ef-ficient excursion. Of course, some decent action was what the rest of my army expected. However, a respite from the pelting rain might suffice so we crammed into the church of St Andrew, adding crosses of holy water to our dripping foreheads.

The parish priest nearly had an apoplexy at the sight of armed men leaning against his font and sullying the floor tiles but when he realised we had a bishop snug among our breastplates, he began to wag his tail. So while he drooled over Morton's ringfinger, I knelt in the gloom with Ned beside me and stared up with humility at the poor tormented face of crucified Christ frozen in perpetual agony on the Rood Screen.

Silently, I pledged a college, two colleges. By Heaven, I would found a blessed monastery, find some fledgling St Benedict to play the abbot, go on crusade! I'd do anything if only the sun would dry the roads. But Christ still looked agonised. All I heard in reply was the endless, endless rain spewing from the gargoyles.

Ned was awed and silent beside me. Brave little fellow. Away from his mother's cloying care, he never whined at all but now he was shifting from knee to knee.

'I need to go and pee,' he whispered, pulling at my cloak, and then, shamefaced, he muttered, 'Well, actually more than that.'

I rose and took his little hand, which was cold as a toad. The men managed smiles for us as we walked out through them. We found his blushing nursemaid in the porch walled in by Delabere's arms in earnest conversation but she instantly slid back into her duty and hurried Ned off to do his business outside the churchyard wall.

'So, is she willing to grant you her favours?' I asked Delabere, but instead of serving me his usual banter, he stood beside me like a stranger full of secrets. 'Another Elizabeth Woodville, eh? A betrothal ring or naught?'

'Her reputation is beyond rebuke, my lord.'

What had I said wrong? He had not even looked at me as he spoke. 'Well, it is time to think about leaving. Play sheepdog, Dick, and whistle up our captains!'

Before we remounted, I jested with them, but my shoulders were tense inside my embroidered surcote. I just hoped sunshine was burnishing the kettle helms of the Woodville men of Maidstone and Ightham and a good wind was blowing Tudor's hired sails to Dorset. And, if not, so be it. I'd manage. The cold of the earth might be seeping up through my soles, yet I was like a horse in the shafts of ambition—unable to turn.

We crossed the Wye as it frothed close beneath the timbers of the bridge then we marched northeast to join the Roman road that led direct to Hereford. The highway, though in disrepair, had retained many of its original stones and the ruts were not so deep. However, I began to grow suspicious when we passed no carts or riders journeying from Hereford and then, while the men were struggling to get the carts across Maddle Brook, one of the scouts, sent ahead of us the day before, returned and we took him aside.

No wonder there were no other travellers: one of my distant relations, Humphrey Stafford, curse him, was ahead of us, felling trees across the narrow stretches and setting bowmen ready to shower us with arrows when we tried to clear the route for the arms wagons.

'Then let us avoid the main road,' I exclaimed.

The weary scout shook his head. 'My lord, I cannot advise it. Sir Humphrey has men on every road and lane into Hereford, and the city gates are closed against you. The King has offered a free pardon to any man who deserts your army and a reward of a thousand pounds or one hundred pounds' worth of land to anyone who takes you prisoner.'

'How very flattering.'

Uncle Knyvett gave a low whistle. 'Lord God preserve us! If the King knows what is happening in Wales, then what of the risings in the south?'

Russhe cleared his throat. 'I hate to be a dampener, my lord, but clearly this Vaughan fellow must have been prepared if he was ready to lay siege to Brecknock the moment we were a day's march away.'

I could hardly tell my London friend to bite his tongue. 'Fetch me the map!' I commanded Limerick.

We stood beneath an oak tree but to prevent the ink from blotching, Bannaster and Pershall held a cered canvas above us. Not the splendid coronation canopy I had planned. This was tasselled by dripping rain and gilded with water.

'If Hereford is blocking us, it is useless trying to pass to the south so I reckon our best chance is to go north to Weobley and still make for the bridge at Tewkesbury. We have to reach Dorset before the King's force sweeps down on us.'

Latimer swallowed unhappily: 'Christ forbid he is making better speed than us in this weather, my lord. But what if he is? Do you think we shall have to face him on our own?'

'I wouldn't know. He'll have to send out commissions of array first.' But in my mind, I knew that if he could put heart in his men like his brother used to, he would be upon us before we could draw breath let alone our swords. I looked intently upon each anxious face in the circle about me. 'Good friends, we *have* to keep this army loyal. That is our dilemma for the present. Too many have deserted because of the weather and the news from home, and now if word of this gets around...'

'It will, it will,' put in Uncle Knyvett dismally.

'Pay them,' interrupted the smooth voice of Morton. I do not know how long he had been standing there listening to every word for he had been napping in one of the wagons when we had halted. 'I've been doing a reckoning. Your army is bleeding men.'

'*Our army*, my lord bishop.' I corrected, staring at the map. I did not need this Jonah and I cursed that I had ever heeded him. 'I know what we shall do,' I declared at last and looked around at my captains with a grin. 'What if tonight we sleep at Lord Ferrers' manor house at Wooton Devereux and grab some stock to replace the supplies we have lost? It lies in our path to Weobley and if Lord Ferrers is at home so much the better. We shall seize the house from him. It will restore the men's morale. What say you?' Their nods were heartening. I turned to Limerick. 'Call the men together. I'll announce it now.'

As I strode towards my horse, Morton puffed after me:

'Buckingham, if you give me an escort, maybe I can get a ferryboat across the Severn and warn our friends of our circumstances.'

'No, Morton, we stay together.' He was my safeguard for Margaret Beaufort's compliance.

MY MEN cheered when I promised them a hearty supper, a blazing fire to warm them to bed plus extra wages for the hardships they had endured, and then we took the road north skirting Garnon's Hill.

It was hard going and the light was fading when we finally left the hollow way through the woods. On the rise, an ugly manor house squatted blackly with no warming light behind its windows, but in the field to the west there were sheep aplenty.

'Ah, roast mutton!' I exclaimed loudly. 'Supper may be late but it will be worth waiting for.'

THE ANCIENT caretakers succumbed willingly to half-scabbarded arguments. We seeped past them into the darkening hall but alas the damned place was damp and as miserable as we were. Naked of tapestries, bereft of rushes, the walls were speckled and smelly with mould.

We bawled at Ferrers' servants to kindle the dusty logs in the central hearth or be hanged for their failure. My men peeled off their wet brigandines and the pong of the vinegar they used against lice reeked through the hall. Once the manor's supply of candles was raided, the light and warmth lifted our hearts somewhat, and with the aroma of Devereux mutton to titillate our nostrils, the men wrung their sodden shirts while the manor's steward wrung his hands. We ate hours after nightfall, greedily filling our bellies with the meat, for there was little else to go with it.

Pershall kindled a fire in the solar and there Lizbeth the nursemaid made up a temporary bed for my tired little boy. Ned had been stoic despite the rain and hours in the saddle and I was proud of him.

Morton dozed off by the hearth in the hall and I was relieved not to have his company. Instead, I sat by my slumbering child, wondering where my royal cousin slept that night.

The rain, oh Christ, if only the beat upon the roof would cease,

FOR several days, we lingered at Wootton Devereux. The rain continued without mercy. It was impossible to return across the Wye and word reached us that the Severn River had burst its banks. The chapman, who brought us the news, said that such a flood had not been seen for decades; with awe he told us how he had seen great beasts struggling in midstream and a wooden cradle, with the mewling babe still in it, rocking on the surge amidst the shattered planks of its mother's dwelling.

But this weather could not last forever. I thought of raising my banner and proclaiming myself king once the sun showed its face but the truth was we could do naught until the floodwaters fell. Our opportunity of reaching the south before the day of the rising was gone.

On the morning of 16th October, Delabere and Uncle Knyvett came purposefully into the solar.

'Where's Ned?' I demanded.

'Collecting mushrooms from the sheep pasture. No, calm yourself, Harry. He can discern the toadstools.' A restraining hand fell heavily on my shoulder. Uncle Knyvett wore a grim determination that boded ill. 'I want you to listen to me.' He glanced at his fellow knight for support. 'Delabere and I have been doing some serious talking. You have to admit it's all up with us.'

'Devil's weather!' They were about to spoon some poisonous decision down my throat.

Uncle Knyvett cleared his throat. 'You're a man grown and can shift for yourself, Harry, but the boy is another matter. Delabere's castle at Kinnersley isn't that far from here.'

Isolde Martyn

'You are suggesting we march on to there?'

'No, your grace.' Delabere was swift to disagree. 'I suggest I take your son there, away from his enemies.'

I was completely floored. 'Enemies!' I spluttered. 'What nonsense is this? The King would not let him come to harm.'

'That's just it.' Delabere glanced suspiciously at the closed door before he lowered his voice. 'King Richard would not, I'll warrant you, but there's others as might. If aught goes amiss with King Richard then your son will be a rival to that bastard Tudor.' He saw the pained astonishment in my face. 'I've followed you in everything, my lord, whether I've thought you were right or not but...'

'But this is no place for a child.' Uncle Knyvett stared me down. 'You have to let him go to safety.'

'I endanger my son?' Pain throbbed through every syllable. I turned to the mantle and stared up at Ferrers' greyhound device. Their silence was my answer. 'I see.' It took me a moment to compose myself to face them before I turned. 'You realise if you do this, Dick, it will take the heart out of every man left to me?'

The lack of compassion in his eyes stoned me. 'With your grace's consent, we'll leave early tomorrow before everyone is awake.'

I swallowed, forcing myself to be realistic. 'Kinnersley may be too close. Once the rivers are passable, every bounty hunter in the Marches will be out.'

'My lord, if that is so, we shall disguise Lord Stafford as a little maid and move him further north.'

I wanted to argue. I wanted to keep Ned with me. Instead, I nodded and turned back to the mantle, playing the brisk commander. 'So be it.'

'Harry. *Harry*.' The soft plea forced me to look round. Christ! Only a blindman could have ignored the battle of emotions in my beloved uncle's face.

'You want to go with them, uncle?' I kept my voice calm and reasonable but, Heaven be my witness, I should have liked to break Delabere's teeth for this. Without William Knyvett...

'I do, Harry. I would give my life for the little rascal.'

'But not for me?' I tightened my lips. 'No, I do not blame you, uncle. I would not want my body parts distributed throughout the kingdom either.'

236

Tears tumbled down his cheeks and clogged in his moustache as he flung his arms about me. 'Harry, I care for you, you know that full well!'

I returned his embrace, loving him for his honesty, for he had been like a father to me.

Delabere coughed as though our embrace embarrassed him. 'We shall leave before tomorrow's dawn, your grace.' The fellow seemed to be relishing his chance to give me orders.

'So be it,' I muttered, disentangling from my uncle, and my angry thoughts were like a rosary prayer to Satan.

Damn you, Dick! Damn you! Damn you!

SAYING farewell to Ned that dusk wrung my heart. I found my boy before the hearth playing knucklebones, becoming skilled at it too.

'Ned.' I dropped on one knee to face him. 'Early tomorrow Uncle Knyvett and Sir Richard are going to take you and Mistress Lizbeth somewhere out of the rain.'

He thought about it as he tossed the bones in the air. 'But you are coming with us, sir.'

'No, I must stay with our soldiers and… Ned, it may be a long time before I see you again.' The cracking of my voice made him look up and the game was forgotten. 'So I…I want you to be a brave, good boy and…and be content with all that God gives you in this life and put your trust in Him.'

He frowned and stood up and came to stand before me like an earnest scholar. His hose was wrinkled and there was a potage stain down his jacket, yet my little rogue's cheeks shone wholesomely. 'You do not have to understand what those words mean, Ned, just remember them when you are older.'

'Why?'

'Because I never had a father to give me advice and I would have welcomed it. Say it back to me: "I-must-be-content-with-all-that-God-gives-me-in-this-life."'

I might have been teaching him *amo, amas, amat* but maybe one day he would remember and avoid the envy that had been my lover ever since I could remember.

I hugged him. He permitted it with childish embarrassment. Ah, he felt so tiny. 'Listen, fledgling, Uncle Knyvett is going to wake you before cockcrow and you will have to creep out like a mousekin.'

'Why?'

'Because mice are very quiet and I do not want you to wake everyone.'

'But mice are not quiet, Father. I have often had mice visit my bed-chamber and they make a great noise.'

'Then you must be a *quiet* mouse. And, Ned...'

'Yes, Father.'

'One day you will be head of our family and you must look after your sisters and brothers. Promise me.'

He nodded solemnly and I pulled his cap down over his eyes. 'Little rascal.'

That night after Mistress Lizbeth had tucked him in the truckle bed in Lord Ferrers' bedchamber, I sat beside him and told him of how I would take him fishing in the Usk when we returned to Brecknock and that one day he must help the town to put a tower on their church—a promise I had never fulfilled. I told him that he was a Plantagenet and descended from kings and that he must serve the King of England with a true heart just as his great-grandfathers had.

'I've been thinking, Ned, see this ring of mine.' I tugged off the ring I wore on the little finger of my left hand. 'See, it has "HS" for Harry Stafford. Well, I want it to be a token betwixt us and if ever I send this to you, you must trust the messenger and let him bring you to me.'

He nodded, so busy moving his pillow that I wondered if he had listened, but then he pulled out the little dagger I had given him last Yuletide. It was scarcely longer than a fisherman's bodkin with a bone handle.

'You might need this, Father.'

'No, I—'

'I know you gave it me, sir, but now I'm giving it you.'

'Oh, Ned.' I gathered him once more in my arms, my heart breaking. Soon, I would make him Prince of Wales but for now we had to part.

I LAY that night with Ned in my arms and Lord Ferrers' bed seemed hard as rock to me. Beside us, Uncle Knyvett snored like a bacon pig until Delabere came to rouse him.

I wrapped Ned tight as a case moth and scooped him into my arms and then mutely, mechanically, I followed them down the stairs. Their esquires had the horses ready saddled. Uncle Knyvett took my son from me then he carried my hand to his lips.

'God keep you, Harry.'

15

I watched them walk the horses to the road bearing my son away and then I closed the door and leaned back against it.

Pershall found me later sitting before the unstoked embers of the bedchamber's hearth. There was no longer the usual laughter in his voice as he set a cup of mulled wine before me.

'Your grace, a dozen of the Newport men have left this morning. Downstairs they are asking whether Sir William and Sir Richard are gone too. Would it please you come and speak with them?'

'Good Pershall, tell them I have sent Sir William back to command the Brecknock garrison, and that every man who stays with me shall have a silver penny and double wages when we've crossed the Severn.' I patted his arm in thanks.

He was gone but a minute when Morton's great bulk blocked the door like a magpie stuffed in a chimney. 'Rats jumping ashore, eh, Buckingham?'

'Pardon?' I clambered stiffly to my feet and picked up the jack of wine.

'It seems that your captains are turning lily-livered. What are you going to do, my boy? Grovel before King Dick and plead for a whipping?' I took a swig of wine, watching through narrowed eyes as he waddled in and sank onto the chest that sat at the foot of Ferrers' bed. The coat of arms carved on its lid creaked in protest.

'Undecided, are you, Buckingham? It looks as though it is not just the King but God who is against you.'

It was hard to keep my temper sheathed. 'Against *me*! I find your choice of words very curious.'

'Where's the child?' He had noticed the empty trundle. 'Ah, so it is true that Knyvett has fled with him.'

I glared at Morton's fat face. Not a flicker of pastoral sympathy was there; he looked so unmoved by our circumstances that I wondered if there was actually any rising planned and whether this had all been some monstrous connivance to detach me from Richard. As if he read my thoughts, he flicked them aside with a wave of podgy hand.

'Doesn't it matter to you that we have failed to meet up with our allies?' I blurted out.

He shrugged, his mouth a scythe of diffidence. 'Quite frankly, if King Dick rounds up the Woodville captains and lops off a few heads, no, it doesn't matter. Just so long as he does not snare Henry Tudor. Still, Margaret's lad is not a fool, he'll hoist sail back for Brittany if there's a hint of doubt.'

By Jesu, was he now saying my claim as the last legitimate heir of Lancaster was of no consequence? That I and the Woodvilles were dispensable? Well, I was not finished yet.

'You've been a disappointment, Buckingham, not raising the numbers we hoped for and now this.'

'*This* is not my fault.'

I had risked everything, believing him my ally, and now he sat there like God at my doomsday. By rights, I should have been riding that very hour to claim the throne yet the curl of his lip told me I was a fool and not worthy of respect.

'You Judas!' I snarled, grabbing him by the neck of his vestments. 'You stinking lump! You've dragged me down to your pit of treason. By Heaven, I should have lopped you straight after Hastings!' I punched my thumbs into his windpipe, determined to choke the air out of that cavernous throat. 'Liar, blasphemer! By God, the Jew priest Caiaphas could learn nothing from you.'

Latimer burst in and grabbed hold of me. 'Your grace, desist, I pray you. The men can hear your quarrel.'

Morton's serpent eyes glittered, unchanging. I let him go and he flopped back on the chest, one bloated hand crawling up like an ugly familiar to knead his flesh but still he could not resist aiming a fist of hoarse words to bruise me further.

'"*More is worth a good retreat than a foolish abiding.*"'

'Get out!' I hissed. 'God grant you burst when they coffin you and, by Heaven, I'll spit on your tombstone. Set a guard on him, Nick, under constant watch!' I would keep him as a hostage. If need be, he would be a peace gift to Richard.

A DAY LATER, they told me he had escaped, taking his guards with him. *They?* Limerick, Latimer, Russhe, Pershall and Bannister. The rest of my army had vanished save for a few indecisive fellows who were fearful of Stafford's men.

We gathered together that morning in final council.

'The river is almost passable, my lord, and then it will be open season for the bounty hunters. Should we not separate? At least that way we may save our lives.' It was Russhe who spoke. Counting out gold pieces in Thames Street had not hardened him to riding in the mire.

'I agree with Master Russhe.' Latimer turned his grey eyes on me. 'We have our families to think of. If we go now, the King will have little evidence against us.'

'Then save yourselves, good friends. I thank you for your service of me with all my heart.' I embraced each of them, promising that once matters improved, I would reward them

'What shall you do, my lord?'

'I shall heed the fox's wisdom and lie low while the hunt is on. There are plenty of possibilities. I could go to Brittany or France. Talk the Scots King into giving me support, perhaps.'

Limerick bowed. 'Then God keep your grace.'

He and Latimer mounted up and took the lane westwards. The remaining soldiers ran after them. Russhe had slipped away too.

Jesu, had every one of them gone? Drawing my sword, I skirted the stable and found Pershall and Bannaster leading out three saddled horses. The dog from Clerk's Well was trotting at their heels.

'Where to, now, my lord duke?' Dear, loyal Pershall.

I eyed the man at his side. 'I gave you a holding north of Shrewsbury, did I not, Bannaster?'

'Aye,' he mumbled. 'It be north of Shreswbury, my lord.'

'Good man! Then guide us there. I purpose to keep my head down for a few weeks until the hue and cry is past. And then I shall quit England or else make my peace with the King Richard.'

Bannaster agreed but he looked fit to piss himself. He had worn my livery all his life and performed his duties efficiently but he was so self-effacing that I could not recall one conversation that did not consist of a command from me and a murmur of compliance from him.

In the solar, I abandoned my expensive German armour for a stained jacket that one of my lily-livered soldiers had discarded in the hall. With my finery gone, I felt naked but it was better so. No one would recognise me now.

I almost had my foot in the stirrup when Thomas Nandik ran out of the house.

'Everyone's gone,' he exclaimed, staring about him.

'Ah, that's what a good education does for you,' jeered Pershall. 'Makes you observant.'

Nandik looked even worse than me. The dye of his new gaudy doublet had run like veins down his long, spindly legs ruining his fine woollen hose.

'Your grace, your stars... I...'

'Jesu ha' mercy, you think I acted on *your* predictions?' I exclaimed contemptuously, easing my crude belt a notch. 'Use your head and go! Every other jack has.' I turned away but he flung his arms around my dirty leggings babbling:

'No, no, my lord, nothing was false, nothing! Remember in Northampton, I warned you to beware rivers. Is that not come to pass? Believe me, this very month the King will die and you may once more prosper.' I tried to shove him away but the sodding fool was clutching at my hose. 'I beg you, lord, return home. Make pretence you were warned of the rebellion and were setting out on King Richard's behest.'

Pershall grabbed him by the shoulders and hurled him from me.

'Fuckin' incubus! Have done with your poxy prophecies! Would we had never set eyes on this accursed wretch, my lord.'

As we galloped away down the sodden track, I realised in hindsight that Nandik had prophesied the truth. It had not been Lord Rivers I needed to fear but the bloody River Severn.

***

ICY damp was in my bones, my liver, my heart, my head but I refused to let courage trickle out of me like piss into the soggy earth. How I longed for the soft comfort of my deerskin boots. The mud-caked hose chafed at every step I took. And the filthy jacket offended me, too. Every spatter that befouled it was only bearable because it made me look less like Harry Buckingham.

Bannaster led us along the contours of the hills and the higher ground was less water-logged than the furrowed highways, but we made pitiful speed at first, our hearts jumping every time we heard a stick snap in the wild woods.

When the sun at last withdrew out of the mist at noon in a belated answer to my prayers, glorious warmth lit the peace of the forest and the bright cloak of the Autumn king swirled around the roots of the trees in a flurry of scarlet and amber. Alas, the radiance lasted scarce longer than a woman's sigh before the clouds again took dominance. No matter, I would survive this, I vowed.

One of the horses cast a shoe at dusk and so, not daring to show ourselves at a blacksmith's, we turned the beast loose. Then the next morning, the second horse began to limp. It had picked up a shard of stone in the frog of its hoof. With one mount between us after that, we made ill progress. I was unused to walking, let alone for hours at a time, and my feet blistered painfully.

My servants conversed sparingly leaving me to hobble along with my thoughts. Taking heed for tomorrow outweighed all else and there were healthy precedents to cheer me. Bolingbroke, Edward IV and Warwick had all returned from exile to rule England. I could, too. And this rebellion had not been a mistake. Richard's friends would have talked him into not trusting me. I'd have been squeezed out between their thumbs like a blackhead. No, that's too distasteful. A splinter is better. A splinter since childbirth, that's me.

But I had no taste for this adventure any more. The wind continually blew in squalls from the south, and trudging through the Malvern Hills, avoiding the villages, was poor sport. Nor was I accustomed to an empty belly. I had to rely on Pershall to forage for us and I despised myself for being so dependent on him and Bannaster. I could not even conjure damp kindling into a fire.

We reached Shropshire and were about half a day's journey from Wem when Pershall returned with ill news. Tudor had sailed back to Brittany, Howard had subdued the rebels in the east and the King had passed through Coventry and was setting out to hunt his 'Cousin of Buckingham' with a deadly vengeance. Proclamations were everywhere. I should definitely have to hole up until the hue-and-cry calmed down.

'I been thinking,' Pershall announced to me as we shared the meagre food. 'I'll go with the pair o' you nigh Shrewsbury but no further.' At that, Bannaster looked up fearfully, and anger drove the blood into my cheeks.

'Why don't you turn me in and have done with it?' I hurled my bread at him and stumbled from their company to lean against a nearby tree.

'I'm now a traitor, am I?' growled Pershall at my elbow. 'Do y' know it's only just dawned on my feeble wits how great a traitor *you* are, my lord of Buckingham! All those letters you and that great turd of a bishop wrote from Brecknock about King Edward's son or that Welsh knave being rightful king when all along it's you who wanted the crown. You've no right to the kingdom.'

I whirled round on him, my hand on my sword hilt. 'A murrain on you for a liar! I've far more right than Gloucester. His brother took the crown in blood.'

'But that's just it, isn't it?' Pershall exclaimed, turning to include Bannaster. 'We just can't have any bloody-minded beggar knockin' the King out of the way and takin' the crown just cos he feels like it.'

'Oh, come now, Pershall...' I knew I could talk sense into him.

'No, you listen to me for a change,' he exclaimed. 'Gloucester is king because Parliament passed a law agreeing to it, an' that was your doing but, bless me,' and here sarcasm dripped from his voice, 'now your grace has had a change of mind. 'By Christ!' he snarled further. 'Your blood are never satisfied. Thirty plaguey years an' more you lords have been slashing at each other an' what good has it done? All your kinsmen slain an' you, a duke, fallen to running like a wretched hare before the hounds. An' here's another thing.' He wagged a calloused finger at me. 'Tell me this, what sort of king does a traitor make? Eh? Eh?'

'I do not follow your reasoning, man,' I protested.

'Well, supposin' a bleedin' miracle occurs and you do become the friggin' king. You won't trust anyone. You'll be even afraid of your own friggin' shadow.'

'No, Pershall,' I began but again he was too anguished to listen.

'Rot you!' he cried, his lips an ugly sneer as he railed further. 'King Richard gave you all a man might dream of and what did you do? Throw it away like it was some soiled rag not fit enough for your grace's hands. O God!' he clapped his hands to his temples as though the pain of his thoughts

246

was agony. 'An riskin' good men's lives to show the bloody world how great you are.'

My tongue froze. I could not believe that Pershall of all people could abuse me so. He had one last insult.

'By Our Lady, you are a fool, Harry Stafford,' he snarled, 'an' I am done with you!' Grabbing up his knife from beside the fire, he stuffed it in his belt. 'God be wi' you, Bannaster, you poor bastard.'

Then without another glance at either of us, the insolent rogue whistled the dog from the field and scrambled down the bank, taking our only horse and leaving Bannaster and I staring at each other in disbelief. I should have sprung down and wrestled the bridle from the bastard but I was not swift enough and Bannaster could not think that fast.

'You ungrateful, stinking, thieving son of a whore!' I yelled. 'After all I've done for you. Damn you, Pershall!'

Wrath and indignation walked with me as Bannaster and I set forth again. We were to sorely miss Pershall's foraging. In truth, the sides of our bellies were almost clanging together in emptiness when we finally reached Wem. We dared not show ourselves until after nightfall and then we crept past the cottages and at long last sighted Bannaster's farm, a crude little holding north of the village with a modest orchard, a few cows and a small flock of sheep.

Three farm dogs barked at us as we wearily stumbled up the track. Bannaster kicked them away, cursing, and smote upon the door. It was scraped open by a pinch-faced, skinny slattern bearing a candle. Bannaster thrust me inside with an oath and swiftly barred the door.

'Can't you recognise your own man, you slut?' he snarled and received the woman's spittle for answer.

The place stank of beasts and cheap tapers. There was a scramble from the loft and I found myself surrounded by curious faces, all of them sleepy, dirty and unkempt: four children, a serving wench and an old gaffer.

'Bring food, wife, an' stop your gapin', the rest o' you. You'll have your pennyworth of tidings in the mornin' an' much joy to you. ' Bannaster shooed the brats away and growled at the woman, 'Say aught, yer mawkin, an' you'll have the back o' my hand!'

His wife bit back her shrewish tongue and sullenly stooped to rekindle the embers below the cooking pot, hanging from the hob. The children scrambled back up the crude ladder and the old wight disappeared behind a ragged curtain.

Mistress Bannaster slapped jacks of thin ale before us and glared at her husband. I dared not say a word but hung my head. I could see this was a mistake but I was too weary to leave. Nor did the tepid broth restore my spirits for it was greasy with fat, lacked flavour and its maker looked as though she wished it full of poison.

Bannaster ignored her. Not one word more was spoken between them until he had drunk and eaten his fill and then he checked to make sure the old man was asleep.

'What pitherin' be you at then? Who be this stranger?' demanded his bawd.

'Been on fut for days,' he muttered. 'Duke's army was flooded out.'

'Need some fuckin' sense shaken into ye, the lot of ye.' Now she had time to inspect me, she seized my hand and jerked it over. I had calluses from holding the reins but her fingers found the soft skin of my palm. 'I tell ye, Ralph Bannaster, ye are not riskin' our necks givin' shelter to one of 'em as is on the proclamation.' She flung my hand back at me, her face ugly with contempt.

'Get you gone then!' growled Bannaster. 'You and 'im.' I started to my feet but he shoved me down. 'Nah, sir, 'er and her da! Ha, see, now yer pipin' to a different tune!'

The slut's rebellion subsided but she was still sullen.

''E's not one of our kind,' she muttered. 'Just look at them nails.' I had put a weary hand to my face. 'Wait on.' Her eyes narrowed to vicious slits. 'Without that beard...'

Pox take the bawd! She must have glimpsed me some time in the past.

'You brainless ful, Bannaster!' She crossed herself as though I was Satan come to visit.

'God nail your tongue to your arse or I'll do it for you, you foolish blabbin' shrew,' snarled Bannaster.

'What you brought him here for?' she mouthed. 'Godssakes, we'll all be hanged!' Her knuckles rose to her mouth and I swear she would have screamed if Bannaster had not grabbed the neck of her kirtle.

'He is our lord, woman,' he growled. 'This place is his.'

'Not any longer,' the woman hissed with sudden glee, looking afresh at me. 'He's naught but Harry Stafford now.'

I stumbled to my feet. Weary and desperate though I was, I did not want her charity and the thought of bearing either of them gratitude filled me with loathing.

'Gracious mistress,' I began and inclined my head grandly. 'My life is in your hands but I'll relieve you of it.'

'Ohh, *gracious mistress,* now, is it?' she mimicked. 'It wanna *gracious* when we was askin' to ha' our rent reduced last Lent. It wanna *gracious* when you denied us new thatch las' winter an' refused us the stewardship at Yald-ing.'

'Good lady, I leave such matters to my bailiffs. My estates are too great for them to inform me of every little grie...matter. If I had known. Bannas-ter, you should...'

'*If?*' she jeered. 'This poor ful 'as worked his guts out for you. Pah, we allus knew you for a hard man.'

Bannaster raised his fist to her but I stayed his arm.

'Mistress Bannaster,' I replied proudly. 'I had hoped that you might give me shelter for a few days until the hue and cry has passed but if you lack the stomach for it then I'll not endanger you further. Ralph, I thank you, and I'll be on my way.'

'Ballocks, ye cannot go any further tonight nor me neither.' He turned on the harridan. 'You drive him out wi' your friggin' tongue an' I'll go too an' God knows when you'll see me again.'

She stuck her hands on her hips. 'You'd do that, for *'im?*' She spat.

I swore, but as I laid my hand upon the doorlatch, Bannaster knocked her to the floor.

'I am the master here!' Then he turned to me. 'If you are minded to remain here, you must dissemble. There's them as would turn you over to the sheriff right willingly. I'll tell 'em you're a soldier an' you deserted Bucking-ham's army, right? But you must do the rest, see?'

'I shall one day make you wealthy beyond your dreams,' I promised.

'We shall most like be dead o' the plague ere that day comes,' sneered Mistress Bannaster. 'An' where would your *gracious* lordship like to sleep, in the grand solar at the end of the great hall?'

'In the barn, I thank you,' I replied tersely and let myself out into the fresh air promising that I must be quit of this harridan, but I had not the strength to run that night. Finding the door to the byre, I stumbled in with several dogs joyously joining me. The place smelled mungy and there was a crack in the roof that let in the moonlight. Ralph followed me with a lantern and a poor blanket. Two labourers roused up but he grunted at them and they settled down again. When he had gone, they tried to question me but I feigned sleep.

Nightmares trampled through my slumber and I dreamed I was still struggling through the mud. I might have slept deeply through the dawn with three happy dogs against my legs but I was woken by prods. Eager, stupid faces, anxious for tales to thrill their humdrum lives loomed over me. I swore at them like a soldier, but they pestered me like children and so I told them how we had fled the traitor Buckingham's army.

Bannaster suggested I work that day lugging bales of hay into the feeble barn against the winter. I did not complain for the work was not arduous and the pale sun on my back was comforting. Besides, the more hardened my hands became, the safer I felt. I even scraped my nails into the dirt to make them ragged. All day I laboured and felt some satisfaction although my belly was gnawing on itself from hunger. I should leave. Yes, I knew that, but my feet still had painful blisters.

Bannaster took off in the farm wagon to Wem next morning without a by-your-leave and returned with a squealing piglet for roasting. His reasoning was that, better fed, I'd recover sooner and he would be quit of me. He was terrified of being hanged. The gossip who had sold him the sucking pig had been right curious, wanting to know why he was back in Shropshire. Bannaster was sure he had dissembled well enough but he also told me that every man and his dog was eager to bring me in for the reward on my head and that Sir James Tyrrell was already in the shire, riding round with the sheriff to seize my holdings.

We agreed that after dark, he would take me to a safer hiding place at Milford, which was a small holding near Barchurch that he had inherited from his family. It was not far, down to the south-west, but when nightfall came, and I sought Bannaster out, he had drank so deeply that he could scarce direct himself to his bed let alone guide me six miles across the fields.

I thought about making my own way but without a local guide, it was too dangerous. Tomorrow night I would definitely move on, maybe make for Chester and thence to the Mersey.

Next morning, Mistress Bannaster took great pleasure in setting me to muck out the byre. I did not argue. If the sheriff's men chanced by, they would not look to find a duke spattered with cowdung. A neighbour came a-calling. Perhaps it was the curious owner of the sucking pig. For sure, my taskmistress made a great show of bawling at us underlings across the yard. Bannaster at least had sobered up. I told him we should leave for Milford.

'At dusk,' he promised.

Towards the late afternoon when my arms were aching and my clothes reeked worse than a swineherd's armpit, one of the children came racing into the yard yelling that soldiers were coming. I heard the hoofs, saw the collars of authority rattling across the breastplates of the first two riders. One of them was Tyrrell. The other, I guessed, was Mytton, the sheriff.

I had no intention of taking off across the fields. Calmly, I pulled my filthy hat down further and leaned on my shovel.

Instead of ordering his men to surround the farmhouse, the sheriff waved a writ at Bannaster. Devil roast them, they were not here to search for me but to seize the farm. For an instant, relief flooded through me and then I realised the irony.

My hands were shaking as I backed into the byre. I exchanged my spade for a pitchfork and forced myself outside again to gape like my fellow labourers.

The Bannasters had taken Tyrrell and Mytton inside the homestead but their half-dozen soldiers were left outside. With naught else to do, these knaves sauntered across to the barn and began to poke the bales with their pikes. They jeered at me, holding their noses, and as I edged towards their horses, I prayed that my churlish companions would not blurt out that I was newly come but the churls, good fellows, said naught.

When Mytton and Tyrrell came out, their men swarmed back for further orders. All's well I thought. But then Tyrrell looked straight at me. I swear the soldiers heard his command in disbelief before they came running.

I was ready.

'No!' I bawled, whirling my weapon in a vicious arc. I hurled the pitchfork at the nearest man, leapt for the closest saddle. As the beast moved forward with me half sprawled across its saddle, I grabbed the mane and dug my heels in hard. I gained the road but they were after me soon enough. I outrode them for a half a mile but the horse was a poor creature with little heart, and soon my hunters surrounded me and dragged me to the ground, wrenching my arms behind my back and twisting a rope around my chest until I was as helpless as a cobwebbed fly.

16

An inn cellar in Salisbury is my duchy now. A makeshift measure since the town gaol is already crammed with Woodville followers.

My face feels swollen. My belly is purple and tender with bruising. My hands are bound in front of me and my head aches. Tyrrell's men did not permit me to sleep during the long journey from Shrewsbury and, when we arrived here, Dick Ratcliffe's whoresons half-killed me as they hauled me in to him for interrogation. Mercifully, because I am of royal blood, they dared not scourge me or drive splinters beneath my nails.

I have some solitude at last and try to keep moving to stay warm. There are no rats—so far—and my keepers have left me a candle. I have had to cram my shirt into the grille that looks out onto the street to stop the children crouching down and spitting. One of them even managed to stick his prick in and piddle at me.

Oh Jesu, how cold it is. Even when I was sodden to the skin, I never felt so cold as this. The winter has come to Salisbury.

Have you ever been so lonely that words with any man are like snow-flakes on the deep drift of your loneliness? Save for my few months of alliance with Richard, I have trod this lifetime alone. But no matter, I can survive. Once I have had speech with my cousin, all will be well. He is coming to Salisbury, they tell me.

The hours labour past. I try not to think. Thinking will bring despair. What if Richard does not come?

Has the landlord left no firkins of ale in this place? Yet again I search the corners of my small prison for some means of forcing oblivion.

If Richard does not come, I have thought about killing myself in Roman style. I still have my son's little dagger hidden in my boot but men say that the ghosts of those who forestall God's will never leave this earth. Haunting this cellar does not appeal.

Perhaps some wrinkled churl can bring me some vipers in a bowl of pippins and I shall sit like ancient Egypt's queen, seeing into the future with dead eyes. 'Look!' they will whisper. 'How noble in death! How proud!'

God help me, Tyrrell and Ratcliffe want to watch me die in the marketplace.

'MY LORD?' It is one of Ratcliffe's sergeants shaking me. The kindliest of the bastards.

'What is it?'

'You cried out, my lord. They could hear you up in the kitchen.'

'Did I?'

'Are you in pain, my lord?'

'No.' I say with faint puzzlement and then wearily, 'no.'

'I'll have some clean water brought down to you, sir.'

Do I still smell? With difficulty I squeeze my fists into my eye sockets and realise my cheeks are wet.

He turns. His toe encounters one of my discarded boots and the interfering beggar picks it up and hears the rattle. 'What's this, eh? Can't have you depriving the crowds now, can we?'

Damn the tidy-headed son of Satan! He's found Ned's dagger.

YESTERDAY, the Devil's Eve, they dragged me with my wrists bound up to a hall packed with Yorkist surcotes; the boar badge was everywhere but not the Boar himself. Grim-faced Ratcliffe, in his soldier's black leather with metal studding, and John, Lord Zouche, a Midlands baron—hardly impartial since he is Catesby's brother-in-law—took their places upon the bench but the central chair was empty.

'Make way for my lord the High Constable!' I assumed it was me they spoke of but the throng parted to let through my deputy, Sir Ralph Assheton—the harbinger of death, the messenger who carried Rivers' death warrant to Pontefract.

God's fist squeezed my heart as I was thrust forward to face him.

'You are Henry Stafford, late Duke of Buckingham?'

How quaint.

'Not late. I think I arrived before you, Sir Ralph.'

The roar of laughter washed around me. My deputy smiled tightly at the double meaning but his face turned a dull red. 'Clear the court!' he ordered. 'This is not a bear-baiting.'

The soldiers closed the door behind the last of my audience and now only the clerks waited for a fresh witticism. Beside Assheton, Ratcliffe lifted cold eyes to mine and I knew the dogs would bite.

The clerk of the court mumbled the litany of charges brought against me and then I was given a chance to answer.

'If it is treachery to raise a banner on behalf of the rightful king, then, yes, I suppose I am guilty.'

I paused. Zouche was staring at me as though I had two horns; Ratcliffe showed no surprise and Assheton merely stroked his forefinger across his jowls.

'However, that was not the sum of things at all, gentlemen, as I have reiterated in the several interrogations you have put me through already. My entire purpose was to lure out the King's enemies and destroy them.'

Assheton had not heard any of this. He drew in a long breath. 'I see from your confession that you have already named your fellow conspirators.'

'Yes, I have provided names, but none of those traitors were my allies. I hope now that you will grant me leave to explain my actions to the King's grace in person.' Swift looks were exchanged between them before Assheton cleared his throat.

'You do not deny that you raised an army against the King.'

'No, it was against the King's *enemies*. I dissembled to let Tudor's supporters use me as captain of their forces. Have I lifted a sword against the King's grace on the battlefield? Never!' I let that sink in before I added, 'Look, Assheton, I agree that it was a dangerous strategy easily misinterpreted. Did my lord the King not receive my letter from Weobley?'

They just stared at me with distaste. Damn them! Assheton should have galloped after that one, but Ratcliffe's snort of disbelief had him sidestepping.

'Why did you refuse to attend your liege lord the King when he requested your presence, giving out you were sick?' he demanded. 'We have testimony from our agents at Brecknock that you were in rude health.'

'Of course, I was in rude health. How else would Morton have believed I could lead a rebellion?'

Isolde Martyn

Zouche asserted himself at last. 'Should you not have sent to the King and told him of your plan to deceive his enemies?'

'I-did-send-to-the King, my lord.' That had become my credo over the last week. Even a beating had not made me change the lie. 'Mayhap someone envious of my friendship with his highness deliberately withheld my letter.' I raised my eyebrows at Assheton, remembering that he had once said that Catesby did not have four limbs like a normal man but tendrils.

Maybe Assheton understood. He looked as though he wanted to chew his lower lip and then thought better of it. 'Stafford, this court does not believe—'

'May I suggest this court does not *want* to believe,' I interrupted. 'My lord, it is my understanding that his highness the King wishes justice to be dispensed impartially in this realm and yet I know full that at least one of you on the bench would cheerfully see me brought so low. Is that not the truth, Ratcliffe?'

A hit! Ratcliffe looked like he was whetting a knife for my throat beneath the board. His tanned visage darkened further, and an uncomfortable silence gripped the chamber until Zouche took up the reins again and leaned forward.

'If you are innocent, Stafford, why did you not surrender your person immediately instead of evading capture?'

'With a price on my head, it seemed risky.' Then I let dismay suffuse my voice. 'My lords, this entire business was not meant to become so messy. If my enterprise has been utterly misconstrued by those I thought friends, I assure you, this can be resolved. If his highness will graciously grant me an audience.' I held up my tethered hands in supplication wondering why at least two of these fools were not moved by my words. 'I assure you even before we left London, the King's grace and I discussed ways to winkle out our enemies'

But these prejudiced judges were not listening. Grey, brown and fair, their heads were together. 'We shall reassemble in an hour,' Assheton announced.

'If it please you, do so,' I added courteously, 'but this is ill done. A duke may only be judged by his peers. The lords of England will see this court as a mockery.'

NOTHING had changed in the upper room except the shadows when they marched me in again. My three judges awaited me bleakly, brooding hawks upon a naked branch.

Assheton read out the verdict:

'Henry Stafford, late styling yourself Duke of Buckingham, you are found guilty of High Treason and I hereby sentence you to execution by beheading.'

Like Hastings? I stared at the row of gargoyles in utter horror. *Beheading?* They are going to behead *me?*

'No! This court is not lawful!' I roared, rushing forward and slamming my bound fists down upon their table.

My head spiked on London Bridge like a traitor's?

'No, no, you cannot do this!' I screamed at them. 'I am the loyalest of King Richard's subjects. You would none of you be here if it were not for me. I shielded you from the Woodvilles' vengeance. *I made him king!*'

Their faces only tightened like fists, and my anger chilled to pleading. 'Ask the King! How can he forget the dangers we have faced together? He will understand how it was.'

But Richard is not in Salisbury yet. They have not asked him.

I CAN hear the fanfares and the bells. Is this my cousin come in a flurry of fur and velvet?

I wrench my shirt down from the grille. It is not easy on my wrists to haul myself up on the bars to look out. All I can see are hooves and feet. The air stinks of wet leaves and horses; their turds dapple the marketplace. Surely there are the dog's slender legs bounding beside the feathery fetlocks of my cousin's destrier? Thank God! This gives me hope.

For an instant, I glimpse the rider's scabbard hanging below the horse's white belly and the spurs spiking out from behind the cloth guard on his stirrups. Richard?

I swear at my helplessness. I'd shout if he could hear me but a forest of legs is hastening towards the horses, and here I am like a hare in a burrow.

The weight of my body has me gasping. I drop down and then heave myself up again.

I can hear the dog's playful bark. It sounds like Loyaulté. He always frisks and barks when his master dismounts. Yes, so it has to be Richard. But this rider's knees are not lapped by fur cuffs or the kiss of velvet. Instead, steel greaves encompass his legs, and as he disappears behind a palisade of pikes and halberd poles, I realise this is an enemy commander's retinue, hungry for vengeance.

An enemy?

Then surely he must see me if only to smash his glove across my face? I shall talk him into seeing sense.

But how soon?

Tense, I pace and pace.

Footsteps are coming. Richard! *Richard?*

Yes, I have a visitor. Francis, Lord Lovell. Good. Perhaps he brings a life-line from Richard.

Lovell's skin is tanned from summer riding but his fair hair is clipped for a helmet and he has aged since I saw him last. The boyishness has fled and spider lines web out from the corners of his eyes. He is in half-armour with a breast plate buckled across his leather jack.

I gesture him to the only stool in my little demesne and take the palliasse for myself but he does not sit down. I try not to show him how desperate I am to see Richard.

'Why did you do it, Harry?' Beneath the blond stubble, his handsome face is compassionate. At last I have an advocate.

'I haven't committed treason, Francis,' I mutter.

My rebellion was no more treason than Richard disinheriting his nephews.

'Will he see me?'

'Who, the King?' To my astonishment, he is indignant. 'Of course he will not see you.'

'But—'

'By Heaven, man, how can you expect it of him after what you've done?'

'I'm sorry, I—'

'Damn you, Harry, when Delabere's news of your treachery reached us, Richard was utterly distraught, almost destroyed. I tell you it was like King Edward's death all over again.'

'*Delabere?*' I echo, appalled to learn of my henchman's betrayal. So *he* was my Judas. God-damned traitor! I need time to digest this but Lovell is in too great an anger.

'By Christ, Harry, Richard gave you everything he could but, no, you wanted his crown as well. The "most untrue creature living," he reckons you, you malicious fool.'

'Oh, I'm an untrue creature, am I? I suppose he planted his spies in my household waiting for me to set a foot wrong so he could kick me away the moment he chose.'

'That is bollocks and you know it.'

I hold my fists to my lips. I'm confused, outraged. *Delabere has Ned* is what I'm thinking!

'My son!' I demand, searching his face. 'Where's my son?'

'Your boy is safe.' He dismisses the matter with impatience. '*Tell me why,* Harry!'

Tell him what?

'*Answer me, God damn you!*'

Such rare anger from Lovell shocks my heart into inner panic. This is not going right. Maybe honesty is the only way from now. I swallow, rise to my feet and pace to the wall.

'It was Brecknock, Francis. I hate the place. I get these black days, these megrims. It's…it's like I'm at the bottom of some monstrous dark well and I can't get out. Away from him, from the King, *I can't get out.*' I turn. 'You have to understand when I arrived back in Brecknock, it was as though the kingmaking had never happened, as if no one believed me. I felt…'

'Go on.' The cold command underscores his ebbing patience but I stumble onwards.

'I felt…well, like a little boy again trying to make myself heard, but no one has ever listened–except Richard. He should not have let me go to Wales, Francis. He should have kept me by him. I should have been all right then and—'

'Wait! You are telling me this rebellion was *Richard's* fault?'

I nod, pleased that Lovell now understands. I long for him to put his arms about me like a brother and forgive me. Perhaps he sees that in my face because he leans away, recoils from me.

'You're talking through your arse!'

'No,' I argue swiftly. 'Upon my soul, it's true, Francis. You see, when I went to see Morton, he treated me like a man, who had achieved something.

Isolde Martyn

Believe me, he can say day is night and you can swear it's gospel. That's what happened.'

'By Our Lady!' Lovell strides back and forth now, his arms clasping his elbows and swirls round on me. 'So all your confession about luring out the King's enemies was a nonsense?'

'Yes...no. I cannot...I cannot reason when I am in the dumps.' But Lovell walks away from me, his face is working as though he is struggling to restrain himself and something nameless begins tying itself into a tight knot in my belly. 'That is truly how it was, Francis,' I plead. 'Please, please tell him what I said. I beg of you. Ask him if he will see me. And ask him to spare my son.'

'Spare your son? What do you imagine—' He turns abruptly and draws so close to me that I can feel his breath upon my beard. '*You* see *him*? You are not worthy to come within ten miles of his bootcaps.' His fist explodes into my belly like a cannonshot and the pain drives me staggering back across the mattress.

He steps back panting with rage. I stare up at him and then as if he sees me as a frightened child, the anger in his eyes gives way to shame, and he smites on the door for the guards and turns his furious face on me.

'You brought me down to your level, curse you! I never did that before to any man.' And then he deals me the coup de grâce. 'But you are beneath a man!'

I AM still reeling from his lack of understanding when the tongue of the door lock withdraws again. It is Thomas Stanley who is escorted in. For an instant, I suppose he is to share my prison but he tells the guards to wait upstairs. I am appalled. How can he be free to do this? I have named his wife the greatest traitor in the realm and yet here he is wearing his fine collar of Yorkist sunnes again. When I get out of here, I'll see it changed to a noose.

Warm in his fur-lined mantle, he looks me up and down. I am conscious of my untrimmed beard, my goose flesh showing through the lacing of my badly fitting gippon. I hope the salt of tears is not staining my cheekbones. I do not want him to see my weakness.

'Come down to Salisbury for my execution?' I ask cheerfully.

He nods dourly, looks round for a seat worthy of his buttocks and finding none, grunts briefly and stands.

260

One must be well mannered. 'May I offer you a cup of congealed gruel, Lord Stanley?'

'I see they haven't yet ripped out that golden tongue of yours, Harry.' He notices the pail in the corner and wrinkles his nose.

'So, did the northern progress go well?' I ask pleasantly, folding my arms and leaning back against the wall.

'All right.' He whirls his little finger round his right earhole. 'Pity old Dick had to cut it short.' He inspects his gingered nail with satisfaction.

'And the Lords Bastard? Safe in some northern fortress, I suppose?'

Stanley seems surprised at my question. 'Nay, the older lad was sick, toothache, trouble with his jaw, like, so Old Dick left 'im int' Tower. As t'other lad...' He shrugs.

I stare down at Stanley's complacent features and suddenly in my head, I hear Nandik's promise: *the King shall die.* And wouldn't some men argue there are in truth two kings in England? And if one king is here in Salisbury, still alive, then Prince Edward.... God's mercy, is it his death written in the stars? Here's matter to chew. I need to think hard about this, keep a shrewd head.

I clear my throat. 'So, enlighten me, Stanley, did you actually know anything of the rising?'

He smiles slowly: 'It would be too dangerous *to know*, wouldn't it? Me being kept right close to Old Dick, but I didn't blab on you if that's what you're thinking, lad.' He pulls a sheepish face that may pass for gleefulness. 'Too many in't secret, eh?'

'Lucky Richard took you with him then, else you'd be a head shorter.'
Like I shall be if I don't talk myself out of this chaos.

'Aye.' His eyes tell me he understands my precarious situation. 'Morton got away then, did he?'

'Oh yes, as far as I know. He came with us as far as Weobley.' I feel like spitting but I do have some manners left. 'So you haven't seen Margaret yet?'

'No, that pleasure to come. She'll have to keep her head down and do some embroidery for a change.'

What am I dealing with here? I close my eyes and run my thumb and finger down my nose, still thinking about a prince with jaw ache. If I wrote out the safe pass to the Tower for Dr Lewes to take to Elizabeth, what became of it? Could it still be used? Was it used? I open my eyes and look hard at Stanley.

'How far will your wife go to make her son king?' I ask aloud.

Suddenly he is standing still, very still. 'What are you witterin' about, Harry Stafford?'

'I'm not sure, in all honesty, Thomas.' I begin walking to and fro like a lecturing divine, my mind frantic.

My plan for the rising was that when the princes could not be found at the Tower, we should spread the news that they were murdered so that Richard's enemies would see me as their rightful king.

But one of the princes was there.

And I gave Bray the cursed pass.

Is Stanley watching the blood draining from my face? I put out a hand to the wall to steady myself.

'Better hie off, eh?' His Lancashire voice grinds through my frantic thoughts. He is looking at me like he knows. 'Can't have Old Dick thinking I'm commiserating with traitors, like.' The timbers of the door shake beneath his fist.

'I don't suppose you'd care to intercede for me, Stanley?'

He shakes his head. 'You haven't a hope, lad.'

***

THE GUARDS are binding my wrists together again. My fingers are ink-stained.

I have written my will and, more importantly, a letter to Richard informing him I know something of importance which I will only tell to him. It has taken me all afternoon, and at last it is ready. You see, I am certain both the princes are dead and that Margaret has had them murdered using the pass to the Tower with my signature.

I have requested a priest, as is my right, and shall ask him to carry my letter to the King.

Surely forewarning Richard will earn me a reprieve?

RATCLIFFE is visiting me, looking down his eagle nose with hate. He wears his dislike of me like a livery now.

'I am here to advise you that you are to be executed at noon tomorrow morning.'

The priest has not come yet. I wonder if I dare trust the letter to Ratcliffe and decide against it. I know he is impatient for the world to heave me off its back.

'Did you hear me, Stafford?'

'Thank you,' I reply diffidently as though he is a servant. 'I shall endeavour to keep the appointment.' But when he turns to go, my control shatters. *'Will he see me?'*

As Ratcliffe shakes his head, my hands pluck his collar. 'He must, he must!'

Lord help me, I don't mean to sound like a whimpering idiot.

Calmly he unfastens my fingers. 'So you can stick a dagger in him, you scum, like the one you had hidden in your bootcuff? Rest your lying tongue! There's no clemency for you tonight.' He runs a disinterested eye around the shadows of the room, impatient to go.

'Listen to me, damn you, Ratcliffe! I have to warn him. He is in such *danger*!'

Danger of being nailed in his coffin as a tyrant and a child murderer.

'Save your fuckin' breath, you Judas!' He shakes his head at me, as unmoved as the Earth itself. 'Even if Christ Himself were to intercede for you, Stafford, I doubt the King would let you have your life.'

He slams the door against my following. I rattle the ringlock, yelling: 'Ask him where his nephews are, Ratcliffe. Tell him to show his nephews to the people!'

The key pulls back the bolt. I step back, pleased, but this time it his sinewy fingers that seize the worn neck of my doublet.

'Just what do you mean by that obscenity?' He is half-choking me. But his mind is clicking. 'Have you had the boys killed? Have you? Have you, you bloody murderer?'

Me? Oh, God! I have to see Richard.

'No! *No!* Don't you see? It's not about me any more. It's about Richard. Oh Sweet Christ, how can I make you understand, Ratcliffe? Use your head! It's still possible to put things right.' I cradle my shivering body, wondering how far a cunning mother will go to make her only son a king? How ruthless is bloody Margaret Beaufort?

'W-warn him, Ratcliffe! Let him look to his son. Warn him for the love of God! Poison, I'd say. A woman's trick. The bitch is so clever, so plaguey clever and patient. That's what he must beware. The bitch's patience, her fucking patience.' Are my words tumbling out all scrambled? Or this ruffian is not even listening?

Devil roast him! Can he not see? Richard is pitched against a mind that has more twists than any rope.

'What in Hell are you babbling about, Stafford? Elizabeth Woodville's a spent force.'

'*Elizabeth?*'

Haven't I made it clear to him that it is Margaret Beaufort? Pious, plain, little Margaret, disguised by works of charity, hiding the ambition of a man and the mind of a murderer behind her woman's face. She wants the throne for her son and she'll kill and kill.

It's then I remember the kerchief Margaret gave Anne at the coronation. 'Warn the Queen about Margaret Beaufort! They must take care of their son.'

I'm losing my objective here. I have to use this news to save my life.

'But I can explain all this to the King, that will be easier. He will understand then. By Christ, Master Rat, even you never smelled her out. You must guard him.'

He lets me go, sneering, 'You've lost your mind, Stafford.'

The door closes behind him and I am locked in with my fears.

I have not lost my mind, but God has snatched back my golden fluency. The stone is cold against my knees, the door timber unfeeling against my burning forehead. How have I failed to make Ratcliffe understand? I who could sway the Lords of Parliament? Yet God Himself has taken away my eloquence and I am naked now. What have I done to Him that I must pay so dearly? I am History's jester.

IT MUST be hours now that I have crouched here in the greyness, my head on my knees, sobbing like a beaten schoolboy silently so that the soldiers cannot hear. My limbs are stiff as I stagger to my pallet, my throat is sore and I am empty and so utterly alone. Words spill out of my memory, the debris of thirty years now. I try to laugh but the sound comes out harsh and brash. I must keep my sanity. Only I can do that and I must keep control, but Jesu, I am terrified.

I am frightened of the coming dark. At thirty, my bones do not promise the nearness of Death that gentles the aged back into passionate prayers and hours of genuflections.

A PRIEST is come at last. He is the Salisbury gaol chaplain, he grandly tells me. He promises to ensure my letter reaches the King, and we talk about redemption between the hour bells.

If I can warn Richard against Margaret, is that not some form of redemption? A way to right the harm I've done? Even if my cousin lets me have my life, I'll probably spend my days chained up at Middleham or Pontefract, but at least I'll have the satisfaction of seeing Margaret hobbled.

Redemption, yes.

Ah, I am trying to find belief but it hangs beyond my reach like a haze of midges on a summer lane. You see, I thought I had no need of God this summer or rather I thought that I was become His favourite. I set up my mirror up as a graven image and the Devil is waiting for my soul.

Can gentle Christ find forgiveness for me? But what I have done to earn his mercy? A camel against the smallness of the needle's eye?

The chaplain witnesses my will and I remember to give him the HS ring for Ned and the letter for Richard.

'God bless you, my son, rest assured I shall return in good time tomorrow to confess you. Remember, as I have said to you, the Son of Man has power on earth to forgive sins. Spend the hours left to you in prayer so you will be in a state of grace to enter Our Lord's kingdom.'

Father, I have no intention of departing this life tomorrow.

Aloud, I thank him. Providing he sees my letter safely delivered, all shall be well.

LIFE HAS become very simple. Left alone, I realise I have no material possessions left. Only my under drawers are mine. Actually, I still owe payment on my finery for the coronation. There's a thought! I wonder if my debtors lit candles on the eve of the rebellion? Lord help me, by now Vaughan must be strutting in my cloth of gold mantle back at Tretower. I hope his balls rot.

Isolde Martyn

Ha, it will be a hard task for the King's creatures if Vaughan and his whoresons have burnt my rent rolls. My smile is gleeful.

I imagine Cat must be spitting. I suppose she will have to survive on some meagre pension like Lady Oxford. No chance of a chantry for me, I'll wager. But my little children concern me. Shall they become royal wards, never permitted to mention their father? That thought stabs me in the gut and twists the blade.

Tomorrow's duke! Ned, my tousled son. Oh Sweet Christ, shall his head be smitten off when he is grown to manhood because he is a threat to Richard's blood?

My breath forms vapour. I cannot stop shuddering. This lousy blanket is plaguey thin, and someone has tugged my shirt from the grille.

What if Richard won't give me a reprieve? What if he doesn't believe my warning? Christ! Maybe he thinks I murdered the princes. Maybe *he* did. Maybe the boy has died from illness joined with melancholy? Maybe the boys aren't even dead and I have jumped to a terrible conclusion. Well, that might be so, given my capacity for stupidity these last weeks.

Stupidity with an 'S' as high as a Colossus. What a fool I have been, envious all my life, wanting to show the world I am more magnificent, clever, wittier, eloquent, powerful. Stupid! Stupid!

I swear like a peasant and kick the palliasse as if it has ribs to be broken. At last, out of breath, I stand still, my heart lurching.

I let Richard have a kingdom; surely he can let me have my life?

THERE ARE voices just above the grille. A Salisbury woman bantering with her swain. They must be watching the carpentry in the square, my platform of death being banged together. They are teasing each other in gentle tones, purring like a tabby and a tom–lovers.

Meg, would she light a candle for me? Had she cared for me at all? If she chose to dally with me, neglect her children, what price her love? Oh God, if only I could have had a loving wife, maybe she could have tethered my restless ambition.

But I did it for my children, Yes, I did. Not just for me. For my little princess, Bess. I fall on my knees whispering my little darling's name. Shall I ever hold her in my arms again?

Oh, God, what have I done?

266

Is this the beginning of contrition? Are you listening, you holy saints? This is your feast day after all. Dare you intercede for me and move my cousin's heart? Else what is there? A millennium in Purgatory, the eternal scourge of Hell with Hastings wielding the lash or shall my soul be blown out by the breath of God? No, what's done is done. Is a kingdom worth eternity in Hell?

Richard, cousin, I shall be waiting for you.

'ROUSE up, my lord!'

'What is it? Who's there? What time is it?'

'Six o' the clock, my lord, the Feast of All Souls.'

'My doomsday already?' The carpenters have worked all night by torchlight, hammering between my thoughts. The flickers of torches play through the grille and caper round the walls like merry demons.

Voices come from the stairs. Yorkshire voices. The change of guard at sparrow's fart.

'No end of beasts lost, they reckon...down far as Bristol. Buckingham's flood, they are calling it.'

'And how is our gobbing traitor? Practising his speech for the scaffold?'

'Crazed in the night, I'm told. Kicked his bed to bits.'

Bread and cheese and a jack of ale are left at my elbow.

I MUST HAVE slept again, despite the hardness of the floor beneath my ragged blanket. Outside there is a rattle of keys. The door to my grand chamber creaks open and Ratcliffe steps in.

'There is no reprieve.' Richard's rat tosses my letter still virgin onto the floor then he prods my untouched platter with his bootcap 'The Last Supper, eh, your grace?' With a wolf's gleam of teeth, he smiles at me then he lopes off back to his master.

No reprieve! Pah, Richard is toying with me! They cannot truly intend to chop my head off. But if Richard hasn't fucking well read my letter, then, well, fucking damn him for a fool!

Oh God, are they going to kill me in the marketplace. The noises from the marketplace tell me people are gathering.

There is still time for mercy. Surely?

17

Someone has come in. I suppose at first it is the chaplain. The man's shoes halt just inches from my nose and I see that the tongues are embroidered with eagle's claws. Stanley is looking down at me, running a hand over his newly shaven jowls. He cocks an eyebrow up at the iron bars no longer wefted by my clothing.

'I've brought you a clean shirt, Harry. You allus like to look your best, eh?' He toes the platter. 'This breakfast doesn't look too bad. You'll be hungry by noon.'

It will not even be digested.

I turn my face to the wall. I want to bawl, and with an obscenity learned from Lacon Farm, I tell the whoreson to go, but perversely he stays, stooping down to set a hand upon my shoulder.

'Come, Harry, eat. It is something to do.' There is kindness in his voice. In the doorway, the soldiers are watching me. He tells them to wait upstairs.

'Here.' He draws out a leather flask from his breast, unstoppers it and holds it out. I sit up scowling, hoist it between my bound hands and take a swig. The liquid fire is welcome but I do not want his charity.

'No, keep it.' He straightens up and folds his arms. The fur trims on his sleeve cuffs bump gently against his knees. 'You worked things out, didn't you?'

Now he has my attention. Is he talking about the boys, the princes?

'Did I?' I knuckle the moisture from each eye and try and find the truth in his face.

First he glances beyond the door to make sure we are not overheard.

'As I see matters like, you'd win prizes for being the most transparent felon in t' country, Harry Stafford, an' it's only because old Dick has got his head down his own hose that you've survived this long.'

Is this why Stanley is here? To gloat?

'Where you went wrong, my lad, was to think you were the only two-faced scoundrel round t' place.'

'Don't tell me you are jealous of my reputation?' I retort sweetly. I heave myself onto my knees and splash the water left in the ewer onto my face.

He is clearly busting to share something. 'Anyroad,' he continues, 'you know what the biggest jest in all this is? I'm the new High Constable of England, Harry, starting tomorrow. Summat, eh?'

I stare up at him, the icy water running down my face. Richard has done this? Oh this is too cruel. I can't even find a jest to prick the bladder of Stanley's vanity. My throat feels dry, corroded. I just stare at him in disbelief. Slowly, slowly the air settles once more between us like castle dust after a bombardment.

He stoops, his face close to mine, his voice a whisper.

'Whatever's happened int' Tower, you are going to get the blame. Well, first away at anyroad.' He straightens, sticking his lower lip out like a jug. 'Reckon by next week old Dick will think he's done the right thing, lopping you this morning, eh.'

This sniggering old Judas is going to nail the children's murder on me. That's it, isn't it? He knows they are murdered, and by his bloody wife.

'What's more, Harry...' I flinch at the familiarity as he steps closer to my rigid back like a gloating Mephistopheles.

I am trying to close my mind but my ears are rebels to my wishes.

'I'm to be the wife's gaoler,' he whispers. 'Yon simple Dick is handing all Margaret's lands over to me.'

I turn my head, my expression contemptuous.

'Nay, lad, it's God's truth.' He is grinning, his fingers playing with the gilded claw upon his chain. 'I'll let Margaret meddle again. This year, next year, when the fancy takes me. All easier now wi' you, Old Dick's great friend, out o' road. Great help to us you were. You pulled down the Woodvilles, you destroyed my good friend Hastings and finally you've put Greek fire up your own arse.'

'Count on nothing, old man,' I sneer. 'You think Margaret's lily-livered boy can best Richard? I hear the craven bastard never even disembarked.'

'Nay, his fleet set sail right enow but the storm that upended you, scattered 'em. His ship reached Poole Harbour an' he hung around waitin' for the rest but only one other vessel made land an' what wi' the King's men waving banners and pretending they were loyal to the Woodvilles, he pulled up anchor an' got out of there 'afore they could send their ships to grapple. Still

270

no matter, gave the lad some experience at any road. Next time, eh? And he won't have you cluttering things up.'

I snort. 'The *lad* may die of the sweating sickness before the year is out or Richard will pay the Bretons to hand him over.'

Stanley chuckles and rubs his hands. 'Doesn't matter to me. I've convinced Old Dick he'd better rely on me to prop his throne up, otherwise he's only got grizzled Howard and young Lovell left to lick his bootcaps among the great lords. Needs me like a whore needs customers, he does.'

'And you're so experienced in licking, Stanley.' He doesn't like it, the disdain.

'Oh, I'll die in my bed, I promise you that, Harry.'

Part of me wants to be rid of this preening old timeserver but the conversation is a distraction from my noon day arrangement and he does not seem to be in a hurry to leave.

'You know what,' he says, 'as we were ridin' down here, I was tottin' up how many lords and their sons have died in these bloody feuds betwixt t' royal Houses an' I'm not talking about newcomers like the Woodvilles. How many do you reckon?'

I shrug.

'At least sixty of the friggin' fools. But not the Stanleys, never the Stanleys.' He nods. 'We allus hang back lad, watch which way the wind blows.'

What does he want? Applause?

'Well, if I have my way,' I assert, 'I'd unite the Houses of York and Lancaster.' I pick up his flask and take another swig to ease my rusty voice. 'Richard's son married to my daughter. That would have settled things down, but he wouldn't listen.'

'Stuck in your craw, did it?' His stare is crawling over my face. 'Was that what flipped you over like a pancake?'

I do not answer him. I cannot be bothered. I want to gather the blanket round my shivering shoulders.

'Of course, taking things into consideration...' His gloved hands rise like a priest's at the Eucharist. 'Admit it, you were daft not to flee with Morton.' He is thinking of more pellets to lob at me. 'An' the rebellion, lad, too hasty, too hasty. People like things done slow and gradual. You need to prepare 'em, see. Margaret'll manage it eventually an' have 'em burnin' like hell to get rid o' the tyrant.' His gargoyle smile revolts me. 'Aye, we'll daub old

Dick the blackest villain since chronicles began.' He nods to himself, his lips disappearing into his mouth like a tight seam. 'Aye, that'll be two kings he's murdered. Old King Harry back in '71 and now his nephews.'

So they will use gossip and calumny, my old weapons, and continue the malevolence that I began. That I began. *Oh God, Richard, you have to let me speak with you.*

A market barrow creaks past the grille. It reminds Stanley to keep his voice soft.

'Old Dick will blame you for the princes' murder but the people of England will blame *him* and when the time comes, no one will mind him getting his come uppance.'

The villainy of it poisons the air I am breathing. Bastard!

I turn away from him. 'I have heard enough. You may go.' I say haughtily and I am surprised at how calm I sound, but the old rogue is still enjoying his sport with me.

'You haven't eaten anything, lad—'

I pick up the plate and consider how the potage will stain his velvet mantle.

'No, truly,' I maintain, with as much hauteur as I can muster, 'I've had enough of this conversation and I do have a last speech on the scaffold to consider.'

That at least needles him. 'Nay, don't you try accusing the wife with some lofty speech ont' scaffold neither or I'll—'

I raise my eyebrows and look down my Stafford nose at him.

He sticks out his lower lip and bares his claws. 'Or I'll make certain tomorrow's Duke of Buckingham, your precious son, hears it was actually his da who murdered his royal cousins.'

'*Get OUT!*'

I hurl the platter as he runs for the door. I think the gravy spattered him but the gobbets missed. I watch the fatty meat slide slowly down the wall.

Pershall was right, damn him!. I have kicked away the cornerstones from the House of York and ripped away the garland of honour from my cousin. No matter that the Lords and Commons made him king, no matter that Canterbury crowned him with England's diadem and anointed his brow in holy oil, the world already prefers the tastier tale of the wicked uncle.

Cousin, cousin, if only you can sidestep Margaret's snares. You are blinded by her piety and gulled by her gender.

Can you forgive me! I was blind as well.

THE WHISPER of the chaplain's chasuble rustles down the stairs and Holy Church knocks upon the door of my life and is come to shrive me. Nothing I can do now will scrape away the past or change the future unless Richard can find forgiveness.

For all my confessor's mouthing, it is hypocrisy to believe I can wriggle into Heaven on my belly just because I say I am sorry for my life's sins. So maybe I have some nobility of mind left, after all, for I am not going to choose the easy path of Christ's compassion. Instead I shall welcome the thorny path that leads to God's throne on Judgment Day for His justice is pure and I betrayed my greatest friend.

Kneeling, I confess my greed, my ambition, my envy and my hate. My forgiveness is for Bannaster and most of all for Richard. Only in that can I better him, and if I could gain from him an absolution then his loving mercy would speed us both unto the very door of Heaven. I shall meet you in hell, my cousin, for blood is upon both our souls.

'*Pax tecum, fili.*'

'Wait, father, I pray you light a candle this day for me in the cathedral in the chapel of our Lady.'

'Of course, my son.' But he looks reluctant. After all, I am a condemned traitor.

'Not for me, but the woman I love. I promised I would light a candle to her every day of the rest of my life.'

And today is the last day.

THE MORNING AIR is so crisp it drives the shadows from my mind. All my senses are sharp. I can see every leaf, every pebble, the untied tag upon a child's points, the freckles on a woman's arm, the stain on the hose of the pikeman marching in front of me. The cathedral bells are tolling across the meadows by the river and the drumbeats pound. There are obscenities. There is spittle. I am deliberately trying not to keep in step but it is too majestic a measure to deny.

Isolde Martyn

I do not expect the dog jumping up at me, knocking me back into my guards, trying to lick my face. Loyaulté! I cannot fondle you, last and honest friend, because my hands have been tied behind my back. Oh Christ, surely Richard has not come to watch? Has he? My eyes search fearfully for him among the cluster of scarlet, as my guards thrust the dog away and, cursing, close about me. He is not here, thank God, his face like rock above his high fur collar. Thank God, thank God.

But there is still time for him to forgive me.

I climb the wooden steps with a confidence I instantly regret, seeing the silver edge of the resting axe, the strangely familiar grain of the block. It is already stained. Bile rises in my throat. I was in control till now.

'It is the block used for Lord Hastings, my lord. It has been brought from London.'

'On whose orders? The King's?'

'No, my lord, not the King's.'

There is something in that. The ruthlessness of the idea is significant, but there is no time to pull the meaning out of it, to assume it is Stanley's doing. The only conclusion now is that of my life. And there is no word from Richard, no change of heart. It should not end like this. Surely he will...

They are leading me to face the crowd. I am supposed to make my last speech. I hold up my freed hands for a hearing. The marketplace is full. There are jeers but then they hush, waiting for a witticism to outlast my rotting corpse. I have them in my palm just as I had Parliament, that wonderful listening silence. But a gesture to my left distracts me. Stanley has his arm raised and as I draw breath, he lets it fall and the drummers savagely snatch the moment from me.

Now my guards are jerking me away from the edge of the scaffold. I am turned and pushed me to my knees. I can hear the gasp of the crowd's breath beyond the pounding of my blood.

The wood is hard against my cheek. I have to lie my head sideways.

O Sweet Christ, Richard, it will be too late.

Then the drums go silent and I can hear...

I can hear the sad straining whine...oh God have mercy...Loyaul—

HISTORY NOTE

I always had the intention of writing a historical novel on Lady Margaret Beaufort, but every time I started out and surveyed the cast of characters, Harry put his hand up, just like a boy in the classroom: 'What about me, Miss? Write about me, Miss!' And, yes, there was this fascinating young man, who supported Richard of Gloucester, made him king and then betrayed him? Why? That was when my research began, an exploration of Harry's childhood and then a journey that took me to Brecon and into a search for the route taken by his army.

Little is left of Buckingham's castle at Brecon but there is a picture in the Castle Hotel that shows how his castle may have looked in its glory. The manor house at Wooton Devereux has vanished as well but some of the lovely architecture in nearby Weobley recaptures the era of the fifteenth century, and there is a house dating back to 1323.

Some of the palaces in London that were familiar to Harry still exist. The Manor of the Red Rose is long gone but Westminster Hall and the Guildhall where he made his speeches are open to visitors and so, too, is the chamber in the White Tower of the Tower of London, where the famous meeting with Lord Hastings took place. The great hall of Richard III's beloved Crosby Place was moved, stone by stone, from Bishopsgate to Chelsea and is now under private ownership.

How true is Harry's account of what happened in 1483? Who did murder the princes? Probably, we shall never know. Fifteenth century political history is scraps pieced together by historians. What clouds the truth for us even more is that contemporary histories, just like bestiaries, were designed to teach morality. 'All is written for our doctrine, and for to beware that we fall not to vice,' commented William Caxton. The Tudor Dynasty would agree with him.

Isolde Martyn

Printed in Great Britain
by Amazon.co.uk, Ltd.,
Marston Gate.